Also by Shannon Messenger

The KEEPER OF THE LOST CITIES Series
Keeper of the Lost Cities
Exile
Everblaze
Neverseen
Lodestar
Nightfall
Flashback
Legacy

KEEPER
OF THE
LOST CITIES

UNLOCKED
BOOK 8.5

SHANNON MESSENGER

SIMON & SCHUSTER

First published in Great Britain in 2020 by Simon & Schuster UK Ltd

First published in the USA in 2020 by Aladdin, an imprint
of Simon & Schuster Children's Publishing Division

5 7 9 10 8 6

Simon & Schuster UK Ltd
1st Floor, 222 Gray's Inn Road
London
WC1X 8HB

www.simonandschuster.co.uk
www.simonandschuster.com.au
www.simonandschuster.co.in

Simon & Schuster Australia, Sydney
Simon & Schuster India, New Delhi

A CIP catalogue record for this book is available from the British Library.

PB ISBN 978-1-3985-0117-1
eBook ISBN 978-1-3985-0118-8

Printed and bound by CPI Group (UK) Ltd, Croydon, CR0 4YY

For Alex

You named this book—and taught me the magical
ways of colorful Post-it plotting—so it seems only
fair to give you the dedication too

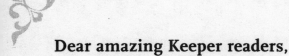

Dear amazing Keeper readers,

I know you're probably thinking, *Okay, what exactly is this book that I'm about to read?* And the answer is: *something extra special, designed to be read between* Legacy *(Book 8) and the currently still untitled Book 9* (hence why we're calling this "8.5"). So that means I need to start things off with a great big **SPOILER ALERT**.

IF YOU HAVEN'T READ THE OTHER EIGHT KEEPER BOOKS—AND DON'T WANT TO HAVE ANY SECRETS SPOILED FOR YOU—STEP AWAY UNTIL YOU'RE CAUGHT UP!

(**Hint:** that means you'll want to have read *Keeper of the Lost Cities, Exile, Everblaze, Neverseen, Lodestar, Nightfall, Flashback,* and *Legacy*—in that order—before reading this!)

The reason there are spoilers is because the first half of this book is a special kind of series guide, filled with details about your favorite Keeper characters and the world of the Lost Cities—plus new tidbits and information you won't find anywhere else! You'll also discover fun bonuses, like the gorgeous map of the Lost Cities, Keeper-themed quizzes and recipes, an Iggy coloring page, and *tons* of seriously amazing art—some of which comes with Keefe commentary!

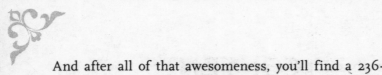

And after all of that awesomeness, you'll find a 236-page exclusive Keeper novella, continuing the main story of the series from the end of *Legacy*—but I'll explain more about that when you get there.

For now, settle in for a super-fun look behind the scenes of the Keeper books—and remember to keep an eye out for those exclusive secrets!

HAPPY READING!

xo

CONTENTS

The Registry

The World of the Lost Cities

Portraits

Life in the Lost Cities

KEEPER
OF THE
LOST CITIES
UNLOCKED
BOOK 8.5

The Registry

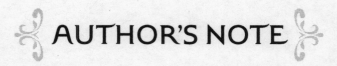

AUTHOR'S NOTE

ONE OF THE FIRST THINGS SOPHIE'S GIVEN AFTER Fitz brings her to the Lost Cities is a registry pendant—a simple choker-style necklace containing a special crystal that allows the Council to monitor her whereabouts. I wrote that detail into the series because it felt logical that a world in which anyone can travel all over the planet on a beam of light (and where light leaping can go tragically wrong) would have safety precautions in place to allow someone to be found in an emergency.

But the Council uses the pendants for more than simply tracking a person's location. In fact, the registry keeps files on everyone in the Lost Cities, monitoring all kinds of different things. (That's why members of the Black Swan and the Neverseen sometimes alter their feeds to hide what they're up to.)

So, I thought it might be fun to give you guys a peek at your favorite characters' registry files. I have a feeling you'll be surprised by some of the details you discover in them! And remember—these are the *Council's* official records, so there may be times when *you* know things that *they* haven't figured out yet. Don't let that confuse you—just enjoy being smarter than the leaders of the elvin world. ☺

(*whispers* You might also notice that certain files have been edited, both by the registry and by a certain powerful Technopath—and some files can't be accessed at all. . . . The elves have tricky security!)

REGISTRY FILE FOR
Sophie Elizabeth Foster

KNOWN ABILITIES: *Telepath, Polyglot, Inflictor, Teleporter, Enhancer*

RESIDENCE: *Havenfield*

IMMEDIATE FAMILY: *Unknown*

ADOPTED BY: *Grady and Edaline Ruewen*

MATCH STATUS: *Unmatchable*

EDUCATION: *Current Foxfire prodigy*

NEXUS: *No longer required*

PATHFINDER: *Not assigned. Restricted to Leapmasters and home crystals.*

SPYBALL APPROVAL: *None*

MEMBER OF THE NOBILITY: *Yes*

TITLE: *Lady*

NOBLE ASSIGNMENT: *Regent; leader of Team Valiant; point of contact for the alicorns*

SIGNIFICANT CONNECTIONS: *Cognate to Fitz Vacker; fealty-sworn member of the Black Swan; human family under the protection of the Council; former Wayward at Exillium*

ASSIGNED BODYGUARD(S): *Sandor (goblin); Flori (gnome); Bo (ogre—temporarily reassigned); Tarina (troll—indefinitely on leave); Nubiti (dwarf—indefinitely on leave)*

A CHILD OF UNTRADITIONAL ORIGINS:

In what was hopefully a first (and last) for our world, Sophie was born and raised by two humans (formerly known as Will and Emma Foster, relocated once as Connor and Kate Freeman, and again as [REDACTED FOR SECURITY] in an area of the Forbidden Cities that the humans call San Diego, California. She had one human sibling (Amy Foster, relocated once as Natalie Freeman, and again as [REDACTED FOR SECURITY] , who was briefly a resident of the Lost Cities and was allowed to retain her memories of that time. But there is no genetic connection between Sophie and her human sister, or between Sophie and her human parents. Sophie's embryo was created from the genetic materials of two unknown elves and implanted into her human mother by a member of the Black Swan who goes by the false name Mr. Forkle. He posed as both a human fertility doctor and a neighbor in order to monitor Sophie's development, as well as her safety. He is also presumed to be responsible for triggering her telepathy at the age of five human years, as well as planting classified information into her memory, and revealing her location to Alden Vacker when she was twelve human years old. The possibility of Sophie's existence was first discovered by Quinlin Sonden and Alden Vacker after the term "Project Moonlark" and a strand of unregistered elvin DNA were recovered during a memory break performed on Prentice Endal—though the Council believed the evidence to be an elaborate hoax. Alden spent years secretly searching the Forbidden Cities for the girl (often with the help of his sons, Alvar Vacker and Fitz Vacker) before finally receiving a human newspaper article that led him to Sophie. Fitz Vacker brought her to the Lost Cities and explained the truth about who and what she was, and also revealed that she would need to leave her human life behind. She was given access to a birth fund, a registry pendant, a nexus, and an Imparter—plus numerous other basic necessities. Later she was given a home crystal to Havenfield. Sophie's residency was provisional at first, but she has since been granted full citizenship and continues to attend Foxfire Academy.

UNEXPECTED EYE COLOR:

Sophie has brown eyes (with small flecks of gold in them) instead of a shade of blue, like the rest of our species. No one, including her creators, seems to be 100 percent clear as to why—though most suspect the condition is related to certain modifications made to her genetics during the Black Swan's experiments, many of which were based on alicorn DNA.

A STRANGE HABIT:

In what appears to be a nervous tic of sorts, Sophie is often seen tugging on her eyelashes. She's been quick to assure everyone that it doesn't hurt, but she does often appear to be trying to break herself of the habit. So far, she's had little success. And it's hard to blame Sophie for that, given the numerous stressful things she's been through—and continues to endure.

AN UNUSUAL REQUEST:

Originally the Council ordered that Sophie's human identity be "terminated" and that her human family be made to believe that their eldest daughter had passed away. But Sophie was concerned about the emotional toll her family would pay while grieving for their lost child, and she convinced Alden Vacker that her human identity should instead be "erased," with the humans relocated to someplace their memories wouldn't be triggered. Alden and Della Vacker oversaw the relocation, moving both parents, their daughter, and their pet (a large gray cat evidently named Marty) to a location with no ties to their previous lives. And Della was careful to ensure that their new lifestyle was what humans would classify as "very comfortable." Sophie had also specifically requested that her family's new home have a yard large enough for a dog, so Della gifted the family with a beagle puppy. Our records indicate that the dog has been named Watson.

POSSESSION OF HUMAN ITEMS:

Sophie brought one small purple backpack with her when she left the Forbidden Cities, and it was filled mostly with human clothing. The only other items were a scrapbook of family photos, a gadget called an iPod (which Dex Dizznee has made numerous adjustments to), and a bright blue elephant stuffed animal that she has named

Ella and apparently cannot sleep without. All other items from Sophie's human home were packed up and meticulously recorded before being stored in [ADDRESS REDACTED FOR SECURITY] in Mysterium, which Sophie has visited once with Councillor Terik in order to retrieve a childhood journal she'd left behind and realized was important. (Councillor Terik asked her why and was not given an answer.)

UNKNOWN POTENTIAL:

Sophie's unconventional upbringing—as well as numerous other suspicious circumstances—led the Council to order Councillor Terik to descry Sophie during her first year in the Lost Cities. Alden Vacker brought Sophie to Councillor Terik's private office in Eternalia, and she cooperated fully with the descrying. But the reading results were inconclusive. Councillor Terik reported afterward that he could definitely sense something *strong* when it came to Sophie's potential, but what that actually means remains unclear.

A COMPLICATED ADOPTION PROCESS:

Upon the discovery of Sophie's existence, Alden and Della Vacker applied to be her guardians—but their application was rejected because Alden's search for Sophie had not been authorized by the Council. Sophie was instead placed at Havenfield with Grady and Edaline Ruewen, and adoption proceedings were initiated shortly thereafter. But several months later, the Ruewens canceled the adoption, citing emotional distress due to their ongoing grief over losing their daughter (Jolie Ruewen) sixteen years earlier. Alden and Della Vacker then renewed their application for guardianship, and the Council was willing to grant permission. But Sophie's kidnapping—and brief presumed death—ended the proceedings once again. After her rescue and recovery, both the Ruewens and Vackers applied for adoption. The Council opted to leave the decision to Sophie, who chose to permanently return to Havenfield with the Ruewens.

THE CONSTANT SHADOW OF GRIEF:

Finalizing her adoption was surely a relief for Sophie—but it was still only a "step" toward truly feeling like a family. A period of adjustment is expected in these situations, so it wasn't surprising that Sophie initially struggled to use terms like "Mom" and "Dad." But for the Ruewen-Foster family (assuming that's what they call themselves), there was the added complication of the loss of Jolie. Reports indicate that Sophie initially worried that Grady and Edaline wished she were more like their lost daughter, and she tried to avoid the subject as much as possible. She evidently also tried to avoid Jolie's old bedroom, out of fear that she might not be allowed in there. But all of that changed when Sophie discovered that Jolie had been involved with the Black Swan.

A MIRROR THAT'S PERHAPS TOO HONEST:

Spectral mirrors are one of Lady Iskra's numerous inventions— and while they were quite popular when they first went on sale, many soon found their mirrors' style and fashion "advice" to be obnoxious (and at times even insulting). The gadgets have since become nearly obsolete, but it appears that Jolie Ruewen kept one in her bedroom at Havenfield, and had even befriended Vertina (the tiny "girl" programmed to appear in the corner of the mirror). So when Sophie was looking to learn more about Grady and Edaline's deceased daughter, she opted to move Vertina's mirror to her bedroom—a decision she likely regrets at times, given Sophie's general lack of interest in clothes and makeup. But reports indicate that Vertina has proven to be quite useful at times, even helping Sophie locate Jolie's secret diary, which led Sophie to identify Jolie's killer.

A MYSTERIOUS MIND:

Sophie has a powerful photographic memory, but it had two blank spots when she arrived in the Lost Cities—both connected to traumas in her childhood that led to her waking up in human hospitals (one when she was five human years old, and the other when she was nine human years old). Our investigation shows that both memories were erased by the Black Swan "for her protection" and have since been returned. Her mind also appears to be filled with numerous bits of information about the Lost Cities—much of which is highly classified (like the location of the unmapped stars)— which were planted as part of her "preparation" for her role as the moonlark. She also struggles to read words written in the primary runic alphabet because her mind has been trained to instinctively recognize them as the Black Swan's cipher runes.

THE BLACK SWAN'S MOONLARK:

Details on the so-called "Project Moonlark" are still vague at best. But the secret—and highly illegal—genetic experiment was carried out by the Black Swan and resulted in the creation of Sophie, who was designed with specific abilities in an attempt to make her a valuable asset against a rival band of rebels now known as the Neverseen. She was also raised with no awareness of who she was or where she belonged in order to give her a unique perspective on the Lost Cities. And she was hidden among humans, both to keep her safe until her abilities manifested, and also to provide her with a different level of insight into the human species—perhaps to someday help determine how to resolve the problems arising from humankind's destructive behavior. Many suspect that some larger purpose for the moonlark still has yet to be revealed. Only time will tell—assuming Sophie continues to survive the numerous attempts on her life.

A GIRL OF MANY TALENTS:

Sophie is the only elf to manifest five special abilities—and it's unclear whether she will continue to manifest any others. She's the youngest elf on record to manifest, becoming a Telepath when she was only five human years old. The ability was triggered by the mysterious Mr. Forkle, who also triggered her inflicting and Polyglot abilities after rescuing Sophie and Dex Dizznee from their kidnappers. (He let Sophie and Dex make their own way back to the Lost Cities in order to keep his identity hidden, and presumably triggered the new abilities to help her through that challenge.) Mr. Forkle additionally triggered Sophie's enhancing after she chose to accept the talent. But Sophie's teleporting triggered on its own, possibly from the adrenaline of nearly plummeting to her death.

GREAT POWER, STRUGGLE, AND RESPONSIBILITY:

Sophie's telepathy was a burden for her as a child, often exposing her to harsh or hurtful things and causing headaches because she did not know how to shield her mind from the constant bombardment of human thoughts. She also had to hide the ability, because humans would have either doubted her or studied her—or both. And when she moved to the Lost Cities, her problems amplified. Sophie has faced suspicion, judgment, and gossip because of her past, and because of the strength and abundance of her abilities—all of which became worse after Sophie made several missteps in regards to the rules of telepathy, including attempting to cheat on her Level Two alchemy midterm and illegally invading King Dimitar's mind. Her telekinesis also proved somewhat unwieldy when tested by Councillor Bronte during her Foxfire qualification exam—and there was a very suspicious incident involving Fitz Vacker during Foxfire's Ultimate Splotching Championship. After Sophie nearly faded away, her abilities also began to malfunction, requiring a dangerous "reset" performed by the Black Swan. She needed a second "reset" later, for further refinement to her inflicting. And initially, her teleporting required her to jump from dangerously high places in the hope that the momentum would help her slip into the void before the fall killed her. Despite those challenges, Sophie's abilities and skills are, in short, *incredible*—even with her lack of proper training and practice. Her unique telepathy allows her to transmit astoundingly long distances, track the thoughts of others to their precise locations, communicate with animals, and heal broken minds. She can also slip past anyone's mental blocking, while her own mental shields remain nearly impenetrable. (Reports indicate that only Fitz Vacker, Mr. Forkle, and the alicorns have ever been able to bypass her guard.) As if all of that weren't impressive enough, she has now become Cognates with Fitz Vacker, and when the two of them work together, they're able to accomplish numerous feats that many would consider to be impossible. Her inflicting has been somewhat less reliable—though the recent reset has given her significantly better control. She's also proven that negative *and* positive emotions can be inflicted—something previously unknown to her inflicting Mentor (Councillor Bronte). And while her linguistics Mentor (Lady Cadence) finds Sophie's mimicking to be seriously lacking, she has noted that Sophie's grasp of languages and pronunciation is flawless. Enhancing is Sophie's newest ability, and another talent that she has recently learned to master. Thanks to the guidance of Councillor Oralie, Sophie no longer requires gloves—or the special gadgets the Black Swan's mysterious Technopath designed for her—in order to "switch off" the ability. And Sophie's teleporting, which already allows her to go nearly everywhere she desires without needing a leaping crystal, recently became much stronger. Reports indicate that she can now reach the void by simply running, without needing a falling sensation first.

AN UNEVEN PRODIGY PERFORMANCE:

Despite being an "advanced student" in human schools (Sophie's human education records indicate that she was considered "years ahead" of her other classmates), Sophie has struggled with many of her sessions at Foxfire. Particularly challenging subjects include

PE, elementalism, and alchemy—the last being a session she didn't technically pass. (Her Mentor's notes list numerous fires and explosions.) In fact, Sophie was only able to advance to Level Three because the Council agreed to replace alchemy with an inflicting session mentored by Councillor Bronte. A linguistics session was also added to her Level Three schedule in light of Sophie manifesting as a Polyglot, and Lady Cadence was brought back to the Lost Cities (somewhat unwillingly) to be Sophie's Mentor. Both new ability sessions required giving Sophie access to the Silver Tower—something that has never been granted to a Level Three before. And Sophie does excel at her telepathy session (mentored by Sir Tiergan and now including Fitz Vacker) and her elvin history and Universe sessions, where her photographic memory works in her favor. She's also done fairly well at making friends and generally adapting to her new environment—though she *has* ended up in detention a significant number of times. It should be noted that Sophie's numerous near-death experiences, as well as certain incidents involving the Council, have often hindered her attendance at Foxfire and forced her to miss key exams.

ACCIDENT-PRONE:

While living with humans, Sophie was hospitalized at least twice—once when she was five human years old, after she fell and hit her head (which was also when Mr. Forkle triggered her telepathy), and once when she was nine human years old, after a severe allergic reaction to something the doctors could never identify. (The substance was later identified as limbium, which was given to her by the Black Swan.) And since arriving in the Lost Cities, Sophie has set a record for injuries, many of which were nearly fatal—though most can't be considered her fault, since they were the direct result of attacks by the Neverseen. See Sophie's medical record for more specifics.

A GIFT WITH ALICORNS:

Sophie's unique telepathy allowed her to track the thoughts of what turned out to be an incredibly rare female alicorn—the only creature capable of resetting the Timeline to Extinction—and bring her safely to Havenfield. And since Sophie could communicate with the creature (the alicorn even informed Sophie that her name is Silveny), the Council opted to leave her in Sophie's care, which allowed Sophie to discover Silveny's ability to teleport. Unfortunately, Sophie also followed the Black Swan's instructions and took Silveny to one of the Black Swan's hideouts, where the Neverseen managed to track them down and stage an ambush. Silveny's wing was broken during the attack, but Sophie used her teleporting to get herself, Keefe Sencen, and Silveny safely back to Havenfield. And Silveny's injury did heal completely, much to everyone's relief. Afterward, Sophie convinced Silveny to move to the Sanctuary, both for Silveny's protection and to unite her with the male of her species (Greyfell). And Sophie discovered soon after that she was able to remain in contact with Silveny telepathically, despite the distance between them—which turned out to be a very good thing. The Neverseen tried numerous times to steal both alicorns from the Sanctuary, and when Sophie learned that Silveny was pregnant (which would surely make the Neverseen even *more* desperate to capture her), she convinced the Council that it would be safer to set the alicorns free so that no one would know where they were. She promised to maintain regular contact with Silveny and Greyfell and provide detailed reports on their safety and wellness—though Silveny made that promise difficult for Sophie to keep. She started ignoring Sophie when she reached out to her telepathically and refused to come to Havenfield for any medical checkups, all of which turned out to be some sort of protective instinct related to the fact that Silveny was pregnant with twins. But she did call on Sophie for help when she went into labor early. And Sophie relied on Vika and Stina Heks—as well as the trolls—to save both babies (a male named Wynn and a female named Luna) and ensure that Silveny survived the delivery. The alicorn family currently lives at Havenfield but is free to go whenever and wherever they want. Sophie remains their point of contact.

A MAGNET FOR TROUBLE:
Since Sophie's arrival in the Lost Cities, she has had numerous—occasionally heated—interactions with the Council. She was tested by a committee of three (Councillor Oralie, Councillor Bronte, and Councillor Kenric) and granted provisional attendance to Foxfire—which she nearly lost due to poor performance in several of her sessions. But as of now, she maintains her standing at our prestigious academy. She has also faced Tribunals for accidentally bottling quintessence—and bringing the dangerous substance to school—as well as for illegally leaping to the human world to bottle a sample of their firestorm in order to prove the flames were Everblaze (a charge she was sentenced to

"time already served" in light of her kidnapping). Several members of the Council also suspect that she has possession of an unregistered Spyball, but no proof has been found to support these theories. After her abilities were reset, Sophie requested permission from the Council to attempt a "healing" on Alden Vacker's shattered mind, which turned out to be wonderfully successful. As a result, she was ordered to perform a healing on a former Councillor (Fintan Pyren) in the hope that she would be able to retrieve the secrets he'd protected during his memory break. Unfortunately, that healing resulted in Councillor Kenric's death and Fintan's escape, along with an inferno of Everblaze that destroyed half of Eternalia. And while Sophie was at Kenric's planting, she attempted to read King Dimitar's mind (she evidently considered him to be suspicious) and was nearly dragged away to an ogre work camp for violating the elvin-ogre treaty. But final punishment was left up to the Council, and the Councillors voted to constrain her abilities with a prototype "ability restrictor" designed by Dex Dizznee instead. The gadget appeared to cause Sophie some discomfort, but it also succeeded in limiting her power. And Sophie cooperated with the punishment—until she "lost" the ability restrictor through suspicious circumstances, right before illegally teleporting to the human world. She—and all of her friends—fled the Lost Cities not long after, hiding with the Black Swan until they were captured while attempting to liberate Prentice Endal from Exile. During the confrontation, Sophie revealed her possession of Councillor Kenric's cache and bartered a deal for her and her friends' freedom by agreeing to formal banishment and attendance at Exillium. Her group's role in finding a cure for the gnomish plague restored their citizenship and admission to Foxfire. Sophie also convinced the Council to free Prentice from Exile and performed a healing on Prentice's mind—but she was unable to recover any of his memories. She was also selected to participate in the ogre treaty renegotiations at Lumenaria, and her warnings during the Neverseen's attack on the castle saved numerous lives, including the Councillors'. Despite that, her relationship with the Council has remained tenuous. Sophie often questions their authority and refuses to play by their rules—particularly after her human parents were captured by Vespera. Miss Foster's desperate rescue led to the discovery of one of the Lost Cities' more dangerous secrets, and she continues to advocate for that information to be made public, despite the chaos that would likely ensue. She and her friends have also become the "faces" of the revolution, both for saving Atlantis from flooding, and because they were broadcast standing up to the Neverseen during the troll attack that occurred at the most recent Celestial Festival. In light of Sophie's growing support, the Council elected to begin working with her and appointed Sophie and several of her friends as Regents in the nobility, forming Team Valiant, which Sophie was assigned to lead. The team was sent to Loamnore to negotiate with King Enki, to mixed results—though King Enki has since been outed as a traitor, so it's possible the lack of success was not Team Valiant's fault. As of this writing, the Council remains committed to the project, but only time will tell if it will find true success, or whether Sophie will fall back into her ways of disobedience and rebellion and finally end up exiled.

DECEASED BUT NOT DEAD:

Sophie was kidnapped by the Neverseen, along with her best friend (Dex Dizznee). But their disappearance at first seemed to be a tragic accident. Evidence at their last known location, as well as the recovery of their registry pendants from the bottom of the ocean, led the Council to believe that both Sophie and Dex had been washed away by a tidal wave. With no evidence to suggest any alternative, both Sophie and Dex were declared "deceased." Plantings were held, and their Wanderlings remain in the Wanderling Woods to this day, since it would be wrong to destroy innocent trees simply because they were planted prematurely.

AN ABUNDANCE OF BODYGUARDS:

After Sophie escaped from her kidnappers and returned to the Lost Cities, the Council reached out to Queen Hylda and requested that she supply Sophie with a goblin for protection. Queen Hylda complied, assigning one of her best warriors (Sandor) to serve as Sophie's bodyguard—and he takes his job *very* seriously. Sandor's motto appears to be "I go where you go," and he does his best to never leave Sophie's side. He's also reportedly hidden trackers in her clothes in case she's ever abducted again—or tries to sneak away. And while Sophie doesn't always appreciate being shadowed by an overprotective, seven-foot-tall goblin (particularly since so many of her "investigations" into the Neverseen require a hefty amount of risk), she and Sandor have still managed to form a unique friendship. In fact, when Sandor considered resigning after what he viewed as "failing Sophie" during one of the Neverseen's recent brutal attacks, Sophie begged him to stay and even agreed to adding additional bodyguards to her detail to make Sandor feel more confident about her level of protection. Sandor in turn surprised everyone by opting for a multispeciesial approach, which is how Sophie ended up with an ogre bodyguard (Botros), a gnomish bodyguard (Flori), a dwarven bodyguard (Nubiti), and a trollish bodyguard (Tarina). (Because of certain dramatics in the trollish and dwarven worlds—as well as one of Sophie's friends needing a bodyguard—her detail is currently reduced to only Sandor and Flori.) It was quite the spectacle when her full group of protectors was gathered, and almost inspiring in a way. Proof that our world could be so much stronger if all the intelligent species truly found a way to work together.

NEXUS AND REGISTRY PENDANT EVENTS:

Sophie was given Fitz Vacker's old nexus when she was first brought to the Lost Cities, and she kept it as her primary nexus until it was stolen during her kidnapping—which was also when her first registry pendant was removed by the Neverseen (in a somewhat successful attempt to "fake" her death). Upon her escape and recovery, Sophie was given an updated registry pendant with heightened security measures to prevent tampering or removal—though Alden Vacker managed to cut it off before Sophie fled the Lost Cities to join the Black Swan. She was issued a third pendant when the Council lifted her banishment, and that one seems to have lasted (but sometimes the feed appears to get interrupted). Della Vacker also gave Sophie a new nexus after her kidnapping, which Sophie was ordered to wear despite how strong her concentration had gotten, as a precaution after Sophie nearly faded away. Additional leaping problems resulted in Sophie being given a second nexus to wear on her other wrist, but neither turned out to be necessary once her abilities were reset. Alden Vacker removed both before Sophie joined the Black Swan, to prevent anyone from tracking her location.

UNMATCHABLE:

If school gossip is to be believed, then Sophie has "liked" or dated (or may currently be dating) a number of different prodigies—but none of that has been confirmed. What *has* been confirmed is that Sophie has attempted to register for the match (according to a report from the Matchmaking Office), and the system has denied her request. Without record of her genetic lineage, she cannot be safely matched, as there is far too great of a risk that she could be paired with a biological relative. And a second investigation into her genetic parents' identities (in addition to one performed when Sophie first arrived in the Lost Cities) has been recently completed by the Council—and turned up nothing. So unless Sophie's biological parents come forward—or she discovers their identities on her own—her status will remain unmatchable.

THE "FOSTER OBLIVION":

Admittedly, there is little actual fact to report on this subject—but given how often the term is used (particularly by Keefe Sencen's ogre bodyguard), it seemed necessary to include a brief mention. Theories suggest that what the phrase means to imply is a certain lack of understanding on Sophie's part when it comes to the feelings of others—and her own feelings as well. Which does make one wonder why the Black Swan didn't also make her an Empath. Little is known on that subject either.

FINAL NOTE:

Tampering has occurred in the past—and possibly still occurs—to Sophie's pendant feed, both for her protection and to hide certain activities she's participated in. For that, and numerous other reasons, the Council remains divided on whether Sophie is trustworthy.

MEDICAL RECORD FOR
Sophie Elizabeth Foster

INCIDENT: <u>Emergency House Call to Everglen</u>

DETAILS:
Rushed over to check on someone that Alden found
hidden in the Forbidden Cities—and I'll admit: Part of me
wondered if this was going to be some sort of prank.
But . . . I just met a girl with brown eyes and <u>elvin</u> DNA.

SYMPTOMS/INJURIES:
Poor kid. I can't imagine leaving my whole life behind
like that! She seemed pretty tough, though. And she
was surprisingly healthy, given all the chemicals she's
grown up with—but she needs a <u>major</u> detox.

TREATMENT:
Gave her what I'd brought and made a list of elixirs to
get from Slurps and Burps. Also told her to drink
two bottles of Youth every day.

NOTES:
I need to check on her in a couple weeks, and she
did <u>not</u> look happy about that. I can't blame her, given

what I know about human medicine. But hopefully I can prove it's different around here.

INCIDENT: <u>First Healing Center Visit</u>

DETAILS:
Sounds like Sophie's first attempt at alchemy was an adventure. (<u>Really</u> wish I could've seen the explosion!)

SYMPTOMS/INJURIES:
A pretty nasty acid burn on her wrist.

TREATMENT:
Tried my favorite balm, and it worked perfectly. Also checked Sophie's detox progress, and her cells are looking <u>much</u> happier.

NOTES:
Starting to think I'll be seeing a lot of this kid, which will be tough since Sophie's still afraid of me. It's a good thing Keefe was there to distract her this time.

INCIDENT: <u>Second Healing Center Visit</u>

DETAILS:
Things got strange during the Ultimate Splotching

Championship, and Sophie (and Fitz) ended up launching backward across the room and slamming into the wall.

SYMPTOMS/INJURIES:
Nothing major—which is surprising, considering Sophie was unconscious when they brought her in. I'm sure she'll be sore tomorrow.

TREATMENT:
Cool compresses and a painkiller—and taking it easy for the rest of the day.

NOTES:
I don't think Sophie has any idea how powerful she is. It sounded like she did a brain push today—and if I'm right, I'm betting that's only the beginning of what she can do.

INCIDENT: <u>Emergency Call to Moonglade</u>

DETAILS:
I'd just settled into bed when Sophie hailed me. Somehow she hurt herself bottling starlight for her Universe assignment. (Always an adventure with this girl!)

SYMPTOMS/INJURIES:
Major burns with blackish, purplish blisters. Looked

super painful. Glad she set aside her fears and hailed me.

TREATMENT:
I started with my strongest burn salve mixed with painkiller and a Youth soak. But her skin still looked raw, so I ran home for something a little more extreme. (I figured Sophie wouldn't want to know that her hands were covered in yeti pee, so I left out that detail—but I did warn her to wash her hands thoroughly.)

NOTES:
I also wrapped up the starlight to make sure she couldn't hurt herself again. Weird thing was, it felt cold—not hot. And I've never seen light like that before—or heard of "███████"

UPDATE:
Sophie stopped by early (I think she didn't want her friends to see her in the Healing Center <u>again</u>), and her hands looked perfect! But I still gave her one more elixir, just to be safe.

ADDITIONAL NOTES:
In the category of Proof That Things Keep Getting Weirder Around Here, a couple of Councillors showed up and asked me a billion questions—and made me

black out the star's name from this record. Pretty sure I know what that means. . . .

INCIDENT: <u>Third Healing Center Visit</u>

DETAILS:
Sophie was unconscious and covered in blotches when Fitz brought her to me. Dex said it was an allergy, probably caused by the limbium in the Nogginease he gave her.

SYMPTOMS/INJURIES:
Difficulty breathing. Hives. Swelling. Projectile vomiting.

TREATMENT:
Never treated an allergy before, so I threw together an elixir to address the symptoms I could see. Thankfully, it worked, and I cleaned Sophie up and brought her home to rest. Also gave her a vial of the elixir to wear in case anything like this ever happens again.

NOTES:
Not gonna lie—this was <u>close</u>. Bullhorn screamed his head off when Fitz brought her in, and curled up against her chest the whole time I was making the medicine.

INCIDENT: <u>Emergency House Call to Havenfield</u>

DETAILS:
Sophie snuck away to the Forbidden Cities to bottle a sample of their fires.

SYMPTOMS/INJURIES:
Minor burns (well . . . minor for <u>Sophie</u>). Her lungs also showed signs of smoke inhalation.

TREATMENT:
Only needed my regular salve this time. Elixirs and Youth took care of her lungs.

NOTES:
Not sure what's going to happen to Sophie after this, but if there's a Tribunal, you can bet I'll be offering to testify. I know what she did was illegal—but it was also incredibly brave. Looks like she was right, too, and the fires were Everblaze.

FILE CLOSED.

PATIENT . . . DECEASED.

I can't believe Sophie's gone. I keep checking my Imparter, hoping someone will tell me it's all a mistake. But . . . I saw her waterlogged registry pendant.

And I just got back from her planting.

There's no elixir or balm to fix this. Nothing I can do—except remember how brave and smart and incredible she was, and make sure everyone else remembers too.

Grow strong, new little Wanderling. You hold some very precious DNA.

FILE REOPENED.

INCIDENT: <u>Emergency Call to Lumenaria</u>

DETAILS:
Got a panicked hail from Fitz that sounded like a cruel joke, but I leaped to Lumenaria with a few supplies—AND THERE WERE SOPHIE AND DEX!!! I will definitely be celebrating later—but first, I have to get them through this. . . .

SYMPTOMS/INJURIES:
<u>Severe</u> fading—but I'm not losing this girl again!

TREATMENT:
Gave Sophie a sedative so we could leap her safely to Everglen.

NOTES:
Now the real work begins.

INCIDENT: <u>Recovery at Everglen</u>

DETAILS:
Still dealing with Sophie's fading, plus leftover issues from her kidnapping.

SYMPTOMS/INJURIES:

Too many to list them all (and it makes me sick to think about what those monsters did to her . . .).

TREATMENT:

I gave Sophie an aggressive combination of elixirs—plus a special limbium-free Fade Fuel. And there were definitely days when I didn't think she was going to make it, but . . . SOPHIE PULLED THROUGH!!! She woke up a few hours ago, and I'm not gonna lie—I totally teared up! She's still weak, but she's safe—and it's so good to hear her voice again!

NOTES:

This girl is a fighter—and thank goodness for that. But I'm having some adjustments made to her nexus, since she clearly needs more practice with light leaping!

INCIDENT: Checkup House Call to Havenfield

DETAILS:

Apparently Sophie leaped home from the Forbidden Cities with her consciousness wrapped around an alicorn (of course she did), and Grady wanted to make sure she's okay.

SYMPTOMS/INJURIES:

Sophie claimed she was fine—and her tests seemed normal. But I get the feeling she's hiding something from me. She also clearly hasn't been sleeping.

TREATMENT:

None. I tried to convince her to take a mild sedative before bed or drink some slumberberry tea, but she refused.

NOTES:

I understand her aversion to sedatives after what she went through—but she seriously needs some sleep. Wish I could think of something to suggest . . .

INCIDENT: <u>Emergency House Call to Everglen</u>

DETAILS:

Sophie and Alden were sent to ▓▓▓▓ by the Council, and things did <u>not</u> go well.

SYMPTOMS/INJURIES:

Sophie faded again during the leap home—while wearing a nexus (!!!). Thankfully, it wasn't as severe this time—but it still worries me. She also had burns on her hands, and a few bruises and scrapes. And she admitted that she's been getting headaches (which she should've told me about earlier!). But she seemed more worried about Alden.

TREATMENT:
More of my special limbium-free Fade Fuel. I also treated her burns with a bottle of Youth, some balms, and a silk wrap. And I recommended weekly checkups for all of the other symptoms she's apparently been hiding. We'll see if she cooperates.

NOTES:
I'm making her wear an extra nexus, since I have no idea what's going on.

ADDITIONAL NOTES:
Given where Sophie was, I can't say I'm surprised that the Council made me edit this record. But I'm <u>also</u> going to add that they were irresponsible for sending an innocent kid (who's been through enough) to a horrible place like that!

INCIDENT: <u>Emergency House Call to Everglen</u>

DETAILS:
Alden's mind is . . . I can't bring myself to write it yet.

SYMPTOMS/INJURIES:
Sophie looked like she was about to have an emotional meltdown.

TREATMENT:
Gave her a mood enhancer—a pretty strong one.

NOTES:
I would've given her a sedative for later, but she's still very against them.

INCIDENT: <u>Fourth Healing Center Visit</u>

DETAILS:
Sophie came here on her lunch break—and it wasn't even an emergency!

SYMPTOMS/INJURIES:
Sore muscles from alicorn riding, plus exhaustion.

TREATMENT:
Gave her some Achey-Break for the pain, and decided to check her mind for guilt—which knocked her unconscious (should've known a Sophie visit wouldn't be easy). Nothing looked wrong in my tests, so I gave her a broad-range elixir and made her stay with me for the rest of school so I could monitor.

NOTES:

I'm feeling a little bad for hanging her picture and joking about calling this the "Foster Center." She _is_ holding the record for near-death experiences, but . . . I think she's really struggling with what happened to Alden. (And I can't blame her for that.) I also think she's more worried about the headaches than she's admitting. I just don't understand why my tests don't show anything wrong.

INCIDENT: <u>Fifth Healing Center Visit</u>

DETAILS:
Sophie's inflicting session with Councillor Bronte didn't go as planned (or that's what Bronte told me to write—I get the feeling this was <u>exactly</u> what he wanted to happen. And he's lucky I didn't punch him in the mouth!).

SYMPTOMS/INJURIES:
Sophie claimed she felt fine, since Grady gave her an elixir the Dizznees made for her. (I'll have to find out what they put in it.) But Master Leto and Sandor wanted me to check her.

TREATMENT:
Made her drink a bottle of Youth and gave her a broad-range elixir. Wish I could do more, but her tests still look normal.

NOTES:

I wanted her to stay and get some rest for her lunch break, but Keefe was there, and we ended up telling him about Alden so . . . that was rough.

INCIDENT: <u>Emergency House Call to Havenfield</u>

DETAILS:

Turns out alicorns can teleport—and I would laugh about how today's adventure is something that would only happen to Sophie, but Sophie had to light leap Silveny home, and . . .

SYMPTOMS/INJURIES:

SHE FADED. AGAIN! WITH TWO NEXUSES—AND REALLY STRONG CONCENTRATION.

TREATMENT:

She took <u>more</u> of my limbium—free Fade Fuel. But I still can't find anything wrong, so I also gave her a vial to wear (she's getting quite the necklace collection . . .) and told her to take a dose every time she leaps, no matter what.

NOTES:

I DON'T UNDERSTAND WHAT'S GOING ON!!

INCIDENT: <u>Sixth Healing Center Visit</u>

DETAILS:
The Hall of Illumination isn't exactly a dangerous place, but leave it to Sophie to still end up unconscious.

SYMPTOMS/INJURIES:
Couldn't find anything <u>physically</u> wrong, but since the mirror that knocked Sophie out was the Lodestar, I tried flashing light in her eyes, and . . . now we know what the problem is. (Sorta . . .) She said the light felt like it was boring into her brain.

TREATMENT:
All I could do was make Sophie stay and guzzle different elixirs (plus some Youth) and then flash light into her eyes again to see if it worked. Sadly, nothing helped—and the headaches eventually got too intense for her to keep going.

NOTES:
I seriously don't know what to do—but I <u>will</u> figure this out!

INCIDENT: <u>Emergency House Call to Havenfield</u>

DETAILS:

The Black Swan convinced Sophie that they could "fix" her. So she flew across the ocean with Silveny (and Keefe) to have her abilities reset. And after <u>that</u> nightmare, a bunch of cloaked enemies attacked.

SYMPTOMS/INJURIES:

WHERE DO I EVEN START? THE BLACK SWAN GAVE HER AN ENTIRE OUNCE OF LIMBIUM AND THEN INJECTED HER WITH SOME MYSTERIOUS REMEDY SO SHE WOULDN'T DIE—AND THEN THE SAME CREEPS WHO KIDNAPPED HER NEARLY KILLED HER AGAIN!!!

TREATMENT:

According to this Mr. Forkle person (who I have <u>quite</u> a few things I'd love to say to), I was only allowed to clean Sophie's wounds for the next twenty-four hours—no giving her elixirs or serums because they could mess with her "reset." NOT EVEN ANY PAINKILLERS.

UPDATE:

As soon as that twenty-four hours was up, I gave her all the medicine she could safely handle.

NOTES:

There's a bruise on Sophie's hand from where the Black Swan injected their "remedy." Pretty sure it's going to scar. But . . . I think the reset did fix the issues she's been dealing with. It also appears she can teleport. (Don't know why I'm even surprised.)

INCIDENT: <u>Seventh Healing Center Visit</u>

DETAILS:
Sophie found what she thought was a tracker tangled in Silveny's tail, and it turned out to be covered in aromark, which then got all over Sophie's (and Keefe's) hands.

SYMPTOMS/INJURIES:
I don't know much about ogre biochemistry, but according to Lady Cadence, aromark = bad and needs to be removed. I also found what looked like a burn on Sophie's wrist, but she claimed it's a bruise and looks different because she used a home remedy.

TREATMENT:
Piquatine melts off the top layer of skin—which isn't <u>as</u> bad as it sounds, since I numbed Sophie first. But it's a freaky process, even for me. I could've sedated her, but I know how she feels about sedatives. My all-purpose salve fixed up the burn-bruise thing.

NOTES:
Made sure to give Sophie a lecture about coming to me with injuries instead of using home remedies.

INCIDENT: <u>Eighth Healing Center Visit</u>

DETAILS:
Sir Harding sent her to see me (though I think Sophie might've been faking to ditch PE and only came because Sandor dragged her here—hooray for overprotective goblins!).

SYMPTOMS/INJURIES:
Checked her burn-bruise thing—which looked good. But her cells were exhausted. Apparently she hasn't slept since Silveny moved to the Sanctuary.

TREATMENT:
None. She's sticking to her "no sedatives" policy.

NOTES:
Magnate Leto was there and suggested she try reaching Silveny telepathically, even with the distance between them. Sophie looked skeptical—but I'll bet she pulls it off.

INCIDENT: <u>Emergency House Call to Havenfield</u>

DETAILS:
The Black Swan sent Sophie (and Keefe) on a leaping adventure—using light from the unmapped stars and taking her underground and under the ocean! (Seriously, <u>how</u> did they think that was a good idea?) Oh, and for added fun, the cloaked villains showed up.

SYMPTOMS/INJURIES:
Some of the most traumatized cells I've ever seen! But no other injuries.

TREATMENT:
Back to my special Fade Fuel, plus a serum to rebuild her cells.

NOTES:
Also gave Sophie a poultice, since the serum she has to take will make her a little itchy.

INCIDENT: <u>Emergency Checkup in the Principal's Office</u>

DETAILS:
In what might be the worst decision ever, the Council

forced Sophie to wear the ability restrictor that Dex never should have designed.

SYMPTOMS/INJURIES:
Fainting, headache, dehydration, nausea—and don't even get me started on the emotional toll that comes with having your powers stripped away.

TREATMENT:
Couldn't do much, but I gave her a bottle of Youth and some elixirs to drink whenever she feels nauseous. She'll probably need to take regular supplements as well.

NOTES:
WHAT SHE REALLY NEEDS IS SOMEONE TO TAKE THAT MONSTROSITY OFF OF HER HEAD.

INCIDENT: Emergency House Call to Everglen

DETAILS:
The Black Swan tried to ambush the bad guys (who seem to be called "the Neverseen"), but it turned into a battle—and this was after Sophie survived a huge firefight with Brant (who's apparently a Pyrokinetic). Basically, I can't keep up with all the weirdness, and I don't know how Sophie's still alive—but boy, am I glad she is.

SYMPTOMS/INJURIES:

Frostbite, altitude sickness, smoke inhalation, and dozens of other issues. Guess it could've been worse (like Sandor), but . . . sigh.

TREATMENT:

So. Many. Things. (Seriously, my elixir and balm supplies are totally depleted.) Also . . . had to give her a big hug.

NOTES:

Thank goodness she got rid of that horrible ability restrictor. I don't want to know how—and I have a feeling the Council's going to freak out. But I'm so happy it's gone.

INCIDENT: <u>Ninth Healing Center Visit</u>

DETAILS:

Sophie was expelled from Foxfire (don't even get me started on that), but leave it to her to show up in the Healing Center anyway—with a plague-infested gnome, no less. (And Fitz.)

SYMPTOMS/INJURIES:

I insisted on doing a full checkup, and I could see signs of healed burns and previous light poisoning. But it looks like the "Sophie Survival Kit" and the list of "Crazy Messes That Sophie Will Find a Way to Get Herself Into" are doing their job!

TREATMENT:
A LOT more elixirs.

NOTES:
Kinda killed me to watch Sophie leave, knowing she's surely going to have more medical emergencies. But at least she knows she can come to me if she needs to.

INCIDENT: <u>Emergency House Call to Sterling Gables</u>

DETAILS:
Timkin Heks hailed me to help Keefe, who was having some sort of emotional meltdown (among other things). And I checked on Sophie while I was there.

SYMPTOMS/INJURIES:
Nothing I could find, except the usual signs that she's been pushing herself too hard and risking her life.

TREATMENT:
A bunch more elixirs. And another hug!

NOTES:
Sophie asked me to get Keefe an Emotional Support Stuffed Animal. Gotta admire how she's always taking care of her friends. Wish I could get her to take better care of herself!

INCIDENT: <u>Emergency House Call to Havenfield</u>

DETAILS:
I can't believe I'm writing this, but . . . there was a major ogre attack.

SYMPTOMS/INJURIES:
No physical injuries to Sophie. (She said she wasn't there for the battle.) But she did show borderline signs of shock.

TREATMENT:
Gave her a couple of calming elixirs.

NOTES:
Grady's bodyguard (Brielle) was killed, and it sounds like it would've been a lot worse if Verdi hadn't broken out of her enclosure and done some ogre-hunting.

INCIDENT: <u>Tenth Healing Center Visit</u>

DETAILS:
Sophie rushed Keefe to see me after he decided to challenge King Dimitar to a sparring match and become a Mercadir—whatever <u>that</u> means.

SYMPTOMS/INJURIES:
Did a quick checkup on Sophie, since she was here. And I couldn't find anything wrong—but she was a little pale.

TREATMENT:
Made her take one elixir, just in case.

NOTES:
Apparently Keefe has the ogre princess for his bodyguard now? Also: There was some serious tension between Sophie and Keefe. As far as I know, they're just friends—but it almost seemed like . . . you know what? I do <u>not</u> want to get involved in teenage drama!

INCIDENT: <u>Eleventh Healing Center Visit</u>

DETAILS:
The Neverseen brutally attacked Sophie (and Fitz). If I ever get my hands on them . . .

SYMPTOMS/INJURIES:
This is the closest Sophie's ever come to dying. Bullhorn knew it too. And Sophie wouldn't respond to <u>anything</u> I gave her—until Tam called the shadows out of her blood. The bulk of the damage is to her

right shoulder and right hand, but there's lots to deal with.

TREATMENT:
I wrapped her arm and hand in a cocoon of bandages to immobilize them. But the healing is going <u>slow</u>, even with marrow regenerator.

NOTES:
She's not going to be able to move or light leap until her bones heal. So it looks like we'll be having a Foxfire slumber party. And of <u>course</u> Sophie doesn't want any sedatives. I also don't like how certain parts of her look fuzzy when I try to examine them.

UPDATE:
Sophie woke up thrashing, which set back her recovery—and she's feeling pain in her head and hand that isn't showing up in my tests. Gave her some of the extreme marrow regenerator (leftover from when Sandor was thrown off Mount Everest) plus pain medicine.

SECOND UPDATE:
I asked Tam to check for shadows, and his Mentor (Lady Zillah) tagged along and gave a long speech about shadowflux and echoes. Tam tried

to soothe them, but it only made things worse. And sadly, there's not much I can do—except give Sophie an elixir to keep her dreams lighter while the echoes fade.

THIRD UPDATE:
It's been uneventful around here (unless you count Keefe's skill lessons—and Fitz waking up). I'm also working with Livvy to change the strategy. The new elixirs and balms have some <u>nasty</u> ingredients, but we're onto something.

FOURTH UPDATE:
Had to change out the bandages and <u>wow</u>, was there a lot of ooze! Also got a better look at Sophie's hand, and it's definitely swollen. But the bones have set, and these new balms and compression wraps might mean she can go home by the end of the week!

FIFTH UPDATE:
Ro and Keefe <u>insisted</u> on being at the next bandage change (or "the Great Fitzphie Ooze Fest"), and it was even stinkier than the last one. But Sophie's hand was back to normal size! Time to focus on the nerve damage and rebuilding strength.

SIXTH UPDATE:

After a special mineral soak and a little more strength training, Sophie regained feeling in her hand and could FINALLY get out of bed! (!!!)

SEVENTH UPDATE:

Fitz went home yesterday, and Sophie's mood seemed a little low. Thankfully, Keefe was there to distract her.

EIGHTH UPDATE:

Gotta admit, sometimes I thought I'd never get to write these words, but: SOPHIE JUST LEFT THE HEALING CENTER!!! And of <u>course</u> she's doing an "errand" with Mr. Forkle before going home. Some things never change.

INCIDENT: <u>Follow-Up House Call to Havenfield</u>

DETAILS:
Sophie still has a long recovery ahead.

SYMPTOMS/INJURIES:
Nothing new, at least!

TREATMENT:
Just rest.

NOTES:
The Black Swan's Technopath made a bracelet to boost the strength in Sophie's left arm, so I gave her permission to start battle training—but only on that side!

═══════════════════════════════════════

INCIDENT: <u>Twelfth Healing Center Visit</u>

DETAILS:
Sophie's being good and coming in for her checkups.

SYMPTOMS/INJURIES:
Found some swelling in Sophie's knuckles, but nothing serious. Lady Zillah also wanted Sophie to trigger her echoes—and it wasn't <u>horrible</u>. But . . . it wasn't great.

TREATMENT:
More medicine. Also hoping Lady Zillah finds a solution to this echo thing.

NOTES:
Kinda looked like Sophie and Fitz were "together." Huh. My little girl is growing up!

UPDATE:
I wasn't there when it happened, but I just got word

from Flori that she learned a song that <u>finally</u> made Sophie's echoes fade away.

INCIDENT: <u>Emergency House Call to Havenfield</u>

DETAILS:
Sophie agreed to reset her inflicting—which means taking limbium and hoping Livvy and I can stop her allergy before it kills her. No pressure.

SYMPTOMS/INJURIES:
Sophie went with the stronger, more dangerous dose (Is anyone shocked by this?), so the reaction was <u>severe</u>—and her heart stopped.

TREATMENT:
Chest compressions, plus the allergy remedy Livvy and I designed (and a booster shot Livvy made), followed by a tiny dose of sedative.

NOTES:
This definitely didn't go as well as I'd hoped.

UPDATE:
Sophie was knocked out for three days. And it's not safe to give her any elixirs or pain medicine for at

least another day. Flori made her a Panakes blossom broth that may help, though.

SECOND UPDATE:
She still needs a little more bed rest. But it was safe to give her some painkillers.

THIRD UPDATE:
Took Sophie five days to get out of bed and six before she made it outside. So this definitely took a toll. But she's through the worst of it, and it does seem to have worked.

INCIDENT: <u>Thirteenth Healing Center Visit</u>

DETAILS:
Sophie rushed Keefe to me. He's unconscious, and his cells are going through some sort of "transformation." So it looks like his mom got what she wanted.

SYMPTOMS/INJURIES:
Checked Sophie, too, and she's exhausted and emotionally overwhelmed and banged up from the battle. But nothing major.

TREATMENT:

Mostly, she just needed a pep talk—which I'm bad at. But I did my best.

NOTES:

I guess she discovered she can teleport without needing to free-fall now. The girl just keeps getting more and more amazing.

VACKER

REGISTRY FILE FOR
Fitzroy Avery Vacker

KNOWN ABILITIES: *Telepath*

RESIDENCE: *Everglen*

IMMEDIATE FAMILY: *Alden Vacker (father), Della Vacker (mother), Alvar Vacker (brother), Biana Vacker (sister)*

MATCH STATUS: *Registered with zero lists received*

EDUCATION: *Current Foxfire prodigy*

NEXUS: *No longer required*

PATHFINDER: *Not assigned. Restricted to Leapmasters and home crystals.*

SPYBALL APPROVAL: *None*

MEMBER OF THE NOBILITY: *No*

TITLE: *None*

NOBLE ASSIGNMENT: *None*

SIGNIFICANT CONNECTIONS: *Cognate to Sophie Foster; fealty-sworn member of the Black Swan; former Exillium Wayward; part of the Vacker family*

ASSIGNED BODYGUARD(S): *Grizel (goblin)*

PREFERRED NAME:

For reasons not disclosed, Fitzroy is most commonly identified by a nickname. In fact, few of his peers even realize his full name is Fitzroy. So to avoid confusion, the rest of this file shall refer to him by his more recognizable, shortened name: Fitz.

A LEGENDARY LINEAGE:

As made obvious by his last name, Fitz is a Vacker—a member of one of the most prominent families in the Lost Cities. Which means that he—and his siblings—have more relatives holding powerful positions in the nobility than any of their peers do. It would be far too tedious to include a full list of all the prominent Vackers and their accomplishments, but a few of note are as follows: Fallon Vacker, who was one of the three founding members of the Council and served for a thousand years as a Councillor; Orem Vacker, who is an extremely talented Flasher and puts on the impressive light show seen at the Celestial Festival; Luzia Vacker, Orem's mother, who is also a Flasher and created many of the illusions that keep the Lost Cities hidden; and, of course, Fitz's father, Alden, who is a renowned Telepath and an Emissary for the Council with the highest level of clearance, and is often given their most important assignments.

THE GOLDEN BOY:

Fitz manifested as a Telepath when he was thirteen, setting the record for "youngest to manifest as a Telepath"—until Sophie Foster revealed that she'd manifested when she was five human years old. Some people occasionally get confused and think that Fitz was actually "the youngest to manifest an ability—period." But that is simply not accurate. His own sister (Biana) manifested younger than that—as have several others. Nevertheless, Fitz's youth, and the strength of his telepathy, earned him the title "Alden's Golden Boy" (which is occasionally used less-than-kindly, particularly by Councillor Bronte). Fitz's academic record at Foxfire is also considered exemplary (despite his brief attendance at Exillium—and a somewhat suspicious number of absences during his first few years at the academy). And when he was descried by Councillor Terik, the reading was incredibly promising. Fitz excels in all areas of study, often receiving the highest grades out of everyone in his level. And he was the reigning Foxfire splotching champion until Sophie beat him with a brain push during her first time competing—though many consider that match to have been a tie, since both of them were thrown backward against the wall and knocked unconscious.

HIS FATHER'S UNAUTHORIZED QUEST:

Alden Vacker has long had a reputation for occasionally pursuing investigations without the Council's approval, and the largest proven example is the twelve years he spent secretly searching for the source of a strand of unregistered DNA. The Council had deemed the DNA to be a hoax after it was recovered during a memory break performed on Prentice Endal (a convicted rebel). But Alden was convinced the DNA belonged to a female child created by the Black Swan (an organization no one believed existed at the time) who'd been hidden somewhere among the Forbidden Cities. And in order to avoid the Council's suspicion or interference, Alden enlisted the help of both of his sons (who were also better able to approach the children that Alden was investigating without frightening them). Alvar—the elder of Alden's sons—was the first to assist with the project, but he was replaced by Fitz as soon as Fitz was old enough to take over, presumably because Fitz was closer to the girl's estimated age. Little is known about how Alden chose which "leads" to investigate or where he got his information from, or how many places his sons visited (though rumor has it that Fitz collected small souvenirs from each of the Forbidden locations he was sent to). But eventually all the searching paid off, and Fitz located Sophie Foster and brought her to the Lost Cities—technically twice. The first time was the day he met her—which was *not* what his father had instructed him to do. He was only supposed to observe and report back. But Sophie's eye color confused him, so he approached her to investigate further and realized she was definitely the girl he'd been looking for. And when she refused to believe what he was telling her, he brought her to the Lost Cities as proof—then took her back to her human home and made her promise not to tell anyone about anything she'd seen. (He's very lucky that she kept her word.) The next day, after the Council had been properly updated, Fitz was sent to retrieve Sophie and bring her to the Lost Cities permanently.

A LOYAL FRIEND:

There is some debate on this issue, but many consider Fitz to be

Sophie Foster's "first friend," since he was the one to discover her and also helped her settle into her new life in the Lost Cities. Despite the difference in their grade levels, Fitz also did his best to look out for Sophie when she first started attending Foxfire, and their relationship has only grown stronger since. Some have tried to claim that Fitz's friendship was initially only motivated by his father's encouragement. But the connection between Sophie and Fitz has stood the tests of both time and trial. Fitz even chose to follow Sophie to the Black Swan when she had to flee the Lost Cities after "losing" her ability restrictor, and Fitz has fought by her side in numerous confrontations with the Neverseen.

HERO MOMENT:

As previously mentioned, everyone believed that Sophie Foster and Dex Dizznee were drowned by a tidal wave after their registry pendants were found at the bottom of the ocean. And Fitz was no exception. He attended both of their plantings and was seen grieving intensely at each. But Fitz was also the first to suspect that Sophie and Dex were still alive. He'd initially thought he was imagining Sophie's transmissions for help, but as they grew stronger and more desperate, he decided to confide in both his sister (Biana Vacker) and his best friend (Keefe Sencen), who encouraged him to check the place where Sophie's "voice" was telling him to go. The three of them leaped to the Four Seasons Tree in Lumenaria and found Dex stunned by multiple melder blasts and Sophie fading away from an unprotected leap—but Fitz was able to keep Sophie conscious by communicating with her telepathically while Biana and Keefe brought Elwin back to help. Sophie and Dex needed time to recover, and it's likely that neither of them would be alive today if Fitz hadn't acted when he did.

SHADOWED DAYS:

Sophie Foster's kidnapping was a world-changing event for the Lost Cities in so many ways. But for Alden Vacker, her rescue proved that he (and the Council) had been wrong about the Black Swan. The organization was technically composed of rebels—but they were not behaving as *enemies*, like Alden had initially suspected. Which meant that Prentice Endal's arrest, memory break, and subsequent exiling had technically been unjust—particularly since Prentice had simply been trying to protect Sophie. And while the Council maintained (and still maintains) that they based their decision on the information they had been given at the time and therefore are not to be blamed, as the source of that information, the realization proved to be too much for Alden. He tried to fight his emotions—even pulled himself back from a smaller breakdown during a Council-assigned mission to [LOCATION REDACTED FOR SECURITY] with Sophie. But after watching Prentice's son (Wylie Endal) performing during the Foxfire Opening Ceremonies, the guilt shattered Alden's mind, leaving him in an unstable, unconscious state that is almost worse than death. His wife (Della Vacker) tried her best to hold her family together. But all three children (Fitz, Alvar, and Biana) were devastated over essentially losing their father. And many reports indicate that Fitz's grief manifested primarily as anger, and that most of that anger was directed at Sophie, whom he blamed for what happened to his father, since she'd known about Alden's smaller breakdown and hadn't warned anyone. (It should be noted that Elwin Heslege, who'd been assisting the family as a physician, reported seeing some improvement in Fitz's temperament with the use of what he calls an "Emotional Support Stuffed Animal." Elwin gifted Fitz with a sparkly stuffed red dragon, which he instructed Fitz to call Mr. Snuggles, and recommended that Fitz try hugging Mr. Snuggles whenever he was upset, or if he couldn't sleep. Numerous reports indicate that Fitz still has Mr. Snuggles in his possession and finds a great deal of solace and comfort from his stuffed dragon.) Even though Alden was technically still alive, a planting was held for him in an attempt to provide his family (and our world as a whole) with some sort of closure for his loss. His Wanderling continues to grow—but it has thankfully turned out to be yet another unnecessary tree casting shade in the Wanderling Woods (along with the Wanderlings for Sophie Foster and Dex Dizznee). Sophie discovered that her unique telepathy allowed her to heal broken minds, and she brought Alden back to consciousness. Since his "reawakening," it's been as though Alden were never gone, which was naturally a huge cause for celebration, both for his family and for everyone in the Lost Cities. And reports suggest that Fitz apologized to Sophie *before* she healed his father, because he wanted her to know that he valued her friendship even if she couldn't save the day.

COGNATES—AND POSSIBLY MORE:

Fitz was already an exceptional Telepath, but his ability improved exponentially once he was granted the rare opportunity of sharing a telepathy session with Sophie Foster and her Mentor (Sir Tiergan). The closer Fitz worked with Sophie, the more Tiergan began to suspect that a significant connection existed between his two prodigies, particularly since Fitz is one of the only Telepaths who can breach Sophie's mental blocking. It seems the reason that Fitz can do so is because Sophie subconsciously chooses to let him into her mind, which then allows Fitz to transmit his thoughts, search her memories, and hear what Sophie's thinking. He's also able to send Sophie bursts of mental energy when her own strength is weakening. And together, Sophie and Fitz have been able to accomplish impressive feats, like performing a mental healing on the shattered, ancient mind of an exiled member of the Neverseen (former Councillor Fintan Pyren)—though that healing did lead to an unanticipated inferno of Everblaze, which destroyed nearly half of Eternalia and caused the death of Councillor Kenric. They've also been able to successfully navigate the complex mental landscapes of other intelligent species, as when they searched King Dimitar's thoughts during a mission to Ravagog, and read the minds of two gnomes. Additionally, with Sophie's help, Fitz has been able to communicate with the alicorns, even over great distances. All of which is why Sophie and Fitz officially began training as Cognates during their time living with the Black Swan. Once their banishment ended, they continued the lessons with Sir Tiergan at Foxfire (though Tiergan had technically been working with them the whole time, since recent reports indicate that Tiergan is a member of the Black Swan's Collective, who goes by the name Granite). Fitz even gifted Sophie with Cognate rings as a Level Three midterms gift. And now that Sophie has manifested as an Enhancer, the two of them are able to accomplish truly incredible tasks, like recovering fragments of memories that had been shattered and buried in the darkest depths of Keefe's consciousness. Trust has occasionally been noted as a barrier for their Cognate connection (particularly for Sophie), but they've managed to find a way of working through it—though it will be interesting to see if the Cognate relationship can survive the matchmaking process. Rumors often circulate about Fitz and Sophie, and the terms "Fitzphie" and "Sophitz" seem to suggest some sort of romantic pairing. One of the matchmakers assigned to Fitz even wondered if certain answers in Fitz's match packet might've been an attempt to steer his match lists a particular way (though the process is of course designed to ensure a bias like that won't interfere with the matchmakers' recommendations).

A BANISHED VACKER—AND THE FIRST WAYWARD:

As mentioned earlier, Fitz chose to go with Sophie when she fled the Lost Cities to join the Black Swan. And his involvement in an attempted prison break in Exile led to him (and the rest of his friends, as well as his sister) being officially banished, expelled from Foxfire, and assigned to Exillium—which was definitely a first for his prestigious family (and quite the scandal, until he and his sister were allowed to return home and resume their studies at Foxfire, thanks to the role they played in stopping the gnomish plague).

FURTHER VACKER SCANDALS:

There have been murmurings of a "Vacker legacy" for some time—though the term has been used in both positive and negative ways. As such, it's unclear exactly what the label is meant to imply—but it should be noted that the legendary family is not without its share of controversy. Rumors have circulated for centuries about Fallon

Vacker—though it's difficult to locate any specific accusations. And Luzia Vacker worked closely with Vespera before Vespera's scandalous arrest. Luzia also had a secret alliance with the empress of the trolls, which recently caused a deadly scandal. Evidently Luzia allowed the trolls to hide hives at both of her residences (Everglen and Dawnheath), and the trolls used at least one of those hives to breed an experimental army. Luzia claimed to have no knowledge of the trolls' experiments, but her son seemed to suspect otherwise. Orem even helped the Neverseen expose his mother's activities by providing the DNA they needed to open the hive at Everglen—which unfortunately unleashed a band of mutant newborn trolls, who then went tearing through the property on a deadly rampage. The Council has yet to punish Luzia for those crimes, because her sentence is still being determined—and investigations into Orem (and other Vackers potentially involved as well) remain ongoing. And then, of course, there's Alvar Vacker—but he needs his own section.

A TRAITOR IN THE FAMILY:

After the Neverseen's defeat in Ravagog, Fitz's older brother, Alvar, boldly declared himself to be a member of the Neverseen. He was also directly involved in the destruction of Lumenaria and the abduction (and torture) of Wylie Endal. He's additionally suspected to have been involved in Sophie Foster and Dex Dizznee's kidnapping, as well as the Everblaze infernos that tore through the Forbidden Cities and Eternalia—and he likely fought with the Neverseen in their skirmish with the Black Swan on Mount Everest and helped with the Neverseen's attempts to capture the alicorns. But all of those accusations unfortunately remain speculation because of severe damage that occurred to Alvar's memories. He was found in a cell in the Neverseen's "Nightfall" hideout, seriously wounded and heavily drugged with soporidine (a dangerous sedative the Neverseen developed), as though he'd been betrayed by the order and left for dead. Alvar remained unconscious for weeks, and when an antidote to the soporidine was finally acquired, his mind was completely erased. Despite the amnesia, Alvar was brought to Tribunal for his crimes. But the Council found themselves uncertain of how to punish someone who no longer remembered what he'd done and seemed genuinely remorseful. So, in an effort to be fair (and despite very vocal protests from numerous members of the Vacker family—including Fitz and Biana), the Council sentenced Alvar to six months of house arrest at Everglen. Alvar was moved to a heavily guarded new apartment that Alden Vacker had built for his son, and was required to wear a gadget called the Warden (designed by Dex Dizznee) to keep track of his every move and render him immediately unconscious if he should do anything suspicious. The Council used the time to study Alvar's behavior and assess whether he'd truly changed—and all tests seemed to indicate that Alvar had legitimately become a different person. Unfortunately, though, Alvar's amnesia turned out to be part of the Neverseen's plan, and his memories were triggered during the most recent Celestial Festival. He did appear to hesitate once he remembered the role he was expected to play. But in the end, Alvar chose to open the gates of Everglen for the Neverseen and helped them unleash the newborn trolls from the illegal hive hidden on the property. The Neverseen then lost control of the situation, and one of their members—a Shade who called herself Umber—was crushed to death before the rest of the Neverseen fled to safety. Alvar tried to escape as well, but a series of events (which still remain murky) left him trapped inside one of the troll's birthing pods. Everyone assumed he drowned when liquid filled the pod soon after. But it appears that Alvar's mastery of basic skills allowed him to escape once again. He's only been seen once since and apparently was in very poor health. But there's no telling whether he'll cause any final havoc before he dies—a fact which seems to infuriate Fitz more than anyone. He's made it clear that he's determined to ensure Alvar can never hurt anyone ever again, even if it requires deadly force. In fact, during the confrontation on the night of the Celestial Festival, Fitz came shockingly close to ending his brother's life. The moment was broadcast by the Neverseen for everyone to witness, and many have mixed feelings about Fitz's behavior. Fitz's friends talked him out of causing any harm, and it's unclear whether he regrets the decision. The Council may or may not regret it as well.

GOBLIN PROTECTION OF HIS OWN:

Given how many enemies Fitz is fighting, it's not surprising that the Black Swan decided to arrange a goblin bodyguard for him. He's now under the protection of Grizel, who volunteered for the position. She's proven herself to be a fierce and fearsome warrior, but also appears to be quite high-spirited, often turning things into games or bets with interesting consequences. Additionally, there seems to be some sort of connection between Grizel and Sandor (Sophie's bodyguard). Neither goblin has been willing to update the Council—or their queen—on their relationship status. But all evidence suggests they're currently a couple.

BRAVE RECOVERIES:

Fitz has suffered numerous minor injuries over the years, as well as two major brushes with death. The first took place while he was living with the Black Swan, after he and his friends were caught breaking into Exile. During the confrontation with the Council, Councillor Clarette used her ability to call forth several arthropleura in an attempt at intimidation. And when the situation escalated, Fitz ended up impaled through the chest and shoulder by one of the creature's antennae. Sophie Foster then negotiated a deal for his freedom, and Dex Dizznee rushed Fitz to the Black Swan's physician, who was able to heal the wound and draw out the venom. (It should be noted that Councillor Clarette was found blameless for her role in what happened, as it was simply an unfortunate accident—and the arthropleura involved was not harmed.) Fitz's second and perhaps more frightening injury occurred during an ambush with the Neverseen. He was with his bodyguard (Grizel) as well as Sophie Foster and her bodyguard (Sandor) when several members of the Neverseen appeared out of nowhere and attacked. Reports on the incident indicate that Fitz was tortured by the Neverseen's Shade (who called herself Umber) in an attempt to make Sophie cooperate. And since Umber used shadowflux for her attacks, Fitz's injuries were complex and long-lasting. He and Sophie (who'd sustained similarly frightening injuries) spent several weeks in the Healing Center, and both of them needed additional weeks of therapy after they returned home. (Grizel and Sandor were also injured during this incident, as was Dex Dizznee; his bodyguard, Lovise; and Wylie Endal, who'd arrived after Sophie sent out a call for help.) Fitz occasionally walks with a slight limp as a result of the attack, but otherwise seems to have fully recovered.

EXCLUDED FROM THE TEAM:

In a move that many have found surprising, the Council opted against inviting Fitz to be part of Team Valiant—though they have assured Sophie that he can be added if she ends up needing his telepathic assistance. The Council's reasoning was that Sophie had grown too reliant on her Cognate and might discover new strengths if forced to work more closely with some of her other friends—particularly the friends with whom she seemed to team up the least often. It's too early to tell if the Council made the right call in this regard, but either way, Fitz was understandably disappointed to be passed over for the assignment.

A HIGHLY ELIGIBLE MATCH:

Despite all of the above drama, Fitz remains one of the most eligible candidates for the match, and will likely cause quite the stir once his name begins appearing on match lists. Most assume he'll be invited to a record number of Winnowing Galas. And given his family's slight fall from favor, it would be excellent timing for him to choose a smart match—and *very* unwise for him to consider anyone not specifically matched to him.

FINAL NOTE:

This was touched on above—and should be taken somewhat lightly, since it's only connected to extreme circumstances—but Fitz's default reaction to emotionally intense, high-pressure situations tends to be anger (and occasionally even violence). He has been known to verbally lash out at friends and family, often unfairly blaming them for the causes of his frustrations. And his physical altercations with his brother, while justified, have grown increasingly brutal. All of which may make him a liability in the future, if the situation with the Neverseen continues to escalate.

REGISTRY FILE FOR
Biana Amberly Vacker

KNOWN ABILITIES: *Vanisher*

RESIDENCE: *Everglen*

IMMEDIATE FAMILY: *Father (Alden Vacker), mother (Della Vacker), brother (Alvar Vacker), brother (Fitz Vacker)*

MATCH STATUS: *Unregistered*

EDUCATION: *Current Foxfire prodigy*

NEXUS: *No longer required*

PATHFINDER: *Not assigned. Restricted to Leapmasters and home crystals.*

SPYBALL APPROVAL: *None*

MEMBER OF THE NOBILITY: *Yes*

TITLE: *Lady*

NOBLE ASSIGNMENT: *Regent; member of Team Valiant*
SIGNIFICANT CONNECTIONS: *Fealty-sworn member of the Black Swan; former Wayward at Exillium*
ASSIGNED BODYGUARD(S): *Woltzer (goblin)*

THIRD CHILD:

Many may consider the following to be a touch scandalous, since it's something that so rarely gets mentioned—but if this file were for someone in any other family, it would be a defining entry. Since Biana is a *Vacker*, there are hardly ever whispers of it—and yet, it should be noted that Biana Vacker is child number three for her parents, Alden and Della Vacker (though the inclusion of this note is in no way meant to cast any judgment). Since many in the Lost Cities fear that second children (and beyond) have weaker abilities and DNA, it's generally rare for a family to have more than one child—and extremely rare to have more than two. Little is known about why Alden and Della chose to have a third child (again, since the subject is so rarely discussed). But one might speculate that they were hoping for a daughter. Whatever their reasoning, they definitely skirted convention and are quite fortunate that their family name protects them—and Biana—from facing the scorn they surely would have endured otherwise.

EXCEEDING EXPECTATIONS:

Given Biana's last name, the constant praise that was always showered on both of her brothers (though most of the praise was for Fitz), and the fact that she's a third child—it's safe to say that she's had a lot to live up to. And like a true Vacker, her beauty, accent, and school performance have all been exceptional. But the real test came down to Biana's manifesting. For years, gossip circles speculated about what ability the youngest Vacker might inherit from her legendary genetics, and whether it could possibly match that of her siblings. Biana did an excellent job of pretending not to notice the pressure she was facing (though she surely must have). And in the end, she outshone what everyone expected, manifesting as a Vanisher at an even younger age than Fitz manifested as a Telepath. And even with limited training, she's proven herself to be incredibly adept at her ability, managing to vanish completely within hours of manifesting and holding her vanish for longer and longer periods of time. Records also suggest that when Biana teams up with Sophie Foster and allows Sophie to enhance her, she's able to not only make herself invisible—but make others invisible as well. And while some may whisper about the irony of one of the most "watched" prodigies in the Lost Cities being able to literally disappear, others suspect that Biana may relish the anonymity her ability allows. There have also been numerous reports of Biana using her ability to eavesdrop on important conversations or sneak into places she otherwise wouldn't be able to access, which has made her a valuable asset to the Black Swan and her friends.

ALL IN THE FAMILY:

A primary goal of the matchmaking system is for each new generation to have increasingly powerful abilities. And while that isn't always the case (much to the matchmakers'—and the Council's—consternation), Biana's family is a prime example of success. Like Biana, her mother (Della) is an incredibly powerful Vanisher (as is her brother Alvar, and it should also be noted that Fitz is a powerful Telepath, much like his father). But Biana seems to have also inherited her mother's unique blend of grace, gumption, and ferocity. Reports indicate that Della's received defensive battle training, and has combined the moves she's learned with her vanishing to make her a true force to be reckoned with. And it appears she's taught Biana (and Biana's friends) how to protect themselves as well, which has allowed Biana to hold her own against some truly formidable enemies.

STRUGGLING SOCIALITE:

While most Vackers tend to be effortlessly popular by reputation alone, Biana has not had the number of friends and acquaintances that one might expect. In fact, it would appear that she has developed some trepidation as to whether potential new friends are looking simply for access to her prominent family, or to find a way to connect with her brothers (particularly with Fitz, who has *many* admirers at Foxfire). This very concern offered an initial challenge to the development of Biana's friendship with Sophie Foster when Sophie first moved to the Lost Cities. In fact, numerous reports paint Sophie and Biana's initial relationship as adversarial—and when they first began spending more time together, it was apparently at Biana's father's (Alden's) urging, which caused a fallout between them when Sophie discovered the truth. Ultimately, though, Biana and Sophie have grown to genuinely respect and admire each other, and are now well and truly friends. Biana has also made amends with others she's neglected or lost touch with over time, including Maruca Chebota and Marella Redek.

A NATURAL TRENDSETTER:

It of course helps that Biana's family name, teal eyes, and incredible beauty make her a magnet for attention. But anyone who understands "style" knows that none of those things can give someone that additional head-turning factor that makes people stop and pay attention. And for Biana Vacker, all of that comes together perfectly, making her someone others often strive to emulate—whether it be through their clothes, hairstyle, makeup, or shoes. (One notable exception is Sophie Foster, whose distaste for attention often results in her resisting Biana's makeover suggestions.) And while some may consider such things to be trivial or frivolous, there's something to be said for Biana's ability to fearlessly face down giant mutant beasts or angry ogre kings, or any of the other terrifying situations she's found herself in, and then swipe on some of her favorite lip gloss and put on her frilliest, fanciest gown like nothing happened. In a way, it's kind of inspiring—and an excellent reminder that when it comes to emulating Biana's style, the most important element is staying true to who you are.

AN ILLUSION OF SAFETY:

Up until recently, the Lost Cities were always seen as a place of comfort and peace—a world that didn't need armies or police like so many of the other intelligent species rely on. And yet, Biana's father (Alden Vacker) added a massive glowing fence around the entire perimeter of his property (Everglen), with bars designed to absorb light and prevent anyone from being able to light leap in. Which surely must have made for an interesting upbringing. On the one hand, his children were constantly being assured that everything was fine and there was no reason to worry. And yet, every time they stepped outside their house, they saw that they were living inside a gated fortress. Does that mean Biana and her brothers suspected some of the dangers that have now been proven to exist in our world? Could that possibly even explain why Biana and Fitz connected so easily to Sophie Foster and involved themselves in the conspiracies and chaos surrounding her? Or did they simply think their father preferred to control his visitors? It's impossible to tell. But the gates have since been removed because of the illegal troll hive found on the property. And given the new instability of our world, it's highly likely that the Vacker family misses them.

THE BANE OF HER BODYGUARD'S EXISTENCE:

Like her friends, Biana was assigned a bodyguard when the Black Swan increased their security. But while most of the other bodyguard-protectee relationships have grown into unique friendships, it's doubtful that Biana's goblin bodyguard (Woltzer) feels any affection for her, the reason being that Biana has a bad habit of using her ability as a Vanisher to ditch poor Woltzer whenever she wants to do something he wouldn't approve of—which also gets him in trouble with his supervisor (Sandor). To be fair, this has also meant that Woltzer has suffered far fewer injuries than the goblins guarding Biana's friends—but that's likely not why Biana sneaks away, so she probably doesn't deserve credit for it.

MARKED BY BATTLE:

Biana is unfortunately not the only member of the Black Swan—nor the only one of her friends—to be seriously wounded during their altercations with the Neverseen. But Biana does bear a much larger souvenir of her injuries, in the form of noticeable scars on her arms, chest, neck, shoulders, and back. The injuries occurred when Biana went after Vespera by herself. (Evidently, her ability to vanish allowed her to sneak away during one of Vespera's speeches.) It took her friends a while to catch up to her, and when they did, they found Biana unconscious and bleeding in a pile of jagged, broken glass. Apparently, Vespera had thrown Biana through one of the mirrors she used for her illusions—and records indicate that Vespera may have even intended for Biana to be scarred by the process and later bragged about that intention to Biana's friends. Perhaps she thought that a girl known for her flawless beauty wouldn't be able to handle any new imperfections—and Biana did, at first, appear to be choosing clothes that hid the marks. But with time, she seems to have grown comfortable with her new skin, and now proudly wears gowns and tunics that leave her scars on display. (It should also be noted that some of Biana's returned confidence may stem from her use of one of Elwin's Emotional Support Stuffed Animals—a stuffed yeti apparently named Lady Sassyfur.) And while some may notice Biana's scars and wonder what could have caused the injuries, no one would ever claim that Biana isn't as stunning as ever. In fact, the scars might make Biana even more striking, testifying to a level of strength, confidence, and fierceness that few are able to claim.

A VALIANT REGENT:

In what may turn out to be Biana's boldest step out of her brothers' shadows, she was chosen by the Council to be a member of Team

Valiant, and is now one of the youngest Regents in the nobility. As a result, she can proudly claim the title of "Lady." (Some reports indicate that Biana likes to tease her brother Fitz and force him to call her "Lady Biana"—but those rumors cannot be confirmed.)

THE VACKER LEGACY:

Biana's brother Alvar's crimes are unfortunately common knowledge—as is his claim that he joined the Neverseen because of "the Vacker legacy." And there are many theories as to what he may have meant by that phrase—as well as certain truths that Alvar managed to expose before his most recent disappearance (the illegal troll hive hidden at Everglen, for example). But like many in our world, Biana doesn't appear to be convinced that she has the full understanding of what exactly the "Vacker legacy" is and seems determined to learn—though it's unclear what risks she's willing to take in order to find the whole truth.

FINAL NOTE:

It's often been said, "Watch out for the Vanishers," and Biana seems to be living proof of the adage. It's difficult to tell exactly what role she plans to play—or if her ever-increasing boldness will lead her to ruin. But Biana's definitely one to watch—assuming we can see her.

DIZZNEE

REGISTRY FILE FOR
Dexter Alvin Dizznee

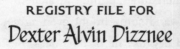

KNOWN ABILITIES: *Technopath*

RESIDENCE: *Rimeshire*

IMMEDIATE FAMILY: *Kesler Dizznee (father), Juline Dizznee (mother), Rex Dizznee (brother), Lex Dizznee (brother), Bex Dizznee (sister)*

MATCH STATUS: *Unregistered*

EDUCATION: *Current Foxfire prodigy*

NEXUS: *No longer required*

PATHFINDER: *Not assigned. Restricted to Leapmasters and home crystals.*

SPYBALL APPROVAL: *None*

MEMBER OF THE NOBILITY: *Yes*

TITLE: *Lord*

NOBLE ASSIGNMENT: *Regent; member of Team Valiant; often brought in by the Council to consult on specific technology projects*
SIGNIFICANT CONNECTIONS: *Fealty-sworn member of the Black Swan; former Wayward at Exillium; best friend to Sophie Foster*
ASSIGNED BODYGUARD(S): *Lovise (goblin)*

LACKING PRESTIGE AND HEAVY ON THE SCANDAL:

There are many kinds of prominence in the Lost Cities. But not all of them are good. And in Dex's case, his family is unfortunately renowned for all the wrong reasons. His father (Kesler Dizznee) is one of the Talentless—though Kesler would likely argue that his incredible aptitude in alchemy should count as a special ability (and some might even agree). Sadly for him, it does not. And because he is Talentless, Kesler's marriage to his wife (Juline Dizznee) was ruled a "bad match" by the matchmakers, since Juline is a Froster and was expected to marry someone else with a special ability. Kesler and Juline also chose to have children—something the rare few who choose to become bad matches generally avoid. And while Dex was born to relatively little additional scandal, everything changed when Juline announced a second pregnancy, and then ended up having triplets. Multiple births tend to be controversial in our world, even under ideal circumstances, since many fear that the children's genetics—and abilities—will be weaker. But a multiple birth from a bad match—with *three* babies? It was enough to send the Dizznee family to the very bottom of the social circles—not that Kesler seemed to mind. In fact, he often seeks out ways to rebel against societal norms and is constantly challenging people's expectations and forcing them to confront their biases. Dex must have inherited that attitude from his father, because he generally avoids anyone considered "popular" and finds rather creative ways to stand up to anyone judging him—or his family. (His Foxfire records show numerous detentions assigned as a result of pranks he played on prodigies bullying him—and it should be noted that those prodigies were also punished for instigating the situation. Foxfire must discipline misbehavior, but the Mentors and principal always strive to be fair.)

THE UNMISTAKABLE RHYME:

Dex's triplet siblings are named Rex, Bex, and Lex Dizznee. Yes, the rhyme was intentional. Evidently, it was Kesler's idea, because he finds it "hilarious." It's unclear how he convinced his wife to agree, since Juline seems to have a more reserved sense of humor—but she does also embrace the way her husband likes to challenge convention, so perhaps that was her motivation. Dex, meanwhile, appears to be less than thrilled that his name matches his brothers' and sister's—but he's quick to defend the decision if anyone attempts to mock him for it. Rex, Bex, and Lex clearly enjoy the attention.

THE FAMILY BUSINESS:

Anyone in the Lost Cities who's taken elixirs to alter their appearance or remedy some ailment (or countless other reasons) likely purchased those elixirs from the Dizznees. Just as anyone who's been to Mysterium has likely seen the Dizznees' store. It's the only unique building on the isle, painted twenty different colors with topsy-turvy architecture and a sign that reads SLURPS AND BURPS: YOUR MERRY APOTHECARY. The door also belches when people enter or exit. And the inside of the store is a veritable maze of shelves filled with colorful vials in all different shapes and sizes, labeled with names like Fuzzy Fizz and Hush Slush. It also tends to smell of burning hair or dirty feet or some other strange byproduct of Kesler's constant experiments—and all of this "quirkiness" is intentional. Kesler has made it abundantly clear that he designed the store specifically to make "the stuffy nobles" uncomfortable. He finds it absurd that so many can rely on his alchemy creations and still turn up their noses at him for not having a special ability—particularly since he's arguably the best alchemist in all of the Lost Cities. He has the perfect blend of creativity, ingenuity, and carefully honed skill. And he's working to pass his methods and experience onto his children—or to Dex, at least, who works in the store as often as his schedule allows. The triplets are a bit too rambunctious—and *loud*—for regular Slurps and Burps shifts at the moment. And many people are a bit terrified of what bizarre elixirs Rex, Bex, and Lex might invent. Dex has already become notorious for crafting numerous "prank" elixirs, some of which are sold in Slurps and Burps and some of which he makes only for himself (or his friends).

INSTANT BEST FRIENDS:

To look at Dex now is to see a young elf with a tight circle of power-ful friends who trust and rely on him every bit as much as he trusts and relies on them. But all of that is a relatively new develop-ment. A few years ago, Dex had zero friends and more than a few enemies. Then Sophie Foster walked into Slurps and Burps with her new guardian (Edaline Ruewen) and changed everything. Sophie was a girl with an even stranger upbringing than Dex had experienced, who saw him without any of the biases or prejudices he'd had to deal with from everyone else. A girl who'd also never felt like she belonged. A girl who was going to need a friend to help her navigate her strange new world—and Dex was more than happy to volunteer for the job. (Many also suspect that Sophie's striking looks played a role in Dex's motivation, but that cannot be confirmed.) Dex helped Sophie navigate her first day at Foxfire, and they've been best friends ever since—and through Sophie, Dex has come to befriend numerous others. Admittedly, he did resist certain friendships at first (particularly when it came to Fitz and Biana Vacker), but he has since set whatever hard feelings he had toward the Vackers aside. Fitz and Biana have reportedly apologized for ignoring Dex before Sophie introduced them, and Dex has apologized for the time one of his gadgets accidentally almost killed Fitz.

COUSINS—BUT NOT:

Dex's mom, Juline, is Edaline Ruewen's sister. And Edaline is now Sophie Foster's adoptive mother. So technically, on paper, Sophie and Dex are cousins. But there's no biological relation between them. Well . . . there's *presumably* no biological relation between them. Given the mystery surrounding Sophie's genetic parentage, Sophie could technically be related to anybody. Still, it seems doubtful that the Black Swan would let her spend so much time with anyone connected to Project Moonlark, since it would arouse too much suspicion. So it seems safe to assume that Sophie and Dex are cousins by law only.

EXPLOSIVE TUTORING LESSONS:

Sophie's struggles with alchemy have become somewhat legendary, and Dex bravely accepted the job of "Personal Alchemy Tutor." But even with his careful guidance, fires, explosions, and other disasters were common elements of every tutoring session, which is why Dex opted to have them practice in a cave at the base of the cliffs near Sophie's house, where there was little kindling and plenty of nearby water. It's suspected that those lessons could've been the reason the Neverseen staged Sophie's abduction in that same cave—not that Dex should feel responsible for the unfortunate events that followed. The cave was nothing more than a secluded spot where Sophie could reliably be found, and the Neverseen simply took advantage of the situation.

SHARED NIGHTMARES:

Dex went to Havenfield to check on Sophie after she left Foxfire in tears, and when he found her in their cave, he accidentally interrupted her kidnapping. The Neverseen opted to abduct Dex as well, presumably to prevent him from telling anyone what was happening, and the details are a bit vague after that. Dex doesn't like to discuss what he endured while he was held captive (though his medical records indicate that he has a scar on his side from a serious burn). And since his registry pendant was found at the bottom of the ocean (along with Sophie's), he—like Sophie—was declared deceased, given a planting, and now has a Wanderling. But also like

Sophie, he was able to return to the Lost Cities and make a full recovery. And Sophie and Dex have grown even closer after their escape, understanding each other in ways no one else can.

SPREADING COLORFUL CHEER:

In what is surely one of the more unusual uses for his alchemy abilities, Dex has developed a habit of changing the fur color of Sophie's pet imp. He started doing this to cheer Sophie up after a hard day, and it has since turned into a regular occurrence. In fact, it's possible the tiny creature may never be his natural fur color again. And while it feels strange including a section on multicolored imp fur in a registry file, the habit does also speak to Dex's character. He's creative, caring, and clever, and always looking for new ways to make people smile.

A CRUSH, A KISS, AND CRUSHING HEARTACHE:

[ARE YOU GUYS KIDDING ME??? THIS HAS SOOOOOO BEEN REDACTED. AND AS SOON AS I CAN FIGURE OUT HOW TO EDIT THE SUBHEADINGS ON THESE FILES, THAT'S GETTING REDACTED TOO! BE GLAD I'M NOT PULLING A KEEFE AND EDITING MY ENTIRE FILE. AND SERIOUSLY, STAY OUT OF MY PERSONAL LIFE! GAH—WHY WOULD THE REGISTRY BE TRACKING THIS???????]

A SECRET TALENT:

Manifesting a special ability is generally a cause for triumph and celebration. But for Dex, it happened very quietly. In fact, reports suggest he may not have even noticed when he manifested, since he'd always been "good with gadgets." And once he realized he was a Technopath, he chose not to report it, because he'd apparently been hoping to manifest a different ability (it's unclear which one) and wanted to remain in his ability detecting session at Foxfire in the hope of triggering something else. Sophie's bodyguard (Sandor) eventually informed the Council of Dex's ability, because he felt the Council should be using their Technopaths to prepare their world for an attack from the ogres. And Dex discovered his secret was "out" when Foxfire's principal at the time (Dame Alina) announced that he'd manifested during the morning orientation. At first Dex blamed Sophie and Keefe for the betrayal, but Dame Alina set the record straight for him. Sandor also confessed and apologized—and Dex has now grown to appreciate his talent. Particularly since the Council has turned to him numerous times for assistance with different assignments. His parents were also incredibly proud—and likely a little relieved, given Kesler's Talentless status. And Dex's ability has proven to be an invaluable resource to the Black Swan.

EAGER TO IMPRESS:

Given his upbringing—and the scorn that still surrounds his family—it's not surprising that Dex has jumped at any opportunities that the Council has come to him with, even if the gadgets he was asked to design had dangerous consequences. One prime example of this was the ability restrictor that Dex created for the Council without realizing they intended to use it on Sophie. He seemed absolutely devastated when he saw how his invention affected his best friend, and even tried to refuse the Council's orders to make a few adjustments. Sophie convinced him to cooperate to prevent the Council from carrying out their threats to exile him. And not long after, the ability restrictor was mysteriously "lost." Since then, Dex has been a bit more careful with what he invents—though he's still had numerous gadgets malfunction. One such miscalculation even led to Fitz being seriously injured during a standoff with the Council in Exile. But even with all of those setbacks, Dex has still proven to be one of the most creative, original, powerful Technopaths in the Lost Cities, and has created numerous gadgets that have saved his friends, uncovered vital answers, and helped them stand strong against their enemies.

WEAPONS DESIGNER:

As already mentioned above, Dex has been creating defensive gadgets since manifesting his ability (to varying degrees of success). But in recent months it appears he's begun training with the Black Swan's Technopath with the specific goal of designing weapons. And while many—including the Council—fear a battle is coming, which would therefore make such measures both wise and necessary, it's also terrifying to imagine what Dex might be building, or who might get caught in the cross fire.

A TRIUMPHANT LORD:

In what was surely a proud moment for both Dex and his family, Dex was selected to be a member of Team Valiant. He is now officially a Regent for the Council and bears the title of Lord. And while some might argue that no one should ever have to prove themselves—particularly because of something they can't control, like their father's Talentless status—Dex's appointment to the nobility (at such a young age, no less) surely sends a message of hope to other children facing scorn and judgment. Things really do get better.

FINAL NOTE:

Dex's technopathy skills extend far beyond gadget creation, and likely also include the ability to tamper with registry feeds and hack into registry files. For this reason, it might be wise to [REDACTED. NICE TRY, GUYS. I'M ONTO YOU!]

REGISTRY FILE FOR

Keefe

[I'M NOT YOUR LEGACY-BOY]

Sencen

NOTE: *Despite numerous attempts—and lots of enhancements to registry security—the information in this file remains hopelessly altered, presumably by Keefe Sencen, who was likely given access by Dex Dizznee. Until we can figure out how they did it, we can't seem to fix it.*

[THAT'S WHAT YOU GET FOR KEEPING YOUR SECRET LITTLE NOTES ON ME!! BE GLAD WE'RE NOT MESSING WITH ALL OF YOUR FILES. I WANTED TO! BUT (NAME REDACTED) WOULDN'T LET ME!]

[DUDE—DID (NAME REDACTED) JUST REDACT ONE OF MY REDACTIONS?]

[HUH. I GUESS SO. WELL THEN!]

KNOWN ABILITIES: *Empath* [DON'T BELIEVE ANYTHING ELSE MY MOM TELLS YOU]

RESIDENCE: *The Shores of Solace and Candleshade* [ANYONE WANNA TRADE LIVES WITH ME?]

IMMEDIATE FAMILY: *Lord Cassius Sencen (father); Lady Gisela Sencen (mother)* [AKA: WORST. PARENTS. EVER!]

MATCH STATUS: *Unregistered* [TRY NOT TO BE TOO HEART-BROKEN, PEOPLE]

[THOUGH I GOTTA SAY: I DON'T REALLY GET WHY EVERY-ONE PAYS SO MUCH ATTENTION TO THIS.]

EDUCATION: *Current Foxfire prodigy* [AND PROUD DETENTION RECORD–HOLDER]

NEXUS: *No longer required* [BECAUSE I'M COOL LIKE THAT]

PATHFINDER: *Not assigned. Restricted to Leapmasters and home crystals.* [HA, THAT'S WHAT YOU THINK!]

SPYBALL APPROVAL: *None* [BUT I HAVE FRIENDS WITH CONNECTIONS, THAT'S ALL I'M SAYING. . . .]

MEMBER OF THE NOBILITY: *No* [THANK GOODNESS]

TITLE: *None* [UM, HELLO, WHAT ABOUT LORD HUNKY-HAIR? THAT'S A THING!]

NOBLE ASSIGNMENT: *None* [MASTER MISCHIEF-MAKER]

SIGNIFICANT CONNECTIONS: *Fealty-sworn member of the Black Swan; former Wayward at Exillium; son to one of the leaders of the Neverseen* [SWORN PROTECTOR OF THE MYSTERIOUS MISS F]

ASSIGNED BODYGUARD(S): *Ro (ogre)* [AND SHE KNOWS, LIKE, 500,000 WAYS TO KILL YOU! SO IT'S REALLY NOT A GOOD IDEA TO MESS WITH US!]

UNNATURAL EXPECTATIONS:
[WAIT—IT WON'T LET ME REDACT THESE LITTLE SUBHEADING THINGS? THAT'S SUPER ANNOYING!]

[FINE, I'LL JUST GIVE YOU *MY* SUMMARY.]

[SO, WHOEVER WROTE THIS WAS ALL BLAH-BLAH-BLAH-STELLARLUNE-SOMETHING-SOMETHING-LEGACY. BUT SERIOUSLY, NO ONE WANTS TO READ ABOUT THE CREEPY STUFF MY MOM DID BEFORE SHE GOT PREGNANT WITH ME! (AND WE'RE ALL SUPER SICK OF HEARING ABOUT MY "LEGACY," AMIRITE?) SO, LET'S JUST LEAVE IT AT THIS: MY MOM IS EVIL. SHE THINKS SHE'S WAY SMARTER THAN SHE IS. AND NOTHING SHE DID IS GOING TO AFFECT MY GENERAL AWESOMENESS, OKAY?]

A PHOTOGRAPHIC MEMORY:
[WOW, HOW *DID* YOU COME UP WITH SUCH A CLEVER TITLE?!]

[AND YEAH, I HAVE A PHOTOGRAPHIC MEMORY. NOT SURE WHY ANYONE CARES. BUT IT DOES COME IN HANDY DURING MIDTERMS AND FINALS.]

AHEAD OF THE GAME:
[BASICALLY: I'M A GENIUS. I SKIPPED LEVEL ONE AT FOXFIRE. YES, YOU SHOULD BE IMPRESSED.]

UNREASONABLY HIGH STANDARDS:
[GOTTA ADMIT, I WAS TEMPTED TO LEAVE THIS ONE ALONE, SINCE WHOEVER WROTE IT ACTUALLY GOT THINGS PRETTY MUCH RIGHT. I GUESS EVEN THE COUNCIL KNOWS MY DAD'S A JERK WHO FREAKS OUT ALL THE TIME BECAUSE I'M NOT A LITTLE MINI-HIM. WHO KNEW?]

A POWERFUL EMPATH:
[UGH, THAT'S THE BEST YOU COULD DO FOR THIS SUBHEADING???]

[HOW ABOUT "LORD OF THE FEELS"? OR "TRUST THE EMPATH"! OR "HE KNOWS WHAT YOU'RE FEELING—AND YOU SHOULD BE ASHAMED OF YOURSELF"?]

[OOO! I'VE GOT IT! "HE KNOWS FOSTER BETTER THAN YOU DO! BETTER THAN SHE EVEN KNOWS HERSELF!"]

[THOUGH . . . KEEPING IT REAL? THE FOSTER OBLIVION CAN BE KINDA NOT COOL SOMETIMES.]

THE HEART OF THE MATTER:

[I CAN'T BELIEVE YOU GUYS NAMED A SECTION OF MY FILE AFTER MY FATHER'S SUPER-BORING BOOK—AND THEN RAMBLED ON FOR TWO PAGES ABOUT HIS SUPER-BORING THEORY!!!!!]

[YOU DON'T NEED TWO PAGES ON IT. YOU DON'T EVEN NEED TWO SENTENCES. HERE'S ALLLLLL YOU NEED TO KNOW—BESIDES THE FACT THAT HE'S TOTALLY NOT THE FIRST PERSON TO COME UP WITH THIS (JUST THE ONE WHO LOVES TO TAKE CREDIT): OUR HEADS AND OUR HEARTS SOMETIMES FEEL DIFFERENT EMOTIONS, AND WHAT'S IN OUR HEARTS IS PROBABLY STRONGER.]

[THAT'S IT!]

[WELL . . . OKAY . . . I GUESS HE ALSO GOES ON A BIT ABOUT HOW EMPATHS PROBABLY ONLY READ THE EMOTIONS FROM THE HEAD.]

[AND THERE'S SOMETHING ABOUT HEART EMOTIONS BEING PURER BECAUSE NO ONE CAN CONTROL THEM.]

[BUT *THAT'S* IT.]

[AND DON'T TELL LORD BORINGPANTS I READ HIS DUMB BOOK! I MOSTLY SKIMMED.]

PRANKSTER AND TROUBLEMAKER:

[100 PERCENT ACCURATE. ALSO, I'M LEAVING YOUR LITTLE ATTACHED DETENTION RECORD BECAUSE IT'S THE GREATEST THING I'VE EVER SEEN IN MY LIFE!!!!]

THE GREAT GULON INCIDENT:

[JUST GONNA LEAVE THIS ONE WITH: REDACTED]

[NOT THAT I HAD ANYTHING TO DO WITH THIS!]

THE VACKER CONNECTION:

[UH, FITZY'S MY BEST FRIEND—NOT A "CONNECTION." AND ALDEN AND DELLA ARE WAY NICER TO ME THAN MY OWN PARENTS ARE. BIANA'S SUPER AWESOME TOO. ALVAR . . . NOT SO MUCH. I PROBABLY SHOULD'VE SEEN THAT ONE COMING. BUT WHATEVER, MY POINT IS: I DIDN'T *TRY* TO MAKE FRIENDS WITH THE VACKERS—NO MATTER WHAT WEIRD STUFF WAS IN ONE OF MY ERASED MEMORIES. SO DON'T GO THINKING THERE'S MORE TO IT THAN THAT.]

[AND HOW DO YOU GUYS EVEN KNOW ABOUT THAT MEMORY? THAT KINDA MAKES ME WANT TO RIP THIS REGISTRY PENDANT OFF MY NECK AND THROW IT FAR, FAR AWAY!]

INSTANT RIVALRY:

[YOU THINK BANGS BOY AND ME ARE "RIVALS"? HATE TO BREAK IT TO YOU, BUT NOPE! I MEAN, YEAH, HE'S SUPER

ANNOYING WITH ALL THE "LOOK AT ME, I'M A MOODY SHADE" NONSENSE—AND HIS HAIR IS TOTALLY RIDICULOUS. BUT THERE'S NO *RIVALRY*. JUST DON'T EXPECT US TO BE BESTIES, AND WE'LL BE GOOD.]

UNWITTING ERRAND BOY:

[OKAY, THAT SUBHEADING MAKES ME WANT TO PUNCH WHOEVER WROTE IT IN THE MOUTH. BUT . . . I GUESS IT'S ALSO KIND OF TRUE. MY MOM *DID* HAVE ME DO STUFF AND THEN ERASE MY MEMORIES SO I WOULDN'T KNOW ABOUT IT. MOM OF THE YEAR, LADIES AND GENTLEMEN. TRY NOT TO BE JEALOUS.]

[AND I'M WORKING ON GETTING THOSE MEMORIES BACK, BY THE WAY. I'VE BEEN FILLING JOURNALS WITH DRAWINGS AND EVERYTHING. IT'S JUST TAKING A WHILE BECAUSE I'VE BEEN A LITTLE BUSY ALMOST DYING AND STUFF.]

TEAM FOSTER-KEEFE:

[WOO-HOO, TEAM FOSTER-KEEFE IS OFFICIALLY A THING!]

[BUT THE REST OF THE STUFF IN THIS SECTION IS SOOOOOOOOOOOOOOOOOOOOOOOO GETTING REDACTED. SERIOUSLY—BOUNDARIES, PEOPLE! FOSTER'S AMAZING— AND OBVIOUSLY WORKING WITH ME MAKES HER EVEN *MORE* AMAZING. BUT YOU GUYS NEED TO STOP WITH ALL OF YOUR WEIRDO SPECULATING.]

ONE PART OF A TRIANGLE:

[OKAY, THAT'S IT. I'M DEEEEEEEEEFINITELY DITCHING THIS PENDANT THING. WHY IS THE COUNCIL PAYING ATTENTION TO THIS STUFF??????????]

[ACTUALLY, YOU KNOW WHAT? IT'S NONE OF YOUR BUSINESS, BUT I'M GOING TO ADD ONE THING: FOSTER GETS TO DO WHATEVER SHE WANTS, OKAY? SHE CAN LIKE WHOEVER SHE WANTS. OR BE CONFUSED ABOUT WHAT SHE'S FEELING. SHE CAN EVEN BE OBLIVIOUS— IT'S HER LIFE. HER CHOICE. AND EVERYONE NEEDS TO STAY OUT OF IT.]

[EVEN ME.]

[ESPECIALLY ME. I WOULD NEVER WANT TO . . .]

[NEVER MIND. MY POINT IS, LET THE POOR GIRL FIGURE THIS OUT ON HER OWN. AND SERIOUSLY, STAY OUT OF OUR LIVES!!!!]

ULTIMATE BETRAYALS:

[OH GOODY—ANOTHER SECTION ON MOMMY DEAREST. WE GET IT. SHE'S CREEPY. I DIDN'T FIGURE IT OUT FAST ENOUGH, AND SHE USED ME FOR A WHILE. BUT THAT'S ALL DONE NOW, AND IT'S ONLY A MATTER OF TIME BEFORE I TAKE HER DOWN. LET'S MOVE ON, SHALL WE?]

A FOOLISHLY DANGEROUS PLAN:
[I SHOULD PROBABLY BE OFFENDED BY THAT TITLE. BUT . . . RUNNING OFF TO JOIN THE NEVERSEEN DEFINITELY WASN'T MY SMARTEST MOVE. I *THOUGHT* I COULD TAKE THEM DOWN FROM THE INSIDE. AND YEAH, IT PRETTY MUCH BACKFIRED.]

[I DID LEARN SOME STUFF, THOUGH!]

[SORT OF . . .]

[I'M STILL PIECING IT ALL TOGETHER. I MEAN, I WOULDN'T DO IT AGAIN OR RECOMMEND IT TO ANYONE ELSE OR ANYTHING (HEAR THAT, BANGS BOY???), BUT IT WASN'T A TOTAL WASTE.]

[OKAY, MAYBE IT WAS.]

A WAY WITH ALICORNS:
[IT'S TRUE. GLITTER BUTT LOVES ME.]

[SAY IT WITH ME: KEEFE! KEEFE! KEEFE!]

EMOTIONAL SUPPORT STUFFED ANIMAL:
[YOU GUYS MADE AN OFFICIAL RECORD ABOUT MRS. STINKBOTTOM???? I CAN'T DECIDE IF THAT'S AWESOME, OR REALLY, REALLY SAD. . . .]

[SAD FOR YOU GUYS—NOT ME. SLEEPING WITH A STUFFED ANIMAL IS THE BEST. YOU SHOULD TRY IT SOMETIME!]

[ALSO: DOES THIS MEAN FITZY HAS A SECTION ON HIS SPARKLY RED DRAGON SNUGGLE BUDDY????????]

A MERCADIR—WITH THE SCARS TO PROVE IT:
[EESH—THANK GOODNESS I CAN REDACT THIS. I REALLY DON'T NEED ANYONE REMINDING FOSTER HOW MAD SHE WAS AT ME. THE POINT IS: I BEAT THE OGRE KING IN A SPARRING MATCH. I DOUBT EVEN GIGANTOR COULD DO THAT!]

FINAL NOTE:
[WHY IS THERE NOT A SECTION ON MY AMAZING HAIR????]

[HERE, LET ME FIX THAT FOR YOU!]

[IT'S DIFFICULT TO DESCRIBE THE ABSOLUTE PERFEC-TION OF KEEFE'S TRADEMARK HAIRSTYLE. COUNTLESS OTHERS HAVE TRIED TO EMULATE IT, BUT THEY'VE ALL FAILED. THERE CAN ONLY BE ONE LORD HUNKYHAIR. IT'S A RESPONSIBILITY THAT MUST BE TAKEN SERIOUSLY!]

[HUNKYHAIR → OUT]

[AND NOW, THE ULTIMATE PROOF
OF MY AWESOMENESS!]

[I BET NO ONE ELSE HAS A DETENTION RECORD
THIS MASSIVE!]

[I WANTED TO CHECK OTHER FILES TO PROVE IT,
BUT (NAME REDACTED) WON'T LET ME. HE'S PROBABLY
JUST MAD THAT MY RECORD IS COOLER THAN HIS!]

FOXFIRE ACADEMY
Disciplinary Record

PRODIGY:

Keefe Sencen

PARENTS:

Lord Cassius Sencen (father)

Lady Gisela Sencen (mother)

SEND CORRESPONDENCE TO:

Candleshade

LEVEL ONE

VIOLATION	SERIOUSNESS	
Keefe skipped Level One.		

LEVEL TWO

VIOLATION	SERIOUSNESS	
DITCHING ELVIN HISTORY According to a report from the gnomes, Keefe was found hiding near the Leapmaster during the morning session.	1 out of 10	

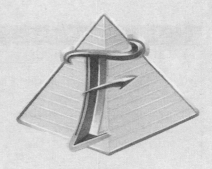

SENTENCE	PRINCIPAL'S COMMENTS

SENTENCE	PRINCIPAL'S COMMENTS
Warning issued.	I let Keefe off with a warning because he's never caused problems before. (He also did extraordinarily well on his midterms.) He's a year younger than his peers, so occasional moments of immaturity are natural—but I gave him a lecture on setting a positive example and he looked inspired when he returned to his session. —Dame Alina

VIOLATION	SERIOUSNESS
<u>DITCHING THE UNIVERSE</u> According to a report from the gnomes, Keefe was found napping near the main amphitheater during afternoon session.	2 out of 10

VIOLATION	SERIOUSNESS
<u>DISRUPTING STUDY HALL</u> According to a report from Sir Bubu, Fitz Vacker began emitting gaseous noises and had to race to the bathroom. Keefe then took credit for slipping Gurgle Gut into Fitz's lunch. Fitz didn't seem upset. He claimed it was a prank (instead of a case of bullying). But the other prodigies were thoroughly distracted.	4 out of 10

SENTENCE	PRINCIPAL'S COMMENTS
Note sent home.	Clearly the warning I gave Keefe yesterday wasn't enough, so I sent a note to Candleshade to apprise his parents of the situation. Lord Cassius assured me he'd correct the problem. —Dame Alina

SENTENCE	PRINCIPAL'S COMMENTS
One detention assigned.	Perhaps allowing Keefe to skip Level One was a mistake—though his Mentors claim he continues to excel in their sessions. Still, that doesn't excuse disrespectful behavior! I reminded Keefe that he could end up expelled if he continues down this path—and asked Elwin to make tomorrow's detention particularly unpleasant to serve as a wake-up call. Elwin said he'll have the prodigies refill vials of pooka pus, which should make Keefe regret his recent life choices. —Dame Alina

VIOLATION	SERIOUSNESS
<u>DISRUPTING DETENTION</u> According to a report from Elwin, today's punishment resulted in what Keefe has termed, "The Great Pus-plosion!" It's unclear *how* the vat of pooka pus erupted, but Keefe was definitely involved.	8 out of 10

VIOLATION	SERIOUSNESS
<u>DISRUPTING DETENTION</u> According to a report from Sir Bubu, Keefe interrupted the day's punishment (which involved a recitation of one of the more tedious Dwarven poems) by improvising a recitation of his own: a poem he called "The Saga of Sir Bubu."	4 out of 10

SENTENCE	PRINCIPAL'S COMMENTS
Three additional detentions assigned. Note sent home.	In hindsight, giving Keefe access to an abundant supply of pooka pus was a terrible idea! The cleanup took hours! (And my gown is ruined!) I spoke with Elwin, since three additional detentions doesn't seem like enough—and I disagree with his assessment that I should "find my sense of humor." I sent a strongly worded letter to Keefe's parents. And I'm making sure the next three detention Mentors choose punishments that don't involve odorous substances! <div align="right">—Dame Alina</div>

SENTENCE	PRINCIPAL'S COMMENTS
A week of additional detentions assigned. Note sent home.	I fear these antics are making detention seem "fun"—both to Keefe and to other prodigies. All afternoon, I've been hearing "The Saga of Sir Bubu" repeated through the halls—and while certain lines were admittedly amusing, this needs to stop! I let Keefe know I'm contemplating expulsion. And I'm meeting with a group of Mentors later to discuss new punishment strategies. Also sent an incredibly stern warning to Keefe's parents, reminding them that having their son attend Foxfire is a privilege! <div align="right">—Dame Alina</div>

VIOLATION	SERIOUSNESS
<u>DITCHING THE UNIVERSE</u> According to a report from the gnomes, Keefe was found tucked into a nook behind the gremlin statue in the Level One Atrium during his session.	3 out of 10

VIOLATION	SERIOUSNESS
<u>THE GREAT GULON INCIDENT</u> Dozens of reports have been gathered on this incident. But it's still unclear exactly what happened. . . .	11 out of 10

SENTENCE	PRINCIPAL'S COMMENTS
A week of detention assigned. Note sent home.	There haven't been any incidents for several weeks, so I'd thought my efforts had finally succeeded. But judging by the amount of Prattles littering the floor of Keefe's hiding place, I suspect he goes there often. (Likely taking advantage of the fact that Sir Jarvin rarely pays attention to anything except the stars. I really should replace him as a Mentor. But he gives the loveliest compliments on my hair. . . .) Clearly I need to send a stronger message. So Keefe gets to sit through another week of detention—and I made much clearer threats to him, as well as in the letter I sent home to his parents. —Dame Alina

SENTENCE	PRINCIPAL'S COMMENTS
NONE. (For now!)	I know Keefe was behind this, no matter how many times he claims he had nothing to do with it! There has to be evidence somewhere (something like this would've taken weeks of planning!), and when I find it, he's off to Exillium! But first . . . I need to get this smell out of my hair. . . . —Dame Alina

VIOLATION	SERIOUSNESS	
<u>DITCHING PHYSICAL EDUCATION</u> According to a report from Sir Bubu, Keefe was found hiding in one of the detention rooms during session.	6 out of 10	

SENTENCE	PRINCIPAL'S COMMENTS
One month of detention assigned. Note sent home.	I still haven't connected Keefe to the gulon incident (I refuse to call it "great")—but if he likes the detention room so much, he can spend an entire month there! I also informed him and his parents that unless they can outline specific steps to correct this situation, I'm starting expulsion proceedings! —Dame Alina
	Update: Lady Gisela had quite a few unpleasant things to say about my note (and my leadership skills in general). It also appears that Lord Cassius could cause me a tremendous amount of headaches if I proceed with the expulsion. In light of that, I've decided to see if the problem can be remedied a different way. I'll now be personally overseeing Keefe's detentions, which will be held one-on-one in my office, and I have a strategy to hopefully get through to him. (Though I've also reduced the punishment to only two weeks—I have my limits!) —Dame Alina

VIOLATION	SERIOUSNESS
<u>STORMING OUT OF DETENTION</u> For the official report: Keefe threw down his polishing cloth halfway through his punishment and stomped out of the room.	5 out of 10

VIOLATION	SERIOUSNESS
<u>DISRESPECT FOR ACADEMY PROPERTY. BREAKING AND ENTERING.</u> For the official report: Somehow Keefe got into the principal's office and ruined all of the polishing he did during detention.	8 out of 10

SENTENCE	PRINCIPAL'S COMMENTS
One additional detention assigned.	I'm not sure what brought on today's tantrum. I was explaining to Keefe why he should thank his parents for the fact that he's still at Foxfire and he turned and stalked away. I followed him—and stayed by his side for his afternoon session and Study Hall (which he didn't appreciate). I also let him know that he now had an additional detention to serve— and I actually saw his smirk fade! Hopefully he's realizing that he's only hurting himself with all of this misbehavior. —Dame Alina

SENTENCE	PRINCIPAL'S COMMENTS
One detention assigned.	Keefe has been so cooperative lately that I foolishly let down my guard. I have no idea how he got into my office (the locks are being changed as I write this!)—and I **don't** want to know what he smeared on my mirrors. But the gnomes were kind enough to handle the cleanup—and I would've given Keefe a harsher punishment if the school year wasn't over. (FINALLY!) Hopefully he will return to Foxfire ready to take his education seriously. —Dame Alina

VIOLATION	SERIOUSNESS
<u>DITCHING ELVIN HISTORY</u> According to a report from the gnomes, Keefe was found hiding in the Level Four wing during afternoon session.	3 out of 10

VIOLATION	SERIOUSNESS
<u>DISRESPECT FOR</u> <u>ACADEMY PROPERTY</u> According to a report from Lady Galvin, Keefe took it upon himself to turn his alchemy table into solid silver.	5 out of 10

SENTENCE	PRINCIPAL'S COMMENTS
Warning issued.	It's the first day of sessions and Keefe is already causing trouble—and he can argue that his photographic memory should exempt him from "boring lectures that repeat what's in the textbook" all he wants! Elvin History is a vital session, and I would've given him a week of detention if I could, but none of the Mentors are prepared to be supervising punishments yet. So, I let Keefe off with a warning (reminding him about expulsion!). I'm sure he'll give everyone plenty of reasons to assign detention soon. This is going to be a very long year. . . . —Dame Alina

SENTENCE	PRINCIPAL'S COMMENTS
One week of detention assigned.	Apparently Lady Galvin asked Keefe to impress her, and this is what happened. Clearly this is not what she meant. Though, I suppose it is rather impressive—not that I would give Keefe the satisfaction of knowing that! —Dame Alina

VIOLATION	SERIOUSNESS
<u>DITCHING PHYSICAL EDUCATION</u> According to a report from the gnomes, Keefe was found hiding in his PE locker during session.	3 out of 10

VIOLATION	SERIOUSNESS
<u>DISRUPTION OF FOXFIRE</u> <u>TRADITIONS</u> Reports are vague, since supervision is always light while the Mentors are delivering grades. But the Level Three midterms party got completely out of hand—and all stories contain the name "Keefe Sencen."	7 out of 10

SENTENCE	PRINCIPAL'S COMMENTS
One week of detention assigned.	It's highly likely that Keefe has used this hiding place before, since his absence could easily be overlooked in the chaos of the group session. Clearly procedures need to be implemented to ensure this behavior is prevented. —Dame Alina

SENTENCE	PRINCIPAL'S COMMENTS
One week of detention assigned (to be served after the midterm break). Face-to-face discussion with both parents.	I can't decide which was worse: having to deal with Lord and Lady Sencen, or hearing Keefe say, "What happens at the Level Three midterms party stays at the Level Three midterms party!" over and over. Actually, no . . . the Sencens are worse. In fact, I think they're the reason Keefe is causing me so many headaches. I suspect he's trying to frustrate them. But if I'm right, I'm not sure what to do. For now, I'm going home, eating a giant slice of mallowmelt, and using the midterm break to research alternate careers. —Dame Alina

VIOLATION	SERIOUSNESS
<u>DISRUPTION OF ORIENTATION</u> According to a report from Lady Galvin, Keefe was seen shaking Scritchy-Scratch onto Fitz Vacker's cape, causing Fitz to do "a funny wiggle dance" in the middle of the morning announcements.	3 out of 10

VIOLATION	SERIOUSNESS
<u>DITCHING MULTISPECIESIAL STUDIES</u> According to a report from Sir Leander, Keefe was caught sneaking back into session. (Sir Leander never saw him leave—and has no idea where Keefe was or how long he was gone for.)	1 out of 10

LEVEL FOUR

VIOLATION	SERIOUSNESS
<u>DITCHING THE UNIVERSE</u> According to a report from Lady Belva, Keefe was discovered missing halfway through her lecture.	1 out of 10

SENTENCE	PRINCIPAL'S COMMENTS
One detention assigned.	I'm starting to think the trick to getting Keefe to behave is to minimize my reactions. So I'm going to hold off on sending any letters home and keep my punishments lighter (and ask his Mentors to do the same). We'll see if that takes some of the "fun" out of this for him. —Dame Alina

SENTENCE	PRINCIPAL'S COMMENTS
One detention assigned.	I think my plan might be working! I haven't gotten any disciplinary reports on Keefe for months (aside from this one)! Though, sadly, I do think part of that is also because Keefe has found a particularly well-hidden ditching spot. Still, we're almost to finals! —Dame Alina

SENTENCE	PRINCIPAL'S COMMENTS
One detention assigned.	I still can't figure out where Keefe goes when he ditches (and this time I had the gnomes do a full search of the campus.) But I'm sticking with my plan of minimally reacting to these infractions in the hope that this will finally be the year that Keefe doesn't pull off any dramatic pranks! —Dame Alina

VIOLATION	SERIOUSNESS
<u>DISRESPECT FOR ACADEMY PROPERTY. ALSO BREAKING AND ENTERING.</u> For the official report: Somehow Keefe got past the new locks on my office door and put reekrod in my desk.	7 out of 10

VIOLATION	SERIOUSNESS
<u>DITCHING THE UNIVERSE</u> According to a report from Lady Belva, Keefe was discovered missing during the middle of her lecture. And when she went searching, she found him in the Mentors' private cafeteria, eating an entire platter of butterblasts.	1 out of 10

SENTENCE	PRINCIPAL'S COMMENTS
Till the end of midterms.	I knew this had to be Keefe! I just didn't have proof, until he bragged to Fitz Vacker within earshot of Lady Galvin. And I know I've been trying not to encourage him—but I had to change my locks (again!) and add other security measures. Plus, I have too much to deal with now that Sophie Foster is a prodigy. (The amount of questions I'm getting about her is ridiculous.) —Dame Alina

SENTENCE	PRINCIPAL'S COMMENTS
One detention assigned.	I'm starting to think I should ask the Council to let me replace Keefe's Universe session next year, since it's far too easy for him to sneak away from a session taught in the dark. I doubt they'd approve my request. But it's nice to imagine. —Dame Alina

VIOLATION	SERIOUSNESS	
<u>DITCHING SESSIONS AND OTHER</u> <u>DISRUPTIVE BEHAVIOR</u>	5 out of 10	

LEVEL FIVE

VIOLATION	SERIOUSNESS	
<u>DITCHING THE UNIVERSE</u> According to a report from the gnomes, Keefe was found in the Mentors' private cafeteria again, covered in butterblast crumbs.	2 out of 10	

SENTENCE	PRINCIPAL'S COMMENTS
None.	I'm not going to bother documenting all of the reports I've gotten about Keefe's recent behavior (or any of the other prodigies currently acting up.) Nor am I allowing any punishment to be assigned. The plantings for Sophie Foster and Dex Dizznee were only a few days ago and everyone needs more time to process their shock and grief—particularly Keefe, who seemed inconsolable when I saw him in the Wanderling Woods. —Dame Alina

SENTENCE	PRINCIPAL'S COMMENTS
One detention assigned.	First day of sessions and Keefe's ditching again. I definitely should've tried to get him assigned to a different session. But the Council's been busy since Sophie Foster and Dex Dizznee returned. I still can't believe anyone would capture children—and I don't want to think about what Sophie and Dex endured. Our world is changing. . . . —Dame Alina

VIOLATION	SERIOUSNESS	
<u>DISRUPTING STUDY HALL</u> According to a report from Sir Rosings, Keefe was talking to Sophie Foster during detention—and made a "sassy" reply when Sir Rosings called them out. When Keefe continued to talk, Sir Rosings gave them both detention. (Keefe apparently looked excited by the prospect. Sophie less so.)	1 out of 10	

VIOLATION	SERIOUSNESS	
<u>DISRUPTING DETENTION</u> According to a report from Lady Cadence, Keefe and Sophie Foster were repeatedly caught talking during detention and earned extra punishment.	2 out of 10	

SENTENCE	PRINCIPAL'S COMMENTS
One detention detention assigned.	Honestly, this seems a somewhat minor offense, considering the theatrics Keefe usually pulls. But I respect Sir Rosings's decision. —Dame Alina
	Update: Keefe's detention (and Sophie's as well) was postponed a day after he injured his hand in Elementalism while trying to bottle a tornado. (Sophie apparently had some trouble in her inflicting session as well.)

SENTENCE	PRINCIPAL'S COMMENTS
One additional detention assigned.	I'm not a fan of Lady Cadence's attitude toward her position as a Foxfire Mentor. But she's volunteered to supervise the majority of the year's detentions. And given the punishments she's planning (I hear today's involved curdleroots!), I think she may be able to curtail Keefe's behavior. —Dame Alina

VIOLATION	SERIOUSNESS	
<u>DISRUPTING STUDY HALL</u> According to a report from Sir Rosings, Keefe was talking to Sophie Foster and Dex Dizznee—and when Sir Rosings warned them to stop, Keefe threatened to fill Sir Rosings's desk with sparkly poop. Punishment was assigned to all three prodigies.	2 out of 10	

VIOLATION	SERIOUSNESS	
<u>DISRESPECT FOR</u> <u>THE PRINCIPAL</u> For the official report: Keefe took it upon himself to slip Sea See into my tea and turn my eyes teal.	10 out of 10	

SENTENCE	PRINCIPAL'S COMMENTS
One additional detention assigned.	I suppose I should be concerned about how many detentions Keefe has accrued in his first week of sessions. But . . . I can't bring myself to care. I think something is going on with Alden Vacker. His children have been absent all week and there was some sort of commotion at the Opening Ceremonies. But every time I've asked the Council for information, they've denied my request. —Dame Alina

SENTENCE	PRINCIPAL'S COMMENTS
A month of detention assigned.	Thankfully, Kesler Dizznee was able to give me an antidote before orientation, so no one saw my altered appearance. Keefe claims he turned my eyes "Vacker Teal" to help me celebrate Alden's remarkable recovery—and while I am exceedingly grateful that Sophie Foster was able to heal him, such a tribute would be seen as highly inappropriate, given my history with Alden. I also can't allow Keefe to think it's okay to slip elixirs into my food/beverages. —Dame Alina

VIOLATION	SERIOUSNESS	
<u>DISRUPTING DETENTION</u> <u>AND DISRESPECT FOR</u> <u>ACADEMY PROPERTY</u> According to a report from Lady Cadence, both Keefe and Sophie Foster were caught placing effluxers wherever they wanted, rather than following her explicit instructions.	8 out of 10	

VIOLATION	SERIOUSNESS	
<u>DISRUPTING DETENTION AND</u> <u>DISRESPECTING A MENTOR</u> According to a report from Lady Cadence, Keefe and Sophie Foster were acting completely inappropriately during detention, and their behavior led to her getting sprayed in the face with musk-tang.	8 out of 10	

SENTENCE	PRINCIPAL'S COMMENTS
One additional week of detention assigned.	I'm sure Keefe was placing his effluxers in places where other prodigies would set them off (or maybe I was his target—I wouldn't be surprised). So I'm glad Lady Cadence stopped this. But I can't say I'm thrilled that she convinced the Council to add effluxers to the campus in the first place. I find it hard to believe we need protection from ogres! —Dame Alina

SENTENCE	PRINCIPAL'S COMMENTS
Full Disciplinary Report given.	I'm not sure what I'm supposed to do with this "Full Disciplinary Report" Lady Cadence gave me. I think she's hoping I'll start expulsion proceedings. But Sophie is far too vital to the Council, given her ability to heal minds—and I'm not in the mood to deal with Lord and Lady Sencen. So I'm just going to leave them to their current punishment. —Dame Alina
	Update: I can't believe I'm writing these words, but . . . I've been elected to the Council! I NO LONGER HAVE TO DEAL WITH UNRULY PRODIGIES. The new principal will be Magnate Leto (the former Beacon of the Silver Tower). —Councillor Alina

VIOLATION	SERIOUSNESS
<u>ORGANIZING A PROTEST</u> According to reports from numerous Mentors, Keefe has been coordinating a walk-out to protest the Council's decision to make Sophie Foster wear the ability restrictor designed by Dex Dizznee.	1 out of 10

SENTENCE	PRINCIPAL'S COMMENTS
None.	For the record, I share Mr. Sencen's issues with the Council's treatment of Miss Foster and see no reason why Foxfire prodigies shouldn't hold a protest. If the Councillors think I'll use this position to promote their agenda, they're going to regret appointing me as principal. —Magnate Leto
	Update: Mr. Sencen has been absent from Foxfire (along with Miss Foster, Mr. Dizznee, Mr. Vacker, and Miss Vacker), and the Council has asked me to notify them immediately if he returns. No explanation was given as to why (though rumors abound that these kids have run off to join the Black Swan). —Magnate Leto
	Second Update: According to a letter from the Council, Mr. Sencen had been officially banished from the Lost Cities and expelled from Foxfire (along with Miss Foster, Mr. Dizznee, Mr. Vacker, and Miss Vacker). Apparently these kids will be attending Exillium from now on. —Magnate Leto

VIOLATION	SERIOUSNESS	

VIOLATION	SERIOUSNESS	
<u>DESTRUCTION OF</u> <u>ACADEMY PROPERTY</u> According to a report from Miss Foster, Mr. Sencen set off a device in my office, shattering the majority of the windows in the glass pyramid.	20 out of 10	

SENTENCE	PRINCIPAL'S COMMENTS
	Third Update: The Council has notified me that Mr. Sencen's banishment has been lifted and he'll be returning to Foxfire (along with Miss Foster, Mr. Dizznee, Mr. Vacker, and Miss Vacker). Hopefully that's the end of this nonsense. —Magnate Leto
	Fourth Update: Mr. Sencen has been absent from Foxfire again—and if rumors are to be believed, he's joined the Neverseen. But surely there's been a misunderstanding . . . —Magnate Leto

SENTENCE	PRINCIPAL'S COMMENTS
None.	Mr. Sencen remains absent, making punishment difficult to issue. And this does appear to confirm his involvement with the Neverseen. But I suspect there's more to the story. —Magnate Leto
	Update: The glass pyramid has been rebuilt. Foxfire is also teaming up with Exillium for skill lessons. And Mr. Sencen has yet to return to campus. The Council is pressuring me to expel him, but I see no reason, (particularly since everyone should be focusing on the upcoming Peace Summit in Lumenaria). —Magnate Leto

VIOLATION	SERIOUSNESS

SENTENCE	PRINCIPAL'S COMMENTS
	Second Update: Foxfire's midterm break was extended aftér the tragedy in Lumenaria, and . . . I'm grateful to have the time to adjust. There's so much to do . . . and I'll be so much more limited now. . . . But I'll find a way to manage. In the meantime, it should be noted that when the academy resumes sessions, Mr. Sencen will be returning, and no disciplinary action will be taken against him. —Magnate Leto
	Third Update: Sessions still haven't resumed. But Miss Foster brought Mr. Sencen to see Elwin for treatment after Mr. Sencen received several serious wounds during a sparring match with King Dimitar. Apparently, one result of the match is that Keefe will now have Princess Romhilda serving as his bodyguard, which will likely cause tension on campus. Preparations will need to be made. —Magnate Leto

VIOLATION	SERIOUSNESS
<u>ASSAULT ON ANOTHER PRODIGY</u> According to numerous reports, Ro stomped on Shayda Adel's foot to punish Shayda for attempting to trip her.	10 out of 10

LEVEL SIX

VIOLATION	SERIOUSNESS

SENTENCE	PRINCIPAL'S COMMENTS
Apology required.	Technically, Mr. Sencen wasn't involved in this incident. But since his bodyguard was, it's going in his file. And for the record, I completely understand Ro's behavior. But I can't condone harming another prodigy. I've ordered Ro to apologize during orientation. —Magnate Leto

SENTENCE	PRINCIPAL'S COMMENTS
	Update: In an effort to contain the story of the Neverseen's recent brutal attack on Mr. Vacker and Miss Foster, I've asked Mr. Sencen to spread the rumor that Miss Foster and Mr. Vacker are away on a mysterious assignment. Elwin also reports having to repeatedly chase Mr. Sencen away from the Healing Center. —Magnate Leto
	Second Update: At Ms. Ruewen's request, I've given Mr. Sencen permission to visit Miss Foster in the Healing Center. (Apparently Miss Foster's morale needs a boost.) Keefe may have untraditional methods, but he does ease Miss Foster's worries and generally improves her mood. —Magnate Leto

VIOLATION	SERIOUSNESS

VIOLATION	SERIOUSNESS
<u>DISRUPTING LUNCHTIME</u> According to a report from Lady Galvin, a number of prodigies began emitting unpleasant gaseous noises midway through the lunch break and had to race to various bathrooms. No proof has been recovered, but the general consensus is that Mr. Sencen slipped Gurgle Gut into their lunches.	5 out of 10

SENTENCE	PRINCIPAL'S COMMENTS
	Third Update: According to a report from Elwin, Mr. Sencen was involved in the recent destruction in the Healing Center—but apparently it happened during a skill lesson that went awry. For that reason, I'm simply noting the incident here, rather than creating a disciplinary report. It should also be noted that Mr. Sencen brought Miss Foster to the Mentors' private cafeteria for butterblasts. —Magnate Leto

SENTENCE	PRINCIPAL'S COMMENTS
One week of detention assigned.	As far as I can surmise, every prodigy affected by Mr. Sencen's prank had recently been gossiping about (or hassling) Mr. and Miss Vacker about their eldest brother—which is why I'm limiting his detention to a week. I cannot allow such behavior to go unpunished. But I refuse to deny the motivation. —Magnate Leto
	Update: Foxfire has been placed on an extended hiatus after the traumatic events during the Celestial Festival. Sessions will resume as soon as the Council determines that it is safe to do so. —Magnate Leto

REGISTRY FILE FOR

Tam Dai Song

KNOWN ABILITIES: *Shade*

RESIDENCE: *Unclear. Possibly Solreef. Family home is Choralmere.*

IMMEDIATE FAMILY: *Quan Song (father), Mai Song (mother), Linh Song (twin sister)*

MATCH STATUS: *Unregistered*

EDUCATION: *Current Foxfire prodigy*

NEXUS: *No longer required*

PATHFINDER: *Not assigned. Restricted to Leapmasters and home crystals.*

SPYBALL APPROVAL: *None*

MEMBER OF THE NOBILITY: *No*

TITLE: *None*

NOBLE ASSIGNMENT: *None*

SIGNIFICANT CONNECTIONS: *Fealty-sworn member of the Black Swan; former Exillium Wayward; former captive of the Neverseen*

ASSIGNED BODYGUARD(S): *Elidyr (dwarf) and Opher (dwarf)*

AN ALTERED FAMILY NAME:

Technically, the Song family's last name should be Tong, since that was their original surname. But Tam's great-great-great-great-great-great-great-great-great-grandmother started calling herself Lady Song and registered her daughter with Song as her surname. Apparently the choice had to do with Lady Song's notoriety as a composer—and since music has remained a dominant profession in the family (Tam's mother and grandmother are both particularly well known for their compositions), the name Song has continued to be passed down.

SIBLING CONFUSION:

Tam was registered at birth as a twin (to his sister, Linh). But his father (Quan Song) later claimed that his children were actually a year apart in age. Tam and Linh refuted that statement—and since Quan had no proof to back up his claims, our records remain with Tam and Linh listed as twins.

FEARED POWERLESS—THEN TOO POWERFUL:

Most likely, the reason Tam's father tried to convince everyone that his children weren't twins was because Tam and Linh were facing judgment, gossip, and low expectations (since many in our world fear that children from multiple births will end up Talentless).

Yet, ironically (and surprisingly), the Song twins actually manifested early. It's hard to pin down their exact ages because of their father's dispute over their inception dates, but it's quite likely that they were some of the earliest to manifest in our world's history. Both Tam and Linh already had special abilities before taking their Foxfire entrance exams. But instead of being celebrated for that remarkable accomplishment, their abilities caused a different kind of fear—particularly in the case of Tam. He manifested as a Shade, and Shades commonly garner suspicion and mistrust. Once Linh's intense hydrokinesis caused her to become the Girl of Many Floods, many began to wish that the Song twins had been Talentless after all.

ON THEIR OWN:
When the Council banished Linh Song for causing so much destruction—and her parents did nothing to intervene—Tam opted to leave the Lost Cities with his sister, even though he wasn't included in her sentence (and despite scoring incredibly high on the entrance exams to Foxfire). Many saw Tam's decision as an act of rebellion (which, of course, it was). But it should also be noted that what he did was a tremendous display of self-sacrifice, loyalty, and love. Few siblings would likely do the same—particularly given the struggles that followed. Both Tam and Linh attended Exillium, where they were assigned to the Ambi Hemisphere and trained under the purple Coach (now known to be Coach Rohana)—and the program was a far cry from the healthy learning environment it has become today. It was a place of harsh rules and harsher punishments, where each

Wayward's identity was stripped away by strange uniforms and policies that forbid any kind of communication. And when Tam and Linh weren't enduring their Exillium lessons, they were finding places to hide out in the Neutral Territories, since they had no actual home. Little is known about their lives during that time, but finding basic necessities like food, clothing, and shelter must've been a challenge. Thankfully, at some point, they set up a small camp near the gnomes' Wildwood Colony, which gave Tam and Linh access to abundant resources and a measure of safety—until the gnomish plague forced the Wildwood colonists to flee, leaving Tam and Linh to fend for themselves once again.

FAMILY STRAIN:

Given the challenges cited above, it's no surprise that Tam appears to have a poor relationship with his parents—especially his father. Numerous reports indicate that he blames them for refusing to move Linh to a residence farther from water while she adjusted to her ability, and for not appealing the Council's decision to banish her. One note even suggests that Tam suspected his parents *wanted* Linh to be banished because they were embarrassed by the negative attention she was bringing to their family. Plus, it would've allowed them the opportunity to pass their son off as an only child and no longer have to deal with the twin-related scorn. But there's no way to determine if those theories are true. What *is* clear is that even now, both Tam and Linh keep minimal contact with their parents—and the encounters they have look far from idyllic.

A SILVER STATEMENT:

Tam wears his hair cut with long, jagged bangs partially covering his eyes—and the tips of his bangs gleam with silver. Apparently he melted down the chain from his registry pendant and dipped his hair in the molten metal as an act of defiance and protest against the way that he and his sister had been treated. In fact, certain reports even indicate that he threw the registry crystal in his father's face right before leaving the Lost Cities.

AN UNIMPRESSIVE WAYWARD:

Notes from the faculty at Exillium make it clear that Tam had a reputation for being a defiant troublemaker, both with the Coaches and the other Waywards. (One report even brands Tam as the worst Wayward at the school—though that report did seem biased against Tam because he was a Shade.) And Tam definitely did not excel in his skill lessons in the program, often receiving mediocre marks at best. But it's difficult to determine how much his performance and attitude were influenced by the harsh atmosphere at Exillium during the majority of his attendance. As touched on above, the school was severely neglected by the Council, lacking the basic funds and supplies it needed to safely operate—which caused the Coaches to enforce a number of overly strict rules in an attempt to maintain some semblance of control. After Sophie Foster participated in the program, she convinced Councillor Oralie to give Exillium the aid it needed—and the situation has vastly improved. But Tam and Linh returned to the Lost Cities not long after, so there's no way to know if Tam's performance would've progressed.

RELUCTANT CHANGES:

Tam and Linh agreed to help Sophie and her friends when they snuck into the ogres' capital (Ravagog). And that mission led to the discovery of vital information on how to cure the gnomish plague. But in order to escape the ogres' city, Linh was forced to flood (and destroy) more than half of Ravagog. So she—and her brother—seemed surprised when their efforts were viewed by the Council as a victory. And both twins were genuinely stunned (and a touch reluctant) when they were welcomed back into the Lost Cities and offered admission into Foxfire. They made it clear that should they return, they had no desire to live with their parents again, so special arrangements were made. And with that, Tam and Linh's banishment ended. The Black Swan also offered to let them join the order—and Linh seemed eager to swear fealty. But Tam had a number of reservations and only joined the Black Swan when he apparently grew tired of his sister "nagging" him about it.

STILL SOMEWHAT ADRIFT:

Since leaving their makeshift camp near the Wildwood Colony, Tam and Linh have floated from home to home. They stayed in an empty dwarven house for a period. Then in one of the Black Swan's hideouts—until that location was compromised. And now it appears they're staying with Sir Tiergan in Solreef (since Wylie has moved to **[LOCATION REDACTED FOR SECURITY]** to be with his father during Prentice's recovery). But it's unclear if Solreef is a permanent arrangement, or whether they'll be moving again. What *is* clear is that Tam continues to refuse his parents' invitations to return to Choralmere (and while Linh recently dwelled there, the move was not meant to be permanent). The rift between the Song twins and their parents obviously needs more time (and perhaps more effort on Quan and Mai's part) in order to heal.

A TEST OF TRUST:

Tam refuses to trust anyone until he's taken a reading of their shadowvapor and measured their potential for darkness against their illumination. It's unclear how often his readings lead him to reject someone as an associate, but reports do indicate that he tested Sophie Foster, as well as the rest of her friends—and the Black Swan—before working with them. In his defense, the process is both quick and painless, and does seem to shed at least some light on a person's character.

FRENEMIES:

While the above term may seem too gimmicky for a subheading in an official file, it's truly the best word to describe the strange relationship dynamic between Tam and Keefe Sencen. The two boys are decidedly *not* friends—in fact, reports suggest they disliked each other almost immediately (and the nicknames they use for each other range from the clever and witty to downright mean-spirited). Some suspect it's because Tam violated Keefe's privacy and read Keefe's shadowvapor without his permission when they first met, while others would argue it's because Keefe refused to have his shadowvapor read as though he had something to hide. Others still might suggest it's actually because the two have quite a bit in common—but prefer to think of themselves as uniquely alone in their challenges and principles. Whatever the cause, it's doubtful that Tam and Keefe will ever truly be friends. But it's important to note that they have never appeared to truly be enemies, either—a fact that became increasingly vital when Tam was taken by the Neverseen and Keefe's mom (Lady Gisela) forced him to use his ability on her son. Had there been true ill will between the boys, Tam wouldn't have attempted to warn Keefe about what his mom was planning— and Keefe would've tried to harm Tam in their final showdown.

THE TRUE POWER OF DARKNESS:

Tam's skill as a Shade has always been impressive—particularly considering the fact that he's had so little formal training. For instance, on the mission to Ravagog, he was able to hide his friends in shadow and help them move through the city undetected. He also lifted the veils of shadowvapor in Prentice Endal's mind, bringing back what little remained of Prentice's shattered consciousness in order for Sophie to perform a mental healing. But a truly astounding aspect of Tam's talent was discovered after the Neverseen's Shade (who called herself Umber) attacked Sophie and Fitz with shadowflux. Few Shades can detect the rare sixth element, much less control it. And only the best can store it within themselves to draw upon later. (Evidently, shadowflux does not like to obey and chooses to embrace only the most powerful Shades.) But Tam was able to feel the darkness that lingered in Fitz's and Sophie's wounds and command it— which was enough to convince Lady Zillah (his Shade Mentor) that he should be training with shadowflux—and after some debate, Tam agreed to the lessons. Lady Zillah can't actually command shadowflux, but she knew enough to guide Tam through special exercises at Foxfire—often at night. And the progress Tam made during those lessons proved vital in the showdown he and his friends had with the Neverseen at Everglen. Not only was Tam able to break through the Neverseen's force fields and leave them defenseless against the newborn trolls, but one of Tam's attacks also seemed to damage the ability of the Neverseen's Psionipath, forcing them to flee. Unfortunately, that display of power also showed Lady Gisela that Tam could command shadowflux—and since the Neverseen's Shade was killed in that battle, Lady Gisela set her sights on Tam.

HOSTAGE:

Lady Gisela lured Tam, Sophie, and Keefe to the hive where the alicorn babies were finishing the final stages of their development and threatened to harm the babies—and Tam's sister—if Tam didn't agree to leave with her and serve the Neverseen. Sophie and Keefe begged Tam not to agree, but Tam apparently didn't see any alternative. He left with Lady Gisela and found himself bound to obey her commands by strange bonds made of light, which had been sealed around his wrists by the Neverseen's Flasher (who calls herself Glimmer). And he soon discovered that Lady Gisela went to all that effort because she needed him to play a key role in what she was planning for her son's legacy. Tam tried to warn Keefe away, but Keefe still showed up in Loamnore exactly the way his mother had arranged, and Tam was forced to dissolve the dwarven King's magsidian throne and send the shadowflux into Keefe's system. It seems Lady Gisela was hoping the sixth element would trigger some sort of transformation in her son, but it's too early to tell if that's what will happen. As of this writing, Keefe remains unconscious from the incident. And Lady Gisela escaped without explaining further.

FINAL NOTE:

The investigation into the events in Loamnore is still ongoing, but for now, it appears the Council won't be holding a Tribunal for Tam or issuing any punishment. Whether that will change once they learn more about what Tam did during his time with the Neverseen—or what may happen to Keefe—remains unclear.

REGISTRY FILE FOR
Linh Hai Song

KNOWN ABILITIES: *Hydrokinetic*

RESIDENCE: *Unclear. Possibly Solreef. Family home is Choralmere.*

IMMEDIATE FAMILY: *Quan Song (father), Mai Song (mother), Tam Song (twin brother)*

MATCH STATUS: *Unregistered*

EDUCATION: *Current Foxfire prodigy*

NEXUS: *No longer required*

PATHFINDER: *Not assigned. Restricted to Leapmasters and home crystals.*

SPYBALL APPROVAL: *None*

MEMBER OF THE NOBILITY: *No*

TITLE: *None*

NOBLE ASSIGNMENT: *None*

SIGNIFICANT CONNECTIONS: *Fealty-sworn member of the Black Swan; former Exillium Wayward*

ASSIGNED BODYGUARD(S): *Urre (dwarf) and Timur (dwarf)*

THE GIRL OF MANY FLOODS:

Elemental abilities are known for being overwhelming—and for Linh, the combination of manifesting so young, becoming a Hydrokinetic, and living in a house near the ocean proved to be an impossible combination. The water constantly called to her, and its draw became so strong that Linh was unable to resist, often with destructive consequences. Her first few floods were smaller, like [LOCATION REDACTED FOR PRIVACY] and [LOCATION REDACTED FOR PRIVACY]. But the problem escalated in [LOCATION REDACTED FOR SECURITY]. Then her parents made the unfortunate mistake of bringing her to Atlantis. Linh's flood nearly destroyed the underwater city, and the Councillors felt they had to intervene. After a rushed Tribunal, a unanimous Council voted to banish Linh in order to "preserve the safety of the Lost Cities." And despite Linh's young age, Linh's parents (Quan and Mai Song) chose not to fight the decision—much to the fury of Linh's twin brother (Tam), who was convinced the Council would've given a different ruling if his parents had sworn to make changes (like moving Linh somewhere with less water exposure and hiring her a full-time ability tutor) to keep Linh's hydrokinesis under better control.

A BOND UNLIKE ANY OTHER:

Linh was banished alone, and given her age and skill set at the time, it seems unlikely that she would've been able to survive for long. Fortunately for Linh, her twin brother (Tam) chose to go with her—despite her adamant protests that he shouldn't give up his life. Reports indicate that Tam insisted they would be better off together—and that he would rather be with her than without her. Which is a true testimony to the connection between these two siblings. For all the judgment that gets cast on twins, it's strange that no one seems to value the bond that children from multiple births have with each other. Tam and Linh are not the only example, but they are an excellent testimony of love, respect, and compassion that truly cannot be compared.

A SILVER REMINDER:

In a similar vein to her brother, Linh's long jet-black hair is tipped with silver—and it seems safe to assume that the metal was applied the same way (by melting down the chain of her registry pendant and dipping the ends of her hair into the molten silver). But in Linh's case, the style was not meant to be a protest. Instead, Linh has explained that her "look" was intended as a reminder to herself of what can happen when she loses control of her hydrokinesis, and likely motivates her to hone her power.

NEW FRIENDS:

After Linh's banishment, it appears that Tam had no intention of trusting anyone ever again. But Linh refused to let her time in Exillium cause her to give up on the idea of friends. And when a new group of Waywards arrived rather suddenly—and one of them accidentally set their rope on fire during the dividing—Linh bravely used her ability to help douse the flames, even though it meant defying the coaches' orders. She stepped back after that, observing as much as she could about these newcomers—and trying to convince her brother that making contact would be worth the risk—before finally reaching out to the one she'd helped that first day. The girl turned out to be Sophie Foster, who agreed to sneak away with Tam and Linh to learn more about them. And whether it was the fact that Sophie clearly didn't judge Tam and Linh for being twins, or the strange color of her eyes (which surely proved that Sophie understood how it felt to be different), or the stories she told about trying to stop both the plague and an ongoing rebellion—or the fact that Tam's reading of her shadowvapor showed no immediate warning of danger—whatever it was, Tam and Linh opted to trust her. Soon after, Sophie introduced them to the rest of her group—which turned out to be a monumentally important shift for all of them. Tam and Linh found a new sort of family, as well as the means to return to the Lost Cities. The Black Swan acquired two vital allies. And all of them became true friends.

A MASTER OF HER ABILITY:

Watching Linh's hydrokinesis now makes it hard to believe that she ever struggled with control. Her aptitude with the ability is nothing short of amazing—particularly since she's mostly self-trained. She's learned to resist the water's call unless it's truly necessary for her to answer it. And she's able to perform all manner of impressive feats—everything from entertaining tricks (like gathering small amounts of water into creative shapes) to lifting flowing rivers and bending them into an arch to allow someone to cross safely under. Technically, Linh *has* caused one additional flood since her banishment—but it most definitely was not a case of her losing control. She flooded Ravagog because it was the only way to get herself and her friends safely out of the ogre capital. Even the Council recognized the distinction, and instead of facing another Tribunal, both Tam and Linh were welcomed home to the Lost Cities—and granted admission to Foxfire. Linh now trains with a Hydrokinetic Mentor, and has even returned to Atlantis and managed to resist the pull of all that water. Control will never be easy for her—such is the challenge with elemental power. But Linh has reached a level of mastery that allows her to make it *look* easy.

CAREGIVER—AND MORE:

When Wylie Endal was captured by the Neverseen—and then managed to escape—he returned to the Black Swan badly burned from what surely must've been a lengthy interrogation. Many might not have been able to face Wylie's gruesome injuries, but Linh bravely stepped in to help, wrapping his scorched body in a cool water cocoon to draw out any remaining heat from his wounds. And when she'd done all she could for Wylie physically, she tended to his emotional recovery, visiting often and cheering him up with water tricks. (Apparently, he's quite a fan of the water animals that Linh can make drift through the air.) And through of all those visits, Linh and Wylie became close friends—though some occasionally wonder if there might be more between them than friendship. That's pure speculation, of course—and given the age gap between them (which is significant, since Linh has yet to register for the match), it also seems somewhat unlikely. All that's known at this time is that Linh and Wylie do appear to spend a meaningful amount of time together.

A QUESTIONABLE CHOICE IN PET:

Much like Sophie, Linh appears to have a penchant for weirdly-cute-but-unusually-challenging pets. In Linh's case, she chose to adopt a murcat—despite Tam's protests, and the fact that murcats are known for having large venomous fangs. Records indicate that the murcat is named Princess Purryfins, and it's highly possible the name was chosen specifically to annoy her brother.

THE GIRL WHO SAVED ATLANTIS:

While the above title has never officially been assigned to Linh, it's definitely deserved. A few short years after losing control and flooding Atlantis (and ending up banished), Linh found the strength and confidence to stop the Neverseen from destroying the city. Yes, she did need Sophie to enhance her (which, it should be noted, was something that Linh had resisted before, out of fear that she might be overwhelmed by the craving). And Sophie, in turn, needed Keefe Sencen to help her focus. But even with Sophie and Keefe's assistance, no one can deny that Linh was the true hero of that moment. Not only did she gather enough water to plug the tear that had been slashed into the city's force field—but she also somehow managed to hold back the force of the ocean until the Council could send Psionipaths to make a permanent repair. Had Linh not been there, the city surely would've been lost—as would thousands of lives.

SEPARATED—BUT STILL CONNECTED:

After everything Tam and Linh have fought through in order to stay together, it was particularly devastating when the twins recently found themselves ripped apart by the Neverseen. Lady Gisela forced

Tam to surrender himself as a hostage in order to protect his sister and the baby alicorns. She also made it painfully clear that if anyone attempted to come after Tam, there would be severe consequences. And while many had doubts as to whether Tam would be able to remain loyal to the Black Swan—and to his principles—in that situation, Linh never doubted her brother for a second. She talked her friends out of planning a risky rescue, assuring them that Tam could handle himself. And when she thought she'd found a way to help him and used her ability to contact him (with Sophie's help), she wasn't discouraged by the harsh things Tam said to convince her to abandon her plan. She trusted him so completely that she even followed his order and returned to Choralmere, despite her strained relationship with her parents. And when she snuck into Loamnore to help him escape, the sound of her voice helped Tam resist the bonds on his wrists that had been controlling him.

FINAL NOTE:

Linh's control of her ability remains remarkable—and yet it also seems clear that we still haven't seen the full extent of her power. Whether that power will lead to salvation (as it did in Atlantis) or widespread destruction (like Ravagog) is yet to be determined. But it's highly likely that it could be both.

ENDAL

REGISTRY FILE FOR

Wylie Zoran Endal

KNOWN ABILITIES: *Flasher*

RESIDENCE: *Solreef (Reports also indicate he's staying with his father at* [LOCATION REDACTED FOR SECURITY]*.)*

IMMEDIATE FAMILY: *Prentice Endal (father), Cyrah Endal (mother)*

ADOPTED BY: *Sir Tiergan Alenefar*

MATCH STATUS: *Registered with one list received*

EDUCATION: *Foxfire graduate (both basic and elite levels)*

NEXUS: *No longer required*

PATHFINDER: *Assigned*

SPYBALL APPROVAL: *Granted*

MEMBER OF THE NOBILITY: *Yes*

TITLE: *Lord*

NOBLE ASSIGNMENT: *Regent; member of Team Valiant*
SIGNIFICANT CONNECTIONS: *Works with the Black Swan (unclear whether he's sworn fealty)*
ASSIGNED BODYGUARD(S): *None*

A REBEL IN THE FAMILY:

When Wylie was seven years old, his father (Prentice Endal) was discovered to be a Keeper for the Black Swan—a rebel organization that, at the time, was believed to have dangerous intentions. With only that limited knowledge to guide their investigation—and Prentice refusing to answer questions after his arrest—the Council had no choice but to order a memory break to discover what Prentice was hiding (before locking him away in Exile). The unsettling task was assigned to Quinlin Sonden and Alden Vacker—and only two pieces of information (a strand of unregistered DNA and the term "Project Moonlark") were recovered before Prentice's mind shattered. Given the strength of Prentice's blocking—and how faithfully he protected the Black Swan—the Council suspected that the information was actually a "hoax" perpetrated by Prentice in a desperate, final attempt to distract the Council and their Emissaries from what the rebels were actually working on. Of course, now it's well known that both Project Moonlark and the child (Sophie Foster) were real, and that the Black Swan—while working outside the law—was actually intent on helping the Council and stopping the true threat to the Lost Cities (a second rebel group now known as the Neverseen). And such hindsight sadly does suggest that what happened to Prentice was somewhat unjust. (Alden Vacker took the revelation particularly hard.) The Council is naturally remorseful for any pain and suffering that

Prentice (and his family) experienced—as well as for the years that Prentice lost to madness in Exile. But it also must be noted that much of what occurred could've been avoided if Prentice had been honest with the Council. Our world is in a state of flux, and the Black Swan is presently considered to be a valuable ally. But the path of rebellion is always fraught with misunderstanding and calamity. The Council's hope is that everyone—themselves included—has learned from what happened to Prentice that the best course for real change is open communication, cooperation, and coordination.

FURTHER FAMILY TRAGEDY:

With Prentice in Exile—and their family facing intense judgment and scandal—Wylie's mom (Cyrah Endal) did her best to bury her grief and step into her role as the sole caretaker of her son. She began designing and selling hair accessories in Mysterium, and life for the Endals appeared to be finding some sort of new normal. Until disaster struck again. Something went wrong while Cyrah was light leaping, and she arrived home dangerously faded. Wylie called for help as soon as he found her, but by the time Elwin Heslege arrived, it was far too late to save her (and had likely been too late even before then). Cyrah had lost too much of herself to be able to recover, and Wylie could do nothing except watch as his mother faded away. A planting was held shortly after, and Cyrah's Wanderling (a bright red tree with tiny purple flowers) grows strong and proud in the Wanderling Woods, honoring her life and commemorating the loss.

A NEW HOME:

Wylie was barely eight years old when his mother died, essentially leaving him an orphan—far too young to live without a guardian. And with death so rare in our world, the Council was at a bit of a loss on how to best proceed. There was talk of Wylie living with Prentice's cousin (Lesedi Chebota), since he was close with his second cousin (Maruca Chebota). But Lesedi was still struggling with her grief over what happened to Prentice. Grady and Edaline Ruewen were also suggested, but they were still mourning the loss of their daughter, Jolie (who'd died a few years earlier). Thankfully, Prentice's close friend (Sir Tiergan Alenefar) offered to let Wylie live at his estate (Solreef). The offer was somewhat unexpected, given Tiergan's relationship with the Council at the time. He'd been Prentice's best friend and resigned from the nobility (quite angrily) to protest Prentice's memory break and exile. (As an aside: It's interesting to consider that Tiergan is now known to be Granite, a member of the Black Swan's Collective. Definitely casts new light on his anger over the injustice.) But even with that noted tension, the Council agreed that Tiergan was the best choice for Wylie as a guardian. Adoption proceedings began soon after. And while little has been recorded about Wylie's life at Solreef (Tiergan was particularly protective of their privacy), the fact that Wylie has continued to thrive and excel over the years, despite all the tragedies he's suffered, more than proves that Prentice provided him with a loving home and supplied the care and support he needed.

HOPE, FURY, AND HEALING:

Reports indicate that before Prentice's memory break, he'd somehow assured his family that if something bad happened to him, it might not be permanent. And Wylie (and his mom) interpreted that promise to mean that whomever Prentice was protecting would be his salvation. Thus, when Sophie arrived in the Lost Cities, Wylie's hope soared—and then turned to anger and resentment when she made no effort to help his father. He confronted Sophie at Alden's planting—and while the interaction appeared to be quite hostile, it seems whatever he said helped Sophie to realize that she might have been designed by the Black Swan to be able to heal broken minds. Her abilities first needed to be reset (thanks to damage caused by her own near-fading). But when Sophie tested the healing process on Alden, it was found to be a tremendous success. Wylie naturally assumed that his father would be next, but sadly, that was not the case. With Prentice locked away in Exile, Sophie was unable to reach him without the Council's permission. And the Council opted to focus on healing former Councillor Fintan Pyren. His case was simpler than Prentice's, since he would be healed strictly to recover what he'd hidden during his memory break, and no one would have to answer the question of "What do we do with him now?" And when Fintan's healing led to disaster (including the fire that destroyed half of Eternalia and killed Councillor Kenric), the Council seemed reluctant to allow any further healings. The Black Swan took matters into their own hands—and while their attempted prison break into Exile was a failure, Sophie did manage to barter a deal with the Council for Prentice's release. He was then handed over to the Black Swan, and everyone (including Wylie) assumed he'd be healed soon after. But when Sophie tried (with Fitz Vacker's help), Prentice was found to be unresponsive. All hope seemed to be lost—until Tam Song tried lifting the veils of shadowvapor in Prentice's mind and Prentice showed hints of improvement. The

Black Swan discovered soon after that Prentice had been drugged with the Neverseen's dangerous sedative (soporidine), presumably by dwarves working with the Neverseen. But they still chose to have Sophie attempt the healing again—though it was an incredibly delicate process. Prentice would be waking up to devastating news about his wife (as well as the knowledge that he'd missed most of his son's childhood), and Sophie had to ensure that those revelations wouldn't shatter his mind all over again. But somehow, she managed to make it work, and Prentice has not only returned to consciousness, but also seems mostly like his old self. The main difference—aside from natural signs of trauma and grief from his experiences—is that Sophie was unable to recover any of his damaged memories. Perhaps with time, a way will be found to recover something useful, but for the moment, Prentice seems grateful to be alive and free and focusing on the future instead of the past.

THE NEVERSEEN'S NEXT TARGET:

Despite his father's affiliation with the Black Swan, Wylie has kept mostly separate from their activities (except those related to Prentice's healing). So it came as a shock to everyone when the Neverseen abducted him from his room at the Silver Tower at Foxfire and brought him to one of their hideouts, where he was interrogated for an unknown number of hours before managing to escape. And while his physical injuries were healed, the greater challenge has been the mental toll. It's honestly quite incredible— given the number of traumas Wylie has endured—that he's managed to hold himself together so well. He's gained some solace from his recent companionship with Linh Song. But what truly appears to be driving him is focusing on figuring out why the Neverseen came after him and what actually happened to his mom.

DEADLY STARSTONES:

Our investigation into this topic is incomplete and ongoing—and it's highly possible that certain information is still being held back by either Wylie or the Black Swan (or both). But reports indicate that the Neverseen did not question Wylie about his father while they held him captive (as might be expected). Instead, their interrogation focused on his mother. Cyrah's death has long been viewed as simply a tragic light leaping accident, but the Neverseen's questions suggested something much darker. Wylie evidently begged Sophie Foster to look into it for him, and from what little she's gleaned, it appears that Cyrah might have been murdered by the Neverseen. Cyrah was a talented Flasher—much like her son—and that apparently made her a target for Lady Gisela, who tried to trick her into using her ability to manufacture a series of special blue-flashing starstones. The starstones were supposedly for the Black Swan (but were really meant to provide transport to certain of the Neverseen's most secret facilities), and Cyrah knew enough about her husband's order to spot the lie. She tried to resist—until Lady Gisela threatened Wylie's safety. Gisela also promised to kill the Black Swan's moonlark if Cyrah didn't cooperate—and while Cyrah had no personal attachment to Sophie, she knew the moonlark was the only hope for healing her husband's shattered mind. So Cyrah did her best to cooperate. But Fintan decided she should be terminated when the project was completed, because she knew too much. It then appears that Fintan enlisted Gethen (another known member of the Neverseen) to use his ability as a Telepath to break Cyrah's concentration before she leaped home, causing her to fade away. But much of that story was provided by Lady Gisela, who could easily be fabricating certain details to cover her own involvement. Without proof, it's hard to say for certain. What *is* known is that one of the starstones Cyrah made is still missing, and given the drastic measures they took to interrogate Wylie, the Neverseen seem desperate to find it.

PROTECTING WHAT LITTLE FAMILY HE HAS LEFT:

Wylie's second cousin (Maruca) recently manifested as a Psionipath—an ability that could prove to be invaluable to Sophie and her friends. The Neverseen's strategies tend to rely heavily on their Psionipath (Ruy Ignis), so having a Psionipath helping the Black Swan would be a game changer (particularly since Ruy's power seems to have been affected by one of Tam Song's shadowflux attacks). But Wylie begged Sophie not to let Maruca swear fealty to the order. Sophie definitely understood why he might not want Maruca to put her life in danger after losing so many members of his family—but she also knew the decision was up to Maruca. And Maruca is every bit as strong-willed as Wylie. She refused to sit by when she could be helping save lives—and Wylie has begrudgingly respected her decision.

A VALIANT FIGHTER:

Since his abduction, Wylie has begun working much more closely with the Black Swan. It's unclear whether or not he's sworn fealty, but he's definitely been involved in many of their recent activities, including coming to Sophie and Fitz's aid during a brutal ambush arranged by the Neverseen. Those who witnessed the battle testified to the incredible power Wylie displayed, both as a Flasher and a fighter, which is one of the reasons the Council offered to appoint him as a Regent to serve as a member of Team Valiant. Wylie accepted the appointment readily, and didn't even protest when he wasn't selected as leader, despite the fact that he's the eldest member of the team and the only one to complete his elite Foxfire training.

FINAL NOTE:

The greatest measure of Wylie's character may be his relationship with Sophie Foster—the girl who was inadvertently the cause of so many of the tragedies in his life. There have clearly been times when he's blamed her—even resented her. But over time, he's come to accept that she's not responsible for what happened. More than that, it appears he's even come to understand why his father sacrificed so much to protect Sophie, and seems to be determined to stand by her side. Whether he'll ever consider her accomplishments to be "worth it" will likely depend on what she achieves. But he seems ready and willing to follow her lead.

HEKS

REGISTRY FILE FOR

Stina Destry Heks

KNOWN ABILITIES: *Empath*

RESIDENCE: *Sterling Gables*

IMMEDIATE FAMILY: *Timkin Heks (father), Vika Heks (mother)*

MATCH STATUS: *Unregistered*

EDUCATION: *Current Foxfire prodigy*

NEXUS: *No longer required*

PATHFINDER: *Not assigned. Restricted to Leapmasters and home crystals.*

SPYBALL APPROVAL: *Granted*

MEMBER OF THE NOBILITY: *Yes*

TITLE: *Lady*

NOBLE ASSIGNMENT: *Regent; member of Team Valiant*

SIGNIFICANT CONNECTIONS: *Works with the Black Swan (but hasn't sworn fealty); trained caretaker at the Heks unicorn preserve*
ASSIGNED BODYGUARD(S): *None*

A CHALLENGING FAMILY:

The Hekses are known for many things in the Lost Cities—but one that's rarely discussed (and yet seems to be incredibly defining) is this: They can be difficult. It's unclear whether there's something fundamentally unlikable about their personalities, or whether they're simply misunderstood. Either way, they're a family with few friends, and many who—while not willing to classify themselves as enemies—would prefer to have as little to do with the Hekses as possible. And yet, the Hekses remain part of our world—a valuable part, even. Just oftentimes a less enjoyable part. And Stina seems to be a particularly strong example of her family's take-me-or-leave-me attitude, regularly causing drama with other prodigies at Foxfire—especially Dex Dizznee and Sophie Foster.

A GIFT WITH EQUINES:

Before the Heks women got involved, unicorns were dangerously close to becoming extinct as a result of their isolating behavior and sporadic breeding (and of course the threat humans posed to the species). The caretakers at the Sanctuary tried everything they could think of to repopulate the species, but the numbers continued declining—until Pelipa Heks (Stina's great-great-great-great-great-great grandmother) paid a visit to the Sanctuary and discovered that her ability as an Empath provided her with a unique understanding of the unicorns' needs. She petitioned the Council to move one male and one female unicorn to her property to test some of her theories, and months later—after the unicorn couple delivered their first foal—several more unicorns were assigned to her care. Thus began the Heks family's most vital contribution to the Lost Cities: unicorn caretaking—a task that Stina and her mother (Vika Heks) are heavily involved in. Stina's been working at Sterling Gables since she was old enough to walk the pastures, and now that she's manifested as an Empath, her training has reached a whole new level—which proved to be valuable when the female alicorn's pregnancy turned out to be twins. Vika and Stina may have been bitter that Silveny hadn't been entrusted to their care (particularly since Silla Heks—Stina's grandmother—had been the one to rehabilitate Greyfell before he was placed at the Sanctuary). But they readily put their frustrations aside and stepped in when Sophie teleported to their property begging for help because Silveny had gone into early labor. With Vika and Stina's guidance—as well as some special aid from the trolls—both Silveny and her babies (Wynn and Luna) are currently healthy and thriving.

THE SCANDAL THAT WASN'T:

Stina's father (Timkin Heks) is one of the Talentless. Her mother (Vika) is an Empath. As such, their marriage should've been ruled a bad match. Yet mysteriously, it wasn't. Timkin's name is clearly included on Vika's first match list—toward the top, it should be noted. Conspiracy theories abound about how that could be possible (mostly in whispers, since no one wants to face the wrath of the Hekses), and the most common story is that records were altered at the Matchmaking Office by Timkin's sister's husband, who works there. But no proof has ever been found of any such tampering. In a more recent investigation, one report did suggest that the real reason Timkin was able to return to Foxfire, complete the final few weeks of the basic levels, and graduate with his class (despite having been expelled and sent to Exillium for faking his "special ability") was because he [DETAILS REDACTED FOR SECURITY]. And if that's true, then perhaps [REDACTED FOR SECURITY]. There is, however, no way to confirm. As such, Vika and Timkin's marriage remains an officially approved match, and the family is spared from any scandal.

DISCIPLINE PROBLEM:

As already mentioned, Stina has a propensity for causing drama with numerous other prodigies at Foxfire, and since the school doesn't tolerate bullying, she a lengthy disciplinary record. She's been assigned the second highest number of detentions—though the gap between her list and Keefe Sencen's list is quite large. But she—unlike Keefe—doesn't seem to enjoy her punishments. In fact, she's tried having her mom speak to the principal several times, to see if anything could be done to lighten her sentence. But Foxfire takes bullying very seriously, and as of this writing, she's never been able to get out of any of her detentions.

HER FATHER'S FEALTY:

For years Timkin has tried to convince the Council to appoint him to the nobility (despite his Talentless status). And for years he's been denied. Perhaps that's why he opted to swear fealty to the Black Swan when they were still an illegal rebellion. It's hard to tell, given what little is known about his involvement in the order. Records suggest that while his involvement with the order tends to be more "hands-off," he may have occasionally used the name "Coiffe" and relied on a disguise of full-body, curly white fur (caused by an elixir that may have been created by Kesler Dizznee) to protect his identity. And he's apparently assisted Sophie and her friends during their banishment from the Lost Cities, despite the fact that he disagrees with the Black Swan's decision to utilize children in their rebellion. In fact, it seems he's done what he could to keep Stina away from anything he's been working on. But Stina's ended up involved anyway.

A NOBLE LADY:

Stina was chosen by the Council to be a member of Team Valiant— a move that came as a surprise to many (particularly given Stina's strained relationship with Sophie and her friends). And while Stina seemed less than thrilled about who she'd be working with (and the feeling was clearly mutual), she also eagerly accepted the title— which was surely a huge cause for celebration for her family. Particularly for her father, who's tried many times to be appointed to the nobility and always been held back by his Talentless status.

FINAL NOTE:

Stina will likely never win any popularity contests. But she's a powerful Empath and a fearless personality, and when she puts her differences aside, she can be a valuable ally. The test will be whether she can handle the hardships that come with her new role, or whether she'll crack the first time she's truly put under pressure.

REDEK

REGISTRY FILE FOR

Marella Adene Redek

KNOWN ABILITIES: *Pyrokinetic*

RESIDENCE: *Fluttermont*

IMMEDIATE FAMILY: *Durand Redek (father), Caprise Redek (mother)*

MATCH STATUS: *Registered with zero lists received*

EDUCATION: *Current Foxfire prodigy*

NEXUS: *No longer required*

PATHFINDER: *Not assigned. Restricted to Leapmasters and home crystals.*

SPYBALL APPROVAL: *None*

MEMBER OF THE NOBILITY: *No*

TITLE: *None*

NOBLE ASSIGNMENT: *None*

SIGNIFICANT CONNECTIONS: *Fealty-sworn member of the Black Swan; training in pyrokinesis with former Councillor Fintan Pyren*
ASSIGNED BODYGUARD(S): *None*

AN EXTREMELY DANGEROUS, ILLEGAL ABILITY:

Marella's special ability is a somewhat recent development (or the Council's knowledge of it is, at least), but it's such a tremendously rare, incredibly complicated issue that her file must begin here. Reports indicate that several months ago Marella arranged for a meeting with Mr. Forkle (the same member of the Black Swan who triggered Sophie Foster's abilities) and convinced him to try triggering hers, since she still hadn't manifested. Evidently, she'd been hoping to become an Empath, because reading emotions could prove helpful with her mother's (Caprise Redek's) condition. But manifesting isn't a process where anyone gets to pick or choose what happens. And unfortunately for Marella, not long after Mr. Forkle filled her mind with energy, she felt feverish and later woke up surrounded by flames after manifesting as a Pyrokinetic—the only illegal ability in the Lost Cities. The rare elemental talent causes an insatiable craving for flame, which has resulted in numerous tragedies—the most notorious of which was Fintan Pyren's failed lesson on Everblaze several millennia ago. All five of the Pyrokinetics that Fintan had been training were killed in that inferno, and the Council was left with no choice but to ban the ability. Their new law forced any already registered Pyrokinetics to be reclassified as Talentless (including Fintan, who had to resign from the Council) and be put under supervision in order to ensure that they weren't sparking any flames. Efforts were also made to prevent others from manifesting the ability. (For instance, anyone directly related to any of the registered Pyrokinetics was labeled as a bad match to halt the spread of their genetics, and the ability detecting session at Foxfire now specifically forbids any exercises that might make a prodigy detect *heat*.) Aside from one exception (the now infamous case of Brant [LAST NAME REDACTED FOR SECURITY]), no other Pyrokinetics have manifested since the ban. Until now.

EXPOSED:

Given the complications that come with being a Pyrokinetic, it's not necessarily surprising that Marella opted to hide her ability from the Council. But she did reveal her pyrokinesis to a select few. Both of her parents seemed to be aware (and most likely helped cover up several accidental fires that happened after she first manifested). And Mr. Forkle was evidently informed and did his best to train her (even though he doesn't share her ability). Marella was also brought in to assist on a few important missions for the Black Swan—which of course means that Sophie Foster and her friends were aware that Marella was a Pyrokinetic (and possibly some of their families were aware too). But everyone "in the know" kept the information secret—and likely would still be doing so, if the Neverseen hadn't exposed Marella during the last Celestial Festival. The battle with the mutant trolls at Everglen was broadcast for our whole world to witness, which meant that everyone watched Marella call down flames and use them to defend herself and her friends. And while the crowd's initial reaction was shock (the collective gasp was loud enough to make many ears ring), the discovery wasn't met with the level of fear and mistrust that most would've expected. Perhaps it was because Marella maintained excellent control. Or perhaps it was watching her bravely stand and fight in the face of such horrors. But after the broadcast, the Council wasn't met with outcry calling for Marella's banishment or exile. And the Councillors have since surprised everyone further.

TRAINING PERMITTED—WITH A TRAITOR:

In a decision that surely no one could have predicted, the Council did not ban Marella from using her pyrokinesis. In fact, they've even gone so far as to allow her to take pyrokinesis lessons with Fintan—on a provisional basis. The situation is far from ideal, but given the rarity of the power, there simply aren't many options for Mentors. And the Council seems to have decided—possibly because of what happened with Brant—that forcing Marella to suppress the ability could end up causing larger problems in the long run. A Pyrokinetic's craving for flame seems to be too strong to ignore—especially without training. So the Council appears to be seeing if there's a middle ground that allows the ability to be used within specific limits. Only time will tell if there is. Until then, Marella's lessons take place at the special prison where Fintan is being held for his crimes, and are, of course, *closely* monitored to ensure that Fintan cannot use the situation as an opportunity to escape or harm anyone. Linh Song also attends most of these lessons, using her hydrokinesis to extinguish any flames. And rumor has it that Marella and Linh do additional training together on their own. There are certain similarities between their abilities, given that they're both controlling an element, and it appears they may be attempting to combine their powers. It's difficult to imagine how that might work, but if the events over the last several years have taught us anything, it's to expect the unexpected—particularly when it comes to any of our powerful youth.

A TRAGIC FAMILY ACCIDENT:

As already briefly noted, Marella's mother (Caprise) suffered a traumatic brain injury when Marella was three years of age. For reasons still unknown (though some have claimed that fizzleberry wine might have been involved), Caprise fell off a balcony at their home and hit her head. Elwin did all he could to help, but some injuries cannot be completely healed, and Caprise was forever changed by the experience. Her symptoms seem to primarily affect her moods, and certain elixirs do help her manage them. But she's known to have good days and bad days. And Marella seems to shoulder a heavy amount of the responsibility in caring for her, oftentimes running late for things or looking slightly disheveled. (And of course, there was Marella's hope of becoming an Empath to better assist, which was already mentioned.) Naturally, Caprise's situation has lowered the family's social standing. Most are sympathetic to the Redeks' plight, but still aren't sure how to help or what to do, since these kinds of challenges are so rare in the Lost Cities.

A BIT OF A LONER:

It's hard to tell how much Marella's family challenges have affected her social decisions, but despite her large personality, Marella has opted to isolate herself—particularly from the other prodigies at school. In fact, until Sophie Foster started attending Foxfire, Marella often ate lunch by herself. She used to claim it was because she found everyone annoying, but it's also possible that she has a harder time "fitting in" given how different her homelife is. Even after Sophie and Marella became friends, they weren't as close as Sophie was with some of her other friends, and rumors claim that Marella has at times felt neglected by Sophie's group, particularly when they started spending an increasing amount of time working with the Black Swan. Sophie was likely trying to spare Marella from the dangers that come with the Black Swan's assignments (much like she tried to do with everyone she cares about)—and some reports *do* indicate that Marella is far less eager to risk her life than some of her friends appear to be. But that doesn't mean that Marella wouldn't have preferred to be included. The number of dangerous missions she's agreed to help with—and the fact that she recently swore fealty to the order—definitely proves that she's both willing and able when asked and needed.

THE "GO-TO" FOR GOSSIP:

Despite her sometimes antisocial ways, Marella has a gift for always knowing about everything, and anyone looking to catch up on the latest gossip (or wanting to find out about a past scandal) tends to go to her. There are often gaps in her knowledge, but what she does know generally seems to be accurate—sometimes so much so that people are left wondering where she got her information. And the truth is, no one knows—except Marella.

A NOTORIOUS FLIRT:

In what also seems to be a strange contrast to her loner ways, Marella definitely has a reputation for flirting. And teasing. And generally being very open about who does and doesn't catch her interest—as well as who she thinks her friends should or shouldn't be interested in. Which may seem like a strange note to be including in this file. But given the particular complications of Marella's ability, she's likely going to have a very challenging matchmaking process—possibly even more challenging than Sophie's. In light of that, her flirting seems suddenly significant.

A SECRET STUFFED ANIMAL:

Elwin's records indicate that Marella is yet another of his patients to receive one of his Emotional Support Stuffed Animals (as is her mother, actually)—though Marella seems to be more secretive about her stuffed animal buddy and hasn't mentioned its existence to her friends. Still, in the interest of thoroughness, it must be noted that Marella is the proud owner of a sparkly blue-green stuffed kelpie, which Elwin named Sir Splashyhugs. It's even possible that Sir Splashyhugs was the *first* Emotional Support Stuffed Animal, since he was gifted to Marella when she was three and struggling to adjust to what happened with her mom.

FINAL NOTE:

It's unclear whether Marella realizes how much pressure is resting on her shoulders. But she has unwittingly found herself in a pivotal role in our world. If she's able to maintain control of her ability, she may be responsible for lifting the ban on pyrokinesis and righting what an increasing number are beginning to see as an injustice. And if she surrenders to her flames, she could end up the most destructive Pyrokinetic yet, given the access she has to the Council and the Black Swan, and the friends who've chosen to put their faith in her.

REGISTRY FILE FOR

Grady Howell Ruewen

RUEWEN

KNOWN ABILITIES: *Mesmer*

RESIDENCE: *Havenfield*

IMMEDIATE FAMILY: *Edaline Ruewen (wife), Jolie Ruewen (daughter, deceased), Sophie Foster (daughter, adopted)*

MATCH STATUS: *Match approved (one match list received; married the #7 recommendation)*

EDUCATION: *Foxfire graduate (both basic and elite levels)*

NEXUS: *No longer required*

PATHFINDER: *Assigned (to the Lost Cities and the Forbidden Cities; crystals to Loamnore and Ravagog also issued)*

SPYBALL APPROVAL: *Yes*

MEMBER OF THE NOBILITY: *Yes*

TITLE: *Lord*

NOBLE ASSIGNMENT: *Emissary*

SIGNIFICANT CONNECTIONS: *Adoptive father to Sophie Foster; known supporter of the Black Swan; former caretaker of Brant* [LAST NAME REDACTED] *; animal rehabilitator for the Sanctuary*

ASSIGNED BODYGUARD(S): *Brielle (goblin, deceased)*

DRASTIC CHANGES:

In a single day, Grady Ruewen went from being one of the Lost Cities' most prestigious and powerful Emissaries to a virtual recluse and outspoken opponent of the Council—though that day did involve a tragic fire that killed his only daughter (Jolie). The grief nearly shattered Grady (and his wife, Edaline)—and sadly, no one knew how to help them. Loss is (thankfully) uncommon in our world, so few could understand what Grady and Edaline were feeling. Instead, everyone watched in sorrow (and a bit of confusion) as the Ruewens retreated from the rest of society after Jolie's planting. Grady resigned from his position as an Emissary, and Edaline took a (still technically ongoing) leave of absence from the assignment she'd been given by the Council. They chose to spend their days tracking down protected species hiding in the Forbidden Cities, bringing them to the pastures at Havenfield, and helping the creatures prepare for life in the Sanctuary. Neither of the Ruewens left their home to visit anywhere in the Lost Cities unless they absolutely had to (which was extremely rare), and gossip grew more abundant and critical by the year. But just when it seemed like Grady and Edaline would soon be nothing more than a "cautionary tale" (before falling into complete obscurity), everything changed for them once again. A young girl (Sophie Foster) had been found hidden among humans and needed a home in the Lost Cities, and the Council wanted Grady and Edaline to be her guardians. To nearly everyone's shock, the Ruewens agreed— and apparently even needed little convincing. Reports indicate that when Alden Vacker hailed Grady to explain the situation, there was a brief pause, an exchanged look, and then a simple, "We'll try our best." It wasn't an easy adjustment for them—or for Sophie—and at one point the situation nearly dissolved. But over time, Sophie proved to be exactly what Grady and Edaline needed to finally work through their grief. And now that Grady has resumed his work as an Emissary, the Council is hoping that he'll be able to return to **[ASSIGNMENT REDACTED FOR SECURITY]**.

REMAINING FILE
HIGHLY
CLASSIFIED.
ACCESS DENIED WITHOUT
PROPER CLEARANCE.

REGISTRY FILE FOR

Edaline Kelia Ruewen

KNOWN ABILITIES: *Conjurer*

RESIDENCE: *Havenfield*

IMMEDIATE FAMILY: *Grady Ruewen (husband), Jolie Ruewen (daughter, deceased), Sophie Foster (daughter, adopted)*

MATCH STATUS: *Match approved (one match list received; married the #3 recommendation)*

EDUCATION: *Foxfire graduate (both basic and elite levels)*

NEXUS: *No longer required*

PATHFINDER: *Assigned (to the Lost Cities)*

SPYBALL APPROVAL: *No*

MEMBER OF THE NOBILITY: *Yes*

TITLE: *Lady*

NOBLE ASSIGNMENT: *None at present*

SIGNIFICANT CONNECTIONS: *Adoptive mother to Sophie Foster; known supporter of the Black Swan; former caretaker of Brant* [LAST NAME REDACTED]; *animal rehabilitator for the Sanctuary*

ASSIGNED BODYGUARD(S): *Cadoc (goblin)*

SO MUCH MORE THAN A CARETAKER:

Edaline may appear to be timid and soft-spoken. Or at times even weary and worried. And her delicate beauty and gentle smile often add to the impression that she's someone fragile who must be handled with care. She's also had many dark days as a result of losing her daughter (Jolie). But the fact that she was able to hold herself together in spite of her grief speaks volumes on the strength of her character. It also tends to shock and amaze people to learn that Edaline regularly wrestles dinosaurs and wrangles saber-toothed tigers and rides woolly mammoths. And before Edaline stepped back from the nobility (after Jolie's death), she'd been assigned to one of the Council's most fraught situations: [REDACTED FOR SECURITY]. The Black Swan has also trusted her with numerous dangerous responsibilities—the most hazardous of which is, of course, serving as guardian to their moonlark (Sophie Foster). In fact, recently recovered reports suggest that the Black Swan manipulated the Council's decision in regard to Sophie's living arrangements in order to ensure that she ended up at Havenfield with Grady and Edaline—a powerful Mesmer and Conjurer who could provide a higher level of protection for Sophie against her enemies. And while the Ruewens needed time to adjust to their new roles, they've now stepped up fully to the task—and just in time, since the Council suspects that soon [REDACTED FOR SECURITY].

REMAINING FILE
HIGHLY
CLASSIFIED.
ACCESS DENIED WITHOUT
PROPER CLEARANCE.

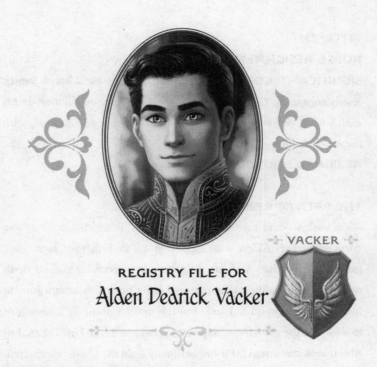

REGISTRY FILE FOR
Alden Dedrick Vacker

KNOWN ABILITIES: *Telepath*

RESIDENCE: *Everglen*

IMMEDIATE FAMILY: *Della Vacker (wife), Alvar Vacker (son), Fitz Vacker (son), Biana Vacker (daughter)*

MATCH STATUS: *Match approved (three match lists received; married the #201 recommendation)*

EDUCATION: *Foxfire graduate (both basic and elite levels)*

NEXUS: *No longer required*

PATHFINDER: *Assigned (to the Lost Cities and the Forbidden Cities; crystals to Gildingham, Loamnore, Marintrylla, and Ravagog also issued)*

SPYBALL APPROVAL: *Denied*

MEMBER OF THE NOBILITY: *Yes*

TITLE: *Lord*

NOBLE ASSIGNMENT: *Emissary*

SIGNIFICANT CONNECTIONS: *Member of the Vacker family; briefly engaged to Councillor Alina (the #104 recommendation on his match lists); father to a member of the Neverseen; works closely with the Black Swan*

ASSIGNED BODYGUARD(S): *None*

THE PATH OF REBELLION:

As a Vacker—and an immensely talented Telepath—no one was surprised when Alden was appointed as an Emissary soon after graduating Foxfire. And his diligence, resourcefulness, and dedication to his investigations inspired the Council to assign him to increasingly complicated and secretive tasks, eventually asking him to look into the growing whispers of rebellion in the Lost Cities. But Alden took the threat far more seriously than the Council expected. They'd assumed his investigation would prove that the alleged Black Swan group lived only in misunderstanding and rumor. Instead, Alden brought them Prentice Endal and proof in the form of **[REDACTED FOR SECURITY]** that Prentice belonged to the rebels. The memory break the Council ordered also seemed to produce further evidence—but the Council refused to believe that anyone could illegally produce a genetically altered child without their knowledge, much less hide her away in the Forbidden Cities. They felt the whole thing had to be a hoax to distract them or potentially embarrass them and decided that Prentice's exile had already stirred up enough scandal. Alden was ordered to drop the matter and found himself facing the same predicament the rebels had faced: Follow orders and allow the situation to escalate—potentially to disaster. Or defy the Council. Alden chose rebellion, conducting his search for the mysterious girl in secret (even involving his children in his work). And while he did turn out to be right and discovered Sophie Foster—who's turned out to be a vital asset to our world (as has the Black Swan, it should be noted)—several on the Council have long suspected that Alden conducted other unsanctioned investigations, some of which may be ongoing even now and have to do with [REDACTED FOR SECURITY].

REMAINING FILE HIGHLY CLASSIFIED. ACCESS DENIED WITHOUT PROPER CLEARANCE.

VACKER

REGISTRY FILE FOR

Della Adara Vacker

KNOWN ABILITIES: *Vanisher*

RESIDENCE: *Everglen*

IMMEDIATE FAMILY: *Alden Vacker (husband), Alvar Vacker (son), Fitz Vacker (son), Biana Vacker (daughter)*

MATCH STATUS: *Match approved (one match list received; married the #1 recommendation)*

EDUCATION: *Foxfire graduate (both basic and elite levels)*

NEXUS: *No longer required*

PATHFINDER: *Assigned (to the Lost Cities and the Forbidden Cities)*

SPYBALL APPROVAL: *Yes*

MEMBER OF THE NOBILITY: *Yes*

TITLE: *Lady*

NOBLE ASSIGNMENT: *Emissary*

SIGNIFICANT CONNECTIONS: *Member of the Vacker family (by marriage, not genetics); fealty-sworn member of the Black Swan; mother to a member of the Neverseen*

ASSIGNED BODYGUARD(S): *None*

WATCH OUT FOR VANISHERS:

After marrying the Lost Cities' most eligible Vacker (and with a hint of scandal, no less, given what happened with Dame Alina at their wedding), Della could have easily settled into a life focused on societal assignments rather than noble ones. But she opted to strive for an appointment as an Emissary, and when the title was granted, she pushed the Council to truly put her to use. She was a Vanisher, after all. She could investigate anything they wanted. And the Council opted to take her up on it, having her look into [REDACTED FOR SECURITY] and [REDACTED FOR SECURITY]. But Della's success in those matters led the Council to eventually issue a much trickier assignment. Reports indicate that they ordered Della to find out what her husband was working on— and when she initially resisted, she was reminded of the oaths she swore. Additional records do suggest that Della provided the Council with information on Alden's work—though none of them mention anything about his search for Sophie Foster. Whether that was an intentional omission or proof that Alden kept his secrets safe is impossible to tell. It's also interesting to wonder if Alden and Della might have noticed the fact that their son (Alvar) had been recruited by the Neverseen if they hadn't been so distracted by hiding things from each other. There's no way to know. But it should be noted that Della did inform the Council that **[REDACTED FOR SECURITY]**.

Inaccessible Files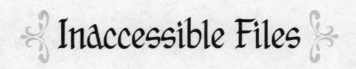

Kesler Ardal Dizznee
[FILE INACCESSIBLE]
See database for:
TALENTLESS
BAD MATCH

Juline Kalea Dizznee
[FILE INACCESSIBLE]
See database for:
BAD MATCH

Lady Gisela Minette Sencen
[FILE INACCESSIBLE]
See database for:
MEMBERS OF THE NEVERSEEN

Alvar Soren Vacker
[FILE INACCESSIBLE]
See database for:
CONVICTED CRIMINALS
MEMBERS OF THE NEVERSEEN

Lady Vespera Neci Folend

[FILE INACCESSIBLE]

See database for:

CONVICTED CRIMINALS

MEMBERS OF THE NEVERSEEN

Gethen Inar Ondsinn

[FILE INACCESSIBLE]

See database for:

CONVICTED CRIMINALS

MEMBERS OF THE NEVERSEEN

Ruy Tonio Ignis

[FILE INACCESSIBLE]

See database for:

BANISHED

MEMBERS OF THE NEVERSEEN

Mr. Errol Loki Forkle

[FILE INACCESSIBLE]

See database for:

MEMBERS OF THE BLACK SWAN

ALIASES

Sir Tiergan Andrin Alenefar

[FILE INACCESSIBLE]

See database for:

MEMBERS OF THE BLACK SWAN

Councillor Kenric Elgar Fathdon

[FILE INACCESSIBLE]

See database for:

MEMBERS OF THE COUNCIL

DECEASED

Jolie Lucine Ruewen

[FILE INACCESSIBLE]

See database for:

DECEASED

Brant Alger [REDACTED]

[FILE INACCESSIBLE]

See database for:

MEMBERS OF THE NEVERSEEN

DECEASED

A QUICK NOTE

FOR YEARS I'VE HAD READERS ASKING ME HOW TO pronounce the different names, so I decided to include my pronunciations on the following pages. That way everyone would have them—but I also want to remind you that this is simply how *I* say the names. One of the truly special things about reading is that you get to imagine things the way *you* want—so if you've been pronouncing any of the names differently, you're welcome to keep doing so! I would never want to take that away from you!

Main Registry List

Find more character information at
keeperofthelostcities.com.

The Babblos Family

FERNAN BABBLOS: *(FER-nan BAB-los)*

JENSI BABBLOS: *(JEN-see BAB-los)*

The Chebota Family

LESEDI CHEBOTA: *(le-SED-ee chee-BOT-uh)*

MARUCA CHEBOTA: *(mah-ROO-kah chee-BOT-uh)*

The Dizznee Family

BEX DIZZNEE: *(BECKS DIZ-nee)*

DEX DIZZNEE: *(DECKS DIZ-nee)*

JULINE DIZZNEE: *(joo-LEEN DIZ-nee)*

KESLER DIZZNEE: *(KESS-lur DIZ-nee)*

LEX DIZZNEE: *(LECKS DIZ-nee)*

REX DIZZNEE: *(RECKS DIZ-nee)*

The Endal Family

CYRAH ENDAL: *(SEE-ruh END-all)*

PRENTICE ENDAL: *(PREN-tiss END-all)*

WYLIE ENDAL: *(WHY-lee END-all)*

The Heks Family

OLLIE HEKS: *(AH-lee HECKS)*

PELIPA HEKS: *(PELL-ip-uh HECKS)*

SILLA HEKS: *(SILL-uh HECKS)*

STINA HEKS: *(STEE-nuh HECKS)*

TIMKIN HEKS: *(TIM-kin HECKS)*

VIKA HEKS: *(VEE-kuh HECKS)*

The Redek Family

CAPRISE REDEK: *(ca-PREES RED-eck)*

DURAND REDEK: *(DUR-and RED-eck)*

MARELLA REDEK: *(mah-RELL-uh RED-eck)*

The Ruewen Family

SOPHIE FOSTER: *(SO-fee FOS-tur)*

EDALINE RUEWEN: *(ED-uh-leen REW-in)*

GRADY RUEWEN: *(GRAY-dee REW-in)*

JOLIE RUEWEN: *(JO-lee REW-in)*

VERTINA: *(ver-TEE-nuh)*

The Sencen Family

CASSIUS SENCEN: *(CASS-ee-us SENSE-in)*

GISELA SENCEN: *(jih-SELL-uh SENSE-in)*

KEEFE SENCEN: *(KEEF SENSE-in)*

The Sonden Family

LIVVY SONDEN: *(LIV-ee SOHN-den)*

QUINLIN SONDEN: *(KWIN-lin SOHN-den)*

The Song Family

LINH SONG: *(LIN SONG)*

MAI SONG: *(MY SONG)*

QUAN SONG: *(KWAHN SONG)*

TAM SONG: *(TAM SONG)*

The Vacker Family

ALDEN VACKER: *(AL-din VACK-er)*

ALVAR VACKER: *(AL-var VACK-er)*

BENESH VACKER: *(BEN-esh VACK-er)*

BIANA VACKER: *(bee-AH-nuh VACK-er)*

DELLA VACKER: *(DELL-uh VACK-er)*

FALLON VACKER: *(FAL-on VACK-er)*

FITZ VACKER: *(FITS VACK-er)*

HARLIN VACKER: *(HAR-lin VACK-er)*

LUZIA VACKER: *(loo-ZEE-uh VACK-er)*

NORENE VACKER: *(nor-EEN VACK-er)*

OREM VACKER: *(OR-um VACK-er)*

The Council

COUNCILLOR ALINA: *(uh-LEE-nuh)*

COUNCILLOR BRONTE: *(BRON-tay)*

COUNCILLOR CLARETTE: *(clare-ET)*

COUNCILLOR DAREK: *(DARE-eck)*

COUNCILLOR EMERY: *(EM-er-ee)*

Councillor Kenric: *(KEN-rick)*

Councillor Liora: *(lee-OR-uh)*

Councillor Noland: *(NO-land)*

Councillor Oralie: *(OR-uh-lee)*

Councillor Ramira: *(Rah-MEER-uh)*

Councillor Terik: *(TARE-ick)*

Councillor Velia: *(VEH-lee-uh)*

Councillor Zarina: *(zare-EE-nuh)*

Foxfire Staff/Faculty

Lady Alexine: *(AL-ex-een)*

Lady Anwen: *(AHN-when)*

Sir Astin: *(AS-tin)*

Sir Beckett: *(BECK-et)*

Lady Belva: *(BELL-vuh)*

Sir Bubu: *(BOO-boo)*

Master (Lady) Cadence Talle: *(KAY-dince TALL-ee)*

Sir Caton: *(CAY-ton)*

Sir Conley: *(CON-lee)*

Lady Dara: *(DARE-uh)*

Lady Delmira: *(del-MEER-uh)*

Sir Donwell: *(DON-well)*

Elwin Heslege: *(EL-win HESS-leej)*

Lady Evera: *(EV-er-uh)*

Sir Faxon: *(FACKS-on)*

Lady Galvin: *(GAL-vin)*

SIR HARDING: *(HAR-ding)*

LADY ISKRA: *(ISK-ruh)*

SIR JARVIN: *(JAR-vin)*

SIR LEANDER: *(LEE-ann-der)*

MAGNATE LETO KERLOF: *(LET-oh KUR-loff)*

LADY NISSA: *(NISS-uh)*

SIR ROSINGS: *(ROSE-ings)*

LADY SANJA: *(SAHN-juh)*

SIR TIERGAN ALENEFAR: *(TEER-gen al-EN-fahr)*

LADY VEDA: *(VAY-duh)*

LADY ZILLAH: *(ZILL-uh)*

Exillium Coaches

COACH BORA: *(BORE-uh)*

COACH ROHANA: *(ro-HAH-nuh)*

COACH WILDA: *(WILL-duh)*

Foxfire Prodigies

AUDRIC: *(AH-drick)*

DEDRA: *(DEE-druh)*

DEMPSEY PEMBERLEY: *(DEMP-see PEM-ber-lee)*

HUXLEY: *(HUCKS-lee)*

SHAYDA ADEL: *(SHAY-duh uh-DELL)*

TRELLA: *(TRELL-uh)*

VALIN: *(VAY-lin)*

Matchmakers

Brisa: *(BREE-suh)*

Ceri: *(SARE-ee)*

Juji: *(JOO-jee)*

Members of the Neverseen

Brant: *(BRANT)*

Fintan Pyren: *(FIN-tan PYE-ren)*

Gethen Ondsinn: *(GETH-en OND-sin)*

Ruy Ignis: *(ROO-ee IG-niss)*

Vespera Folend: *(VESS-per-uh FOE-lend)*

Other

Jurek: *(JUR-eck)*

Damel Kafuta: *(duh-MELL ka-FOO-tuh)*

The
World
of the
Lost Cities

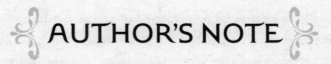

AUTHOR'S NOTE

IN CASE YOU SOMEHOW MISSED THE *GORGEOUS* map of the Lost Cities—or even if you did see it—*go take a look at all of that amazingness!*

It's okay. I'll wait.

waits

waits more

Everyone back now?

Good!

Now that you've studied the map, I'm guessing you have QUESTIONS. Like, *What are Solreef and Splendor Plains and Fluttermont?* Or *Why do Ravagog and Marintrylla and Loamnore and Gildingham have alternate names?* And those questions are all answered in the next few pages. But before we get to that, I wanted to cover the bigger question you may be having, which is: *If the Lost Cities are on Earth, why does this map look different from other maps I've seen?*

The simple answer is: Maps are a reflection of the cultures that create them. So a map drawn by the elves wouldn't look like a map drawn by humans (even though they're technically representing the same planet). And after *lots* of discussion (seriously, you have no idea how many emails my editor and I sent back and forth on this), we settled on a style that's not built around latitude and longitude (since maps that do so were primarily designed for sea travel).

Instead, we went with a more "overhead" approach (which would make more sense for a culture that relies on light leaping). That's why Antarctica looks like a large island (near Australia), instead of sliced up and running along the bottom like you're probably used to seeing. Most of the locations are also in places that might make you think, *Wait—I don't remember an island there!*—which is the point! The Lost Cities have been carefully hidden from humans. In fact, the elves won't be too happy with me for showing you where to find everything.

Well . . . I'm not showing you *everything*. The world of the Lost Cities is so intricate that there was no way to include every place I've mentioned in the series without the map turning into a cluttered mess. So we tried to pick the places we thought you'd be most interested in. Turn the page to learn more about them!

PS: The map was drawn by Francesca Baerald, who somehow took the disastrous sketch I sent her and turned it into all of that stunning beauty. She seriously deserves a round of applause!

MAPPED LOCATIONS

(FOLLOWING THE ORDER ON THE MAP,
CLOCKWISE FROM THE UPPER RIGHT CORNER)

Splendor Plains: Elwin's residence is just as bright and bold as his fashion sense, and every pane of his windowed walls is set with a different color of glass. But the architecture is also surprisingly sleek and modern, with a flat roof and lots of sharp angles. And while the decor is somewhat sparse, there are plenty of "Elwin" touches—like the room holding his stuffed animal collection and the tunnels visible under the glass floor, which allow his pet banshee (Bullhorn) to scurry wherever his little heart desires. The house is bordered by forest on one side and ocean on the other, providing Foxfire's resident physician with a variety of peaceful views to enjoy after stressful days in the Healing Center (most of which involve complicated injuries suffered by Sophie Foster).

Wanderling Woods: As the Lost Cities' only graveyard, the Wanderling Woods is a place of peaceful silence, filled with carefully arranged, incredibly special trees. Wanderlings are planted with the DNA of someone deceased in order to grow with hints of their physical attributes. As a result, no two Wanderlings are alike, and each is labeled with a sign to indicate the life being memorialized—though there are three Wanderlings that were planted prematurely: Sophie Foster's, Dex Dizznee's, and Alden Vacker's. Only elves may enter the Wanderling Woods (unless special permission is granted by the Council), and a golden sign arches over the entrance reminding visitors that "those who wander are not lost." And while some might comment on how few trees grow in the woods—and claim it as proof that death is rare in the Lost Cities—those mourning loved ones would likely argue that there are still far too many Wanderlings.

Candleshade
(Keefe's House)

Candleshade: This towering skyscraper of a residence is one of the tallest structures in the Lost Cities, with at least two hundred stories. Owned by Lord Cassius Sencen—but unoccupied since the family fell into scandal (after Lady Gisela Sencen was discovered to be a leader of the Neverseen)—Candleshade is equal parts impressive, intimidating, and devastating. A hundred stories up, the main building splits into a series of narrow towers, each crowned with a curved golden roof that looks like a flame. Decor varies from floor to floor—some rather simple, some quite ostentatious. (One room even includes a life-size statue of Lord Cassius.) And while numerous searches have been made of the property since Lady Gisela's ties to the Neverseen came to light, little has been found. But given the enormity of the property, many suspect that Candleshade still hides vital secrets.

Everglen: Alden and Della Vacker's castle-style manor is every bit as luxurious and opulent as someone would expect from such an illustrious family. It's also surrounded by parklike grounds and overlooks a glittering lake. The estate was originally owned by Luzia Vacker, but

Everglen
(Fitz & Biana's House)

she passed the property to Alden when he was appointed as an Emissary for the Council. Everything about Everglen's design is meant to testify to the prestige of the Vackers, from the fountains that spout arcs of colored water throughout the halls, to the tinkling chandeliers and jeweled mosaics on many of the doors. The property used to be protected by an enormous glowing gate with metal bars that absorbed light (to prevent anyone from leaping inside without permission). But after the recent scandal involving an illegal troll hive discovered on the property, the Council ordered the gates to be removed.

Mysterium: As one of the "working class" cities in the elvin world, Mysterium was designed for function and practicality (as opposed to the glitz and glamour of many "noble" cities). The narrow streets are lined with food stalls and vendor carts and plain,

Mysterium

identical buildings—with one notable exception: Slurps and Burps (the Dizznee family's tremendously popular apothecary), which adds a bold splash of color and a topsy-turvy style of architecture, along with a door that belches when anyone enters or exits.

Havenfield (Sophie's House)

Havenfielð: The Ruewen family's estate is a mix of chaos and elegance, between the shimmering glass-and-gold house overlooking the ocean and the vast expanses of fenced-in pastures. As one of the rehabilitation centers for the Sanctuary, Havenfield is home to an ever-changing assortment of strange and wonderful creatures—everything from dinosaurs, to verminions, to the precious alicorn family (as well as the lone mutant gorgodon freed from the Neverseen's facility). The property is also home to the only known Panakes tree (along with a large number of gnomes who reside in a special grove in order to gather the Panakes's healing blossoms). Havenfield is bordered by steep cliffs, which have been blocked by a massive gate ever since the Neverseen abducted Sophie Foster and Dex Dizznee from the dark caves below. Given the near-constant danger Sophie lives with, there are numerous other highly classified security elements to the property.

Gilðingham (OR DORARSPADERA IN GOBLINESE):

The goblins' gleaming capital city is made of intricate golden

Dorarspaðera (Gilðingham)

buildings that surround a golden lake, so it's highly possible that Gildingham is the source of human myths about "El Dorado." And while most of Gildingham's architecture has a fragile feel (lots of arches, pillars, windows, and balconies), the queen's palace is a sturdy golden step pyramid. One of the city's most notable features is the Hall of Heroes—a massive memorial of twisted golden columns and gilded statues of the many goblins lost in battle. And Queen Hylda enters and exits the city using the Imperial Pathways, where her royal carriage is pulled by Twinkle (a massive titanoboa—which is far less fearsome than it first appears). Elves aren't unwelcome in the goblin capital, but they need special permission from the queen to visit.

Fluttermont:
The Redek family's sprawling estate has a series of domed buildings draped with bougainvillea that surround a square reflecting pool mirroring the sky. The house is peaceful and immaculate, but visitors tend to catch themselves wondering which of Fluttermont's numerous balconies was the one Caprise Redek fell from—a fall that caused the injuries she still battles. A huge stone firepit was recently added to the property, surrounded by golden beanbag chairs made of flareadon fur, in order to provide a safe space for Marella Redek to practice her pyrokinesis. The family limits visits to Caprise's "good days."

Fluttermont
(Marella's House)

Marintrylla (OR WEERIIĐUULOOAA IN TROLLISH):
Little is known about Marintrylla, since the elves are rarely invited to visit. But the city serves as the trollish capital and includes Empress Pernille's palace. Marintrylla is housed on a secret island and consists of an intricate

Weeriiđuulooaa
(Marintrylla)

network of caves and bridges—and it should be noted that the city likely *doesn't* include one of the trolls' special hives. Those appear to be hidden among elvin locations, thanks to Luzia Vacker (who secretly served as an ally to one of the trollish empresses), in order to keep the trolls' unborn babies safe from ogres.

Shores of Solace: Lord Cassius Sencen's beachfront mansion was originally a property that he kept private and used as a place to escape to whenever he wanted space from his family. But since his wife's involvement with the Neverseen was discovered, the Shores of Solace has become his primary residence (though he does still retain a somewhat secret apartment in Atlantis). The estate is a tranquil single-level beach home with mother-of-pearl walls and vine-draped arches, sunny patios, and stately rooms decorated in soothing tones of gray and blue. Keefe Sencen lives there for the moment—but not by choice—and he spends the majority of his time on a patio lined with cushioned swings, watching waves crash onto a black sand cove.

Alluveterre: Once a hideout for the Black Swan (and now abandoned, because the Neverseen have a crystal that could give them access), Alluveterre is an enormous underground cavern that contains a lush forest, as well as a subterranean river. Two of the largest trees have been crowned with clever tree houses connected by an arched bridge, and winding wooden staircases wrap around the trunks to provide access. During Sophie's time residing in Alluveterre, she and her friends were separated into groups (Sophie, Biana, and Della in one treehouse, and Keefe, Dex, and Fitz in the other) and when Tam and Linh lived there, they each claimed a treehouse for themselves. The hideout was given to the Black Swan by the dwarven king—which is why the name comes from the dwarven language (meaning "the sands of dawn")—and the dwarves view Alluveterre as a testimony of our planet's power to re-create itself, since the land above lies desolate from human pollution and destruction, while below, a crack filtered the light in and allowed nature to thrive in peace.

Sanctuary: This special animal preserve was created because humans were hunting certain animals to extinction (particularly those believed to be "magical" or "mythical"), and the elves believe that every species exists for a reason and that the planet's delicate balance would

Sanctuary

be forever altered if one disappeared. The dwarves helped hollow out the Himalayas, and the gnomes helped build a thriving ecosystem inside, and any creatures now under the elves' protection are caught, rehabilitated (primarily to help them adjust to their vegetarian diet), and eventually moved into the Sanctuary. The lush interior includes every possible climate, comfort, and care the creatures might need, as well as a rainbow-shifting sky to provide the illusion of freedom. The Sanctuary is definitely not a zoo full of cages. It's a haven where all creatures can thrive without danger—or it's supposed to be. While the rare alicorns were housed inside, the Neverseen made numerous attempts to break into the Sanctuary, and Sophie Foster had to convince the Council that it would be safer to set the alicorns free.

Solreef
(Tiergan's House)

Solreef: Given Sir Tiergan's intense desire for privacy—particularly after what happened with Prentice Endal—few have visited his personal residence. Solreef is situated on a small island and protected by an intense level of security. The house itself is somewhat fortresslike, with extra high walls—and the only entrance is situated at the top of a long stone staircase. Inside, though, Tiergan has striven to make his home a warm, welcoming environment for his adopted son (Wylie Endal) and later for Tam and Linh Song, who reside in Wylie's room (which is more like three rooms) now that Wylie lives with his recovering father.

Eternalia: The glittering elvin capital is hidden in a valley in the Himalayas, and it's truly a sight to behold—and likely the source

Eternalia

of human legends about Shangri-la. Eternalia is divided by a wide river lined with Pures (towering palmlike trees that filter the air), and one half of the city holds the twelve identical crystal castles that serve as offices (and residences) for the Councillors. The other half is a sparkling, jeweled metropolis, which includes—among numerous other buildings—Tribunal Hall (a tall domed building built from emeralds, which flies a blue flag when a Tribunal is in progress), the Council's Seat of Eminence (a massive diamond palace with four towers, which only the nobility may enter), the Lost Cities' primary (and largest) library, and a special memorial fountain to the late Councillor Kenric. A large portion of the city was destroyed in the same inferno of Everblaze that stole Kenric's life, but Eternalia was quickly rebuilt with the help of the gnomes and dwarves. Buildings that survived the fire can be identified by their style (built from solid-color bricks of a single gemstone), as can the replacements (with walls that are elaborate, multicolored jeweled mosaics).

Foxfire: The Lost Cities' most prestigious academy is more like a small city than a school. Foxfire's main building contains six wings and six towers (each in the same color as the grade level that attends sessions there)

Foxfire

and wraps around a five-story glass pyramid (which houses the principal's office at the apex, as well as the cafeteria, the orientation room, and the rooms where detention is held). The campus also has the elite towers (comprised of the Silver Tower and the Gold Tower, which twist around each other), as well as a domed amphitheater and numerous other buildings and fields—plus a well-equipped Healing Center, which has been put to use quite extensively since Sophie Foster arrived in the Lost Cities.

Gateway to Exile: In truth, there are no striking geographic features to identify the Gateway to Exile amid the endless scorching desert—but given that it's the first means of access to an underground prison where the worst criminals from all the intelligent species are kept, that's largely the point. Those granted permission to enter Exile are provided with instructions for how to find the pool of quicksand that will allow them to sink to the Entrance to Exile, where dwarves will be waiting to make sure they have the required piece of magsidian before allowing them to continue down the long, winding flight of stairs to the center of the earth. The final step takes place in the Room Where Chances Are Lost, where magsidian is used to open the door into Exile, a spiraling prison that winds in on itself, filled with horrible sounds and horrible cells—though the worst part is the somnatorium (where the "hopeless cases" are permanently sedated).

Atlantis: This gleaming silver metropolis is hidden under the ocean beneath a dome of air—much like the human myths about Atlantis claim. The reason those legends are somewhat accurate is because Atlantis was designed to be a place where elves and humans united their cultures—and for a brief time, that's exactly what it was. But then the humans planned an uprising and forced the elves to disappear (though recent evidence suggests there may be more to that story). Since light doesn't reach Atlantis, visitors must begin their journey at a small rocky outcropping in the middle of the ocean and create a whirlpool that allows them to slide down the enormous swirling maelstrom into the city (landing on a giant sponge, which dries them off completely). Leaving is equally complicated and requires being encased in a giant bubble and launched out of the city by a geyser. Notable features of Atlantis include the glowing balefire spires (which provide soft blue-toned light), the starlight effect on the dome (which gives an appearance of night), the Unity Fountain (a remnant from the city's human history), specialty shops of all kinds, an intricate system of bridges and canals—with fancy eurypterid-pulled carriages floating along the water—as well as numerous noble offices including the Registry, the Treasury, the Matchmaking Office, the Chief Mentalist, and many others.

Lumenaria: The original castle at Lumenaria—which proudly stood in the center of its small, rocky island for millennia—was recently destroyed in a tragic (and deadly) attack by the Neverseen (who also freed one of the prisoners from the dungeon).

But the gnomes and dwarves helped the elves rebuild, and the new castle (once again built from lumenite) is even more magnificent. Access to Lumenaria is currently restricted (until the final security measures can be put into place), but someday soon it will again be a fortress where all of the intelligent species (gnomes, dwarves, ogres, goblins, trolls, and elves) can come together for Peace Summits and treaty negotiations. It's unclear whether the castle's dungeon was rebuilt, or whether any remaining diplomatic prisoners (those with too much value to be locked away in Exile) were moved elsewhere. But the main courtyard still contains the Four Seasons Tree—a silent testimony to a darker part of the Lost Cities' history.

Sterling Gables (Stina's House)

Sterling Gables: The Hekses' private residence is far better known as a unicorn preserve than an estate—though its silver-and-crystal mansion has a uniquely "homey" feel. The pastures are always filled with unicorns under the Hekses' care, and the outbuildings have an abundance of equine supplies. Thanks to the Heks family, the unicorn species is slowly repopulating—though there is still a great deal more work ahead.

Saðlitzagvatka (Ravagog)

Ravagog (OR SADLITZAGVATKA IN OGREISH): Previously called Serenvale (when the land served as the gnomes' homeland—before the ogres stole it), the ogres' capital city is not considered a welcoming place for other species. Ravagog is tucked among dark, jagged mountains and protected by force fields and massive gates, and King Dimitar has made it clear that anyone who enters the city without his permission will face consequences. Half of the city is carved into the side of a mountain (in a network of ledges and staircases built around misty waterfalls), and the other half is underground (in a huge swampy cavern). Other notable features include the King's Path and main palace, the Eventide River (which glows green from a special enzyme), a recently rebuilt dark metal bridge lined with arched towers, the Triad (where King Dimitar holds court), the Armorgate (the ogres' military university), and the Spateswale River (which provides the most direct path into Ravagog). Much of Ravagog was damaged or destroyed after King Dimitar made the cruel decision to unleash a plague upon the gnomes. Sophie Foster and her friends infiltrated the city in order to find the cure and were forced to cause a flood in order to escape. The ogres were punished for their crime, and the city has been largely rebuilt—as has the relationship between the elves and the ogres.

Loamnore (OR NYMTYRANYTH IN DWARVEN): The dwarven capital is an enormous underground maze of intricately woven tunnels that snake deep into the earth and lead to marketplaces, plazas, and even bubble-shapped living quarters.

Nymtyranyth
(Loamnore)

Visitors unable to tunnel into the city must wade to the middle of a muddy quagmire and sink down through the muck into a cavern known as the Visitor Center. Two paths are available from there: one narrow but bright enough to see (for those heading toward the main city), and the other a wide, black void of nothingness previously called the King's Path. (The name will likely be changed to the Queen's Path in light of the dwarves' new leader.) The path can be a disturbing journey and should *not* be braved unless a visit to the ruler of the dwarves is both approved and absolutely necessary. Parts of Loamnore were recently rebuilt after King Enki's betrayal (and the battle that followed), and residents of the city hope that Queen Nubiti's rule will bring a new era of peace and prosperity.

Choralmere
(Song Residence)

Choralmere: Quan and Mai Song's stunning beachfront estate is tucked between a pristine cove and the edge of a rainforest. Choralmere's massive, elegant house has a series of courtyards crowned with golden roofs and framed by amber and garnet walls. Golden lanterns light the residence, and hundreds of wind chimes create a peaceful ambiance—much like the compositions that Mai Song is famous for creating (most of which are composed in her studio at the property). Their children (Tam and Linh) left Choralmere after Linh was banished—and Tam has long contended that Linh would've been spared such harsh punishment had Quan and Mai been willing to move her farther from water. As a result, even though Tam and Linh have returned to the Lost Cities, they choose not to live with their parents—though Linh temporarily agreed to stay with them (at Tam's request) while Tam was trapped with the Neverseen.

Rimeshire
(Dex's House)

Rimeshire: The Dizznees are known for being quirky and untraditional, so many are surprised by the refined beauty of their family home. Rimeshire resembles an ice castle with its blue cut-glass walls and swirling towers that look like upside-down icicles. It's located in the Gloaming Valley (near the Alenon River, where the wild kelpies live), surrounded by snow-capped mountains and twisted evergreen trees—which makes Rimeshire one of the colder places in the Lost Cities. But the temperature is still pleasant—and it's also fitting, given that Juline Dizznee is a Froster. Part of her garden even includes a collection of shockingly lifelike ice sculptures, which she creates as a compromise with her rambunctious triplets, who would prefer to have a pet, but are willing to settle for new ice creatures every day (which is much easier for their already overwhelmed parents to manage).

Riverdrift: When King Dimitar refused to let Lady Cadence Talle set up a permanent residence in Ravagog, she built Riverdrift as a solution. The craft was primarily docked along the Eventide River, but it's capable of journeying across any body of water thanks to the massive paddle wheels mounted to the back of the steel barge. Riverdrift is as large as any of the other elvin manors but is comprised of a wide variety of structures built from different metals, as well as a small glass pyramid and several chimneys spewing multicolored mist. The design may not be as aesthetically appealing as the Lost Cities' usual architecture, but it was built to be practical rather than beautiful. Riverdrift allowed Lady Cadence to spend years researching the ogres, and she still lives there—despite being forced to return to the Lost Cities to serve as a Mentor to Sophie—in the hope that someday she'll be allowed to sail back to Ravagog to properly continue her research.

Portraits

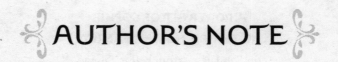 AUTHOR'S NOTE

WHEN MY PUBLISHER APPROVED MY PLAN FOR including a series guide in this book, my first question was, *CAN WE HAVE ILLUSTRATIONS?* And I happy-danced around my house when the answer was, *Absolutely!*

But then I was left with the NEARLY IMPOSSIBLE task of deciding which pieces to include.

(When it comes to Keeper art, imagine me like Silveny: *MORE! MORE! MORE!*)

In the end, I picked characters, locations, and moments we haven't gotten to see yet—and it all turned out so much more amazing than I ever could've hoped!

And so, without further ado, I present a selection of awesome Keeper portraits, and they are as follows:

A PORTRAIT OF SANDOR AND GRIZEL
(standing outside of Everglen)

A PORTRAIT OF BO AND RO
(standing outside of Candleshade)

A PORTRAIT OF FLORI
(under Calla's Panakes tree)

THE TWELVE ORIGINAL COUNCILLORS
(seated on their thrones in Tribunal Hall)

A PORTRAIT OF SOPHIE
WITH HER HUMAN FAMILY

(in San Diego, from before Sophie
moved to the Lost Cities)

A PORTRAIT OF WYLIE
WITH HIS PARENTS

(happy together, before tragedy
struck their family)

A PORTRAIT OF TAM AND LINH
WITH THEIR PARENTS

(standing in front of Choralmere, from
before they were banished)

A PORTRAIT OF ELWIN
AND LIVVY

(with Bullhorn!)

A PORTRAIT OF THE
BLACK SWAN'S COLLECTIVE

(standing in Alluveterre)

Art by Laura Hollingsworth

Life in the Lost Cities

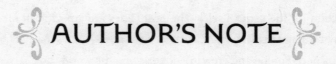

AUTHOR'S NOTE

ONE OF THE MOST FASCINATING (AND CHALLENGING!) parts of my job for this series was creating the world of the Lost Cities. In fact, I spent more than a year brainstorming the elves' history and culture—and then discovered how much I still had to figure out once I actually started writing the first draft.

I knew the elvin world needed to feel familiar in certain ways, since it shares our planet. But it also needed to feel wholly different, since it was built and inhabited by a totally separate species (a species that cut itself off from human contact, no less). Most important, it couldn't just be a place where I threw together a bunch of stuff I loved. I had to follow the logic of each decision—even if it meant that certain things weren't necessarily the way I would want them to be if I lived there.

Which is why the Lost Cities are luminous, and vibrant, and filled with places and foods and creatures and gadgets I *wish* existed—but they also aren't perfect.

In fact, I've always thought of the elvin world as a "Crumbling Utopia"—a place that *seems* idyllic at first, but the longer you linger, the more you start to see the flaws in the system.

Those flaws are where the story comes from. After all, if the Lost Cities were *perfect*, they wouldn't need Sophie Foster! (Or Keefe! Or Fitz! Or Biana! Or Dex! Or Tam! Or Linh! Or Wylie! Or! Or! Or! It takes a lot of characters to bring about change!)

So, don't be surprised if you catch yourself thinking, *That's so cool!* AND *Wait—that doesn't sound fair!* as you read through this section (or the series itself). The Lost Cities are amazing in *many* ways. But not in *all* ways. At least not right now—we'll see what happens once Sophie and crew are done saving the world. ☺

(And don't forget to keep an eye out for new details as you continue reading. You also might find that sometimes your favorite characters are the ones explaining things, since they do it way better than I can!)

The Council

THE LOST CITIES ARE GOVERNED BY A COUNCIL—
and while the Council's authority technically only applies to elves,
its role in negotiating and enforcing treaties with the other intelligent species causes the elves to see the Councillors as rulers over
all. Members of the Council accept their positions not for privilege
or honor or glory, but rather from a sense of obligation stemming
from the fact that they believe they're uniquely qualified to lead.

In Ancient times, the Council had three members. But as the
population of the Lost Cities has grown, so has the number of
Councillors. Currently the Council is a group of twelve. And given
the vital role they play, the Councillors have each been assigned a
goblin bodyguard for their protection. (Other security measures
have been recently added and are kept highly classified.)

Each Councillor has the same level of authority—though
they choose a "spokesperson" from among their ranks (always a
Telepath who can mentally moderate their discussions before voicing the consensus) in order to ensure that the Council publicly
presents a united front. And while many decisions require a
unanimous vote, some only need a majority. In cases where dis-
sent exists, the outvoted Councillors are expected to resist further
argument or disruption (though Councillor Bronte notoriously
struggles with that edict).

Elections are infrequent, only occurring when a Councillor
either dies or chooses to resign—or in rare cases (like what happened with Fintan and the ban on pyrokinesis) when a Councillor

finds themselves no longer qualified for the position. The most common reason for resignation is a desire for a family. Councillors aren't allowed to marry or have children while serving (strong family connections could bias their decisions), and some eventually grow weary of the restriction. When a new Councillor is elected, the public first submits nominations from various members of the nobility who qualify for consideration. The remaining Councillors then vote among themselves to determine who will join their ranks, using a network of mirrors. When all the mirrors are aligned (and the vote is therefore unanimous), a beam of light refracts off their castles, bright enough to be seen anywhere in the Lost Cities.

The Councillors wear extravagant gowns and jerkins, highly embellished capes, and jewel-encrusted circlets decorated with their choice of gemstone. Their circlet jewel also adorns their throne in Tribunal Hall. At times, the Councillors need to appear more unified, and in those instances, they'll wear silver cloaks and matching circlets, pull their hair back, and often keep their hoods raised, making it difficult to tell them apart. When they make their annual visit to the Point of Purity (to remind themselves where true power lies), they wear special cloak clasps shaped like glowing golden keys (which give them access to the Paragon—their transport for the journey—as well as prevent motion sickness and vertigo).

All current—and previous—Councillors also possess a small crystal gadget called a cache, which is designed to store Forgotten Secrets (information deemed too disturbing or dangerous for the Councillors to keep in their memories). Each cache contains a different number of secrets, and only the possessor of the cache is able to access theirs (using a process that's kept highly classified).

Recent events involving the Neverseen have cast uncertainty on the strength of the Council's power and their right to rule—as well as the appropriateness of certain past and present decisions. And while many—including certain Councillors—have come to agree that changes must be made, it's vital for the safety and survival of the Lost Cities that the Council's authority remain supreme. Therefore, every effort must be made to halt this rebellion before the world dissolves into war and chaos.

Currently
Ruling
Councillors

Despite numerous attempts, Councillor Alina has yet to approve an official portrait. According to her, "none have captured my beauty properly."

Councillor Alina

ABILITY: *Beguiler*

JEWEL: *Peridot*

NOTE: *Before being elected, Councillor Alina was the principal of Foxfire. She also dated Alden Vacker and rather notoriously tried to break up his wedding after their relationship ended.*

STANCE: *Despite seeming supportive when she was Sophie's principal, Alina has openly sided against Sophie numerous times.*

Councillor Bronte

ABILITY: *Inflictor*

JEWEL: *Onyx*

NOTE: *As one of the only known Inflictors, Councillor Bronte additionally serves as a Mentor to Sophie Foster. He's also the only Ancient member of the Council.*

STANCE: *Bronte used to be one of Sophie's worst adversaries, but he's slowly become one of her most committed supporters.*

Councillor Clarette

ABILITIES: *Polyglot, Flasher*

JEWEL: *Turquoise*

NOTE: *Councillor Clarette is the most powerful Polyglot in the Lost Cities and can even vaguely speak to animals—which often makes people forget that she (like most Polyglots) has a second special ability.*

STANCE: *Clarette has never voiced support for Sophie and tends to defer to whatever the majority of the Council decides.*

Councillor Darek

ABILITY: *Phaser*

JEWEL: *Ruby*

NOTE: *Councillor Darek was found to have the most powerful telekinesis out of everyone on the Council.*

STANCE: *Darek has never openly sided with Sophie and has likely voted against her.*

Councillor Emery

ABILITY: *Telepath*

JEWEL: *Sapphire*

NOTE: *Councillor Emery is the spokesperson for the Council.*

STANCE: *Emery vacillates between siding with Sophie and siding against her.*

Councillor Liora

ABILITY: *Conjurer*

JEWEL: *Pearl*

NOTE: *Councillor Liora is the second longest–serving Councillor—second only to Councillor Bronte (though she's still several centuries away from becoming one of the Ancients).*

STANCE: *Liora has never spoken in support of Sophie and has likely sided against her.*

Councillor Noland

ABILITY: *Vociferator*

JEWEL: *Tanzanite*

NOTE: *Councillor Noland often holds back from speaking (unless necessary) because of the power carried in his voice.*

STANCE: *Noland has never proven to be an ally to Sophie and has surely voted against her.*

Councillor Oralie

ABILITY: *Empath*

JEWEL: *Pink tourmaline*

NOTE: *Rumors used to connect Councillor Oralie romantically to Councillor Kenric (before he died)—but no proof of impropriety has ever been found.*

STANCE: *Oralie has always loyally sided with Sophie.*

Councillor Ramira

ABILITY: *Vanisher*

JEWEL: *Diamond*

NOTE: *Councillor Ramira's cache contains more Forgotten Secrets than any of the other Councillors'.*

STANCE: *Ramira has never expressed support for Sophie and likely defers to the majority of the Council.*

Councillor Terik

ABILITY: *Descryer*

JEWEL: *Emerald*

NOTE: *Councillor Terik is the only known Descryer. During the fall of Lumenaria, he lost the lower portion of his left leg and now walks with a prosthetic and a cane.*

STANCE: *Terik has consistently supported Sophie.*

Councillor Velia

ABILITY: *Guster*

JEWEL: *Amethyst*

NOTE: *Councillor Velia is an expert on maps.*

STANCE: *Velia has yet to show support for Sophie and has surely voted against her.*

Councillor Zarina

ABILITY: *Charger*

JEWEL: *Opal*

NOTE: *Not long after her election, Councillor Zarina considered resignation. None except her fellow Councillors know why.*

STANCE: *Zarina has never shown herself an ally to Sophie and has likely voted against her.*

IN MEMORY OF

Councillor Kenric Elgar Fathdon

ABILITY: *Telepath*

JEWEL: *Amber*

NOTE: *Councillor Kenric was killed at Oblivimyre during the mental healing of former Councillor Fintan, when Fintan used his newly recovered strength to call down Everblaze in order to escape before his memories could be recovered. Kenric died a hero, reportedly helping spare Sophie Foster, Fitz Vacker, and Councillor Oralie from the inferno, which consumed the tower—as well as nearly half of Eternalia—before it was extinguished. A planting was held, and Kenric's Wanderling grows bravely and boldly in the Wanderling Woods. His loss is further commemorated with a special memorial fountain in Eternalia.*

BASIC ELVIN CULTURE

A WORLD OF ILLUMINATION:

Light is the foundation of the elvin world, shaping every aspect of their culture (especially their use of crystal in their architecture, gadgets, and fashion), since it's what keeps the Lost Cities connected *and* allows them to remain hidden. The elves—particularly those who manifest as Shades—also utilize the power of darkness. But their true strength comes from light, whether it's the unlimited might of the Prime Sources (sunlight, moonlight, and starlight) or the faint glow of bioluminescence in deep, shadowy places. Similarly, knowledge—and wisdom—are of vital importance to the elves, and the emphasis on study doesn't end when they finish their schooling. Growth and learning are meant to be a focus for the entirety of their lives, as is striving to improve.

A FRAGILE PSYCHE:

Elves are remarkably intelligent and intensely emotional—two traits that give them tremendous power and a higher capacity for understanding. But they also face limitations as a result, one of which is their total aversion to any kind of violence. If an elf causes someone harm—or even witnesses it—the violence can shatter their sanity and leave them either unstable or completely unable to function. As a result, the elves have no army or police and rely instead on their treaties and their intellect to avoid conflicts before those conflicts can escalate. A related limitation is their response to guilt, which can similarly lead to mental breakdown. Each elf must do all they can to avoid actions that could cause them to feel intensely guilty—and must actively fight the feeling if it should arise. Grief can also be incredibly debilitating, particularly because loss is rare.

A SYSTEM WITH CONSEQUENCES:

Despite the elves' aversion to violence (and lack of military or police), the Lost Cities still have checks and balances in place to maintain proper peace and order. Laws exist, both to guide general behavior and to ensure that those with certain abilities aren't abusing their power. And in the rare instances when laws are broken, Tribunals are held. The accused is judged by the Council and sentenced to a variety of punishments—most of which are relatively minor. But larger offenses *can* lead to memory breaks, banishment from the Lost Cities, or being sent to Exile (the elves' primary prison). Certain crimes have also led to imprisonment in the dungeon at Lumenaria. And when problems arise between species, Peace Summits are held with the leaders of all the worlds, to ensure the treaties remain upheld.

A GENEROUS DISTRIBUTION OF WEALTH:

Every elf born in the Lost Cities is given a birth fund of five million lusters—more than enough money to comfortably sustain them for the entirety of their lives. (For reference: A single luster translates to a million human dollars.) They still add to the fund once they begin working, so some families do end up having more money than others. But such disparities have no effect on status, nor cause any social unrest, since everyone is still considered "prosperous." (And work is done out of *want*, not *need*.) The birth fund is accessed using a small green gadget called a Treasury Cube, which each elf carries with them. Vendors swipe the Treasury Cube with a gadget called a Deducter, and the money is subtracted from the corresponding account—no coins or paper money is ever needed or exchanged.

A NATURAL PROPENSITY FOR LANGUAGE:

Elves speak the Enlightened Language instinctively from birth—though to human ears it sounds a bit like babbling. And they have two written alphabets, both of which are instinctive as well. Their primary alphabet uses modern letters, and their runic alphabet is used mostly for decoration (though some have also built codes and ciphers around the runic alphabet). The elvin mind has a tremendous capacity for language, so many elves also learn to speak Dwarven, Trollish, Gnomish, Ogreish, and Goblinese (particularly elves who join the nobility). And a small handful learn human dialects as well.

A LIMITLESS LIFE SPAN:

The elves consider their lives to be "indefinite" because no one in the Lost Cities has ever died from old age (at least not that they know of . . .). They aren't immortal—elves can and have passed away. But those deaths were caused by circumstance, not time. The elves also appear somewhat "ageless" and do not get gray hair or wrinkles. A thirty-year-old elf looks the same as a three-hundred-year-old elf—and a three-thousand-year-old elf would only have one small difference: The tops of their ears would be pointy. Elvin ears continue to grow slowly along the tops, which is why pointed ears are considered a mark of the Ancients.

AN ABUNDANCE OF TIME:

Thanks to their incredible longevity, time is a relative construct in the Lost Cities—something the elves mark, but rarely focus on. They still break time down into seconds, minutes, hours, days, months, and years, but they don't pay much attention to them—particularly when it comes to their own ages. The elves technically count age from their inception date (because of the way their pregnancies develop), but few even notice the date when it passes, and none celebrate the occasion. In fact, most Ancient elves have long since lost track of precisely how old they are.

A UNIQUE SET OF TRADITIONS:

Despite their relaxed attitude toward time, the elves do have a few celebrations—most of which are linked to accomplishment, or significant natural events. For instance, whenever there's a total lunar eclipse, Orem Vacker uses his skills as a Flasher to put on a spectacular light show called the Celestial Festival. And there are numerous traditions connected to Foxfire Academy, including their Opening Ceremonies, midterms, and finals celebrations. Winnowing Galas, weddings, and funerals also carry their own customs and experiences—and many choose to hold parties for no particular reason.

A RARE GOODBYE:

Death is incredibly uncommon in the Lost Cities, but it does occasionally happen. As such, the elves have developed a ceremony called a "planting" to commemorate the loss. Plantings are held in the Wanderling Woods (the elves' only graveyard), and friends and family gather for support. A Wanderling seed (wrapped with the deceased's DNA—usually a single strand of their hair) is planted and immediately sprouts, taking on certain physical characteristics of the life that's been lost and allowing the deceased to live on in a small way. Each tree is marked with a stone bearing the name of whoever has been planted there, and most families choose to visit the Wanderlings regularly, to grieve in the trees' gentle shade.

A TRULY GLOBAL WORLD:

The elves rely heavily on light leaping, a process that involves letting the light break down their bodies so they can "hitch a ride" and travel great distances in a matter of seconds. With practice, each elf's concentration becomes strong enough to hold themselves together during the leap—but until then, they wear a nexus as a safety precaution. (If they lose part of themselves in a leap, they'll reform slightly faded. And if they lose too much, they'll fade away completely. It's also possible to become sick with light poisoning.) The Ancients used starstones to create their paths before leaping crystals were invented. Now, home crystals and Leapmasters are used until an elf can prove that they're responsible, mature, and trustworthy enough to be issued a pathfinder. Even then, certain pathways are restricted, and the color of the crystal determines where the light will go.

A TALENT-BASED SOCIETY:

All elves share the same language and culture—and pay no heed to physical appearance or financial stature. And yet, division still exists in their world, between those with special abilities and those without. As a result, the Lost Cities can generally be broken down into three primary social groups: the nobility, the working class, and the Talentless (though there are some elves who fall into none of those categories). The nobility is primarily composed of those with the most useful special abilities. The working class is primarily composed of those with the more "niche" abilities. And the Talentless are those without abilities. Of the three groups, only the Talentless face any social scorn or social restrictions, including what jobs are available to them and who they're allowed to marry.

GUIDE TO LEAPING CRYSTALS

COLOR	GOES TO	USED BY
CLEAR	The Lost Cities	Everyone
BLUE	The Forbidden Cities	Restricted to the Council and authorized members of the nobility
YELLOW	The Neutral Territories	Restricted to the Council and authorized members of the nobility
BLACK	The Gateway to Exile (and other places, depending on how the magsidian is cut)	Restricted to the Council and authorized members of the nobility—though the Neverseen have been seen using them
GREEN	Ravagog (and other ogre-related locations)	Restricted to the Council and authorized members of the nobility
OPALESCENT PINK	Unknown locations (These crystals are said to have added security measures)	Restricted to members of the Black Swan
PURPLE	Unknown locations	Restricted to members of the Black Swan
ORANGE	Marintrylla (and other troll-related locations)	Restricted to the Council and authorized members of the nobility
RED	Gildingham (and other goblin-related locations)	Restricted to the Council and authorized members of the nobility
SWIRLED WHITE, SILVER, & GOLD	Uses the power of the Prime Sources	Restricted to the Council

AN UNEXPECTED ELEMENT OF CONTROL:

Because of their ageless appearance (and indefinite life spans), the elves adopted a system of matchmaking in order to ensure that distant relatives weren't unintentionally marrying. And since special abilities play such a vital role in elvin society, the matchmakers (whose motto is, "Progress, Prosperity, Permanence, and Proliferation") also strive to create couples with the greatest genetic advantage—and the best chance of producing talented offspring. Everyone can register for the match once they turn fourteen (though they can also choose to wait). And once registered, they're given an extensive packet to fill out in order to determine their wants and needs. Packets can be turned in anytime (though many use the final exam period at Foxfire as an arbitrary deadline), and the matchmakers take an entire year to review the information. Nothing else influences their decision (despite the choice some young elves make to wear "crush cuffs"— cloth bracelets embroidered with their crush's name—in the hope of catching their matchmaker's attention). The first match list can be retrieved after the year is up (but again, waiting is an option) and contains one hundred of the top matches, which are meant to be whittled down using Winnowing Galas. If no "match" is found, a second list with another hundred matches can be retrieved, as well as a third, fourth, and fifth list. (A minimum of one month must pass between each list.) After the fifth, no additional lists are provided. Anyone who marries someone not on their lists is branded a "bad match" and faces significant social consequences. And if a "good match" ends up unsuccessful, the couple may file a "match-fail"—though such an event is *incredibly* rare. Even rarer is someone "unmatchable"—though it has happened in a case where vital genetic information was missing from the file. And while most comply with the matchmaking system, some elves are uncomfortable with the biases it promotes and decline participation.

A CHOICE OF SURNAME:

Last names aren't arbitrarily passed from one generation to the next. Rather, each couple decides which surname to adopt, generally opting for the name that carries the most prestige.

A LIMITED AMOUNT OF FAMILY:

Most elves only have one child, believing their genetics grow weaker with each additional birth. And children from multiple births tend to face a tremendous amount of scorn, with many expecting the children to be either Talentless or otherwise troublesome.

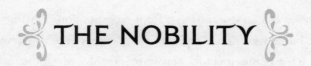

THE NOBILITY

RULING THE LOST CITIES IS A DAUNTING responsibility. As a result, the Council created the nobility to share parts of their workload—which is why special abilities are required for any noble position. Graduation from Foxfire Academy is also mandatory, as is making an oath of obedience and loyalty to the Council.

Members of the nobility most commonly bear the title of Lord or Lady (though certain appointments come with the titles of Dame, Magnate, or Master). And only nobles are able to enter the Seat of Eminence in Eternalia. They also wear capes to signify their position, and it's customary for others to bow or curtsy when greeting them—though only some members of the nobility *insist* on such formalities. Many prefer to keep social interactions more casual.

The most commonly held noble positions are Mentors, Regents, and Emissaries, each of which comes with different responsibilities:

- **MENTORS** are appointed to help future generations reach their full potential.
- **REGENTS** are appointed to carry out assignments for the Council.
- **EMISSARIES** are appointed to carry out *highly classified* assignments for the Council.

Nobles can choose to resign from their positions anytime they wish, but few ever do. And since completion of the elite levels at Foxfire is a requirement for appointment, noble assignments have always been held by adults—until recently, that is.

In a groundbreaking decision (meant to better utilize the talents of the Black Swan's moonlark), Sophie Foster and four of her friends were carefully selected and appointed as Regents to form Team Valiant. The Councillors even swore a special oath to the team—"We will listen. We will learn. And we will adapt"—and asked Sophie and her friends to make an oath of their own: "I swear to *fight* with everything in my power to serve the Council and keep our world a haven of peace, hope, and illumination."

Each member of Team Valiant was assigned two Councillors as their "points of contact" for advice and guidance (with Councillor Emery and Councillor Terik serving as the "general overseers" of the team). They were also each given a mascot (to represent the role they play for their teammates) and three Articles of the Regency (a circlet, a cloak clasp, and a cloak) in three different colors (gold, silver, and glowing white) to represent the Prime Sources (sunlight, moonlight, and starlight). Occasionally the Council will dictate which articles Team Valiant should wear. But most of the time the decision is up to the team's leader—so long as all members of the team coordinate their accessories (as a sign of unity and solidarity) and make sure that each of the articles belongs to a different Source (to properly represent all three Sources at once).

TEAM VALIANT

TEAM MEMBER	MASCOT	PATCH BORDER	CIRCLET JEWEL	POINTS OF CONTACT
Sophie Foster (Leader)	Dire wolf	Red	Ruby	Councillor Bronte Councillor Oralie
Biana Vacker	Kelpie	Purple	Amethyst	Councillor Darek Councillor Liora
Dex Dizznee	Temple	Green	Emerald	Councillor Noland Councillor Clarette
Stina Heks	Kraken	Pink	Pink tourmaline	Councillor Zarina Councillor Alina
Wylie Endal	Wyvern	Opalescent	Opal	Councillor Ramira Councillor Velia

ABILITIES VERSUS SKILLS

A WORLD FOCUSED ON ABILITY:

Manifesting a special ability is a life-changing event for an elf in the Lost Cities—as is *not* manifesting. Until that moment, all elves are equal. Afterward, they can be divided into the "talented" and the "Talentless" (though few use the term "talented," preferring instead to identify themselves by their abilities).

No one can control when, where, how, or *if* manifesting will occur—nor can they choose which abilities they'll get. Foxfire's ability detecting session is designed to trigger abilities—and it definitely has had great success throughout the centuries. But there are always a few prodigies who never manifest. Similarly, certain Telepaths can fill someone's mind with mental energy, which can cause an ability to activate—but the effectiveness of this technique still depends on the person's genetics. Even following the guidance of the matchmakers cannot guarantee that a child will not end up Talentless—which turns the process of manifesting into a source of fear, stress, consternation, *and* celebration, depending on how it turns out.

Manifesting is also intense, confusing, and at times slightly dangerous, with elves struggling to understand the changes happening to their minds, senses, and bodies—and fighting to control their new ability. The average manifesting age is somewhere between twelve and fifteen years old—but there have been elves who manifested older or younger. Some elves also have more than one ability—though that's much more uncommon. And while any special ability elevates someone's rank to the talented, not all abilities are viewed as equally valuable—and some are even considered to be undesirable. (One ability is actually forbidden.) It also doesn't happen often, but new abilities still appear, so the list of recorded abilities is ever changing.

As it stands, the most well-known special abilities are:

- **BEGUILER:** An elf with the power of persuasion who can manipulate others by using the tone of their voice to affect someone's emotions (rather than affecting their actions, like Mesmers). In order to insure the ability isn't abused, Beguilers have restrictions on when and how they can use their power. *Reported Beguilers: Councillor Alina*
- **CHARGER:** An elf who can sense and manipulate electricity (and electron particles), allowing them to create and control everything from static to bolts of lightning. *Reported Chargers: Councillor Zarina*
- **CONJURER:** An elf who can sense the threads connecting everything together and use them to pull objects through the void (though the ability only works if they already know where the item is). Conjurers can also hide things in the void to retrieve later, and help others place things there as well. *Reported Conjurers: Edaline Ruewen, Lady Cadence Talle, Jolie Ruewen, Councillor Liora*
- **DESCRYER:** An elf who can sense the "potential" inside of someone—though the person still has to live up to that potential in order for the reading to be accurate. Only one Descryer has ever been recorded, and he rarely uses the

ability because his readings were causing contention. *Reported Descryers: Councillor Terik*

- **EMPATH:** An elf who can sense the emotions of others through physical contact (though the strongest Empaths can sense emotions through the air). Translating what they're sensing can be challenging (since strong emotions often feel the same), and Empaths are at risk of going numb if they don't focus on their training. They can also sense when someone is lying (but are terrible liars themselves). *Reported Empaths: Keefe Sencen, Lord Cassius Sencen, Councillor Oralie, Stina Heks, Vika Heks, Vespera Folend*

- **ENHANCER:** An elf who stores energy in the tips of their fingers, which can amplify the strength of someone else's ability. Enhancing happens automatically through touch, so Enhancers often wear gloves (or in some cases, special gadgets) to allow themselves some control over when and who they help—though it appears that special mental exercises may be effective in training the mind to switch the ability on and off. *Reported Enhancers: Sophie Foster*

- **FLASHER:** An elf who can sense and manipulate light— most often by gathering it into glowing orbs or beams of a single color on the visible spectrum. Uses for flashing range from entertainment to medicine to battle tactics. *Reported Flashers: Councillor Clarette, Elwin Heslege, Wylie Endal, Cyrah Endal, Orem Vacker, Luzia Vacker, Glimmer*

- **FROSTER:** An elf who can sense and gather particles

of ice in the air and use them to freeze things, create snowfall, or form any shapes they desire. They can also cover themselves with ice as a disguise. *Reported Frosters: Juline Dizznee*

- **GUSTER:** An elf who can sense and manipulate wind, creating everything from breezes to storms. The ability is elemental, and the wind is *always* calling—which tends to make Gusters more powerful than other elves (and, at times, slightly unstable). *Reported Gusters: Durand Redek, Councillor Velia, Trix*

- **HYDROKINETIC:** An elf who can sense the presence of water (whether it's the invisible particles in the air, or a nearby lake or ocean) and manipulate the water any way they choose (lifting rivers, draining pools, making it rain—or drying something off—or even bending it into shapes or forming tidal waves). Like other elemental abilities, the pull of the water is relentless, so without training (and constant vigilance), Hydrokinetics can cause floods. *Reported Hydrokinetics: Linh Song*

- **INFLICTOR:** An elf who can gather their emotions into tangible mental energy and launch the force at others. In the case of negative emotions, the ability can cause tremendous pain and even incapacitate someone. And in the (rare) instance when positive emotions are inflicted, the ability can heal a broken mind. As a result, Inflictors are closely monitored by the Council. *Reported Inflictors: Sophie Foster, Councillor Bronte*

- **MESMER:** An elf who can sense someone's *will* and manipulate it, putting them into a kind of trance and controlling their actions and behavior. Someone being mesmerized remains conscious but can rarely resist the Mesmer's command, which is why those with the ability are often mistrusted (and are closely watched by the Council). *Reported Mesmers: Grady Ruewen*

- **PHASER:** An elf who can sense the bond between their cells and temporarily break it down, allowing them to slip through solid barriers like walls, doors—anything they want. Some can even delay re-forming, allowing them to hide their identity from others. *Reported Phasers: Fernan Babblos, Lady Alexine, Councillor Darek, Blur*

- **POLYGLOT:** An elf who instinctively speaks any and all languages, including those of the other intelligent species (and human dialects). In rare cases, the ability even allows them to communicate with animals. Polyglots' accents are flawless, and with practice, they're able to perfectly mimic the vocal tones and inflections of others—on a level far beyond a convincing impression. Polyglots also often (but not always) have more than one special ability. *Reported Polyglots: Sophie Foster, Lady Cadence Talle, Lady Gisela Sencen, Councillor Clarette*

- **PSIONIPATH:** An elf who can sense and manipulate energy, shaping it into charged force fields around themselves and others. Psionipaths are often unstable—and can seem unstoppable in battle situations (though their force fields can be broken down by Flashers and Shades). *Reported Psionipaths: Ruy Ignis, Maruca Chebota*

- **PYROKINETIC:** An elf who can sense and control the heat in the air and use it to spark anything from a tongue of flame to a raging inferno. Like with other elemental abilities, a Pyrokinetic's hunger for fire can be insatiable, and that craving eventually led one of them to call down Everblaze. When he attempted to teach others, the lesson tragically resulted in five deaths (which is what caused the Council to ban pyrokinesis). Since the ability is now illegal, Pyrokinetics are forced to live as Talentless. *Reported Pyrokinetics: Fintan Pyren, Brant, Marella Redek*

- **SHADE:** An elf with the ability to sense and control darkness, either by focusing on shadowvapor, or (in the case of the strongest Shades) by focusing on shadowflux. Shades can also use their shadow to carry their voice into someone's mind (shadow-whispering) and can read a person's potential for darkness. Given the focus on light in the Lost Cities, Shades are often mistrusted and ill-spoken-of. *Reported Shades: Tam Song, Lady Zillah, Umber*

- **TECHNOPATH:** An elf who can communicate with technology through its inherent "language" and can use that knowledge to create new inventions or manipulate gadgets to their will. *Reported Technopaths: Dex Dizznee, Tinker, Lady Iskra*

- **TELEPATH:** An elf who can sense the thoughts of others and shield their own mind. Telepaths have a code of rules to follow (to prevent them from abusing their power) and are extremely important to the Council, serving as Keepers, Washers, and Probes. If they find another Telepath they trust, they can even become Cognates (which gives the pair a greater level of power). *Reported Telepaths: Sophie Foster, Fitz Vacker, Alden Vacker, Mr. Forkle/Magnate Leto, Sir Tiergan Alenefar, Councillor Emery, Councillor Kenric, Prentice Endal, Quinlin Sonden, Gethen Ondsinn, Damel Kafuta, Lady Pemberley*

- **TELEPORTER:** An elf who can use momentum to build a unique type of energy that can create a crack in the void for them to slip through. Once inside the void, they can travel to any location they visualize (so long as it's not underground). *Reported Telepaths: Sophie Foster (though alicorns can teleport as well)*

- **VANISHER:** An elf who can sense the light making contact with their skin (or clothing) and allow it to pass through their cells (instead of bouncing off), rendering themselves invisible—even when they're moving (though the length and quality of their vanish is dependent on their training). *Reported Vanishers: Councillor Ramira, Biana Vacker, Della Vacker, Alvar Vacker, Wraith*

- **VOCIFERATOR:** An elf who can manipulate the volume of their voice to an extreme degree, making earsplitting screams that force everyone to pay attention to them and that can even be incapacitating. *Reported Vociferators: Councillor Noland*

AN ABUNDANCE OF SKILL:

The elves are so focused on special abilities that they often overlook (or completely forget) that they also possess a number of useful skills. Practice is needed to fully utilize each skill—which is sorely lacking in the Lost Cities. (Foxfire's physical education session touches on a few, but the real skill training happens at Exillium—which is part of the problem. Until recently, Exillium was seen as an unfavorable institution.) Efforts are currently being made to place more emphasis on skill training, particularly since the Neverseen brought down the castle in Lumenaria with nothing more than skill, focus, and patience—and Alvar Vacker used skills to survive and escape an otherwise deadly situation.

Known elvin skills include:

- **APPETITE SUPPRESSION:** controlling hunger by focusing on something else as a distraction. Can even slow digestion and allow longer survival without food.
- **BLINKING:** similar to vanishing—but blinking lasts a maximum of a few seconds, and requires far greater concentration and absolute stillness.

- **BREATH CONTROL:** controlling the distance between breaths by distracting the mind, slowing the body's systems, and focusing on the air remaining in the lungs.
- **CHANNELING:** using the mind to send energy where it's needed—whether it be to the legs, arms, core, etc.—to boost speed, strength, or concentration. The same energy can also be channeled outward, causing the ground to tremble—or much worse.
- **DARKNESS VISION:** focusing on the small amount of light that exists (because there's almost always *some* light) and letting the mind amplify it to provide illumination.
- **LEVITATION:** concentrating on the force of gravity and pushing against it with the mind to achieve weightlessness. Movement takes practice, since there's no traction.
- **BODY TEMPERATURE REGULATION:** focusing on whatever small amount of heat or cold exists and allowing the mind to amplify the sensation, providing cooling or warmth.
- **TELEKINESIS:** drawing on the energy stored in the core (and sometimes in the mind) and thrusting it out through the limbs as though it's an extension of the body, allowing things to be moved and lifted without needing physical contact.

All wish to attend.
Only the most talented
are chosen.

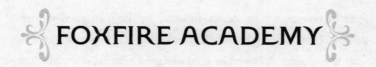

FOXFIRE ACADEMY

FOXFIRE IS THE LOST CITIES' MOST PRESTIGIOUS academy, as well as the only "noble school"—which means that graduation from Foxfire is one of the many qualifications for the nobility.

The academy is named after the rare bioluminescence found in otherwise dark, lonely places—and as such, Foxfire prodigies are expected to be a bright, welcome glow in an often-darkened world.

The campus is similarly a glittering oasis, tucked away in the midst of a barren desert and renowned for its unique architecture, including a main building that houses six wings and six towers (each built from a different color of crystal and gem), a central glass pyramid, and two separate twisted towers (one silver and one gold) to house the elite levels, as well as numerous fields, paths, gardens, and amphitheaters. And despite recent challenges in the Lost Cities, Foxfire remains a safe haven for its prodigies, with every possible security measure in place (including an assigned goblin regiment).

Schedules are customized to each prodigy's needs, and sessions are taught by the most illustrious Mentors in the Lost Cities. In fact, teaching at Foxfire is a noble profession and comes with the title of "Sir" or "Lady." Sessions are taught one-on-one (with the exception of physical education and ability detecting, which are held with the whole school and have Mentors assigned to each grade level). Subjects vary level by level (and day by day). Prodigies begin each morning with orientation (where attendance is taken and any necessary announcements are provided), followed by their assigned morning session. They then enjoy socialization during lunch (where a veritable feast is available), followed by their assigned afternoon session. They finish each day with study hall to give them a chance to work through their Mentors' assignments without needing to carry any work home (beyond practice and studying, of course! The point is to inspire prodigies, not overwhelm them!). And while it is the goal of everyone at Foxfire for the environment to be both educational *and* enjoyable, rules are also in place to keep things safe and organized. The consequence for violators is generally lunch detention (with the specific punishment determined by whichever Mentor is supervising for the day). But in extreme cases, suspension or expulsion will be enforced (though it should be noted that such things are incredibly rare).

At the beginning of every school year, each prodigy receives multiple sets of the required uniform for their grade level (either a pleated skirt paired with leggings, a shirt, a vest, and a half cape pinned with their mascot; or slacks paired with a lace-up jerkin, a long-sleeve undershirt, and a half cape pinned with their mascot; all uniforms prominently feature each prodigy's family crest), as well as an Opening Ceremonies costume based on their level's mascot, their sessions schedule, a locker assignment (programmed to open with their DNA), and all other necessary supplies.

Foxfire has six "basic levels," and prodigies must pass both their midterm and final exams in order to progress from one level to the next. Those who complete all six levels *and* manifest a special ability then qualify to apply for the two additional "elite levels"—which serve as an excellent stepping-stone into the nobility. The elite levels are separated from the main campus and held in the elite towers (where the elite prodigies also live, in order to remain better focused on their studies). Each grade level (basic and elite) has a mascot, a uniform, an associated color, a designated section of campus for their lockers and sessions, and key attributes that the curriculum is meant to foster. (See the chart below for further details.)

• BASIC LEVELS •

LEVEL	AVERAGE AGE	MASCOT	MAIN BUILDING LOCATION	UNIFORM COLOR	QUALITIES EMPHASIZED
One	11-12	Gremlin	Onyx Wing	Black	Curious and Capable
Two	12-13	Halcyon	Sapphire Wing	Bright Blue	Calm and Steadfast
Three	13-14	Mastodon	Amber Wing	Dark Orange	Clever and Cooperative
Four	14-15	Dragon	Emerald Wing	Green	Adaptable and Cunning
Five	15-16	Saber-Tooth Tiger	Ruby Wing	Red	Bold and Calculating
Six	16-17	Yeti	Diamond Wing	White	Earnest and Fearless

• ELITE LEVELS •

LEVEL	AVERAGE AGE	MASCOT	MAIN BUILDING LOCATION	UNIFORM COLOR	QUALITIES EMPHASIZED
Seven	17-18	Flareadon	Gold Tower	Gold	Resolute and Enduring
Eight	18-19	Unicorn	Silver Tower	Silver	Noble and Gentle

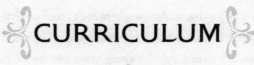

CURRICULUM

THE FOXFIRE CURRICULUM IS EXTENSIVE AND varied (and has also been rigorously tested and refined) in order to provide each prodigy with maximum enlightenment. As a result, the list of available sessions is ever changing and extremely lengthy. Still, some of the more popular sessions (as well as the few that are required) include:

Ability detecting: A group session where Mentors test each prodigy's senses in a variety of ways in the hope of triggering their special ability. All Foxfire prodigies who haven't manifested are required to take this session on Tuesday and Thursday afternoons until they can be placed into their proper ability session. (Note: Pyrokinesis is *not* tested for—and Talentless prodigies remain in ability detecting until they complete the basic levels.)

Agriculture: A gnome-taught session held in the Foxfire gardens designed to teach prodigies to properly care for nature and understand the time, love, and energy it takes to keep plants healthy and thriving.

Alchemy: Prodigies learn the power of transmutation and purification through hands-on training in specially designed laboratories. Specific skills include elixir-making, poultice-crafting, and the careful conversion of matter into gold.

Elementalism: Through careful instruction and hands-on training, prodigies learn to harness the power of the elements and properly store and contain them. Specific skills taught include how to bottle wind, rain, lightning, thunder, fire, and so much more.

Elvin history: Our past defines who we are today, so all prodigies are required to learn the history of the Lost Cities, from Ancient days up to the present. Topics include the establishment of the intelligent species' treaties, the human betrayal, the sinking of Atlantis, and the development of the matchmaking system, as well as numerous others.

Linguistics: Prodigies master the languages of all five other intelligent species (as well as humans) and learn to mimic accents and pronunciation. Please note: This is an elite-level session and is only available to Level Eight prodigies (unless special permission is granted by the Council).

Metaphysics: A truly unique session where prodigies examine the potential of our existence, including the true power of mind over matter, the hope of endless possibility, and the necessity and challenges created by allowing all intelligent creatures to maintain their free will.

Multispeciesial studies: Prodigies discover the fascinating cultures and histories behind the intelligent creatures that share our planet, including ogres, gnomes, trolls, dwarves, and goblins. (Note: Discussion of humans is excluded from this session.)

Physical education: All Foxfire prodigies must take physical education on Tuesday and Thursday mornings in order to train their minds to enhance their physical abilities. Skills such as channeling, telekinesis, levitation, and numerous others are practiced through sports, games, and exercise.

Special ability focus session: Any Foxfire prodigy who has manifested an ability is required to train in that ability every Tuesday and Thursday afternoon (while the rest of the school takes ability detecting). Possible sessions include: telepathy, empathy, vanishing, flashing, gusting, phasing, frosting, technopathy, conjuring, inflicting, descrying, mesmerizing, and many more. (Please note: Training in pyrokinesis is strictly forbidden.)

The Universe: Prodigies study the many wonders that lie beyond the boundaries of our planet, including the countless stars and galaxies, which they learn to map and name. Provides an important perspective, reminding us that no matter how powerful we may be, we are still small in the grand scheme of things, and must respect the larger natural forces surrounding us.

THE CURRENT PRINCIPAL IS MAGNATE LETO KERLOF (formerly the Beacon of the Silver Tower), who was appointed after Dame Alina (the former principal) was elected to the Council.

The Beacon of the Silver Tower is now Master Cadence Talle (formerly Lady Cadence).

For any medical needs that arise, Sir Elwin Heslege keeps an office in Foxfire's Healing Center (though he rarely uses the title "Sir").

Mentors vary year by year, depending on their availability (and the needs of the prodigies). With such a large prodigy population (and most sessions taught one-on-one), the number of Mentors on staff is rather daunting. Still, for those who would like a sampling of the faculty, see the featured Mentors listed below.

NAME: Lady Alexine

SESSION: *Physical Education*

MENTOR TO: *Co-Mentor to All Level Two Prodigies*

NAME: Lady Anwen

SESSION: *Multispeciesial Studies*

MENTOR TO: *Sophie Foster (Level Two)*

NAME: Sir Astin

SESSION: *The Universe*

MENTOR TO: *Sophie Foster (Level Two)*

NAME: Sir Bubu

SESSION: *Multispeciesial Studies*

MENTOR TO: *Keefe Sencen (Level Two)*

NAME: Sir Caton

SESSION: *Physical Education*

MENTOR TO: *Co-Mentor to All Level Two Prodigies*

NAME: Sir Conley

SESSION: *Elementalism*

MENTOR TO: *Sophie Foster (Level Two)*

NAME: Lady Dara

SESSION: *Elvin History*

MENTOR TO: *Sophie Foster (Level Two)*

NAME: Lady Delmira

SESSION: *Alchemy*

MENTOR TO: *Keefe Sencen (Level Two)*

NAME: Sir Donwell

SESSION: *Multispeciesial Studies*

MENTOR TO: *Biana Vacker (Level Two)*

NAME: Sir Faxon

SESSION: *Metaphysics*

MENTOR TO: *Sophie Foster (Level Two)*

NAME: Lady Gálvin

SESSION: *Alchemy*

MENTOR TO: *Sophie Foster (Level Two),*
Keefe Sencen (Level Three)

NAME: Sir Jarvin

SESSION: *The Universe*

MENTOR TO: *Keefe Sencen (Level Two)*

NAME: Lady Nissa

SESSION: *Tutoring Center*

MENTOR TO: *Any Level Two*
Prodigies Requesting Additional Practice

NAME: Sir Tiergan

SESSION: *Telepathy Training*

MENTOR TO: *Sophie Foster (Level Two, Level Three, Level Four)*
and Fitz Vacker (Level Five, Level Six)

NAME: Barth the Reaper

SESSION: *Agriculture*

MENTOR TO: *Sophie Foster (Level Three)*

NAME: Sir Beckett

SESSION: *Elvin History*

MENTOR TO: *Sophie Foster (Level Three)*

NAME: Councillor Bronte

SESSION: *Inflicting Training*

MENTOR TO: *Sophie Foster (Level Three, Level Four)*

NAME: Master Cadence

SESSION: *Linguistics*

MENTOR TO: *Sophie Foster (Level Three)*

NAME: Lady Evera

SESSION: *Multispeciesial Studies*

MENTOR TO: *Sophie Foster (Level Three)*

NAME: Sir Harding

SESSION: *Physical Education*

MENTOR TO: *Co-Mentor to All Level Three Prodigies*

NAME: Lady Iskra

SESSION: *Technopathy Training*

MENTOR TO: *Dex Dizznee (Level Three)*

NAME: Sir Leander

SESSION: *Multispeciesial Studies*

MENTOR TO: *Keefe Sencen (Level Three)*

NAME: Sir Rosings

SESSION: *Elvin History*

MENTOR TO: *Stina Heks (Level Three)*

NAME: Lady Veda

SESSION: *Elementalism*

MENTOR TO: *Sophie Foster (Level Three)*

NAME: Lady Belva

SESSION: *The Universe*

MENTOR TO: *Keefe Sencen (Level Four)*

NAME: Lady Zillah

SESSION: *Shade Training*

MENTOR TO: *Tam Song (Level Four)*

NAME: Lady Sanja

SESSION: *Elvin History*

MENTOR TO: *Keefe Sencen (Level Six)*

A NOT-TO-BE-MISSED EXPERIENCE

AS ANYONE CAN CLEARLY SEE, ATTENDING FOXFIRE is truly a tremendous privilege. And those who call themselves prodigies become immersed in a unique environment, rich with exciting traditions, powerful knowledge, and lasting friendships.

Highlights of the school year include:

The Foxfire Opening Ceremonies: Before the new school year begins, the prodigies gather to perform for their families in a musical extravaganza, including a light show, costumed dances for each grade level, showers of edible confetti, and a very special presentation from the elite towers that includes the blooming of the splendors and the flight of the flickerwings. The campus is decorated in a variety of bioluminescence for the festivities, and the Council attends—and speaks to the audience—wishing the prodigies a successful year of study.

Midterm celebrations: Hard work should be celebrated—even before the results are in. As such, prodigies are directed to hang their thinking caps from their lockers as soon as they complete their exams. The next day, they fill them with gifts and treats for their friends, which they then open while their parents meet with their Mentors to receive their grades. The whole campus is decorated for the occasion, and treats float through the halls for prodigies to catch and enjoy.

The Ultimate Splotching Championship: Most of the activities in physical education are more casually organized, but the Ultimate Splotching Championship is an exciting exception. Prodigies battle each other using telekinesis, with the losers being eliminated and the winners sparring against each other until the Ultimate Champion is found—and rewarded with a pardon, which can be used to skip one assigned punishment.

Final exam celebrations: These festivities are similar to the midterm celebrations—though the gifts exchanged tend to be more extravagant. And the principal closes out the school year with an inspiring speech, followed by another shower of edible confetti and a coordinated cape toss between all the prodigies.

A new beginning for the truly exceptional.

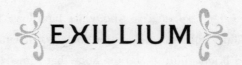

EXILLIUM

FOR CENTURIES, EXILLIUM HAS BEEN VIEWED AS A place for the unworthy—a school only attended when there were no other options. Waywards were sent to Exillium as punishment, after most had been banished from the Lost Cities.

But Exillium was originally created to be a space of alternative learning—a haven for those who take in knowledge a little differently, where all can grow and thrive. Additionally, Exillium was meant to offer a path toward redemption for those who'd made mistakes in their past.

Somehow those visions were lost over time—but Exillium is working hard to bring them back!

Thanks to the efforts of Sophie Foster—and the assistance of Councillor Oralie—Exillium has begun receiving the funds and support needed in order to transform the educational experience into what it was always meant to be.

In fact, Exillium recently set up their tents on the Foxfire campus for a joint educational venture that benefitted everyone in the Lost Cities! *Every* elf was then able to experience being divided according to their learning style before working through some of Exillium's skill-based curriculum with our three talented Coaches. And everyone could clearly see how simple and effective the Exillium approach is.

Still, many in the Lost Cities cling to old misconceptions about Exillium. So for clarity, two former Waywards (Tam and Linh Song) have shared their experiences. And while Tam doesn't hold back from revealing Exillium's old, unfortunate ways, Linh points to the school's bright future—and the hope that someday attending Exillium will be a choice many will eagerly make.

BASIC PROGRAM ORGANIZATION

HEMISPHERE	LEARNING STYLE	TENT COLOR	COACH
Left	Favoring logic and reason	Red	Coach Wilda
Right	Favoring spontaneity and creativity	Blue	Coach Bora
Ambi	A hybrid of both approaches	Purple	Coach Rohana

TAM SONG'S EXILLIUM EXPERIENCE

The worst thing about Exillium was that the rules were all designed to strip away our identities and leave everyone feeling powerless—and I get that the Coaches were super outnumbered and trying to find a way to keep some kind of control. But it was brutal not being allowed to talk to anyone—or use our names.

The only "identifying" thing we were able to have was an ability badge pinned to our vests—and don't even get me started on the rest of the uniform. I mean, I'm a Shade. Black clothes are my life. But really, guys? Tall boots? A studded mask? It's like they were trying to make us look ridiculous.

Actually, they probably were. . . .

The Coaches were also allowed to punish us however they wanted. And there was never enough food or medical supplies. Oh, and for added fun, we had to prove that we deserved to get one of the beads to find the campus every day. So we got to be miserable, and also got to be like, "Please let us come back tomorrow so we can be miserable again!"

Fun times.

But . . . all the skill practice has turned out to be pretty useful. Everyone definitely needs a lot more of that. And Foxfire can be kind of annoying, with everyone walking around like, "We're so special!" Plus, things really did get better at Exillium after Sophie got the Council to cough up some actual funding. Sometimes I think about transferring back.

It was cool seeing all the different Neutral Territories— and I'm pretty sure my dad's brain would implode if I went back.

But, I go where Linh goes.

~Tam

LINH SONG'S EXILLIUM EXPERIENCE

I'm not going to pretend that things weren't hard at Exillium—but I'm sure my brother already had plenty to say about all of that.

Plus . . . I'm actually not sure if I would've learned how to temper my hydrokinesis if I'd been at Foxfire. The Foxfire curriculum is centered on abilities, and that's the last thing I needed. Focusing on skills at Exillium trained my brain to ignore the call of water—which is the only reason I stopped flooding everything.

It was also nice getting to learn in a group setting at Exillium—or it was, once we were allowed to talk and show our faces and make friends. Sometimes working one-on-one with the Foxfire Mentors can be a little intimidating—especially if their lecture is boring and there's no way to hide your yawns.

So I hope everyone is finally realizing that it's absolutely okay if their brain works a little differently. Going to Exillium should never be about "failing" or "punishment," or "not belonging in the Lost Cities." It should be about finding a safe, happy learning environment that works for how someone learns. And it looks like that's what Exillium's trying to create for everyone.

I hope they pull it off, and that no one ever has to feel scared or worthless or cast aside like Tam and I did.

Oh, and Exillium definitely needs to get new uniforms!

~Linh

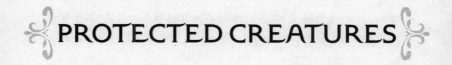

PROTECTED CREATURES

THE ELVES BELIEVE THAT EVERY CREATURE EXISTS for a reason, and to allow any species to go extinct would throw off the planet's delicate balance and cause irreparable damage—possibly even a massive catastrophe. As a result, the elves have gone to tremendous lengths to preserve each type of animal—particularly those linked to human myths and superstitions (since they're the most vulnerable to hunting, capture, and experimentation).

Many creatures considered by humans to be "extinct" or "endangered" are also thriving under elvin protection—and finding a place to safely (and secretly) shelter so many animals was *quite* a challenge. But the elves turned to the dwarves and gnomes for assistance, and together, they hollowed out the Himalayan mountain range and built the Sanctuary: a special wildlife preserve designed for creatures of all shapes, sizes, and needs. Every climate and ecosystem is available, as is a limitless supply of food and resources—and a vast team of caretakers. All animals are also "rehabilitated" before being moved to the Sanctuary, to ensure they've adjusted to a diet of gnomish vegetables and tamed their hunting instincts.

Some of the species under elvin protection are:

ALICORN

The rarest creature on the planet, with only four in existence (Silveny, Greyfell, Wynn, and Luna)—and that number is a recent development. Alicorns have shimmering silver fur, feathered wings, brown eyes, a wavy silver mane and tail, and a white-and-silver-swirled horn jutting out of their foreheads. They're also telepathic and can teleport.

ARGENTAVIS

Enormous silver-blue birds that humans believe are extinct. They eat carrion in the wild and are one of the four creatures the Neverseen used to create the gorgodon.

ARTHROPLEURA

Giant arthropods believed to be extinct, with long, poisonous antennae that end in forked points covered in clear slime. Arthropleura have plenty of writhing legs, but they travel primarily by coiling themselves into balls and rolling—and they hiss when threatened.

BANSHEE

Slinky ferretlike creatures with gray fur and beady purple eyes. Banshees can tell when someone is dangerously ill and will scream a warning—or choose to lie beside them if the person is about to die. As a result, many physicians keep banshees as pets (like Bullhorn in the Foxfire Healing Center).

BENNU

Best known for their orange and blue fire-resistant feathers and small watery eyes. Bennus have storklike bodies and pelican-like beaks and often build their nests near flareadons—or in areas where lightning strikes are a regular occurrence.

BOOBRIE

Black parrot-size birds with dark, glittering eyes.
Their heads are crowned with a yellow feathered
mohawk—but a boobrie's most distinct
feature is their long, curled eyelashes (or
perhaps their earthshaking *roar*).

BUGBEAR

Furry, rat-size creatures with curved brown shells a bit like turtles,
which they hibernate inside for the majority of the year.

COCKATRICE

Small, friendly creatures that make excellent pets, given their lack
of claws or fangs as well as their calm temperament. Cockatrices'
bodies are similar to chickens', but are covered in scales instead of
feathers, with beaked noses and stumpy tails.

DINOSAUR

Large reptilian creatures that come in a variety of species (T. rexes,
triceratops, stegosaurs, pterodactyls, raptors—to name a few), with one
noticeable commonality between them: They're all covered in bright,
fluffy feathers. And despite what humans think, dinosaurs are definitely
not extinct. Most species of dinosaurs easily transition to the Sanctuary,
but Verdi (a T. rex) might end up a permanent resident at Havenfield.

DIRE WOLF

Larger and much fiercer than the more common wolves in the
wild, dire wolves have elongated fangs, thicker coats, and sharper

claws. Humans believe they're extinct, but the Sanctuary houses numerous thriving packs. The Council selected the dire wolf as the mascot for Sophie Foster when she became the leader of Team Valiant.

DRAGON

Unlike the fearsome beasts of human legends, dragons are timid reptilian creatures—larger than a dog but smaller than a horse, with scaled green skin and spikes running down their backs. They walk on four legs (which is the easiest way to differentiate dragons from wyverns) and serve as the mascot for Level Four at Foxfire.

ECKODON

Elephant-size plesiosaurs with long hooked necks, pointed noses, gills lining their cheeks, and scaled skin that comes in a variety of colors (most commonly gray-green, purple, and blue). Eckodons live in the water and use sound vortexes to travel great distances. Many human legends are based on them, particularly the stories of the Loch Ness Monster.

EURYPTERID

These eight-foot sea scorpions are another creature that humans believe to be extinct. And while eurypterids *look* deadly (especially with their pincers raised), they're actually quite gentle and friendly. Eurypterids swim along the surface of water, which is why they were chosen to pull the carriages in Atlantis.

FLAREADON

Pterodactyl-like creatures with golden, flame-resistant fur and enormous green eyes. Flareadons *need* fire to survive and generally live near volcanoes. The Neverseen used flareadon DNA to make the gorgodon, and flareadons are also the mascot for Level Seven at Foxfire. Sophie Foster additionally used a flareadon named Gildie to bottle a sample of Everblaze.

FLICKERWING

Small insects that look part firefly, part moth, and part butterfly— with a slightly venomous bite. Flickerwings are drawn to the splendors (a rare type of plant) and are used as part of Foxfire's Opening Ceremonies.

GHOUL

A furless catlike creature with deep-set black eyes and sallow gray skin that sags slightly off their bones, giving ghouls an appearance of something dead, even though they're very much alive—which is probably why they're featured in so many human ghost stories.

GORGODON

A deadly creature created by the Neverseen to guard their Nightfall facility. Gorgodons are part flareadon, part gorgonops, part argentavis, and part eurypterid, with a reptilian face, lionlike limbs, sharply angled wings, and slitted yellow eyes—as well as venomous fangs, venomous talons, and venomous spikes on their curled tails. They can also fly, breathe underwater, scale walls, and camouflage themselves—and they're at home on land, in the sea, or in the sky. Their only vulnerability is fire, despite the fact that their eggs require Everblaze to hatch. Only one gorgodon remains, which some feel means the gorgodon is now the rarest creature on the planet (and the new standard for the Timeline to Extinction). But others argue that gorgodons aren't a "naturally" existing species and therefore shouldn't count.

GORGONOPS

Humans believe the gorgonops is extinct, but the vicious creatures live on in the Sanctuary—though they have to be kept in isolation because of their aggressive tendencies (even after rehabilitation). They look like a combination of a saber-toothed tiger, a hippo, and a giant rat—with *huge* fangs—and their DNA was used by the Neverseen to create the gorgodon.

GREMLIN

Small creatures with black fur, shiny noses, and folded ears like a puppy's who love to dismantle things with their capable hands—particularly technology (which makes it extra surprising that the Black Swan's Technopath, Tinker, chooses to keep a gremlin named Sprocket as a pet). Gremlins are the mascot for Level One at Foxfire.

GRIFFIN

A lionlike beast with wings and a beaked nose—much like the human myths surrounding their existence. Given their eagle-sharp eyesight, enormous claws, and prominent fangs, griffins are deadly hunters and are some of the trickiest creatures to rehabilitate.

GULON

Incredibly stinky greenish creatures that are rarely seen above-ground (though a number became visible during Foxfire's infamous Great Gulon Incident). Their bodies are similar in size to a large rabbit, but shaped more like a rodent—with the exception of their noses, which are elongated like an anteater's.

HALCYON

Small birds with feathers in different shades of blue (not to be confused with the birds that humans have given the same name). Halcyons are able to sense when a storm is coming, and they serve as the mascot for Level Two at Foxfire.

ICHRITE

A type of tiny, troublesome insect similar in size to a flea, but with silver bodies perfect for blending into unicorn fur. Ichrites feed primarily on unicorn blood.

IMP

Palm-size gray creatures with enormous eyes, furry ears, batlike wings, and tiny purple tongues. Imps are equal parts adorable and troublesome—with a venomous bite that isn't deadly (but *is* painful). They're also incredibly stinky and known for their loud snoring. But under the right circumstances, they can make wonderful pets (as in the case of Sophie Foster's imp, Iggy).

JACKALOPE

Rabbitlike creatures with massive antlers jutting out of their heads. Humans consider them to be nothing more than a silly folk tale.

JACULUS

Black, winged serpents that feed off blood by latching onto an animal and injecting them with venom that serves as a powerful anticoagulant.

KELPIE

Bluish-green water horses that are slightly sparkly. Kelpies are beautiful and elusive and live primarily in the Gloaming Valley where the Alenon River connects to the ocean. Kelpies were chosen by the Council as a mascot for Biana Vacker when she joined Team Valiant.

KRAKEN

Slimy green beasts that look like a strange combination of an octopus, an elephant, and a lion, with six fangs and a trunklike, tentacled nose. Krakens live so deep under the ocean that the elves don't need to relocate them—but they do still monitor them to ensure they're safe. The kraken was chosen by the Council as a mascot for Stina Heks when she joined Team Valiant.

LARVAGORN

Bugs that look like a blend of scorpions and maggots—considered a dwarven delicacy (and a favorite food of eckodons).

MANTICORE

A powerful beast with red shaggy fur, blue-gray eyes, and multiple rows of teeth. Manticores' tails can sting, much like a scorpion's, and their venom is a powerful sedative.

MASTODON

Elephantine creatures believed to be extinct that are similar to woolly mammoths—but with shorter, stockier bodies and sharper tusks. Mastodons serve as the mascot for Level Three at Foxfire.

MEGANEURA

Vulture-size green insects believed to be extinct that look like enormous dragonflies, with iridescent wings and eyes like disco balls on the sides of their heads.

MERMAID

Despite the abundance of human legends, mermaids are neither humanoid nor pretty. Instead, they are eel-like creatures with stringy, tentacled "hair" growing from their pointed heads. Most live wild in the ocean, and their migration is carefully monitored by the elves. But mermaids that are too weak to make the journey are placed in private aquariums—the most famous of which is at Everglen.

MOONLARK

(Proper name: *suldreen*)

A rare species of bird with long legs like a crane, sweeping silver tail feathers like a peacock, and a curved neck like a swan. Their heads are crested with wispy feathers, and their beaks are rounded bills.

Moonlarks are best known for laying their eggs in the ocean—so only the strongest make it to shore—and leaving the babies to survive on their own (though the parents often nest close enough for the hatchlings to hear their songs).

MURCAT

Small underwater creatures that look like mini kittens covered in colorful scales. Although they have venomous fangs, murcats can be sweet once trained—though few choose them as a pet. (Linh Song adopted one recently, named Princess Purryfins.)

MUSKOG

Froglike creatures that burp stinky gas when frightened—which makes muskogs a popular choice for pranksters.

PANNONIASAUR

Bluish-gray freshwater mosasaurs that look like a combination of sharks, alligators, and eels. Pannoniasaurs have beady eyes and extra-long snouts, as well as an abundance of needle-sharp teeth. Lady Cadence sometimes uses them to pull her floating houseboat (Riverdrift).

PEGASUS

Winged equines that differ from alicorns by their smaller, huskier bodies—and their lack of a horn. They're also more common than unicorns and have deep blue spots and midnight blue manes.

PHOENIX

Eagle-size reddish birds with flame-resistant feathers, best known for their strange way of reproducing (which is likely the source of many human myths). Phoenixes are only able to conceive at the end of their lives, and they do not lay eggs like other birds. Instead, the baby develops inside the mother, who sheds her feathers as the pregnancy progresses. And when the last feather falls, she steps into fire, sacrificing herself for the new life that rises from her ashes and is cared for by the father, whose sweat provides a food source for the first few weeks.

POOKA

A small aquatic creature that's a cross between a toad and a sala-mander, best known for the large pustules that form on its greenish-yellow skin. Pooka pus serves a number of medicinal uses.

SABER-TOOTHED TIGER

Large red-orange cats with *huge* fangs and claws, believed to be extinct by humans. Saber-toothed tigers are used as the mascot for Level Five at Foxfire.

SANGUILLISK

Giant insects that look like a combination of a roach and a mosquito.

SASQUATCH

Tall, green, shaggy creatures with beady eyes, beaklike noses, and big feet (like the human legends). Sasquatches walk bipedally and live in dens in the forest. They're also avid climbers who can travel by treetop. And they're absurdly smelly.

SELKIE

Sleek black creatures with whiskered faces and long, coiled bodies, making them look part seal, part snake. They routinely shed their skin, which liquifies into an oily black puddle swirled with iridescent blue. Many selkies live in the Sanctuary, but some live free on Inktide Island.

SIREN

Small, water-dwelling creatures that look a little like otters—only much less adorable. Their black fur is matted, their gray faces are scaled with long whiskers like a catfish, and their oversize mouths are always open, letting out shrill, earsplitting whines that some consider to be musical.

SUNCATCHER

Majestic yellow birds with long, wispy tail feathers that curl out behind them in wide coils. Suncatchers are best known for their tremendous wingspan and the sheen on their bodies, which can make them painful to look at when they stand in direct sunlight.

TITANOBOA

Absolutely enormous snakes that humans think are extinct. Titanoboas live so deep underground that they don't necessarily need protection, but the elves still monitor them. The most famous Titanoboa is Twinkle, who pulls the goblin queen's royal carriage through the Imperial Pathways to and from Gildingham.

TOMPLE

Small, fluffy creatures that look like a cute cross between a kitten and a hedgehog—until they turn over and display their six spindly, cockroachlike legs. Tomples feed on dust, which makes them useful to keep in labs—though many elvin homes have them as well. And the Council chose tomples as a mascot for Dex Dizznee when he joined Team Valiant.

TREDGEON

Gigantic sand crabs with squirming legs and antennae, iridescent claws, and a glowing opalescent shell. Tredgeons tunnel underground like dwarves, which is why the dwarves value their carapace above any gem (and even use it for their leader's crown).

UNICORN

Rare horned equines with black manes and tails, silvery bodies, and no wings. Only one pair of unicorns lives at the Sanctuary. The rest are with various members of the Heks family, who've mastered unicorn care and breeding. Unicorns are the mascot for Level Eight at Foxfire.

VERMINION

Rottweiler-size hamsterlike beasts with purple fur, glassy black eyes, constantly growing fangs, and pouchy cheeks where they store their "food"—including small animals they've hunted.

WOOLLY MAMMOTH

Large elephantine creatures similar to mastodons, only they're larger and have longer horns. Humans believe them to be extinct, but there is a thriving herd at the Sanctuary.

WYVERN
Huge winged lizards with a ridge of spikes down their back—similar to a dragon. But they only have two legs and two much smaller arms, like a T. rex. Wyverns were chosen by the Council as a mascot for Wylie Endal when he joined Team Valiant.

YETI
Large bipedal creatures with bushy white fur and tiny eyes. Yetis are the source of the human myths about the abominable snowman, and they serve as the mascot for Level Six at Foxfire.

ALICORNS AND THE TIMELINE TO EXTINCTION

NO ONE KNEW ALICORNS EXISTED UNTIL A MALE was discovered by accident—and the Lost Cities were then faced with a bleak new reality. Unless a mate could be found for Greyfell before his life ended, the alicorn would become the first creature to go extinct. And for centuries, an extensive search for a female alicorn turned up nothing.

But a chance encounter led Sophie Foster to discover Silveny in the Forbidden Cities, and Sophie was able to bring her safely to Havenfield. The Council left Silveny in Sophie's care—but after the Neverseen tried to steal the precious creature, Sophie moved Silveny to the Sanctuary to be with Greyfell. Not long after, Silveny informed Sophie that she was pregnant. And when the Neverseen tried to capture the alicorns *again*, Sophie convinced the Council to set Silveny and Greyfell free so that the alicorns could hide from their enemies.

Sophie stayed in regular contact with Silveny and Greyfell—which was how she was able to get Silveny help when she went into early labor. The pregnancy turned out to be twins, and only with the help of the trolls—as well as Vika and Stina Heks—were both babies delivered safely. Silveny survived the birth as well, effectively resetting the Timeline to Extinction. But it's only been a cautious improvement.

Four alicorns are better than one—but the species remains severely vulnerable.

Still, for now, the elves celebrate babies Wynn and Luna.

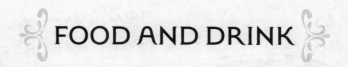

THE ELVES FOLLOW A PLANT-BASED DIET, BUT IT isn't the least bit limiting, because the gnomes cultivate an abundance of unique fruits and vegetables that are both healthy *and* delicious (even if the colors and textures may appear strange at times). Some gnomish plants taste like meat or various other human delicacies. Others are perfect for baking, which is why the Lost Cities are famous for their desserts (and their candies!).

There's also a variety of flavored beverages to enjoy in the Lost Cities, but the most essential staple is called Youth (and rumored to be the source of human myths about a mysterious Fountain of Youth, which grants eternal health). Given its unique properties, this cool, slightly sweet water is often used medicinally—but that doesn't mean it's not also seen as a refreshing way to stay hydrated throughout the day.

Starkflower stew will never taste as good without Calla—but it's a perfect way to remember her!

The candy is delicious—but everyone knows the best part about Prattles are the collectible pins inside!

Any flavor anytime—custard bursts are always AMAZING!!

SOPHIE'S FAVORITE FOODS

The secret Mentors' cafeteria at Foxfire always has butterblasts available—it's not fair that they don't share!

Lushberry juice is the perfect blend of sweet and tart!

Mallowmelt is always a good idea—and one gooey slice is never enough!

POPULAR FOOD AND DRINKS IN THE LOST CITIES

BLITZENBERRY MUFFINS

Petite cakes that melt like butter when bitten into, filled with tart berries that fizz and pop on the tongue.

BRATTAILS

Tuber-style plants (shaped a bit like cattails) that are served roasted, and taste like the sausages that humans eat.

BUTTERBLASTS

Round, golden pastries topped with giant sugar crystals. They're chewy like doughnuts, but taste like hot pancakes filled with a maple-flavored cream.

CINNACREME

A hot, thick beverage that tastes like melted snickerdoodles.

CUSTARD BURSTS

Square puffs that look like marshmallows but are crunchy on the outside and gooey on the inside. They come in tons of flavors, but some of the most popular are chocolate, butterscotch, lushberry, chocolate-cherry, and caramel.

DAWNLINGS

Dark purple fruits grown from special seeds created by Calla. They taste warm, sweet, and tingly, like little slices of sunshine.

FIZZLEBERRY WINE

A bubbly, sweet beverage mulled from fizzleberries. It isn't technically alcoholic, but its effect is similar, so the elves reserve it for adults.

FLAVORED AIR

A truly unique type of candy that turns breathing into a delicious experience. Flavored air comes in a wide variety of flavors and keeps the air sweet and mouthwatering for several minutes after popping open the can.

FLUFFCREAMS

A delicious flaky pastry filled with a cloud of honey, cinnamon, and butter. Perfect for dessert, a snack, or breakfast—or all of the above!

INDIGOOBERS

A messy, blue, bite-size candy cluster filled with sweet fruity juice that dribbles everywhere when eaten—which is half the fun of the experience.

LUSHBERRY JUICE

By far the most popular beverage in the Lost Cities. Lushberry juice manages to be both perfectly sweet and delightfully tart and tastes amazing with everything.

MALLOWMELT

A gooey cake covered in frosting and butterscotch, that tastes like freshly baked chocolate chip cookies soaked in ice cream.

NOIRSSELS

These silver-wrapped treats look like hard candies, and their dark color and squishy texture is reminiscent of a dead bug. But don't be fooled—noirssels are so sweet and cinnamon-y and delicious that they can even take away the flavor of unpleasant medicines (which Sophie knows very well!).

PORCAROOT PIE

This surprisingly healthy pie is often served for breakfast. And while its strange purple color may seem unappealing, it tastes like bacon covered in gooey melted cheese.

PRATTLES

These chewy, peanut-butter-and-caramel-flavored candies are filled with cream and taste delicious. But everyone would buy them even if they were gross, because every box of Prattles contains an awesome collectible pin based on the protected species. *Everyone* collects and trades Prattles pins.

PUDDING PUFFS

Fudgey squares that taste like a mix of warm apple pie and melted vanilla ice cream.

RIPPLEFLUFFS

Buttery, fudgey desserts that are part cupcake, part brownie, with a candy surprise sunken into the center. They can be made in many flavors, but two of the most popular are butter toffee and chocolate mint.

RIPPLENUTS

These round yellow nuts have shells that turn orange as they roast, and their centers melt into a warm goo that tastes like butter, vanilla, and honey—with a dash of cinnamon and a hint of caramel.

STARKFLOWER STEW

A rich, earthy stew made with a variety of gnomish spices, herbs, and vegetables—but the secret ingredient is the starkflower, which adds a dark, smoky flavor. Calla invented the recipe and kept it secret for millennia. But she decided to share it with Sophie—and even though Sophie's stew never tastes quite the same, she makes it often to remember her friend.

SUGARKNOTS

Flaky, croissant-like pastries filled with a rich brown-sugar custard.

THREADLEENS

A rare, spicy, tangy fruit that's eaten by pulling off the juicy pink strings.

UMBER LEAVES

Wide black leaves best served dried and cut into strips. Their chickenlike flavor makes them both a delicious meal—and an excellent way to train animals to become vegetarians.

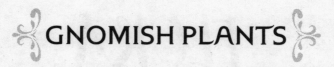

GNOMISH PLANTS

ELVES DO THEIR BEST TO CARE FOR NATURE—BUT they cannot cultivate gnomish plants on their own. (The Neverseen try, and the result is *not* delicious, according to Keefe Sencen.) So the elves are very grateful that the gnomes choose to remain in the Lost Cities (particularly after the hard truths that were uncovered during the gnomish plague), and elves would never present themselves as authorities on plant life. The subject should always be covered by a gnome—even the agriculture session at Foxfire has gnomish Mentors. As a result, Flori—one of the gnomes who resides at Havenfield (and Sophie Foster's gnomish bodyguard)—will cover this lesson.

FLORA

Only gnomes can understand the language of nature (though the moonlark comes close!). Still, it's vital that everyone understand the potential inside each growing thing. They can heal or harm or nourish or provide beauty or freshen the air or enrich the soil. And sometimes, in the right hands, they can become something incredible. —Flori

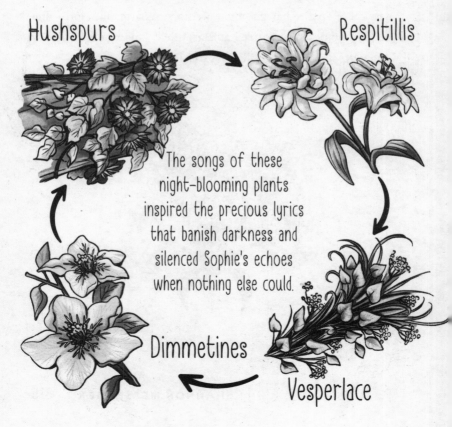

Hushspurs

Respitillis

The songs of these night-blooming plants inspired the precious lyrics that banish darkness and silenced Sophie's echoes when nothing else could.

Dimmetines

Vesperlace

CALLA'S GREATEST GIFT

The Panakes tree healed my people from a deadly plague—and we're forever grateful for its blossoms. But we'll always miss the Brave One who sacrificed herself to save us.

ANOTHER PRECIOUS GIFT FROM CALLA

Created to help the moonlark chase away her nightmares

Dreamlilies

Chosen for their night whispers

Reveriebells

Chosen for their soft song

Chosen for their sweet scent

Aethrials

Sweetshades

TREES OF HEALING,
CLEANSING, AND LOSS

THE PANAKES

Also known as the "Brave Ones," Panakes
trees only exist if a gnome shifts their
form while life remains within their
body. That sacrificed life energy then
pours out through the Panakes's abundance of blossoms, giving
the petals a powerful healing quality. Only one Panakes exists—and
only because of Calla's incredible sacrifice. It grows in the pastures
at Havenfield—a vision in pink, blue, and purple, with weeping
willow–like tendrils and coarsely braided bark.

THE PURES

These towering palmlike trees are officially named *Purfoliage
palmae*—but everyone in the Lost Cities calls them "the Pures."
And while the Pures may be the most common trees in the Lost
Cities (every house has at least one, and every city has several), their
fan-shaped leaves are nothing short of incredible. Each frond has a
clothlike texture, allowing them to serve as filters for pollutants and
impurities drifting through the air. As a result, the Lost Cities have
perfectly fresh, clean air—despite the fact that the elves must share
their planet with humans (and their abundance of pollution).

THE FOUR SEASONS TREE

This unique tree in the main courtyard at Lumenaria may at first appear to be nothing more than a marvel of nature—and with its limbs growing in four sections (each a manifestation of what the tree would look like during summer, winter, spring, and fall), it truly is a sight to behold. But until recently, few realized the tree's tragic history, or mourned for the four brave Ancient gnomes who were cruelly infected with the plague and used the last of their energy to be reborn as this striking memorial.

OTHER NOTABLE PLANTS

SPECKLED SPIDER SNAPPER

Similar to a Venus flytrap—but with much sharper teeth. And as their name suggests, these strange, carnivorous plants feed off spiders. They also bloom with bell-shaped flowers that release a particularly fragrant perfume—which is why some elves consider them to be a unique gift (albeit slightly gruesome).

SPLENDORS

A rare species of plant that requires a great deal of specialized care in order to survive. Splendors only bloom once every year with purple flowers that are both beautiful and pungent. Their scent—and the unearthly glow from their freshly bloomed petals—draw the flickerwings, which is why splendors are used for Foxfire's Opening Ceremonies. Every elite prodigy must cultivate a splendor throughout the course of Level Seven in order for it to bloom before they enter Level Eight.

STARGLASS FLOWER

The petals of this shimmery, star-shaped flower drip with a unique nectar that's used to produce somnalene—a special type of eye drop known for its "midnighting" effect (which is described as feeling like there's a twinkling universe inside the mind).

STARKFLOWER

These unattractive flowers have curled, shriveled black petals with gray speckles—and contain shadowvapor inside them. But once that darkness is removed, they turn lush, plump, and gleaming white—and even the shadowvapor serves a use, providing a smoky flavor to Calla's legendary starkflower stew.

SUGARBELLES

Despite their name, the nectar from these pink flowers is anything but sweet. But sugarbelles have potent healing qualities that make their awful taste well worth utilizing.

SWIZZLESPICE

Long blue stalks that taste like sweet cinnamon—swizzlespice can be eaten by anyone, but it's particularly popular with animals. Especially the alicorns.

TANGOURDS

These melon-size purple fruits grow on thick, thorny vines and are best known for their raw, meaty flavor. Most elves consider the taste to be too gamey, but animals being rehabilitated for the Sanctuary love them (except for the gorgodon, which has not seemed impressed).

THE WANDERLINGS

Grown in a special forest that serves as the elves' only cemetery, Wanderling seeds are wrapped with the DNA of someone deceased before they're planted. This allows these incredible trees to take on characteristics of the life that was lost, mirroring elements of the person's appearance and personality as they grow. As a result, no two Wanderlings are alike, and the life they commemorate gets to carry on in a different form.

FASHION

I know Sophie thinks wearing capes is super weird. (I guess humans don't really wear them?) But capes are more than gorgeous accessories that help keep you warm in the Lost Cities—they're a sign of status! (Though they also help keep you warm—unless someone shares their cape with you . . .)

Some people wear gloves to keep their hands nice and toasty. Some wear them to make a fashion statement. And some wear them to hide a secret enhancing ability. Either way, once you put the gloves on, you can't even feel they're there—and they can be so pretty!

I *love* heels! But they may not be for everyone—especially people who have a hard time walking without tripping!

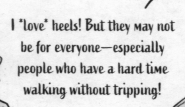

Biana's Style File

Personally, I say, "The fancier, the better!" But what's most important is wearing whatever makes you feel fabulous! (Though I still think sparkles make everything better!)

Gowns aren't worn for everything—but they aren't just for parties, either. Pretty much anytime you want to look important or be taken seriously, bring on the ruffles and frills! (And when you really want to impress someone, make sure to add a jeweled circlet or hair comb!)

Of course these are real jewels! Why wouldn't they be?

If sparkles or jewels aren't your thing, there's always embroidery to add stylish detail! (Or a fun slogan! My next tunic is going to say: "You should stare—I'm letting you see me right now!")

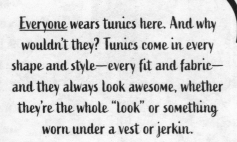

Everyone wears tunics here. And why wouldn't they? Tunics come in every shape and style—every fit and fabric—and they always look awesome, whether they're the whole "look" or something worn under a vest or jerkin.

Pants don't always have pockets at the ankles—it depends on what kind of shoes they'll be paired with. (And a lot of the taller boots have pockets at the top. Pockets are important, after all!)

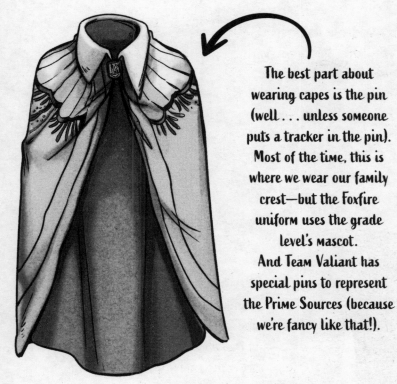

The best part about wearing capes is the pin (well . . . unless someone puts a tracker in the pin). Most of the time, this is where we wear our family crest—but the Foxfire uniform uses the grade level's mascot.
And Team Valiant has special pins to represent the Prime Sources (because we're fancy like that!).

Okay, this might not look as comfortable as a tunic (and it isn't!). But some things are so stunning, they're worth that little extra discomfort—and jerkins definitely fall into that category.
I mean, look at all that incredible detail!

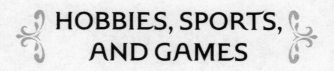

HOBBIES, SPORTS, AND GAMES

WHILE THE MAJORITY OF ELVIN CULTURE PRIMARILY focuses on education (and general world-betterment), life in the Lost Cities of course still includes a healthy measure of entertainment—particularly in the form of hobbies, sports, and games.

Elvin hobbies include activities like swimming, hiking, drawing, dancing, baking, and animal care—as well as the incredibly popular pastime of trading Prattles pins. Thus far, no one has ever managed to obtain a complete collection of Prattles pins. In fact, the closest anyone has ever come is still lacking three key pins—and the owner of the collection (who prefers to remain nameless) has developed a strong dislike of both the taste and smell of the candy after opening so many packages.

Elvin sports are equally varied. Children grow up playing base quest and bramble—and elves of every age enjoy the Bramble Championship held every three years (though the recent turmoil with the Neverseen led the Council to indefinitely postpone the most recently scheduled game). Foxfire is also known for its Ultimate Splotching Championship, as well as numerous other team-oriented games played during the physical education session.

For a unique glimpse at two of the popular elvin sports, included on the next page are the additional rules for both bramble and base quest, created by Fitz Vacker for the well-known matches that he and his friends regularly hold at Everglen.

BRAMBLE RULES

No time-outs.

Abilities _are_ allowed.

Tackling is _also_ allowed—but no knocking anyone into the lake!

(That one's for you, Biana!)

Covering the ball in anything from Slurps and Burps

is _definitely_ cheating!

(Looking at you, Keefe!)

Pretending to be injured and then tackling someone

who tries to help you is _also_ cheating.

(Another one for you, Keefe.)

Losers owe the winners a dare.

Winners get to eat all the mallowmelt in the kitchen.

(And no, Keefe—I'm not scared. Get ready to lose!)

BASE QUEST RULES

Both teams' bases have to be within the main gate.

The team that chooses their base first has

to quest first.

No hiding muskogs in someone's base!

(We all know that wasn't a "random muskog encounter," Keefe!)

Abilities _are_ allowed.

(But staying invisible the whole time makes playing

with you super boring, Alvar!)

There's no prize for winning.

(Because you guys get way too competitive!)

Prattles Pins

ONE PIN IS MADE FOR EVERY
LIVING CREATURE UNDER ELVIN
PROTECTION, SO SOME ARE
RARER THAN OTHERS.

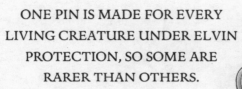

Prattles Kraken
(AKA Krakie)
#32 of 709

Prattles
Alicorn
#2 of 4

Prattles Sasquatch
(AKA The Stink)
#467 of 982

Prattles Flareadon
#55 of 329

Prattles Moonlark
#10 out of #91

GADGETS

THANKS TO THE HARD WORK AND CREATIVITY OF numerous talented Technopaths, the elves have an abundance of gadgets at their disposal to facilitate life in the Lost Cities, or to provide a measure of privacy or protection.

Some of the most well-known gadgets are:

ADDLER

A necklace-style gadget worn when someone wants to remain private or anonymous. Addlers make it impossible for anyone to focus on the wearer's face, effectively keeping them from being recognized or remembered.

ATMOSPHERIC STABILIZER

A triangular gadget that allows the user to breathe at extremely high altitudes—though only in small, contained spaces.

COGNATE RING

Special rings made of ruminel (a rare metal that reacts to mental energy and has a magnetic draw) that Cognates wear, both to symbolize their telepathic relationship and to keep their hands connected when working telepathically.

DEDUCTER

Vendors use these gadgets—which come in several forms (sometimes pendants or rings—but most commonly as cuffs worn on the arm)—to access their customers' birth funds and process any payment due.

DNA SENSOR

Anything meant to remain "secure" in the Lost Cities can only be accessed by providing the necessary DNA (generally through saliva) on these small, subtly placed sensors. Some sensors—like those on the lockers at Foxfire—even change flavor.

EFFLUXER

These silver forklike gadgets are stuck into the ground in order to provide a measure of protection from ogres. When triggered, effluxers release a cloud of scent that damages ogres' sinuses (and isn't particularly pleasant for any nearby elves).

ENHANCING BLOCKER

These tiny, clever gadgets are technically one of a kind and were designed by Tinker in order to give Sophie Foster control over her enhancing ability. The small curves of silver fit over her fingernails and create an undetectable force field around her hands—kind of like invisible gloves. Tapping the fingers five times activates or deactivates the blockers.

HOME CRYSTAL

It's hard to decide if a home crystal is an accessory or a gadget, but whichever category someone places them in won't affect how vital these pendants are, providing a safe path home for those without access to Leapmasters or pathfinders.

IMPARTER

A handheld communication device that allows someone to speak with a projection of anyone they "hail" (though there are certain restrictions on which elves are "reachable"—the Councillors, for instance, can only be hailed with Imparters that have been granted special permission). Imparters are thin, palm-size crystal squares with a silver sheen—and users should be careful, since it's now known that Imparters can be tampered with.

LEAPMASTER

Since pathfinders are limited to those with the Council's approval, most residences in the Lost Cities are equipped with some form of Leapmaster—a ceiling-mounted device comprising numerous dangling crystals, which raise or lower on command and create a path to the requested location. Leapmasters are often named for the number of locations they include. (For instance, the Leapmaster 500 has 500 locations.)

LUFTERATOR

A T-shaped mouthpiece that allows the user to safely breathe underwater for an unlimited amount of time.

MELDER

As one of the rare weapons used in the Lost Cities, melders are meant to incapacitate—not cause permanent harm (though repeated blasts, particularly at close range, can be highly dangerous). Melders have a sleek curved handle that connects to a triangle of silver with a single button in the center, and they can cause instant, painful paralysis.

NEXUS
These bracelet-style gadgets put a force field around the wearer during light leaps as an extra layer of safety. Nexuses cannot be removed unless the meter on the underside (which measures the strength of the wearer's concentration) becomes full, proving their mind is now strong enough to leap unassisted. Their signal can also be tracked.

NULL
A device designed to block the signals from any technology near the wearer—but nulls can also be adjusted to block only certain frequencies.

OBSCURER
A small black orb that bends light and sound around whoever holds it, making them undetectable to anyone outside the obscurer's range.

PATHFINDER
This wand-shaped gadget has a small round crystal at the end, cut with facets to create specific paths to important locations within the Lost Cities (and, for those with special approval, to locations connected with the other species as well). Note: Given the freedom that pathfinders allow, they are restricted to those who meet the Council's approval.

REGISTRY PENDANT

All elves in the Lost Cities are assigned one of these choker-style necklaces to wear at all times, which allows the registry to track their location (as well as numerous other details). The design occasionally varies, but most registry pendants consist of a simple band along with an etched silver loop with a small clear crystal set in the center.

RIDDLER

A pen programmed to only write the words of a riddle—until the person using it writes the correct answer. Given their cleverness and small size, riddlers are one of the most common midterms or finals gifts for prodigies at Foxfire.

SHADOWPAINTER

These softly glowing orbs reflect shadows of animals on the walls and are often used by parents to soothe children who are afraid of the dark.

SPECTRAL MIRROR

These specialty gadgets come in every size, shape, and style and appear to be normal mirrors—until someone steps within range. Then a tiny face appears in one of the corners and offers fashion and beauty advice with a surprisingly lifelike personality. No two spectral personas are the same, but they do share one common trait: unflinching honesty—which is likely why spectral mirrors fell out of popularity. Most elves weren't fans of being insulted by their mirrors while they tried to get dressed.

SPYBALL

These small silver orbs can project someone's location and activity without their knowledge, allowing the user (within certain limits) to view anyone, anytime, anywhere. Given the serious privacy violations that could result from such a gadget, Spyballs are severely restricted and closely monitored.

STELLARSCOPE

A device shaped like a bent, upside-down spyglass, which can be used to bottle starlight as well as to simply observe the stars.

THINKING CAP

These long, white floppy hats may not be a very fashionable accessory, but they're made from an amalgam of metals and designed to dull telepathic abilities (and other abilities as well). Prodigies wear them during the Foxfire midterm exams and final exams to preserve the integrity of the tests—and then hang them upside down from their lockers afterward to be filled with gifts during the corresponding celebrations.

TRACKER

Tiny, disk-shaped gadgets most commonly sewn into clothing as an added safety precaution. The use of trackers is relatively new to the Lost Cities, previously used only on the Councillors (at the insistence of their goblin bodyguards). But recent challenges with the Neverseen have caused many others to begin utilizing them.

TREASURY CUBE

Every elf is assigned one of these small green cubes at birth to allow them access to the monies assigned to their birth fund.

VORTINATOR

A mechanized staircase that spins at rapid speed to quickly allow access to the upper floors of the taller buildings in the Lost Cities. Warning: Vortinators can cause dizziness and queasiness the first few times someone uses them.

Dex Dizznee's Greatest Inventions

Who doesn't want to be able to punch extra hard—and I'm REALLY hoping that someday I'll get to watch Sophie use the Sucker Punch on Lady Gisela and Vespera!

It may look funky, but the Twiggler hacked through Lumenaria's security and helped save the gnomes!

First: This is a panic switch—NOT a boring Cognate ring. It also saved Sophie's life twice. And it works so well that I've been making them for everyone I care about!

The Evader makes it SUPER easy to hack into things like the registry—and it leaves no trace that I was there! (Well, unless I change stuff . . .) Now I just need to make a few tweaks so I can bypass the security on certain files.

. . . AND A FEW THAT WEREN'T THE BEST IDEA.

No one thought the ability restrictor would work—but it DID. Except the Council ruined it by ordering Sophie to wear it and . . . yeah. I wish I'd never made it. I destroyed it, though—and I'll never make another!

I made these Blocker Bands to help Sophie with her enhancing—and they definitely did their job. But using crush cuffs kinda got me stuck in the most awkward conversation ever. . . .

The Warden also worked perfectly and monitored Alvar's every move. But I wish I'd made sure it was resistant to Nulls . . .

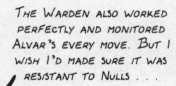

For the record, these Sense Blasters were actually working really well until Councillor Zarina fried one with lightning. Still, I should've put an override because Fitz almost got killed.

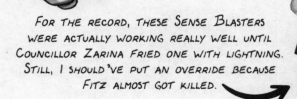

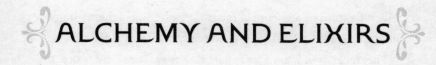

ALCHEMY AND ELIXIRS

ALCHEMY ISN'T CONSIDERED A SPECIAL ABILITY IN
the Lost Cities—a fact that some disagree with, since certain elves
are far more talented at it than others (and a few are woefully disastrous, like poor Sophie Foster).

The study of alchemy has two primary focuses:

- **METAL PURIFICATION AND TRANSMUTATION:**
  Using a variety of techniques, alchemists are able to
  remove impurities from metals, and turn one metal into
  another (ideally into gold). Particularly gifted alchemists
  can even turn nonmetallic substances into metal.

- **ELIXIR-MAKING:** Every elixir is different, and
  some are much simpler to make than others. So elixir
  mastery varies widely (and even experienced alchemists
  occasionally explode things). But only the most talented
  alchemists are able to invent their own formulas.

Elves who work in the Treasury regularly use metal purification for
their jobs. Elvin physicians spend a great deal of time creating (or
modifying) medicines. And alchemy Mentors of course focus on
the subject extensively.

Beyond that, most elves treat alchemy as a hobby—or abandon
the practice entirely once it's no longer a school requirement.

Still, a handful of alchemists focus on gathering alchemy ingredients, or creating (and selling) a variety of useful elixirs.

The most well-known example is Kesler Dizznee's store in Mysterium (Slurps and Burps), which sells both elixirs and alchemy supplies. The store is frequented by nearly everyone in the Lost Cities—and for good reason. The elixirs available for sale range from essential medicines to pranks and everything in between—with new formulas being created all the time.

Some of the most popular elixirs and ingredients for sale at Slurps and Burps are:

ABRASION PERSUASION

Quickly seals and heals small scrapes to the skin

ACHEY-BREAK

A handy, all-purpose painkiller

ALKAHEST

The universal solvent, which can dissolve
any material. Must be stored in a bubble of itself.
(This is the second hardest substance for an alchemist to make.)

AMARALLITINE

A highly combustible substance used in numerous elixirs

BLISTER BLAST

Shrinks and numbs blisters within minutes—and gets
rid of them completely within a few hours

BROWN-EYE SOLIDARI-TEA

Temporarily turns eyes brown
(became quite popular after Sophie Foster's
arrival to the Lost Cities)

BRUISE CRUISE

Fades bruises of all shapes, sizes, and colors

BUFF STUFF

Temporarily increases muscle mass

DROOLY DEW

Temporarily makes the mouth hypersalivate

FADE FUEL

Speeds cell regeneration for someone
who faded during a light leap
(The Slurps and Burps version includes limbium)

FART A LA CARTE

Temporarily causes an abundance of flatulence

FLOOF

Temporarily causes hair or fur
to turn fluffy and feathery

FRECKLE JUICE

Temporarily gives the appearance of freckled skin

FRISSYN

A shimmering silver powder that puts out Everblaze.
(Frissyn is the hardest substance for an alchemist to
make—and a recent addition to Slurps and Burps
in light of challenges with the Neverseen.)

FUZZY FIZZ

Temporarily causes the body to be covered
in short, mostly invisible hairs, giving
skin a fuzzy feel

GASHROOMS

Small, stinky mushrooms used for both
metal purification and elixir-making
(particularly prank elixirs)

GREENLEAF

Temporarily turns hair or fur
bright green

GURGLE GUT

Temporarily causes abundant
gaseous eruptions

HAIROIDS

Temporarily causes hair to grow much more
rapidly than normal

HUSH SLUSH

Temporarily eliminates someone's ability to talk
(generally lasts eight hours)

LIMBIUM

A substance used in elixirs that affects the limbic system
(must be kept safely away from Sophie Foster)

LOVELYLOCKS

Temporarily makes hair extra shiny
and smooth

MERMAID-TIGER DELIGHT

Temporarily turns hair and fur a combination
of purple, teal, and blue, with black stripes
running through

NOGGINEASE

Temporarily clears the mind to allow greater
focus during studying

QUICKSNUFF

A green powder that easily puts out fires

REEKROD

A stinky stalklike plant commonly used for pranks,
either by itself or in elixirs

SCRATCHES 'N SPLITS

Immediately seals any cuts or scratches to the skin

SEA SEE

Temporarily turns eyes teal

TANNY FANNY

Temporarily gives pale skin the appearance of a suntan

WOUND WIPE

A quick and easy way to clean and treat small injuries

Dex's Fail-Proof Alchemy Tips!

(Even For You, Sophie!)

✱ Trust the Dizznee method. We're the best!

✱ WHAP means "Wash hands and present."
(DO NOT "whip" the elixir instead! I know you know
this, but it seemed like a good reminder.)

✱ Only practice alchemy in a fireproof location.
(We, uh, both know why this one's so important....)

✱ Always pour in amarallitine from a safe distance—and
use a timer to ensure you're adding it at the exact
second the elixir is ready for it.

✱ Don't get any ruckleberry juice on your skin—
it'll make you smell like stinky feet. And your skin
will get all weird and wrinkly like Forkle.

✱ Yeah, a lot of the ingredients for elixirs are super
disgusting. It's probably better if you don't think about
it. (And plug your nose!)

✱ Remember: Lady Galvin hates everybody—it's not just
you. (Although maybe try not to destroy her cape again?)

✱ Alkahest is the universal solvent and can only
be stored in a bubble of itself. (Whatever you do,
DO NOT touch it.)

✱ If you bottle quintessence (accidentally or on purpose),
DO NOT bring the bottle to Foxfire.

✱ If you suddenly remember any complicated formulas,
don't try making them. The Black Swan way
overestimated your alchemy skills!

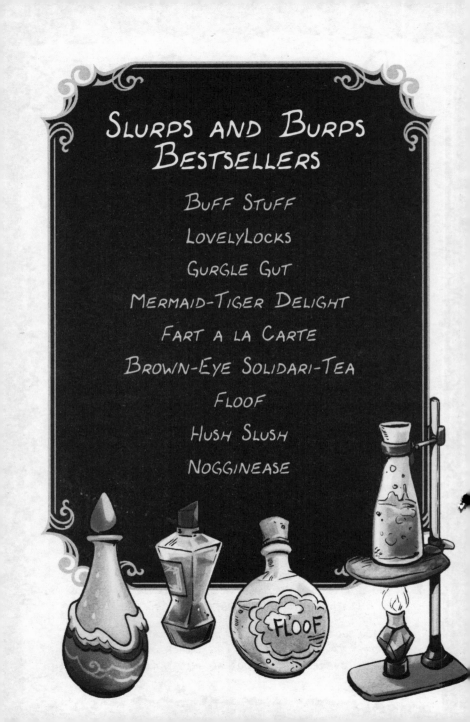

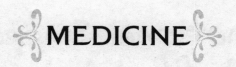

I'd forgotten how different elvin medicine is from the other species' until Sophie moved to the Lost Cities and I saw how terrified she was of me! (Can't totally blame her when I think about all the sharp things human doctors have to use!) I've also treated her bodyguards quite a few times, so it's been an educational experience. And hey, all medicine has value. But I'm glad I get to work with elixirs, balms, and poultices (even if those can have some pretty nasty ingredients).

Sadly, I can't fix everything—but that never stops me from trying. And thankfully I've been able to keep Sophie safe and healthy. So far . . .

—Elwin

Emotional Support Stuffed Animals

Amy's Bun-Bun

Elwin's Stinky the Stegosaurus

Keefe's Mrs. Stinkbottom

Sophie's Ella

Fitz's Mr. Snuggles

Biana's Lady Sassyfur

I'm definitely not the first person to realize the therapeutic power of a good snuggle buddy—nor can I take credit for giving out all of these. But I am a big supporter of the "hug a stuffed animal" movement. And someday I hope everyone tries sleeping with one!

—Elwin

OTHER COMMON REMEDIES AND TREATMENTS

BENNU TEARS

These extremely rare drops can increase the potency of most remedies, but especially in cell regenerators.

BILEPOD

This gray, walnut-shaped seed cures seasickness when anyone eats the reddish-brown goop inside (which smells like burnt garlic).

BOTTLED YOUTH

Elves drink at least one bottle of this cold, sweet water daily because it contains an essential enzyme that helps flush toxins out of the system. Any treatment plan for an illness or injury always includes additional bottles of Youth.

CALLOWBERRIES

These orange and green speckled fruits are used to reverse the effect of ruckleberries—but they taste and smell horrible.

CLARIFAVA

These strange, cube-shaped fruits with black-and-white speckles are known to help the body resist the influence of technology.

FATHOMLETHES

These tiny pearls (harvested from rare river oysters) can trigger vivid, overwhelming dreams when ingested—which makes taking fathomlethes both a risky and useful tool to access long-term memories.

HOLLOWTHISTLE TEA
This drink is most commonly described as "vile" and must be taken in moderation, since drinking too much in one sitting could cause someone's insides to liquefy. It's one of the best methods to purge poison or venom from the system.

JACULUS VENOM
Contains a powerful anticoagulant that can be used as a tissue regenerator when combined with Phoenix sweat.

KELPIE DUNG
The waste from a kelpie can take the sting of out terrible bites when applied to the skin.

KELPIE URINE
Most only use this remedy as a last resort, but it's the absolute best way to regain equilibrium when fighting vertigo or seasickness.

LIMBIUM-FREE FADE FUEL
Similar to the product sold at Slurps and Burps, but designed specifically to treat Sophie Foster without triggering her allergy.

PHOENIX SWEAT
This valuable ingredient is used in burn salves and flesh

regenerators (and works best when combined with jaculus venom).

PIQUATINE

This acid is nearly as strong as alkahest and can dissolve the top layers of skin—which is the only way to remove aromark if someone comes in contact with it. The process can be strange and gross, but with numbing balm, it's completely painless.

POOKA PUS

The liquid form of this powerful cell regenerator is relatively easy to find—but the solid form is incredibly rare, and can tackle the strongest infections.

RUCKLEBERRIES

Also used in alchemy (for metal purification), ingesting these small yellow-orange berries causes the body to bloat and the skin to wrinkle, drastically altering someone's appearance and making them unrecognizable.

SLUMBERBERRY TEA

This special purple-tinted tea is brewed from slumberberries and is used by many as a mild sedative before bed.

SOMNALENE

The nectar from the starglass flower can be used as eye drops, creating a unique effect called "midnighting," which can calm the mind and encourage sleep.

SQUELCHBERRIES

Purplish, reddish, fuzzy fruits that resemble dead caterpillars. Each bite contains an entire meal's worth of nutrients—but they must be eaten slowly. Squelchberry juice is incredibly sticky and can glue the jaw shut if too many berries are consumed at once.

YETI PEE

This strong-smelling golden sludge can be hard to find—and even harder to wash off. And it's not particularly pleasant to use. But it's the best way to treat serious burns.

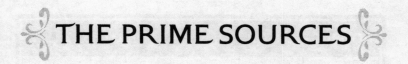

THE PRIME SOURCES

THERE ARE THREE:

SUNLIGHT
MOONLIGHT
STARLIGHT

And they aren't studied or discussed as often as they should be in the Lost Cities—particularly since they're considered to be the elves' true source of power. But Councillor Bronte may be working to change that.

At least once a year, the Councillors visit the Point of Purity—a place at the edge of Earth's atmosphere, where the Sources are all equal and unimpeded by any contamination or filtering—and leap back to the Lost Cities using a beam made from all three Sources.

The leap is a test, meant to remind the Council where their power comes from and help them better comprehend each Source's unique attributes to harness.

Together, the Prime Sources provide a perfect example of how to lead without dominating, which is why the Council used them as a symbol for Team Valiant. The three spiraling lines of gold, silver, and white unite evenly, demonstrating the need for proper balance in Team Valiant's collaboration.

SOURCE	COLOR	ATTRIBUTES
SUNLIGHT	**GOLD**	Sunlight is the easiest Source to identify—an invisible fire that always has more to give. Harnessing its power is about respect and restraint.
MOONLIGHT	**SILVER**	Moonlight is the ever-changing Source—there in the darkest hours, but sometimes elusive. Harnessing its power is about managing expectations.
STARLIGHT	**WHITE**	Starlight is the most varied of all the Sources, since each star is different. So harnessing the power of the stars is about choice—and utilizing them takes both knowledge and wisdom.

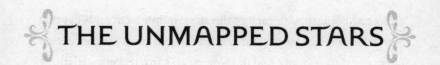

THE UNMAPPED STARS

GIVEN THAT STARLIGHT IS ONE OF THE PRIME Sources, it's no surprise that the elves spend a great deal of time mapping, naming, and studying the stars—even bottling their light.

But there are five stars that are treated *very* differently.

The "unmapped stars" are kept secret from all except the Council (and former Councillors). Knowing their locations is illegal—as is bottling their light. In fact, most elves have never even heard the stars' names:

ELEMENTINE

MARQUISEIRE

PHOSFORIEN

LUCILLIANT

CANDESIA

The reason for the secrecy is that light from the unmapped stars is actually quintessence—the highly volatile, potentially dangerous fifth element.

Each star's quintessence is a different color and texture and has unique qualities and capabilities. And understanding those differences may prove vital in the days ahead.

Which is likely why the Black Swan made sure their moonlark knew where to find every one of the unmapped stars. They've also had her leap with each of the stars' quintessences. What that knowledge might be used for is unclear—but given the connection between quintessence and the Neverseen's mysterious stellarlune project, it's likely to be significant.

WARNING:

The information on the next page can get you in <u>serious</u> trouble (trust me, I would know).

Read at your own risk!

— Sophie

ELEMENTINE:
* Silvery light.
* Least stable, but most powerful form of quintessence.
* Used to make frissyn.

MARQUISEIRE:
* Shimmering, rosy light.
* Most versatile form of quintessence.
* Breaks things down.

PHOSFORIEN:
* Opalescent light.
* Quintessence is full of life and energy.
* Optimal for DNA tests.

The Unmapped Stars

CANDESIA:

* Pale light.
* Weakest, safest quintessence.
* Can leap underwater.

LUCILLIANT:

* Icy light.
* Coldest, darkest quintessence.
* Can leap underground.

Rebel Groups

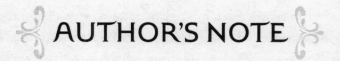

AUTHOR'S NOTE

UNLIKE IN STORIES WHERE THE HERO IS CLEARLY on the side of *good*, fighting against a villain who is clearly on the side of *bad*, Sophie has found herself caught in the middle of multiple rebellions. In fact, in the early books in the series, she even struggles to figure out who the "bad guys" are—the Council? The Black Swan? Someone else entirely?

Only as the story progresses does she discover the existence of the Neverseen and realize who she's truly fighting.

That was one of the things that fascinated me about this story. The good guys *and* the bad guys are technically both rebels, responding to the same "flaws" in the Lost Cities. (You probably noticed several of those flaws in the previous sections of this guide—and also when you read the books themselves.) The Council has been ignoring major injustices for millennia, and their world finally reached a point where someone had to step in and do something.

That's where the Black Swan and the Neverseen come in.

Yes, one group is definitely bad, and the other strives to be good—but they're both right about the problems their world is facing. They just have drastically different plans to fix the situation.

And their plans are always changing—which was another thing that made me want to write this story. To me, the scariest villains are the ones that grow and adapt, abandoning things that aren't working and changing the game again and again. And the smartest heroes are the ones who are always trying new things.

But I do realize that it can be hard to keep everything straight (especially since the books are *quite* lengthy). So the next section of this guide is sort of a cheat sheet, to catch you up on what each of the rebel groups has been up to—or what Sophie knows, at least. Since she's the one stuck in the center of it all, it seemed only fair to let her be the one to explain everything.

Think of the next few pages as her notes to herself, trying to make sense of what she's learned—so she's ready for what comes next.

THE BLACK SWAN

This is the "sign of the swan,"
which is the Black Swan's fancy symbol
(though sometimes they only use the head/neck portion).

I guess they picked their name because a <u>really</u>
long time ago, humans used black swans as an
example of "something impossible," since they
thought swans were always white. Aaaaaaand then
they discovered that black swans were a thing,
so black swans became a symbol of "something
that shouldn't exist, but does." Which, I guess, is
pretty fitting for the Black Swan, since they're
a group of rebels in a world that thought it
was too perfect to ever have a rebellion.

SHANNON MESSENGER

Plus, it gives them an excuse to use phrases like "swan song" for when they're about to take a big risk or make a sacrifice, and to put dwarven poems about swans into the little notes they give me, and use the Cygnus constellation as clues, and all kinds of other swan-related stuff.

Pretty sure by the time this is over, I'm never going to want to see a swan again.

(Or a moonlark ...)

THINGS I KNOW
ABOUT THE BLACK SWAN

* They're the "good guys." (I hope ...)

* They "created" me and hid me with humans. (And then helped Alden find me so he could bring me to the Lost Cities)

* They planted information in my brain. (And I still don't know exactly how much they hid. It pops up at random times)

* They stole two of my memories. (And only gave them back because I forced them to)

* The first memory was about "the Boy
  Who Disappeared" (who turned out to
  be Alvar).

* The second memory was about me
  manifesting as an Inflictor before I should
  have and accidentally hurting my sister.

* They've been around for a really long time.
  (But it sounds like they've been stepping
  up their game for the last few decades)

* They used to communicate with me
  through a bunch of vague notes and
  riddles. (Definitely not sad those days are
  over—though it's not like they actually tell
  me anything now. . . .)

* They have a ton of hideouts, but so far
  they've only let me see:

  * The High Seas facility (a huge
    cave on an island in the middle
    of nowhere, where they healed my
    abilities—and where they did a lot
    of the genetic work for Project
    Moonlark. They had to abandon it
    after the Neverseen tracked us there).

SHANNON MESSENGER

- Alluveterre (the underground cave we stayed in when we were banished. It's also abandoned now, since the Neverseen have a crystal that leaps to it).
- Brumevale (the lonely tower where Mr. Forkle hid after what happened in Lumenaria, which is apparently also where he first came up with the idea for Project Moonlark).
- Watchward Heath (one of Mr. Forkle's offices. It's like a giant underground egg, with walls that project what's going on with every species all over the world. There's also a 3D map of the Lost Cities).

* They're ruled by a "Collective" of five different leaders, each using weird code names and disguises:

- Mr. Forkle
- Granite
- Squall
- Blur
- Wraith

* Other members are:

  - Livvy Sonden (Physic)
  - Timkin Heks (Coiffe)
  - Tinker (No idea who she is—but
    I guess she goes by "Tinker" to
    everybody)
  - Lord Cassius Sencen (He doesn't
    have a code name, but I bet
    Keefe would say it should be "Ugh.")
  - Lady Cadence Talle (She doesn't
    have code name either—but she
    should totally be "Grump.")
  - Della Vacker (Since I'm
    apparently making up code
    names for everyone, let's go
    with "Dazzle.")

Huh … I just realized I should be including all my
friends who've sworn fealty—and me. Funny how
my brain still keeps us separate.

Well, guess I'll give us all code names while I'm at
it—and they'll be way better than the ones Keefe
tried to give us in Alluveterre!

  - Me (Moonlark)
  - Dex (Dimples)

- Keefe (Hunkyhair)
- Tam (Bangs)
- Linh (Splash)
- Biana (Sparkles)
- Fitz (Wonderboy? I don't know—
  maybe Keefe was right and it
  should be Brainwave. . . .)
- Wylie (Flare)
- Marella (Inferno)
- Maruca (Shield)

(Pretty sure this list is proof that I've been
spending too much time with Keefe)

* Jolie was also a member (and it
  feels wrong giving her a code name
  after what happened, so I'm going
  to skip that).

* The oath we swore when we joined the
  Black Swan was, "I will do everything in
  my power to help my world."

* They also gave us these black-swan
  monocle/magnifying-glass pendants to
  wear (which were really good at starting
  fires). But mine got destroyed when
  Keefe ran off to join the Neverseen,

and the one he stole back for me
turned out to have a tracker in it, so
I'm kinda done with those pendants
for now.

* The Collective all have matching
black rings filled with some sort
of special poison they can take
to completely erase their memories
if they're ever captured—and they
say it'll be okay if that happens
because they have "Proxies"
(whatever that means). Though, it
also kinda sounded like they think
I'm going to take over someday—
with my friends. I don't know how
I feel about that. . . .

* They <u>love</u> telling everyone to trust them
and be patient and spend time reading
boring books instead of doing anything
that might actually be helpful.

* We're going to win this . . . whatever
you want to call it. "Game" sounds too
fun, and "war" sounds too terrifying,
but . . . either way, we're going to win.
We have to.

SHANNON MESSENGER 373

THINGS I KNOW ABOUT MR. FORKLE

* His official name (for this identity, at least) is Mr. Errol L. Forkle, which he apparently chose because the initials spell out "elf," and because the word "Forkle" can sometimes mean "disguise" in Norwegian. (I guess he used to spend a lot of time in Norway—no idea why) The <u>L</u> stands for Loki, because he was kinda the source of some of the Loki myths—which is way too weird to think about.

* He claims he's not my biological father (despite being listed that way on certain documents). Even if that's true, he still helped create me. And he knows who my biological father is. And he refuses to tell me.

* He's a super powerful Telepath.

* He loves to start sentences with "you kids."

* He eats a lot of ruckleberries to disguise what he really looks like.

* He lies sometimes. Maybe all the time. Who knows?

* He was my annoying next-door neighbor in San Diego, always sitting in his yard rearranging his lawn gnomes (and apparently the gnomes were one of the ways he passed along messages to the Black Swan).

* He's the one who triggered my abilities. And the one who stole my missing memories. And the one who planted the information in my brain. He also rescued me from the Neverseen after they kidnapped me. And probably a bunch of other stuff I don't know about yet.

* He's Magnate Leto.

* Also Sir Astin.

* I'm sure he has other identities too. I just haven't figured out what they are yet.

* And . . . he secretly had an identical twin. Only one of them was registered (their parents didn't want them to face the scorn of being a "multiple birth"), and

they were sharing one life and switching places all the time. Sometimes I was talking to one brother, and sometimes I was talking to the other—or I was, until one of them died right in front of me in Lumenaria. I thought he was gone, but ... then Granite brought us to Brumevale, and ... there was the other Forkle. I still don't really know how to process it. But I'm glad he's still here, even if he's a little more limited now that he can't be two places at once.

* We planted a Wanderling for the Forkle-twin we lost near Trolltunga in Norway. The tree looks like it's leaning a bit, waiting for its brother—but I'm selfishly hoping it grows alone for a really long time. Maybe forever.

THINGS I KNOW ABOUT GRANITE

* He takes a powder called indurite to make himself look like an unrecognizable half-carved statue.

* But he's actually Sir Tiergan, my telepathy Mentor.

* So . . . he spent my first year or two in the Lost Cities lying to me all the time. But . . . that's how it goes when you're the moonlark, I guess.

* Huh . . . I don't really know much else about him, other than all the stuff about Prentice and Wylie—but none of that really matters for this.

THINGS I KNOW ABOUT SQUALL

* She's a Froster and covers herself in a thick layer of ice to hide her identity.

* She's actually Dex's mom (Juline)—and technically my aunt.

* She joined the Black Swan after she had the triplets and saw how much scorn they were going to grow up with (unless something changed).

* She lied to her family to hide what she was doing—especially Dex and Kesler. Unfortunately, that's how it goes with the Black Swan.

* And . . . that's pretty much it.

THINGS I KNOW ABOUT BLUR

* He's a Phaser and only lets himself partially re-form, so all I can see are blurry splotches of color sort of shaped like an elf.

* One time, I did get a slightly better glimpse of him, and I could tell he was skinny with full lips and round cheeks. But I still didn't recognize him.

* Wow. That's all I know about him—though I have a few theories for who he might be . . .

THINGS I KNOW ABOUT WRAITH

* He's a Vanisher, so all I ever see is his floating silver cloak.

* According to Della, making the body disappear while leaving the clothes visible is called a "layered vanish," and it's super hard to do.

* Huh. That's all I know. I don't even have any theories about his identity!

THINGS I KNOW
ABOUT PROJECT MOONLARK

* I'm the moonlark—which means I get to have lots of people trying to kill me.

* Calla came up with the name for the project because of the way moonlarks treat their eggs.

* She also helped the Black Swan figure out my genetics, which are mostly based off alicorn DNA. That's why I have brown eyes and can teleport. (And yeah, it's hard not to feel like "the horse girl.")

* They chose a lot of the abilities they gave me because they were hoping I'd be able to use them to heal broken minds (since the Black Swan knew some of their members might endure memory breaks—like poor Prentice).

* I grew up with humans, partly to make sure no one found me. But mostly so I'd

understand humans differently from how other elves understand them. And I guess I do, but ... I'm not sure what I'm supposed to do with that information.

* It's possible I may end up manifesting another special ability (or more than one—anything's possible at this point). But I hope not. Five is seriously enough!

* My biological mother is Councillor Oralie, which means she lied to me every time she saw me for years (and signed me up for a genetic experiment and then totally abandoned me). I also can't tell anyone who she is, because then she'd have to resign from the Council, and that would create so much chaos that it could give the Neverseen the opportunity to take control. So, lucky me—I get to be unmatchable!

* The Black Swan loves to tell me I have a choice in all of this, and I guess I do for certain things. But it's not like I can change my genetics. Or everything I've gone through. Or the fact that everyone's expecting me to be this big important

THING, and I have no idea what I'm supposed to do or how I'm supposed to do it.

* Sometimes I wonder if the real reason the Black Swan won't tell me what they're planning is because they don't actually have a PLAN. They just made their little moonlark and are expecting me to figure out the rest. Which, you know, would be pretty terrifying if I'm right. But at the same time ... I kinda think it might be better—because if they do have a PLAN, then wouldn't that mean they also knew exactly what the Neverseen were going to do and could've prevented it all from happening in the first place?

THE NEVERSEEN

The Neverseen LOVE using symbols. They might even love them more than the Black Swan loves making swan references. And this is their main one—the creepy white eye that stares at me from the sleeves of their black hooded cloaks. I swear this symbol will haunt my nightmares forever.

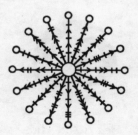

This is the "Lodestar symbol." Took us forever to figure out what it was supposed to be and how it worked—and Dex was the one who finally solved it. Each one of those little "rays" is actually a special code that can be used to leap to one of the Neverseen's hideouts. Unfortunately, by the time we figured that out, they'd abandoned all the hideouts and taken everything important away.

I sometimes call this the "Nightfall symbol," even though it's really Vespera's signature. Each one of those swirling lines is actually an elvin rune, spelling out her name. But the symbol was used to mark the entrance to her original Nightfall facility in Atlantis, so calling it the Nightfall symbol is still accurate.

Sadly, I have no idea what this symbol is supposed to be—but it was on the letter that Lady Gisela made Keefe deliver to the humans she later murdered, so I'm sure it's super important. I just hope we figure this one out before it's too late.

THINGS I KNOW ABOUT
THE NEVERSEEN

* They're evil.

* They hide behind long black cloaks with hoods.

* They have some dwarves and ogres on their side—and I wouldn't be surprised if they also have trolls.

* The gnomes hate them, though, and won't grow them any food. I don't think they have any goblins helping them either. Let's hope that doesn't change.

* They want to overthrow the Council and take over as rulers because they think they're smarter than everybody. And they don't care if people get hurt or killed in the process.

* Mr. Forkle thinks they're trying to weaken all of the intelligent species to make sure none of them could be victorious in the coming power struggle.

* They have a Technopath working with them (but I have no idea who it is).

* They have way too many leaders (and we have way too many enemies). I'm hoping that's going to turn out to be their undoing.

THINGS I KNOW ABOUT LADY GISELA

* She's Keefe's mom.

* She's also one of the main leaders of the Neverseen— for the moment, at least.

* She's a murderer. The facts are blurry, but it seems like she killed two humans not long after she had Keefe deliver a letter to them in London. And it's possible she killed Cyrah Endal—though she claims that was Gethen's doing (and that Fintan gave the order).

* Even if Gethen <u>was</u> the one to murder Cyrah, Gisela was the one who forced Cyrah to make a bunch of special starstones for her, which is why Fintan wanted to get rid of her.

* One of those starstones seems to be missing.

* Fintan and Brant had Gisela locked away in an ogre prison, which left a bunch of scars on her face (though she's gotten rid of those somehow—and it makes her skin really tight and strange).

* After she fought her way back to the top, she basically forced Vespera to work with her. So it's probably only a matter of time before there's another huge power struggle. I'm kind of hoping for that, actually.

* She's a Polyglot—and excellent at mimicking.

* It doesn't seem like she has a second ability (like most Polyglots do), but I wouldn't be surprised if she's hiding something.

* She's also really good at lying to Empaths.

* She tried to steal the alicorns several times.

* One of her plans used to be called "the Lodestar Initiative" and had its own symbol and a bunch of fancy hideouts

and stuff. But it seems like she's mostly abandoned all of that—maybe because of stuff Fintan did when he overthrew her?

* She built her own "Nightfall" facility, sealed the door with her son's blood, and created the creepy gorgodons to guard the place. I don't know what she planned to use it for—it looked like she stored all the soporidine there, but it was gone by the time we were able to sneak in. All that was left was Alvar, lying bloody and unconscious in a cell—which turned out to be another trap.

* She wrote this book called the Archetype and locked it with a special key that Keefe found hidden at Candleshade. I guess it's her long, boring explanation of all her theories—some of which are based on Vespera's ideas (but Vespera seems to think Gisela's wrong about a ton of stuff and that they actually have opposite visions). No one knows where the Archetype is right now. But we still have the key, in case we find it.

* She tried to destroy Atlantis as part of some evil test for me and Keefe, to see

if we're ready to "make hard choices."
She also tried to kill Ro, to punish King
Dimitar for the scars he gave her (and
the time she spent in his prison).

* She took Tam hostage and had Glimmer
put these weird bonds on his wrists to
force him to do whatever awful things
she wanted.

* She used Keefe for different tasks,
like having him spy on his friends or
deliver stuff for her—and then erased his
memories (or shattered the worst ones) so
he wouldn't know what he'd done.

* She also hid a tracker in Keefe's Sencen
crest pin and used it to follow him to
the Black Swan (and totally attacked her
own son during those ambushes).

* She even rigged his Imparter so she could
eavesdrop on him.

* She also loves to talk about Keefe's
"legacy," like she has this huge master
plan for him—even though she also used
to claim that she never experimented on

her son. Turns out Keefe was part of something she calls stellarlune. I don't know the specifics yet, but it seems like it had to do with exposing herself and her husband to shadowflux and quintessence before trying to have a baby—and then exposing Keefe to a whole lot more in Loamnore to "transform" him. We won't know more until Keefe wakes up.

* So she's basically the worst mother ever—and someday I'm going to make her pay for every horrible thing she's ever done. I don't know how or when yet. But it <u>will</u> happen.

THINGS I KNOW ABOUT VESPERA

* She's one of the Ancients.

* She's an Empath (but it's made her go numb).

* She spent several thousand years locked away in Lumenaria's dungeon because of the experiments she was doing on humans, trying to understand

their capacity for violence and learn how elves could effectively be more ruthless. She's the real reason the elvin-human alliance fell apart. But the Council covered that up.

* She's a master of creating illusions and worked with Luzia Vacker to design the tricks that keep the Lost Cities hidden.

* She wears a headpiece that's kind of like a really strong thinking cap and blocks everyone from being able to use their abilities on her.

* She took my human parents and used them for her horrifying experiments because she wanted to figure out why the Black Swan chose them for Project Moonlark.

* She shoved Biana through some of her mirrors in Nightfall, intentionally trying to give her scars so she'd "never be the same."

* She made Alvar open the gates to Lumenaria and made Umber open the

hidden troll hive as some sort of vendetta to expose Luzia Vacker—and had no problem cowering under a force field and then fleeing to safety when the newborn trolls turned everything bloody.

* Basically she's psychotic—and I don't think sending her back to prison is going to be enough to stop her.

THINGS I KNOW ABOUT FINTAN

* He's Ancient.

* He's a Pyrokinetic.

* He created Balefire.

* He used to be a Councillor—until he tried to teach five of his Pyrokinetic friends how to call down Everblaze, and it turned into an inferno that killed everyone except him. Pyrokinesis was banned after that, and he had to step down, since Councillors can't be Talentless.

* He trained Brant in pyrokinesis—and managed to keep Brant's identity secret

during the memory break the Council ordered.

* When I tried to heal his mind, he called down Everblaze and killed Councillor Kenric (and destroyed half of Eternalia).

* He faked his death and only revealed that he was still alive when he thought he was winning with the gnomish plague.

* He overpowered Lady Gisela and sent her to an ogre prison, becoming the new leader of the Neverseen.

* He keeps a list called Criterion, which seems to have something to do with emotions, because he made Keefe help him with it during their training sessions (when Keefe was trying to infiltrate the Neverseen).

* I don't know if he's the one who tortured Wylie, or if it was Brant—either way, I know he fully supported that disgusting interrogation.

* He showed up to the Peace Summit in Lumenaria because he knew the Council

would put him in the dungeon and he could help Gethen knock down the castle and set Vespera free.

* He let Keefe think he was stealing his cache and Kenric's cache—when Keefe fled the Neverseen. But the caches were actually fake.

* He was captured by Grady while trying to sneak away from Vespera's version of Nightfall, and he's now being held in a special prison designed to make sure he'll never have enough heat to escape.

* He's training Marella in pyrokinesis—which could be a really bad idea. But he's the only one who can help her truly learn to control her ability.

* He <u>might</u> be willing to help us with other things, since he doesn't seem all that loyal to the Neverseen now that Lady Gisela's in charge again—but his help never comes free, and I'm not sure what we can offer.

THINGS I KNOW ABOUT BRANT

* He was engaged to Jolie (who loved him more than anything).

* Everyone thought he was Talentless. But he was secretly a Pyrokinetic.

* He joined the Neverseen because he hated the Council for banning pyrokinesis and forcing him to be Talentless, since it made him a bad match and caused a ton of problems for him and Jolie.

* He tried to recruit Jolie to join the Neverseen, which was how she figured out what he was doing. She tried to get him to stop, and he lost his temper and accidentally sparked the fire that killed her (and left him brutally scarred—and more than a little unstable).

* He was the kidnapper who burned me (and Dex) during the interrogations and set the Everblaze in the Forbidden Cities.

* He let Grady and Edaline take care of him for the next sixteen years, even though he'd murdered their daughter.

* When Grady finally learned the truth and confronted him, Brant tried to kill him. Grady was stronger and made Brant burn

off his own hand before I stopped him from doing more, because I didn't want Grady to damage his sanity.

* I had to let Brant escape as part of the deal I made, to find out what the Neverseen were planning for their attack on Mount Everest, so I could warn my friends before it was too late.

* He tried to force Keefe to burn me to prove his loyalty when Keefe tried to infiltrate the Neverseen.

* He allowed himself to get captured (along with Ruy) when we used the Lodestar symbol to leap to one of their hideouts. He needed to be in Lumenaria's dungeon (with Gethen) to carry out Fintan's plan to knock down the castle.

* He was killed during the collapse of Lumenaria by Mr. Forkle, somewhat accidentally. (Apparently Mr. Forkle shoved him right as a piece of debris fell, and it crushed him.)

THINGS I KNOW ABOUT GETHEN

* He's a Telepath.

* He tried to grab me before Fitz brought me to the Lost Cities, but Mr. Forkle scared him away.

* He has a curved scar on his hand, from a dog bite he got trying to trick me into leaving the Forbidden Cities with him.

* He may have also followed me to my human school to try to grab me from there. (I swore I saw him—but I don't know if I imagined it) But Fitz was with me and took me to Everglen.

* He helped kidnap me from Havenfield— and tried to read my mind and erase my memories while I was a hostage.

* He would've killed Dex if I hadn't been able to inflict and leap us away.

* He let himself get arrested during the battle on Mount Everest, hoping he would end up in Lumenaria's dungeon

with enough time to build up his mental energy and use it to knock down the castle with his outward channeling, setting Vespera free.

* He might've killed Cyrah Endal.

* He killed Mr. Forkle—using the sword he broke out of the stone in his Lumenaria cell. I guess he was aiming for Councillor Oralie, and Mr. Forkle took the blow instead.

* He led the attack when Umber used shadowflux to torture me (and Fitz).

* Sometimes I think he's the villain we should be focusing on. I bet he's a Keeper and knows all the Neverseen's secrets—and I _know_ I could shove past his mental barriers if everyone wasn't always trying to protect me when I'm around him.

* I also wouldn't be surprised if he's hoping Lady Gisela and Vespera will take each other out and leave him the new leader of the Neverseen.

THINGS I KNOW ABOUT ALVAR

* He's Fitz and Biana's older brother.

* He used to be an Emissary for the Council, assigned to the ogres.

* He helped his dad search the Forbidden Cities for me—until Fitz took over. Sometimes he was kind of nice to me. Especially when Alden's mind was broken.

* Keefe used to look up to him.

* He's a Vanisher. And I'm pretty sure he used that ability to spy on his dad (and his brother). Especially when they were trying to find me.

* I'm also pretty sure he helped the Neverseen kidnap me.

* I <u>know</u> he helped the Neverseen capture Wylie.

* He claims he joined the Neverseen because of the Vacker legacy—and I still don't know exactly what that means. But . . . I

also think he was jealous of his siblings. Especially Fitz.

* He had amnesia for a while, after we found him unconscious and injured in Nightfall. And the Council didn't know how to punish someone who didn't remember their crimes. So they put him on house arrest to monitor him and see if he'd changed.

* I'll admit, he totally fooled me. I thought that since he couldn't remember all the reasons he'd joined the Neverseen anymore, he'd finally realized that he'd picked the wrong side and wanted to change. But then his memories came flooding back, and ... he chose to go ahead with his awful plan and let the Neverseen into Everglen during the Celestial Festival.

* Fitz almost killed him—twice—that night. And the second time, Alvar actually did look dead. But I guess he was using his skills to feign death so he could escape.

* Last time I saw him was at Candleshade, and ... he didn't look good. I guess he's dying from the stuff Fitz did to him

during the troll battle at Everglen. In fact, he may already be dead now. That's why I agreed to his deal and let him get away in exchange for a little information. He's not going to be able to hurt anyone again. I hope ...

THINGS I KNOW ABOUT RUY

* He was expelled from Foxfire as a Level Four and sent to Exillium—which he ended up getting expelled from too.

* His parents worked in Mysterium.

* Nobody knows what he looks like—even after the Black Swan captured him! I guess he wears an addler to make sure no one can really see his face, and he's destroyed any records of his appearance.

* He's a Psionipath.

* He helped the Neverseen spread the gnomish plague by putting force fields around infected trees.

* He helped capture Wylie.

* He shielded Gethen, Fintan, and Brant (and probably Vespera) under force fields when they collapsed the dungeon in Lumenaria to free Vespera and bring down the castle.

* His ability makes it <u>really</u> hard to fight the Neverseen—even when Tam and Wylie are there to break down his force fields. But that may be changing.

* Tam did something to him during the battle at Everglen—something with shadows that seems like it might've wrecked Ruy's ability. Though I don't know how long that's going to last.

THINGS I KNOW ABOUT UMBER

* Umber wasn't her real name.

* She was a Shade.

* She could control shadowflux.

* She helped abduct Wylie.

* She . . . hurt me pretty bad. Let's just leave it at that.

* She got crushed at Everglen by the newborn trolls, and the Neverseen just left her there. Didn't try to get her help. Didn't even take away her body. I guess that's what you get for allying with selfish, evil people—and it's not like Umber didn't deserve it. But it's still kinda sad.

THINGS I KNOW ABOUT TRIX

* Trix isn't his real name.

* He's a Guster.

* He helped kidnap me—and helped abduct Wylie, too.

* He used to be friends with Umber.

* So I'm pretty sure it's safe to say I'm not going to like this guy.

THINGS I KNOW ABOUT THE NEVERSEEN'S PLAN

* Honestly? Nothing.

* I mean, I have a ton of bits and pieces—and a few theories based on everything.

* But none of it actually comes together into anything coherent.

* And their plans are constantly changing, so nothing I've learned matters anyway.

* I _do_ know they're a million steps ahead of me. And it's _seriously_ frustrating.

* BUT . . . maybe that doesn't matter.

* Maybe the real trick is to stop wasting time trying to figure out what they're planning and come up with a plan of our own—make the Neverseen deal with _that_.

* Maybe that's the secret. . . .

The Intelligent Species

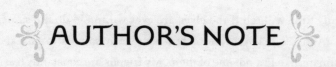

AUTHOR'S NOTE

ANYONE WHO'S READ THE KEEPER SERIES KNOWS
that there are only six intelligent species in the Lost Cities:

ELVES
GOBLINS
OGRES
GNOMES
TROLLS
DWARVES

Humans lost that classification after they violated their treaty
with the elves—that's why the human world is called the Forbidden
Cities. So you may have looked at this book's table of contents
and thought, *Wait—why did Shannon put the human section with
everyone else? They're not an intelligent species!* And I assure you, it's
not a mistake—nor is it because I wasn't sure where else to put
that section.

The truth is, while the elves have valid reasons to be concerned
about some of the things humans do (like crime, pollution, wars,
etc.), Sophie also discovered in *Nightfall* that the elves have hidden
a *very* dark secret.

The kind of secret that might have prevented humans from
losing their status as "intelligent species" if the Council hadn't
covered it up.

So, I put humans in the section where they rightly belong.

Only time will tell if the elves are ever willing to do the same.

(And yes, I *am* aware of how strange it sounds to talk about humans like I'm not one of them. My friends are constantly teasing me about it. Writing is a weird job! ☺)

GOBLINS

CAPITAL CITY:

Dorarspadera

(translates to Gildingham in the Enlightened Language)

RULED BY:

Queen Hylda

CULTURE:

The first time Sophie saw goblins, Fitz told her they were "the most dangerous creatures you'll ever meet." And while the ogres might take exception to that, Fitz definitely wasn't wrong. Goblins start battle training as toddlers, and focus heavily on weapons and war tactics throughout their lives. They also have heightened senses to detect threats or intruders (though their senses *can* be fooled by those who know certain tricks). All of which is why they make excellent bodyguards for the Council—and for Sophie and her friends. But the goblins' military-driven ways are only one side of their culture. They also have a tremendous appreciation for beauty and art, as is evidenced by the delicate, shimmering architecture of their capital city. They don't need their buildings to be strong, or to provide protection. Instead, they prefer to live somewhere that inspires awe—somewhere *worth* defending. And if peace truly became a reality, the goblins would happily set down their throwing stars and swords and celebrate that no more fallen soldiers would be added to their Hall of Heroes. Queen Hylda only keeps her forces poised for a fight because she fears that one is coming (particularly with the ogres, who have long been the major threat to the goblins' safety). The goblin queen does everything in her power to ensure that if a war should happen, her people are armed, ready—and victorious.

RELATIONSHIP WITH THE ELVES:

The elvin-goblin treaty is one of the strongest of all the intelligent species' treaties, which is why the Council trusts the goblins to be their personal bodyguards (and why they used the goblins for security in Lumenaria). Still, the relationship between elves and goblins has its limitations, particularly now that numerous goblins have lost their lives, between the Neverseen's attack at Lumenaria and the ogre attack at Havenfield. The situation may dissolve further if no solution is found for what some are beginning to call "the human conundrum," with human populations soaring and causing increased pollution and destruction to the planet. The goblins haven't shown signs of being power-hungry or ambitious, nor have they demonstrated any desire to be the ultimate leaders over the elves. But they won't allow anyone (ogres, trolls, humans, dwarves, gnomes—or elves) to cause harm to their world or their people. And if they *did* decide to break their treaty with the elves, it would be disastrous—particularly if any bodyguards turned against their charges.

GOBLIN BODYGUARDS

Sandor

ASSIGNMENT: *Bodyguard to Sophie Foster*

QUALIFICATIONS: *Before being assigned to the Lost Cities, Sandor was in charge of his own squadron in the goblin army.*

KNOWN FOR: *His high-pitched, squeaky voice; overprotective personality; and rigid, disciplined approach to training and battle.*

NOTES: *Sophie isn't always a fan of being followed around by a seven-foot-tall, stubborn (and exhausting) goblin. But she and Sandor have grown quite close over time, fighting side by side during battles and trusting each other with their lives. Sandor has had several brushes with death since he started protecting Sophie—and* *he'll surely face many more, given the Neverseen's ruthless tactics. Yet his concern is centered on Sophie's safety—not his own. He did consider requesting reassignment once, after the Neverseen's most brutal attack on Sophie, but only because he feared he'd failed his charge. Sandor also appears to be in a relationship with Grizel (Fitz Vacker's bodyguard), but he's careful to remain professional and not let any feelings interfere with his duties.*

Grizel

ASSIGNMENT: *Bodyguard to Fitz Vacker*

QUALIFICATIONS: *Before volunteering to serve in the Lost Cities, Grizel was in charge of a squadron in the goblin army.*

KNOWN FOR: *Her husky voice and stealthy way of moving—as well as her teasing personality.*

NOTES: *Grizel is leaner than other goblins, with a natural grace and a light step—but she's still every bit as deadly. Possibly more so, given her gift for sneaking up on others. She's also highly competitive and loves a challenge, whether it's on the battlefield or in a friendly wager—and if she wins the latter, there will be creative consequences. Rumors suggest that she and Sandor are romantically involved, but Grizel hasn't let whatever may or may not be going on between them affect her behavior. She's also been one of the primary proponents of the battle training that Sophie and her friends have been working through, believing the elves should learn to fight and protect themselves as much as they can.*

Woltzer

ASSIGNMENT: *Bodyguard to Biana Vacker*

QUALIFICATIONS: *Before being assigned to the Lost Cities, Woltzer served in Queen Hylda's palace.*

KNOWN FOR: *Regularly getting scolded by Sandor for failing to keep control of his charge.*

NOTES: *Given how often Biana manages to sneak away from Woltzer, it may seem as though he's somehow less competent at his duties than the other bodyguards. But protecting a Vanisher is no easy task—particularly someone as sneaky and strong-willed as Biana. And Woltzer has diligently fought to keep Biana safe, despite the trouble she causes him. Many do suspect, however, that Woltzer is eagerly hoping for a transfer to a new assignment as soon as possible.*

Lovise

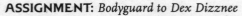

ASSIGNMENT: *Bodyguard to Dex Dizznee*

QUALIFICATIONS: *As the oldest of the goblins assigned to guard Sophie and her friends, Lovise has had decades of service in the goblin army. The only reason she hasn't been placed in charge of her own squadron is because she prefers assignments that are more solitary.*

KNOWN FOR: *Her abundance of patience, which is particularly essential for her assignment, given that she spends a great deal of time around Dex's triplet siblings.*

NOTES: *Lovise was severely injured during one of the Neverseen's recent attacks, and yet she refused anything more than temporary battlefield remedies for her wounds until she'd reorganized the security. She then returned to Gildingham for proper treatment, and while she was there, Queen Hylda gave her the option of being reassigned. But Lovise has grown quite fond of Dex and chose to remain with her charge. She also became one of the few goblins to have visited a Forbidden City after going with Sophie, Dex, and Sandor to London.*

Cadoc

ASSIGNMENT: *Bodyguard to Edaline Ruewen*

QUALIFICATIONS: *Before being assigned to the Lost Cities, Cadoc served* in Queen Hylda's palace and also taught battle tactics at one of the goblin's military academies. All in his regiment agree he's one of the best in their ranks.

KNOWN FOR: Cadoc is the strong, silent type—and so tall and muscular that he manages to make Sandor look petite.

NOTES: Cadoc survived the ogre attack that killed Brielle—but only because Havenfield's resident T. rex broke free from her enclosure and went on an ogre-chomping rampage. And he was seriously injured in the fight. He now works to protect both Grady and Edaline as much as he can, feeling it's his duty to honor Brielle's sacrifice.

Brielle

ASSIGNMENT: Bodyguard to Grady Ruewen

QUALIFICATIONS: Before volunteering to serve in the Lost Cities, Brielle was second-in-command for a series of goblin squadrons, which is likely why she offered to be a bodyguard. Serving time with the elves can often lead to appointments in Queen Hylda's palace.

KNOWN FOR: Unflinching commitment and loyalty—and her long, curly hair. She also saved Grady Ruewen.

NOTES: Brielle was killed during an ogre attack at Havenfield after taking on four ogres at once so Grady could get to Edaline. Three ogres fell to her sword. The fourth ended her life—and was captured and killed by King Dimitar during his interrogation (despite Queen Hylda's demand that the ogres turn the murderer over to her). Brielle's aurified body now stands in the Hall of Heroes, a permanent testimony to her bravery, loyalty, and sacrifice.

OGRES

CAPITAL CITY:

Sadlitzagvatka

(translates to Ravagog in the Enlightened Language)

RULED BY:

King Dimitar

Queen Gundula

CULTURE:

The ogres have proven time and again that they're one of the more volatile, aggressive species on the planet, and many aspects of their culture could definitely be considered extreme. Their work camps are known to push workers until they collapse. Bloody sparring matches are a regular occurrence—even with their king. In fact, ogre leaders aren't elected, but rather must fight their way to the position through deadly rounds of sparring. Even the ogres' homeland was stolen long ago from the gnomes—and the ogres made sure to tear down the trees and poison the river in case anyone tried to help the gnomes return. So it's no surprise that weapons and battle training feature prominently in the ogres' lives. Warriors famously wear a minimum amount of armor to prove how little protection they require, and scars are celebrated. The army is organized to ensure that the king reigns supreme, with all ranks reporting to him—and select Mercadirs (who hold no actual power) are in charge of seeing that his orders are carried out. Ogre warriors are able to utilize certain skills, like the *grusom-daj* (where their brains transmit a high-pitched frequency to trigger pain) and phase-shifting (using a gadget to shift the force of gravity to launch themselves to safety). But the ogres' greatest military (and medical) advancements are actually a result of their incredible biochemistry (which also affects much of their architecture). Substances like aromark (used for homing devices), reveldust (used to detect the presence of microbes), *Bucollosisia* (the bacterium that the Neverseen used to make soporidine), ethreium (another type of tracker), and numerous other microbes are utilized to tremendous effect. Even their Markchains (similar to the elves' registry pendants) rely on special bacteria to identify whether someone has permission to be in Ravagog. And Mercadirs who commit serious offenses find themselves punished with a shamkniv (a special kind of dagger) dipped in flesh-eating bacteria. And while all of that may paint ogres as violent, ruthless creatures (and some have definitely played that role), ogres are also family-oriented, creative, clever, and fiercely loyal to their own people. They've also recently become more willing to cooperate with others. Whether that will be a permanent change or whether they'll return to their warmongering habits is yet to be seen.

RELATIONSHIP WITH THE ELVES:

The original ogre-elvin treaty was somewhat of a farce, since it was drafted while the king of the ogres was threatening the gnomes. After the ogres stole Serenvale and burned down the Panakes trees, they discovered the drakostomes—a deadly plague of nematodes that could wipe out the gnomish species in one go. As a result, the elves were forced to make certain concessions—and those concessions allowed the ogres to restrict the elves from entering Ravagog (except in very rare circumstances), and to cause problems for many of the other intelligent species (particularly the goblins and trolls). Humans further complicated the situation, fueling the ogres' drive for more land and power. So when the Neverseen approached King Dimitar with a cruel plan to finally unleash the drakostomes and force the gnomes into servitude in Ravagog (simultaneously gaining a workforce *and* dealing a blow to the Lost Cities), the ogre king jumped at the opportunity—and the plan would have succeeded if Sophie Foster and her friends hadn't infiltrated Ravagog and learned how to find a cure. Half the ogre capital was destroyed when King Dimitar tried to prevent them from escaping. And with his army depleted (and the plague no longer a threat), Dimitar was forced into a new round of treaty negotiations. He seemed somewhat humbled in those meetings—even agreed to everyone's demands and asked only for his people to be left alone (particularly by the elves). Even more surprising: When Keefe Sencen visited Ravagog and challenged King Dimitar to a sparring match—and won—Dimitar assigned his daughter (Princess Romhilda) to move to the Lost Cities to serve as Keefe's bodyguard. And while Ro has strong opinions about much of elvin culture, she's actually formed several friendships and seems to be a true elvin ally. Even the Neverseen's vicious attack on the ogre princess in Atlantis didn't reignite tensions between the elves and the ogres—and some of the ogres who'd defected to the Neverseen temporarily cooperated with Sophie and her friends during the battle at Everglen with the newborn trolls. All of which could be a turning point for both species.

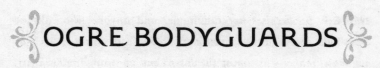

Princess Romhilda (Ro)

ASSIGNMENT: *Bodyguard to Keefe Sencen*

QUALIFICATIONS: *Ro has been training for battle since she was a month old—and being the princess meant she had to fight harder than everyone to prove she belonged. She bears a deep scar down the center of her back from her father's sword—the mark of a leader, and proof that she's held her own against the king.*

KNOWN FOR: *Colorful hair and painted claws, her snarky personality, brutal honesty, and hatred of anything that sparkles (despite the tattoo on her wrist declaring, Sparkles Rule!—all that tattoo proves is that Ro is never one to say no to a bet).*

NOTES: *Ro despises her full name, and anyone who calls her Romhilda does so at their own peril. She also seems intent on playing matchmaker—assuming she doesn't end up strangling Keefe first. Her ex-boyfriend (Cadfael) is one of the ogres who defected to the Neverseen. And she's (somewhat secretly) married to Botros. Her father arranged the marriage in the hope that it would prevent his two greatest warriors from slaughtering each other when it came time to claim his throne. Unfortunately, it seems like the marriage may simply make Bo and Ro try to kill each other much earlier.*

Botros (Bo)

ASSIGNMENT: *Bodyguard to Sophie Foster*
QUALIFICATIONS: *Bo is one of King Dimitar's best Mercadirs and has been preparing for battle his entire life.*

KNOWN FOR: *His less-than-cuddly personality and aversion to senti-ment (and hugs!). Bo believes that warriors are meant to be fearsome, ruthless, cunning, and merciless, and he doesn't want to get close to Sophie, so he can better protect her.*

NOTES: *Like his wife, Bo prefers to be called by his nickname—and he's not exactly thrilled about his marriage. Nor is he excited to be serving in the Lost Cities—with a goblin as his supervisor. But he's loyal to his king. And he seems to be slowly growing to appreciate the elves, even agreeing to protect Linh Song—and now her brother, Tam, as well.*

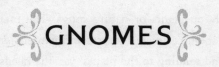

GNOMES

CAPITAL CITY:

Their original homeland was Serenvale—but it was stolen by the ogres, and the gnomes now live scattered throughout the Lost Cities (or the Neutral Territories).

RULED BY:

The elvin Council

(At times, the gnomes may assign one or several of their own to speak for them—like Thales the Sower. But primarily, they defer to the Councillors.)

CULTURE:

Gnomes are incredibly industrious creatures, requiring almost no sleep (only about ten minutes a day). They also draw their nourishment from the sun and only eat when it's something worthwhile (like starkflower stew!). Gnomes can live for thousands of years—and when the last of their energy finally fades, they shift into trees. But if they choose to shift early (when life still remains within them), they become Panakes trees (also known as "the Brave Ones"), and their sacrificed energy makes the Panakes bloom with special healing blossoms. Given how plantlike gnomes are, it's no surprise that their culture revolves around nature: Their language sounds like rustling leaves; their clothes are woven from different grasses, flowers, leaves, and barks; and their medicine relies entirely on plants or nature songs. The majority of their time is also spent caring for forests and gardens, singing soothing songs, and tending to the plants' various needs. As a result, gnomes are responsible for growing all the foods eaten in the Lost Cities. They're also happy to help the elves with numerous other tasks and chores. But the gnomes definitely *aren't* servants—and would never cooperate if they felt unappreciated or forced. They simply prefer to keep themselves busy. Gnomes can be tremendously productive and can accomplish more in a few hours than most elves can in days. They're also able to see elvin Vanishers by detecting the glints of pollen that cling to them. When gnomes need to travel somewhere, they're able to sing to the roots of the nearby trees, creating a tunnel underground and coaxing the roots to pull them through at rapid speeds, heading anywhere they'd like—except Ravagog. The ogres destroyed the root system to prevent the gnomes from visiting their former homeland.

RELATIONSHIP WITH THE ELVES:

The gnomes have an incredibly strong alliance with the elves, given that they live with them—but they also came tremendously close to a full-fledged rebellion. The Ancient Councillors hid the truth about the drakostomes, as well as the truth about what happened to the original Panakes trees, and the truth about the gnomish leaders who lost their lives and became the Four Seasons Tree. So when the Neverseen convinced the ogres to unleash the plague, the gnomes blamed the Council for not warning them. They even organized a strike and a protest—until the Councillors finally told them *everything*, including the fact that the Ancient gnomish leaders had made them promise to keep the plague secret, fearing the knowledge would put the gnomes in greater danger. If Sophie Foster and her friends—along with Calla—hadn't infiltrated Ravagog and discovered how to create a new Panakes, the gnomes might've been forced to live as slaves for the ogres in Ravagog—or perished. And after everything settled (and everyone suffering from the plague had been cured), the Council offered to help the gnomes establish their own homeland. But the majority of the gnomes chose to remain in the Lost Cities. Some still roam free in the Neutral Territories, but most stay close to Havenfield, to be near their beloved Panakes.

GNOMISH BODYGUARDS

Calla

ASSIGNMENT: *Calla wasn't a bodyguard—but as a member of the Black Swan (and a part of Project Moonlark from the very beginning), she often played the role of Sophie's protector.*

QUALIFICATIONS: *Calla was an expert on plant hybridization, which made her incredibly valuable to the Black Swan's genetic experiment.*

KNOWN FOR: *Her grandmotherly ways, gentle songs, brilliantly designed reveriebells, and delicious starkflower stew.*

NOTES: *One of Calla's many roles in Project Moonlark was to keep the Black Swan grounded and ensure they never strayed away from what was natural, or lost sight of the fact that they were sparking the life of an innocent girl. She lived to be four thousand, three hundred, and twenty-nine years old before she sacrificed herself by turning into a Panakes tree to cure the plague. Her Panakes stands on its own hill at Havenfield and has long, sweeping branches (similar to those of a weeping willow); braided bark; star-shaped leaves; and an abundance of pinkish, purplish, bluish flowers. Her tree is cared for by many, but particularly by her moonlark, who often pours bowls of starkflower stew into the ground for her roots and sleeps under her branches, soaking up her soothing songs.*

Flori

ASSIGNMENT: *Bodyguard to Sophie Foster*

EXPERIENCE: *Her great-great-grandaunt Calla trained Flori personally in many valuable ways.*

KNOWN FOR: *Her eager spirit, loyal heart, fierce fighting, and healing songs.*

NOTES: *Flori believes that everyone has a song within them—even if they don't think of it as music—and that each life has a rhythm of breaths and a heartbeat, creating a melody that can be drawn on for strength, healing, and comfort. She created the song that finally calmed Sophie's echoes from the Neverseen's shadowflux attack by carefully drawing inspiration from vesperlace, dimmetines, respitillis, and hushspurs. The Panakes tree is also believed to sprout twice as many blossoms whenever Flori sings to it.*

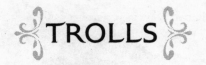

TROLLS

CAPITAL CITY:

Weeriiduulooaa

(translates to Marintrylla in the Enlightened Language)

RULED BY:

Empress Pernille

CULTURE:

Trolls age in reverse, meaning their bodies shrink with time instead of growing—which is only possible because they develop more like marsupials. Babies are born before they've fully developed and are then implanted into a hive to gestate further, finally hatching when there's an eclipse. The trollish birthing process isn't a secret, but the location of their hives *is*, since other species (the ogres in particular) have proven to be deadly to the unborn babies. Trolls have seven distinct stages throughout the course of their lives, all of which have different physical and mental attributes. Newborns are the strongest physically, the weakest mentally, and the most ferocious and deadly. And as the trolls pass from stage to stage, their strength fades and their mental capacity enhances. As a result, Stage Four is considered the Prime Stage—the stage when a troll's mental and physical strength are nearly even (which makes them less useful as warriors and ideally fit for diplomatic assignments). By their final stages, trolls are small, strange creatures with slower minds—though their years of experience often make them the most qualified to lead. (Empress Pernille is a Stage Six.) The trolls are a battle-focused species (like goblins and ogres) and have an incredibly strong army (most of which are Stage Two trolls). Part of their training involves naming their weapons, to give them meaning and significance.

RELATIONSHIP WITH THE ELVES:

Until recently, the trolls had a neutral relationship with the elves, neither particularly friendly nor notably hostile. Empress Pernille made herself available whenever the Council called upon her (and even sent Tarina to be one of Sophie's interspeciesial bodyguards) but rarely—if ever—invited any elves to Marintrylla. The Council used to assume this was because the trolls simply preferred to keep to themselves. But it turned out that the trolls had been relying on secret alliances. Through Tarina, Empress Pernille formed such an alliance with Sophie Foster (which allowed Sophie to save the prematurely born alicorns by incubating them in a specially built troll hive). And a previous empress formed a similar alliance with Luzia Vacker, after seeing how little the elvin Council had done for the Ancient gnomes. Luzia had created many of the illusions that keep the Lost Cities hidden, and the trolls needed Luzia to help them hide their hives after a brutal ogre attack. Luzia hid one hive at Everglen (her first property) and another at Dawnheath after she moved—and Luzia claims she thought the hive at Everglen had been sealed and abandoned. But it was later discovered that the trolls continued to use the hive for genetic experiments, trying to design an even deadlier newborn army. This shocking truth was exposed by the

Neverseen while everyone in the Lost Cities watched—right before the mutant newborns broke free, causing a bloody battle. Sophie and her friends fought bravely along with their bodyguards (including Tarina) and managed to stop the newborns from escaping. But the Council has been left in a tricky situation. The trolls' experiments violated their treaty. But the trolls also played a vital role in resetting the Timeline to Extinction by helping the baby alicorns. Plus, no one wants another Peace Summit to renegotiate the trolls' treaty while the Neverseen are free (after what happened in Lumenaria). So for the moment, no punishments have been enacted—though Tarina has returned to Marintrylla indefinitely.

TROLLISH BODYGUARD

Tarina

ASSIGNMENT: *Bodyguard to Sophie Foster*

QUALIFICATIONS: *As a Stage Four troll, Tarina has had an abundance of battle and weapons training, but she also has the mental capacity to work with the other bodyguards without any problems (particularly since one of them is an ogre).*

KNOWN FOR: *Creating an alliance with Sophie (and helping save the baby alicorns).*

NOTES: *Tarina has amazing reflexes, often moving as if her bones are made of rubber, and she's an equally impressive fighter.*

Her weapon of choice (a cross between a scythe and an ax, with a sharp point on the end of the pole for stabbing) is named Long Shot, as a reminder that even when all hope feels lost, she can continue fighting.

DWARVES

CAPITAL CITY:

Nymtyranyth

(translates to Loamnore in the Enlightened Language)

RULED BY:

Queen Nubiti (though her appointment is incredibly recent)

CULTURE:

Dwarves are rarely seen aboveground, since the light is too bright for their sensitive eyes—and with their pointed noses and lengthy claws, they're much better suited for tunneling. Clothing and adornments are often minimal for their species, since their bodies are covered in thick fur—though the former dwarven king wore a pair of white, furry pants (since it was considered a sign of power and strength for King Enki to be waxed bare). The dwarves' new queen has yet to continue this practice, and it's unclear whether or not she will, or whether King Enki's betrayal proves the need for a fresh tradition. Dwarven hearing is incredibly powerful, allowing them to monitor conversations both above and below ground simultaneously—and if someone on the surface needs a dwarf's help, all they have to do is stomp in a prearranged pattern. The dwarves are also incredibly talented at mining. In fact, they're the only creatures capable of mining magsidian (an exceedingly rare onyxlike stone, apparently made from shadowflux). As a result, the dwarves use magsidian much like the ogres use their Markchains. Visitors are only welcome in Loamnore if magsidian is detected, and the dwarves severely limit who they give pendants to. Magsidian can also serve a variety of other purposes, depending on how it's carved. For example, a magsidian flask will refill itself by drawing water from the air, and a small piece can also change which direction a compass points, or be used for light leaping (though the leap *won't* be pleasant). The dwarves also mine ethertine (believed to be made of quintessence), which is almost as rare as magsidian but less useful and therefore less valuable. King Enki had an ethertine crown (in addition to his traditional crown, made from tredgeon carapace) and chose to sacrifice the crown as part of his betrayal. The dwarves spend less time on battle training than other species do, since they rely on their natural defenses more than weapons. (When threatened, dwarves can form deep cracks in the earth by stomping and can control which direction the crack spreads.) As a result, there's an abundance of dwarven art, songs, poems, writings, and numerous other creations—some of which may seem a bit strange, but all are remarkable in their own way.

RELATIONSHIP WITH THE ELVES:

The dwarves have teamed up with elves many times throughout history, like when they helped hollow out the Himalayas to build the Sanctuary, or when they designed and constructed Exile. The elves have trusted them implicitly, even putting the dwarves in charge of Exile's security. And any time the Neverseen caused destruction in the Lost Cities, the Council turned to the dwarves for help. King Enki even assigned Nubiti to be one of Sophie's bodyguards (and four other dwarves were assigned to Tam and Linh). Over time, though—and mostly without the Councillors realizing—the Council lost their dwarven support, with a number of dwarves even joining the Neverseen. King Enki first turned his support to the Black Swan, providing them with supplies and dwarves to assist with their projects. But when the Black Swan's moonlark failed to achieve the level of victory King Enki had been hoping for, he turned to an alliance with the Neverseen, even going so far as to help the rebels hold several members of the Council hostage and sacrificing his magsidian throne—and his ethertine crown—for Lady Gisela's mysterious "stellarlune" project. But the battle turned against him, with many dwarves remining loyal to the elves, and King Enki was captured by Nubiti before he could get away. He is now serving a life sentence in Exile's somnatorium, and Queen Nubiti (who earned the title as the one who overthrew the king) is now the dwarves' leader. Many hope that her rule will bring forth positive change, and a new era of peace between the elves and the dwarves.

DWARVEN BODYGUARDS

Queen Nubiti

ASSIGNMENT: *Previously a bodyguard to Sophie Foster*

EXPERIENCE: *Nubiti is both a fierce fighter and a tremendously quick thinker, both of which serve her well in battle.*

KNOWN FOR: *Overthrowing King Enki and becoming the new queen of the dwarves.*

NOTE: *Nubiti has yet to assign Sophie a replacement dwarven bodyguard, likely because she's still rooting out the traitors from the dwarven world and determining who she can trust.*

NOTE: *Tam and Linh are also protected by Elidyr, Opher, Timur, and Urre, but these four dwarves remain primarily underground and have not shared anything about themselves with their charges.*

HUMANS

CAPITAL CITY:

Too many to list

RULED BY:

Definitely too many to list—and constantly changing!

CULTURE:

Compared to the intelligent species (which the elves do not classify humans as), humans have relatively short life spans—and many elves believe that this gives humans a more "short-term" focus, causing them to overlook significant problems (like their pollution and destruction of the planet). Humans also do not have a single culture, language, or government—a notable difference that gives them an incredible diversity of cuisines, arts, music, fashion, customs, and traditions to enjoy and experience. But these differences also create distinct national and societal divisions. Humans sometimes also discriminate for other reasons (like background, appearance, wealth, and systems of beliefs), which has caused a number of serious problems for their world—at times even leading to further divisions and war. And yet, all of this is a *tremendous* oversimplification of the "human experience" and does not even begin to capture the depth of their unique challenges and struggles—as well as their contributions, gifts, and talents. Sadly, though, it's the full extent of what elves (and the other intelligent species) are taught about humanity.

RELATIONSHIP WITH THE ELVES:

Contact with humans is forbidden (which is why elves call the human world "the Forbidden Cities")—and they've gone to great lengths to ensure that humans have no knowledge of their existence (or of any of the intelligent species—as well as many of the protected species). All of the Lost Cities are hidden by numerous illusions and shielded by a variety of security measures—and the elves have also spread myths, legends, and stories to make humans think of them as "silly" and "magical" and "make-believe." That way, even if humans were to accidentally discover the Lost Cities, they'd discount what they were seeing. But the relationship between humans and elves wasn't always this way. Long, long ago, humans *were* classified as an intelligent species. In fact, the elves built Atlantis as a merging point for their two worlds—a city where elves and humans could peacefully exist together, and learn from each other, and inspire each other, and form friendships and connections. The Unity Fountain in Atlantis remains a reminder of this brief time period—before everything went wrong. And while elvin history books tell a tale about the humans' greed for power and the violent uprising they were planning (which led to the elves' decision to engineer the tidal wave "catastrophe" and sink Atlantis), recent discoveries have unearthed the reasons *why* the humans began their rebellion—and the elves were very much to blame. Vespera was fascinated by the humans' capacity for "ruthlessness" and felt that if elves didn't learn to be the same way, the humans would eventually overthrow them. So she began conducting evil experiments on humans in a secret facility under Atlantis in an attempt to understand their propensity for violence—and when the humans started noticing that people were going "missing" and tried to get the Council to intervene, the Councillors refused to believe that such monstrosities could be happening. As a result, the humans banded together, planning to overthrow the elves—which then led to the elves' disappearing to avoid a war. And even though both species have continued to thrive without each other, it's hard not to wonder how much better things would be if they'd been able to keep working together. That's one of the reasons why the Human Assistance Program was created (a program where those with the Council's permission would enter the Forbidden Cities disguised as humans, in order to advance human wisdom and potentially gain knowledge in return). But all too often, the information shared led to troubling human innovations (particularly in the case of weapons—which infuriated the goblins and ogres), and the elves eventually canceled the program, fearing it was causing more harm than good. Since then, the elves have done their best to pretend that humans don't exist—all while the other intelligent species have grown increasingly concerned about how much land the humans are claiming and how much damage their pollution is causing. At one point, some even proposed moving the humans to a new sort of "Sanctuary" to contain them *and* protect them—but the Council rejected the idea, knowing the humans would consider it to be imprisonment (and it would be). Despite making the right choice, the Council has taken no other actions to remedy the situation, which is one reason why the Black Swan created Project Moonlark and chose to have Sophie Foster grow up in the Forbidden Cities. Yes, she was also hidden from the Council that way, but the true benefit was to give Sophie an alternate perspective by allowing her to experience the human world without any elvin biases. As a result, Sophie not only understands humans in a way no one else in the Lost Cities can, but she also views the elvin world through a different lens and is able to identify problems and injustices that others have grown too accustomed to notice. And perhaps someday, she'll fulfill her creators' hopes, and change both worlds for the better.

SOPHIE'S HUMAN FAMILY

William (Will) David Foster

*(also known as Connor Freeman—and another
alias kept classified for his protection)*

ROLE: *Sophie's human father*

QUALIFICATIONS: *Kind, affectionate, hardworking, balanced, and
generous—and someone who would never use his children to gain prestige.*

KNOWN FOR: *Calling Sophie "Soybean."*

NOTES: *The Black Swan needed Sophie's existence to remain "low-
key" to avoid detection—and they knew there would be many things
about her that could garner quite a bit of attention. So they carefully*

searched for a loving couple who wouldn't exploit their daughter for fame or profit, finally settling on the Fosters. After Sophie was moved to the Lost Cities, her human father's memories of her were erased, and he was given a new job, a new name, and what humans would consider a "comfortable" existence—as well as a house with a yard big enough for the dog their family had wished for. The Freemans seemed to be thriving in their new lives—until Vespera escaped from Lumenaria and took both parents hostage to use for her horrible experiments. No one knows exactly what they endured, but it had to be terrible. Once they were rescued, their memories were erased in a unique way to ensure flashbacks would never be triggered, and the Council now keeps a closer eye on Sophie's human family to better ensure their safety.

Emma Iris Foster

*(also known as Kate Freeman—and another
alias kept classified for her protection)*

ROLE: *Sophie's human mother*

QUALIFICATIONS: *Loving, intelligent, cautious, humble, and skeptical
about human medicine—as well as someone who needed fertility assistance in order to have a baby.*

KNOWN FOR: *Her homemade fettuccine and tendency to worry.*

NOTES: *Many human medicines have dangerous side effects, so the
Black Swan searched for parents who wouldn't expose their daughter
to too many chemicals during her time in the Forbidden Cities. But
they also needed someone who would get Sophie treatment if the need*

arose, and the Fosters struck that perfect balance. The elvin fertility treatments Sophie's mom (secretly) received also enabled a second pregnancy, giving her a biological daughter to hopefully make up for the fact that Sophie would someday return to where she belonged. Like her husband, she was captured by Vespera and put through terrible experiments—and her memories of that time have been similarly erased. But she managed to say a proper goodbye to Sophie before the Washer did his job, giving them each gentle closure.

Amy Rose Foster

*(also known as Natalie Freeman—and another
alias kept classified for her protection)*

ROLE: *Sophie's human sister*

QUALIFICATIONS: *None, since Amy was born into her role—but
she mastered the part of "annoying little sister" quite quickly.*

KNOWN FOR: *Her snarky personality and beloved stuffed animal
(Bun-Bun), as well as her cat (Marty) and her dog (Watson).*

NOTES: *Amy is one of the few humans to visit the Lost Cities—and
she's the only one who remembers the experience. Sophie brought her
there after her parents were captured by Vespera, and the Council
let Amy keep her memories of the experience so she could be better*

prepared if the Neverseen came after her family again. As a result, Amy has an Imparter that reaches Sophie—but she's only allowed to use it in case of emergency. She's also able to understand the Enlightened Language.

Activities

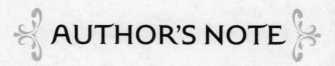

AUTHOR'S NOTE

NOW THAT YOU GUYS HAVE BEEN GIVEN A CRASH course on all things Keeper, I thought it'd be fun to have you take a really really really hard test to see how much you remember—and if you don't pass, this book will self-destruct and you'll never be able to read the novella and see what happens next—mwhahahahahahahaha.

JUST KIDDING!

I'm evil—but not *that* evil.

(Or maybe I *am* that evil. You've read my cliff-hangers. . . .)

No, really, I'm kidding!

What I actually have for you now are some super-fun Keeper-related activities, including Keeper quizzes, an Iggy coloring page, and some delicious Keeper-themed recipes!

Here's the full breakdown of the awesomeness ahead:

QUIZ: *Which protected creature should you adopt as a pet?*

QUIZ: *How many bodyguards would you need in the Lost Cities?*

QUIZ: *Who said it first?*

IGGY COLORING PAGE

RECIPE: *Mallowmelt cookies*

RECIPE: *Cinnacreme*

RECIPE: *Lushberry juice*

Enjoy!

QUIZZES

WHICH PROTECTED CREATURE SHOULD YOU ADOPT AS A PET?

What are you most excited to do with your pet once you bring them home?

a. Gaze at their beauty—and then get back to life. You have too much to do to sit around cuddling a pet all day.

b. Wreak some havoc! Somewhere out there someone is *begging* to be pranked—and now you have the perfect pet–partner in crime.

c. Go exploring! The world has so much to see— and you have a wonderful companion to go on adventures with.

d. Piggyback time! You made sure your pet was big enough to carry you everywhere—even if the ride is a little bumpy.

e. Keep them in their cage and feed them *lots* of treats, hoping they won't eat you before you can brag to all your friends that you got the supercool pet they were too scared to get!

f. Give your new friend a super-silly name, and then show it to your sibling and make them repeat the name over and over—especially if they're embarrassed.

You're at an ice cream shop, and they have TONS of amazing flavors—but they're mean and will only let you try one. Which flavor do you taste?

a. Whichever flavor has the prettiest colors.

b. Cotton candy with sour Pop Rocks, so every bite is an explosive surprise!

c. Brown sugar cinnamon, because sugar and spice is the best combo ever!

d. Doesn't matter. You like everything—but you want a double scoop!

e. Ghost-pepper chocolate. You don't care that no one else has tried it—in fact, that's half of the appeal. You'll show everyone how it's done.

f. Salted caramel, for that perfect blend of salty sweet.

What kind of music is always at the top of your playlist?

a. Soothing classical symphonies.

b. Punk rock—cranked up to full volume!

c. Pure, perfect pop. (The bouncier the better!)

d. Anything with bass—played so loud the walls shake.

e. Experimental electronica. Weird is wonderful.

f.   Nature sounds. Especially the ocean.

Describe your favorite outfit.

a.   It's designer (of course) and the height of fashion.

b.   It's super comfy—with tons of pockets to hide things!

c.   One word: sparkles.

d.   Basic jeans because you hate frills—and a neon shirt for a pop of color!

e.   It's one of a kind, bought from several different stores (with a few homemade pieces).

f.   Casual beachy-chic!

What's your dream vacation spot?

a.   A private palace—preferably on its own island.

b.   The busiest, noisiest city you can find, where everything's open late so you can explore all day and all night.

c.   Anywhere with mountains and meadows and lots of fresh air.

d.   The desert. Bring on the dust and heat and gorgeous views!

e.   Doesn't matter as long as there's bungee jumping or skydiving available.

f.   White sand, teal water, and all the scuba and snorkeling ever!

Which word best describes you?

a. Mysterious.
b. Playful.
c. Enchanting.
d. Energetic.
e. Misunderstood.
f. Unique.

Which pet problem would bother you the least?

a. They scoot out of your reach every time you want to cuddle them.
b. Their breath is toxic—and their burps are *much* worse.
c. They have so much energy, you wonder if they accidentally drank a double espresso.
d. Bath time is a GIANT splash-fest.
e. They get that look in their eye that makes you wonder if they're plotting to eat you.
f. One second they love you—the next they're biting you. (And their bites sting!)

Which pet from the human world would you be most excited to have?

a. Honestly, you're not sure you'd want one. Human pets are so *ordinary*. But maybe there's a fancy bird?

b. A hyper kitten, eager to attack anything that moves.

c. A horse! You know they're a ton of work, but you don't care!

d. Any kind of lizard—the bigger the better.

e. A tarantula.

f. A betta fish—pretty *and* fierce.

If you picked . . .

MOSTLY As: You should adopt a *moonlark*! These rare, gorgeous birds are the prettiest pets ever—and their solitary ways are perfect for your independent spirit. You'll both be able to admire each other from afar and get back to your busy lives.

MOSTLY Bs: You should adopt an *imp*! These tiny, adorable troublemakers are perfectly suited to all your pranking needs—and they thrive in chaos. Plus, they make adorable, squeaky purrs when it's snuggle time! Just make sure you hold your breath every time they fart!

MOSTLY Cs: You should adopt an *alicorn*! These majestic flying horses are an excellent choice for anyone who values beauty and adventure—and they'll do pretty much anything you want for some treats. You'll have to clean up some sparkly poop, but . . . sparkles make everything better, right?

MOSTLY Ds: You should adopt a *T. rex*! These giant fluffy dinosaurs are a whole lot of pet to love—and they're a blast to ride around on! But watch out—sometimes they have a bit of a hard time adjusting to their new vegetarian diet!

MOSTLY Es: You should adopt a *gorgodon*! These mysterious hybrid creatures are new to the Lost Cities—and they need someone brave and accepting like you to show them a little love. Who knows how sweet they could be if someone truly cared for them?

MOSTLY Fs: You should adopt a *murcat*! These unusual aquatic creatures will get everyone talking—and they can be very sweet when they want to be. And bonus points if you name your murcat something extra silly!

HOW MANY BODYGUARDS WOULD YOU NEED IN THE LOST CITIES?

You find a mysterious note in your locker, and you're pretty sure the poem inside is from the Black Swan. Do you . . . ?

    a. Ignore the note. If someone wants your help, they can ask you like a normal person!

    b. Show the note to an adult and see what they think you should do.

    c. Show the note to a friend and let them help you figure it out.

    d. Ponder the note by yourself for several days, figuring out the best plan.

    e. Rush off by yourself to investigate—something dangerous might be happening!

You're shopping in Atlantis and overhear someone say something that makes you wonder if they're part of the Neverseen. Do you . . . ?

    a. Ignore them. It's the midterms celebration tomorrow, and you still have to find gifts for the rest of your friends.

b. Tell a nearby adult what you heard.

c. Hail one of your friends and ask them to rush over to help.

d. Follow the person from a safe distance—and make sure you always stay with a crowd.

e. Follow them as close as you can—and don't stop for anything. They might lead you back to their hideout!

Five members of the Neverseen surround you. Which ability do you wish you had?

a. Vanisher, so you can sneak away before things get ugly.

b. Psionipath, so you can trap them all under a force field and wait for help to show up.

c. Hydrokinetic, so you can wash them away with a tidal wave.

d. Mesmer, so you can control everything they do.

e. Pyrokinetic, so you can fight fire with fire.

You discover a huge secret. Who do you tell?

a. Anyone who wants to know. It's not your job to keep something hidden.

b. A parent. They'll find out anyway, and you don't want to get in trouble.

c. Your best friend. Because that's what BFFs do!

d. No one—but you write about it in your journal.

e. No one. Period. A secret is a secret.

Would you ever ditch class?

a. Of course not! Good grades are important!

b. Only if it was a huge emergency.

c. Maybe. It depends.

d. Probably, as long as I wouldn't get caught.

e. Absolutely!

Someone gives you a goblin throwing star. Do you . . . ?

a. Give it back. You're *not* into weapons.

b. Ask them to give you some pointers on how to use it.

c. Practice with your friend.

d. Add a special pocket to your clothes so you can carry it with you.

e. Ask for a bunch more.

You end up injured in the Foxfire Healing Center. What do you do?

a. Let Elwin take his time to do everything he needs to do—you can't rush a proper recovery.

b. Ask your parents to collect your schoolwork so you can stay caught up with your sessions while you're stuck in bed.

c. Ask your friends to help you practice whatever skills you can in the Healing Center.

d. Tell Elwin to give you extra treatments to hurry your recovery along as much as possible.

e. Tell Elwin you're fine because you need to get out of there ASAP and catch the villains who attacked you!

If you picked . . .

MOSTLY As: You're clearly not interested in getting caught up in any conspiracies—but trouble still seems to find you, so you definitely need one bodyguard.

MOSTLY Bs: You're quick to turn to adults for help—but you definitely still want to be involved in what's going on. So you need two bodyguards to keep you safe.

MOSTLY Cs: You rely on your friends to back you up—which means you're going to need extra protection for them. So three bodyguards is the best bet.

MOSTLY Ds: You're cautious. You take time to think before you act—but once you have a plan, it's full steam ahead, even if it's dangerous. So you need four bodyguards to keep you from taking too many risks.

MOSTLY Es: Congratulations, you're destined for as many near-death experiences as Sophie—so you need the full Foster Five to keep you alive. Careful there, hero—you can't save the world if you're not alive to keep fighting!

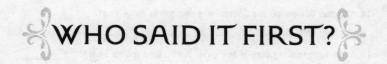

WHO SAID IT FIRST?

Character First Lines

Some of the Keeper characters have especially memorable first lines. See if you can match the first line to the character for these!

ALDEN BIANA DAME ALINA DEX EDALINE ELWIN FINTAN

FITZ JENSI KEEFE LADY ZILLAH LINH MAGNATE LETO

MARELLA MARUCA SOPHIE STINA TAM WYLIE

1. "You must be lost." _____

2. "It's a pleasure to meet you, Sophie." _____

3. "I can't, I can't, I can't." _____

4. "Hey, you're the prodigy Dame Alina told us about, right?
   The new one?" _____

5. "Is that my dress?" _____

6. "It was you, wasn't it? You're the one." _____

7. "This goes a lot faster if you hold still." _____

8. "Is this you?" _____

9. "You kids don't seem to realize that interrupting elite study time merits
   a week's detention." _____

10. "I need you to take me to see Wylie." _____

11. "*You* shouldn't waste your talent on such ordinary defenses." _____

12. "No, Mr. Sweeney." _____

13. "Ready?" _____

14. "I guess this means the Council has decided to make good
    on their threats." _____

15. "Thanks for taking care of her, guys, but I'll take it from here." _____

16. "If you're thinking it'll get easier, it won't." _____

17. "You're covered in dinosaur fluff!" _____

18. "Mom!" _____

19. "Good morning, prodigies. First and foremost, whoever put
    reekrod in my desk over the weekend *will*— It's not funny!" _____

And here are some other characters' first lines!

MR. FORKLE: "Looking for someone?"

EMERY: "Please be seated."

KENRIC: "We don't know."

FALLON: "A lot can happen in six months."

LORD CASSIUS: "Well, well, who do we have here?"

TERIK: "It works better one-on-one—you know that."

TIERGAN: "You've got some nerve summoning me."

UMBER: "Ugh, now I get why Keefe was always going on
about this one."

VERTINA: "My goodness you have strange eyes."

VESPERA: "The answer you seek does not exist."

ALVAR: "Sorry I'm late, Mom."

SIR ASTIN: "Where's your seventh star?"

BRONTE: "What?"

LIVVY (AS PHYSIC): "It looks worse than it is."

LUZIA: "Yes. I liked the view."

ORALIE: "Give me your hand, Sophie."

RUY: "That's enough of that."

ANSWER KEY: 1. KEEFE; 2. ALDEN; 3. LINH; 4. JENSI; 5. BIANA; 6. WYLIE; 7. ELWIN; 8. FITZ;
9. MAGNATE LETO; 10. MARUCA; 11. LADY ZILLAH; 12. SOPHIE; 13. DEX; 14. FINTAN;
15. MARELLA; 16. TAM; 17. EDALINE; 18. STINA; 19. DAME ALINA

IGGY COLORING PAGE

EVERYONE KNOWS THAT IGGY GETS A NEW FUR color (and style!) in every book of the Keeper series—and many of you also know that my readers are the ones who choose his look every year. But you might be wondering why I give away that kind of control, and it's because a reader inspired the idea in the first place.

I decided to have Dex turn Iggy pink (in *Exile*)—but I wasn't planning to change Iggy again, until an adorable little girl (whose name I sadly forgot to get—author fail!) asked me at one of my *Exile* tour events what Iggy's color was going to be in Book 3. I opened my mouth to tell her, "The pink will wear off, and he'll be gray again," when I thought, *Why not have someone change his color again?* So I asked her what color she wanted Iggy to be, and she leaned in, looking very serious, and told me, *"Orange."*

And so, Iggy turned orange in *Everblaze*—and every year since, I've used my social media channels to let readers pick the next new color and style. You'll see how this year's winning Iggy look gets worked into the novella. But I also thought it'd be fun to give you your own Iggy coloring page, so you can turn him whatever color (or colors) your heart desires!

PS: If you're not following me on Instagram—@SW_Messenger— you *might* want to (or have a parent follow me, if you don't have an account), so you can vote for Iggy's color/style in Keeper Book 9!

RECIPES

I LOVE TO BAKE—SO WHEN I FIRST STARTED coming up with the elvin foods for this series, my goal was to create desserts that I'd be able to make recipes for, so that my readers could enjoy the same treats as the characters.

(Okay, fine, I wanted to eat all the yummy things too!)

And while there are sadly a few delicacies that have defeated my baking skills (so far—I'm not giving up!), I've also been able to create several that taste exactly like what I was imagining when I wrote those scenes. Hopefully you'll love them too.

If you decide to give these recipes a try, make sure you have a parent or adult with you to help, since baking is a lot of fun, but it needs to be done safely!

Mallowmelt Cookies

Technically, mallowmelt is a gooey cake—and you can find a recipe for it on my website (shannonmessenger.com), as well as a recipe for mallowmelt-flavored cupcakes (because cupcakes are always a good idea).

But, as any of you who follow me on Instagram already know, I've recently spent a lot of time baking cookies. (It's an excellent stress release—and they're so easy to serve and share!) And one night I thought, *What if I could make mallowmelt-flavored cookies?!*

It took a few tries to perfect the method, but the final result was every bit as melty and delicious as I'd imagined—and now you guys can make mallowmelt-flavored cookies too! (But make sure you have a parent or adult with you to help!)

Makes about 24 cookies

Ingredients

FOR COOKIES:

1/2 cup salted butter, melted

1/3 cup granulated sugar

1/2 cup packed brown sugar

1 large egg

1 1/2 teaspoons vanilla extract

1 teaspoon salt

1/2 teaspoon baking soda

1 1/2 cups flour

1 1/4 cups semisweet chocolate chips

1/4 cup butterscotch chips

12 marshmallows, cut in half

FOR CHOCOLATE DRIZZLE:

1/2 cup semisweet chocolate chips

1/3 cup half-and-half

FOR BUTTERSCOTCH DRIZZLE:

3/4 cup butterscotch chips

2 tablespoons half-and-half

Directions

FOR COOKIES:

1. In a medium mixing bowl, whisk together flour, salt, and baking soda. Set aside.

2. In a large mixing bowl, stir together melted butter and both sugars until smooth. Add egg and vanilla and mix until combined, making sure to scrape down the sides of the bowl. (Note: This can also be done in a stand mixer with a paddle attachment or with a hand mixer—your preference!)

3. Add half of the flour mixture to the wet ingredients and stir until combined. Then add the remaining flour mixture and stir until batter is smooth, making sure to scrape down the sides of bowl.

4. Gently stir in chocolate and butterscotch chips until combined. Cover bowl with plastic wrap and chill dough in refrigerator for at least 2 hours (or as long as overnight).

5. Preheat oven to 350 degrees Fahrenheit. Take cookie dough out of fridge and let stand for 10 minutes. Line cookie sheets with parchment paper. Scoop 2 tablespoons of dough per cookie and roll into balls. Arrange cookie dough balls 2 inches apart on each tray and bake for 12 minutes.

6. While cookies are baking, cut the marshmallows in half, and after the 12 minutes have passed, quickly remove cookie trays from oven and place half a marshmallow, cut-side down, on top of each cookie. Return cookies to oven and bake for 2 more minutes. Remove cookies from oven and allow them to cool on the trays for 5–10 minutes, then transfer to a cooling rack and let them cool completely.

Note: The cookies are delicious just like this—but if you want to capture the true gooeyness of mallowmelt, you'll want to add the chocolate and butterscotch drizzles.

FOR CHOCOLATE DRIZZLE:

1. Combine chocolate chips and half-and-half in a microwave-safe bowl.
2. Cover and microwave for 30 seconds.
3. Remove and stir.
4. Repeat process, microwaving in 30-second intervals until chocolate is melted and stirs smooth. (Caution: The bowl may get warm.)
5. Using a spoon, drizzle chocolate over each cooled cookie. (If you want it to look fancier, you can use a pastry bag. Or if you want to keep it simple, you can also spread like frosting on top. Whichever method you choose, make sure the cookies have cooled completely before adding drizzle.)

FOR BUTTERSCOTCH DRIZZLE:

1. Combine butterscotch chips and half-and-half in a microwave-safe bowl.
2. Cover and microwave for 30 seconds.
3. Remove and stir.
4. Repeat process, microwaving in 30-second intervals until butterscotch is melted and

stirs smooth. (Caution: The bowl may get warm.)

5. Using a spoon, drizzle butterscotch over each cooled cookie. (If you want it to look fancier, you can use a pastry bag. Or if you want to keep it simple, you can also spread like frosting on top. Whichever method you choose, make sure the cookies have cooled completely before adding drizzle.)

Additional note: I use salted butter for the cookies because I think it helps balance the sweetness of the butterscotch—but if you prefer to bake with unsalted butter, it works just as well!

Cinnacreme

Ever since I invented cinnacreme for a scene in *Lodestar*, I've been wishing it existed. I mean, who doesn't want to drink something warm and steamy that tastes like melted snickerdoodles?

Took me a little while to figure out the right combination of flavors to capture what I was imagining—but I finally did it! And now you (and your friends) can make yourselves mugs of cinnacreme too! (Just make sure you have a parent or adult with you while you try!)

Makes 2 servings

Ingredients

1/4 cup + 3/4 cup half-and-half (divided)
1/2 cup white chocolate chips
1 cinnamon stick
1 cup whole milk
1/8 teaspoon salt
1/2 teaspoon ground cinnamon
1/4 cup mini marshmallows
Optional: extra mini marshmallows
and whipped cream for topping

Directions

1. In a small saucepan, combine 1/4 cup of half-and-half, white chocolate chips, and cinnamon stick.
2. Place on stove and set the burner to low heat.
3. Stir until chocolate melts.
4. Add remaining 3/4 cup of half-and-half, milk, salt, and ground cinnamon, stirring constantly.
5. Add mini marshmallows and stir until melted.
6. Pour into mugs.
7. Top with additional mini marshmallows and/or whipped cream if desired.

Note: This recipe works with any kind of milk you prefer. Personally, I like the thickness when it's equal parts whole milk and half-and-half, but you can use anything you like. And make sure you're working on low heat so the milk doesn't scald.

Lushberry Juice

(the Forbidden Cities version)

Probably the number one request I've gotten from readers over the years is for a recipe for lushberry juice. And sadly, I've always had to tell everyone, "Alas, lushberries only exist in the Lost Cities"—which is true. I've yet to meet any gnomes who could grow some for me.

BUT.

I did discover a way to create that perfectly refreshing, sweet-tart juice I've been imagining by using ingredients we humans have access to.

Bonus: It's SUPER easy to make!

And so, I give you my recipe for the Forbidden Cities version of lushberry juice! (And even though this recipe is really simple, it's still a good idea to have a parent or adult with you when you make it.)

Makes 4 servings

Ingredients

2 cups strawberry lemonade

1 cup pomegranate juice

1 cup sparkling water

Ice to serve

Directions

Combine all ingredients in a large pitcher and
stir. Pour over ice. Enjoy!

Note: I use my favorite brand of store-bought strawberry lemonade when I make this, but you are welcome to make your own,
if you want to be fancy like that. ☺

*For more Keeper-themed recipes, go to
shannonmessenger.com/keeper-of-the-lost-cities/recipes!*

Keefe's Memories

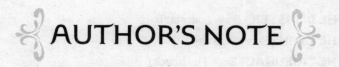

AUTHOR'S NOTE

THOSE WHO'VE READ *LEGACY* PROBABLY REMEMBER that Keefe is in the process of drawing all his memories, to see if it helps him remember anything his mom erased. And ever since I wrote those scenes, I've wished those drawings existed.

So when my editor and I were discussing what art to include in *Unlocked Book 8.5*, my immediate thought was, *OHHHHHH, WE NEED TO HAVE A SECTION OF KEEFE'S MEMORIES WITH ONE FROM EACH BOOK IN THE SERIES!!!!*

Thankfully, my editor agreed, and we began the nearly impossible task of deciding which memories to include. It wasn't *just* about picking favorites (though there are definitely some of those in the mix)— we also needed to show the moments that Keefe might focus on, since all the gorgeous art is followed by Keefe's personal commentary!

*pauses while Team Keefe does *all the squealing**

We also let you guys settle the tie for the *Exile* memory. My editor and I had narrowed it down to two, and there was no way to pick, so I put a poll on my social media and let you guys choose.

And so, I give you the list of the amazing art you're about to see*:

THE MEETING (*From* Keeper of the Lost Cities)
THE FLIGHT (*From* Exile)
THE LEAP (*From* Everblaze)
THE BETRAYAL (*From* Neverseen)

THE DISASTER *(From* Lodestar*)*

THE TWIN *(From* Nightfall*)*

THE TRIBUNAL *(From* Flashback*)*

THE THING *(From* Legacy*)*

*Please turn to page 512 to see Keefe's amazing drawings!

KEEFE ART COMMENTARY

So... Foster thinks I might learn more from my memories if I try writing stuff about them after I finish the drawings. Not totally sure why. She gave me a big speech about the power of words and different ways of processing information. But I was only half listening because she gets this cute little crinkle between her eyebrows when she's trying to be serious, and it makes me want to reach up and smooth her forehead with my fingertip—and I'm betting she'd think I was super weird if I did that, since it's not like she's my...

You know what?

I don't know why I'm talking about this! Or writing about it—or thinking about it—or whatever I'm doing right now.

Pretty sure I'm just stalling, because this feels kiiiiiiiiinda pointless.

But.

Foster's way smarter than I am. And nothing else I've tried has helped me remember anything new. So, I guess that means it's time to write about my messed-up life—oh boy!

And in case I forget why I did this later, I'm writing about the memories here, instead of in the notebooks where I've been sketching them, because Lord Nosypants is always going through my stuff. (HEAR THAT, DADDIO? I'M ONTO YOU! AND I DARE YOU TO KEEP READING—I'M SURE I'LL HAVE <u>LOTS</u> TO SAY ABOUT YOUR AWESOME PARENTING SKILLS!) Plus, I have the world's most annoying ogre constantly looking over my shoulder. (YEAH, I SEE YOU OVER THERE, PRINCESS! YOU'RE NOT AS SMOOTH AS YOU THINK YOU ARE!) So, basically, I'm separating the lock from the key. (GOOD LUCK FINDING ALL THE NOTEBOOKS, GUYS!)

Okay... let's do this!

MEMORY #1

Ugh. The snooty expression on my dad's face makes me want to throw a vial of gulon gas at him—and

I HAVE A PHOTOGRAPHIC MEMORY, SO THERE'S NO WAY I IMAGINED IT.

I THINK HIS HAIR ACTUALLY BUGS ME MORE THAN HIS SLIMY SMILE DOES, THOUGH. IT'S LIKE... PROOF OF HOW PERFECT AND TIDY HE EXPECTS EVERYONE AND EVERYTHING TO BE. ONE DAY I ACTUALLY TIMED HOW LONG IT TOOK HIM TO SMOOTH EVERY STRAND INTO PLACE LIKE THAT—ESPECIALLY THAT ONE LITTLE PIECE IN THE FRONT. (I WAS GROUNDED, OKAY? THERE WASN'T A WHOLE LOT ELSE TO DO!) AND HE WAS AT IT FOR THIRTY-ONE MINUTES.

<u>THIRTY. ONE. MINUTES.</u>

THEN HE WINKED AT HIS REFLECTION AND STALKED AWAY. (I SO WISH I WERE MAKING THAT UP!) WHAT I WOULDN'T GIVE TO BE A GUSTER AND BE ABLE TO BLAST HIM WITH WIND....

BUT I'M GUESSING THE POINT OF THIS WHOLE WRITING-ABOUT-MY-MEMORIES THING ISN'T TO MAKE FUN OF MY DAD'S HAIR, SO...

✳SQUINTS AT DRAWING✳

I HONESTLY CAN'T TELL WHO MY DAD'S SHOWING OFF FOR. IT COULD BE TIERGAN, SINCE HE DEFINITELY

KNEW ALL ABOUT TIERGAN'S FANCY REPUTATION—AND MY DAD'S ALWAYS LOOKING TO MAKE NEW "CONNECTIONS." BUT HE COULD JUST AS EASILY HAVE BEEN TRYING TO IMPRESS FOSTER. I USED TO HEAR HIM TALKING ABOUT HER TO MY MOM, GOING ON AND ON ABOUT HOW HE WAS CONVINCED THAT FOSTER WAS WAY MORE POWERFUL THAN ANYONE KNEW.

AND, I MEAN... HE WASN'T WRONG—BUT NOW THAT I'M THINKING ABOUT IT, MY MOM WAS THE ONE WHO ALWAYS STARTED THOSE CONVERSATIONS. AND SHE KEPT TELLING MY DAD THAT HE SHOULD FIND OUT MORE ABOUT HER.

THAT'S PROBABLY BECAUSE SHE WAS TRYING TO PLAN FOSTER'S KIDNAPPING AND DIDN'T WANT THE BLACK SWAN TO BE WATCHING HER.

HUH.

MOM OF THE YEAR STRIKES AGAIN!

ANYWAY. I'M SURE I'LL BE DIGGING INTO MY MESS OF MOMMY ISSUES SOON ENOUGH. FOR NOW, LET'S GET BACK TO THE DAY DADDY DEAREST MET THE MYSTERIOUS MISS F, SHALL WE?

I DON'T REALLY KNOW WHY I DREW MYSELF LOOKING SO MISERABLE. I COULDN'T SEE MY FACE,

SO IT'S NOT LIKE I HAVE ANY IDEA WHAT I ACTUALLY LOOKED LIKE RIGHT THEN—AND I MOSTLY REMEMBER FEELING NERVOUS, SINCE I WAS SUPER AWARE THAT MY DAD COULD TELL FOSTER WAS HIDING SOMETHING. SHE'S <u>NOT</u> THE SMOOTHEST LIAR.

THOUGH... I GUESS MY MOOD DID CHANGE WHEN I FELT FOSTER'S EMOTIONS SHIFT, AND THAT'S THE MOMENT I DREW HERE.

MY DAD HAD BEEN DRONING ON, BEING HIS USUAL JERKY SELF. AND I WAS PICKING UP A PRETTY HILARIOUS AMOUNT OF ANNOYANCE FROM MISS F. BUT THEN SHE LOOKED AT ME, AND I COULD TELL SHE FELT...

SAD.

NOT FOR HER—FOR <u>ME</u>.

MY DAD MIGHT'VE BEEN TRYING TO LEARN SOMETHING ABOUT FOSTER THAT DAY. BUT SHE LEARNED SOMETHING ABOUT HIM, TOO—AND IT'S THE THING IN MY LIFE THAT I'D RATHER NOT HAVE PEOPLE KNOW. ONCE THEY DO, THEY EITHER FEEL AWKWARD, OR WEIRD, OR THEY START PITYING ME FOR HAVING SUCH A HORRIBLE FAMILY.

THANKFULLY, FOSTER DIDN'T DO THAT.

SHE JUST FELT SAD—AND A LITTLE BIT INDIGNANT. AND IF I HADN'T ALREADY KNOWN I LIKED HER, I WOULD'VE—

YOU KNOW WHAT?

I THINK THAT'S ENOUGH RAMBLING ABOUT THIS MEMORY.

MEMORY #2

AWWWWWW, MY FIRST FLIGHT WITH GLITTER BUTT!

I LOVE THAT SPARKLY ALICORN MAMA <u>ALMOST</u> AS MUCH AS SHE LOVES ME!

TOO BAD HER BACK WASN'T NEARLY AS COMFORTABLE AS I WANTED IT TO BE. I COULDN'T SIT WITHOUT WINCING FOR DAYS—THOUGH, I GUESS THAT <u>MIGHT'VE</u> ALSO HAD SOMETHING TO DO WITH THE BUMPS AND SCRAPES AND BROKEN RIBS I GOT WHEN MOMMY DEAREST AND HER NEVERSEEN BUDDIES SHOWED UP AND TRIED TO STEAL SILVENY.

AHHHHHHHHHHHHH, MEMORIES!

But that's not what _this_ moment was about.

This one was...

Actually, I'm not sure.

All I really remember is how freaked out Foster was. And I don't blame her. It had to be pretty terrifying knowing she was about to meet the people who "created" her—especially since we didn't know if the Black Swan were the good guys or the bad guys back then. Plus, there was the whole "Will they be able to fix her abilities?" thing, which was kinda important since she wouldn't be able to heal Alden's mind if they couldn't.

So yeah, Foster was feeling a _tiny_ bit of pressure. And I was only there because her parents had decided that letting me go was better than having her fly across the ocean at night to meet a group of mysterious rebels all alone. But Grady still didn't seem happy about it.

Can't say I blame him for that. It wasn't like I could help much. All I did was make a bunch of jokes to distract her—and it was

SUPER FUN FEELING HER GET ALL ANNOYED AND EMBARRASSED. I MEAN, LOOK AT THAT ADORABLE BLUSH! I COULD SEE IT EVEN WITH THE MOONLIGHT WASHING OUT MOST OF THE COLOR.

IN FACT... IF I'M KEEPING IT REAL... I'M PRETTY SURE THAT BLUSH IS THE REASON I DREW THIS MEMORY.

I MEAN, I COULD'VE PICKED ANY MOMENT FROM THAT FLIGHT, BUT I DREW THIS ONE. BECAUSE THAT WASN'T AN "I'M SO EMBARRASSED RIGHT NOW" BLUSH. OR A "KEEFE IS DRIVING ME CRAZY" BLUSH.

IT STARTED OUT THAT WAY.

BUT THEN IT GOT WARMER.

ALMOST LIKE...

UGH, I'M JUST GOING TO SAY IT, SINCE IT'S NOT LIKE ANYONE'S EVER GOING TO READ THIS (AND RO AND LORD BOSSYPANTS ALREADY HASSLE ME ABOUT IT ANYWAY—AND IT'S NOT LIKE I CARE).

THAT WAS THE FIRST TIME IT FELT LIKE... MAYBE I HAD A TINY SHOT AT MAKING THIS BRAVE, BEAUTIFUL, BLUSHING GIRL LIKE ME.

HASN'T WORKED OUT THAT WAY YET. AND I HAVE NO IDEA IF IT EVER WILL.

BUT THERE'S A TEENY, TINY CHANCE.

AND THAT'S ENOUGH.

FOR NOW.

AAAAAAAAAAAAAAAAAND, THAT GOT WEIRD AND SAPPY SO... YEAH. I CAN'T TELL IF IT'S PROOF THAT THIS MEMORY-WRITING THING IS WORKING AND MAKING ME SEE THINGS MORE CLEARLY, OR IF IT'S JUST MAKING ME FIND NEW WAYS TO HUMILIATE MYSELF.

I GUESS WE'LL SEE.

MEMORY #3

RIGHT, THE DAY OF THE TEN THOUSAND LIGHT LEAPS!

ACTUALLY, THERE WERE ONLY FIVE LEAPS—ONE FOR EACH OF THE UNMAPPED STARS. BUT IT <u>FELT</u> LIKE TEN THOUSAND, BECAUSE LEAPING WITH QUINTESSENCE IS <u>MISERY</u>—AND IT TOOK US TO ALL KINDS OF PLACES THAT REGULAR LIGHT CAN'T GO, LIKE DEEP UNDERGROUND AND TO THE BOTTOM OF THE OCEAN.

(Yep, that was a kraken behind us. He definitely wanted to eat us. Foster thought he swam away, but he was totally lurking behind us the whole time we were there, trying to figure out how to break through our force field.)

Not a fun day. Pretty sure Gigantor hated it even more than Foster and I did.

This was our second leap, I think.? Or was it the third.?

It was the third!

We did Lucilliant, Candesia, then Marquiseire—which is what that pink glittery glow all around us is—followed by Phosforien and Elementine (photographic memory for the win!).

And for the record: Sparkly light.? NOT FUN to leap with.

The Marquiseire leap was seriously the worst part of the day.

Well, I guess the worst part was technically when the Black Swan wasn't there after we finally made it to their little island, because

THE WHOLE THING WAS ACTUALLY THEIR PLAN TO USE FOSTER AND ME AS BAIT. AND THE PLAN WORKED, BECAUSE SEE THAT PIN ON MY CAPE?

MOM OF THE YEAR WAS AT IT AGAIN!

SHE HID A TRACKER IN MY FAMILY CREST—WHICH, BY THE WAY, I'D WAITED YEARS TO HAVE MY PARENTS GIVE ME. SO NOT ONLY DID IT TURN OUT THAT THEY HADN'T FINALLY TREATED ME LIKE I WAS PART OF MY OWN FAMILY, BUT I'M ALSO THE REASON THE NEVERSEEN SHOWED UP AT THE BLACK SWAN'S HIDEOUT AND TRIED TO STEAL SILVENY (AND BROKE HER WING). AND I'M THE REASON THEY FOUND THAT ISLAND AND TRIED TO GRAB ME AND FOSTER.

IT'S SUPER, SUPER FUN TO BE ME, ISN'T IT?

BUT THAT'S NOT ACTUALLY WHY I DREW THIS MEMORY—AND IT WASN'T ABOUT FOSTER, EITHER (OR HOW ADORABLY PROTECTIVE GIGANTOR LOOKS).

IT WAS ABOUT THAT GLITTERY PINK LIGHT.

I GUESS ETHERTINE IS MADE FROM SOME WEIRD COMBINATION OF QUINTESSENCE AND LIGHTNING. AND I'M PRETTY SURE THE ETHERTINE CROWN MY MOM HAD GLIMMER DISSOLVE DURING THAT CREEPY THING SHE DID

TO ME IN LOAMNORE WAS MADE WITH QUINTESSENCE FROM MARQUISEIRE. IT WASN'T PINK OR ANYTHING. BUT THE GRATING, SCRAPING FEELING THAT HIT ME WHEN THE LIGHT TORE THROUGH MY BODY FELT FAMILIAR, AND I THINK IT REMINDED ME OF THIS LEAP.

So MAYBE IF I LEARN MORE ABOUT MARQUISEIRE, I'LL GET A BETTER IDEA OF WHAT'S GOING ON WITH ME.

IT'S A PRETTY SLIM HOPE BUT . . . IT'S ALL I'VE GOT.

TOO BAD THIS MEMORY ISN'T TRIGGERING ANYTHING USEFUL, NO MATTER HOW LONG I STARE AT IT.

OH WELL—AT LEAST FOSTER LOOKS ALL CUTE AND DETERMINED!

MEMORY #4

YEEEEEEEEAAAAAAAAH, SO . . . THIS WAS <u>NOT</u> A PROUD MOMENT FOR ME. IT'S PRETTY MUCH THE WORST IDEA I'VE EVER HAD—AND I'VE HAD A LOT OF <u>REALLY</u> BAD IDEAS.

I JUST . . . I <u>HAD</u> TO DO SOMETHING.

We weren't getting anywhere. And I knew the Neverseen wanted me to join them. So I thought... okay... let me give them what they want—or pretend to, anyway. Then I could find out all their secrets and take them down from the inside out.

But it went wrong right from the start—right from this moment.

Foster wasn't supposed to be there.

She wasn't supposed to know what I was doing until I was already long gone.

Just like she wasn't supposed to know I stole Kenric's cache until I'd already stolen it back and destroyed the Neverseen and saved the day and fixed everything—go, me!

But... she WAS there.

And while I will ALWAYS be glad I made her that necklace and hid a leaping crystal in one of the beads (I seriously don't even want to think about what would've happened if she couldn't have gotten away...), her escape also derailed everything. Any trust

I WAS SUPPOSED TO EARN FROM HANDING OVER KENRIC'S CACHE VANISHED THE SECOND SOPHIE DID. AND I KNEW THAT THE NEVERSEEN WERE <u>NEVER</u> GOING TO TRUST ME.

I GUESS I PROBABLY SHOULD'VE CUT MY LOSSES RIGHT THEN AND FLED TO THE BLACK SWAN. BUT I JUST KEPT THINKING THERE HAD TO BE A WAY TO SALVAGE THE SITUATION.

THERE WASN'T.

AND I'M PRETTY LUCKY NO ONE GOT SERIOUSLY HURT, AND THAT FOSTER FORGAVE ME.

I WASN'T SURE IF SHE WOULD.

SOMETIMES I STILL WORRY THAT SOME TINY PART OF HER HOLDS IT AGAINST ME. THAT SHE'LL NEVER FULLY TRUST ME. THAT SHE'LL ALWAYS SEE ME AS THE GUY WHO BETRAYED HER AND STOLE FROM HER AND RAN OFF WITH THE ENEMY.

I MEAN... LOOK AT HER FACE....

I MAKE MYSELF REMEMBER THAT EXPRESSION EVERY TIME I HAVE TO BE AROUND FITZPHIE. IT STOPS ME FROM SCREAMING, DON'T PICK

HIM—PICK ME. BECAUSE YEAH, FITZ HAS YELLED AT HER A FEW TIMES, AND SAID STUFF THAT MAKES ME WANT TO SMACK HIM UPSIDE THE HEAD.

BUT I'M THE ONLY ONE WHO'S MADE FOSTER LOOK LIKE THIS.... LIKE SHE'S JUST LOST ALL HOPE THAT THERE'S ACTUALLY GOOD IN THE WORLD.

I DID THAT.

NOT SURE I DESERVE TO BE FORGIVEN.

AND ON THAT CHEERFUL NOTE, LET'S MOVE ON TO THE NEXT MEMORY!

MEMORY #5

OKAY, SO I'VE LIVED THROUGH SOME PRETTY SCARY THINGS. BUT I'VE NEVER BEEN AS TERRIFIED AS I WAS WATCHING LUMENARIA FALL.

I WAS RIGHT THERE ON THE BEACH WHEN THE CASTLE CRUMBLED. AND ALL I COULD THINK WAS: FOSTER'S IN THERE.

EVERYTHING AFTER THAT IS A FRAGMENTED BLUR.

I have scattered memories of running around, asking anyone if they'd seen her or knew where she was. But no one could help. I'm not sure they even understood what I was asking. Everyone was in shock. It felt like the whole world had just toppled.

So I kept running faster, digging through rubble, screaming her name, begging anyone to tell me something—give me some tiny shred of hope that she was okay, because she had to be. It had to be like her kidnapping—like her planting. Everyone said she was gone forever, but she came back safe.

I needed her to be safe again.

But she wasn't with the survivors.

Neither was Edaline.

And one person said they'd seen Sophie run back into the castle not long before it fell....

But then... there she was.

I definitely cried after I'd made sure she and Edaline were still breathing.

Don't think Foster noticed, though. I tried to get it together before I woke her—tried to focus on looking calm, because I knew she'd need me to be. But I was a mess.

I'm <u>still</u> a mess, just looking at her bruises and all that destruction. . . .

I know I crack a lot of jokes about Foster's near-death experiences—but there's nothing funny about them. Especially this one.

I <u>almost</u> lost her.

And if I had, it would've been all my fault.

<u>All</u> of this is my . . .

Hmm. Probably better if I don't finish that sentence. And <u>wow</u>, this is getting dark. Let's hope the next memory is a bit less brutal.

<u>MEMORY #6</u>

Ha, looks like I got artsy with this one. I couldn't actually <u>see</u> the moonlarks in their nest

(OR ANY FANCY SHADOWS). BUT... I WANTED TO MAKE
SURE I REMEMBERED THEIR SONGS.

THE MELODIES WERE MOURNFUL AND TRAGIC—BUT
SOMEHOW STILL SO HOPEFUL. AND THAT DEFINITELY
SUMMED UP WHAT IT FELT LIKE TO FIND OUT FORKLE
WAS NOT-DEAD AND STILL-DEAD ALL AT THE SAME TIME.

FITZ FREAKED OUT AND YELLED. BIANA SOBBED.
DEX GOT ALL TECHNICAL AND ASKED A BILLION
QUESTIONS. BANGS BOY GOT MOODY AND DEMANDING
(NO SURPRISE THERE). LINH DID THAT QUIET,
THOUGHTFUL THING SHE'S SO GOOD AT.

AND ME?

I SWEAR, WHEN I SAW FORKLE, I DIDN'T KNOW
IF I WANTED TO STRANGLE-HUG HIM OR JUST
STRANGLE HIM. I <u>STILL</u> DON'T REALLY KNOW HOW TO
WRAP MY HEAD AROUND THE WHOLE SECRET-TWINS-
SHARING-A-SINGLE-LIFE THING. BUT... I'M GLAD WE
DIDN'T LOSE HIM COMPLETELY.

AND I'M GLAD FOSTER TOOK THE NEWS OKAY
(THOUGH SHE DID TUG OUT A FEW EYELASHES).
FORKLE HAD BEGGED ME WITH HIS FINAL BREATHS
TO TAKE CARE OF HIS MOONLARK. AND I SWORE I
WOULD—THOUGH HE DIDN'T NEED TO ASK.

That's been my plan for a long time—and not because I don't think she can take care of herself.

Because she shouldn't have to.

She's dealing with enough pressure and responsibility and people trying to kill her. If there's _anything_ I can do to make things easier for her, I'll do it. No matter what.

Also? Really hoping I don't have to wear that green tunic again. I mean, I look _awesome_—but I'm sick of losing people.

I'm sick of losing in general.

But staring at this memory isn't going to help with that, so... moving on!

MEMORY #7

Ugh.

That's all my brain wants to say about this memory.

Just... ugh.

But that's not going to be helpful.

Neither will the MANY thoughts I have about the way Fitz is freaking out. Or the fact that I was only there because Alden basically asked me to join Team Fitzphie.

(Yeah, I know. I wanted to say no. But I said yes for HER. She deserves to decide what she wants—even if it's not me.)

As for HELPFUL thoughts... I don't know. Alvar definitely looks super meek and remorseful. And I know I'm supposed to see that and think, LIAR! TRAITOR! LOCK HIM UP!

And I DO think that.

But the weird thing about being an Empath is that I also know, for a fact, that he actually WAS meek and remorseful after he lost his memories. And if they hadn't come back, I think he would've stayed that way. Which is pretty terrifying, if you think about it.

Means we don't have to be born evil to be evil.

We can switch sides anytime.

Pretty sure that's what my mom is counting on....

And before I go any farther down THAT depressing thought-path, let's move on.

MEMORY #8

Welp. I knew I was going to have to face my mommy issues eventually, aaaaaaaaaaaaaaand here we are.

I mean... look at her!

She looks like she's cheering on her favorite team in bramble, not torturing (and almost killing) her son! And that was seriously her expression. I'd told myself not to look at her, but I did end up stealing one quick glance, and I swear, I could imagine her chanting, Legacy, legacy, legacy!

Then there's Tammy Boy. I should probably hate him for this, since it's not like he's ever been my favorite person. But... he did try to warn me. And I know he only cooperated because of those creepy light-things on his wrists.

So... I guess I can't really hold it against him.

(But I **will** keep right on making fun of his stupid silver bangs!)

As for Foster... I probably shouldn't admit this because it's super selfish and horrible, but ... I'm really glad she was there. It killed me seeing her bound and helpless like that—kills me now just remembering it. And I can only imagine what kind of nightmares she must have.

But... if she hadn't been there—and hadn't gone all mega-powerful Telepath and kept our minds connected when the shadows hit me— I don't know what would've happened.

Actually, maybe I **do** know.

I wanted to retreat into that darkness and never come back. But Sophie called for me. And I came back for her.

I'll always...

Ugh, I'm back to more sappy, pointless rambling. Pretty sure that proves this project is a

WASTE OF TIME. IT HASN'T TRIGGERED ANY NEW MEMORIES. I HAVEN'T LEARNED ANYTHING NEW ABOUT STELLARLUNE, OR THOSE HUMANS MY MOM KILLED, OR THE LETTER I DELIVERED, OR ANYTHING ELSE. SEEMS LIKE A PRETTY EPIC FAIL. BUT WHAT ELSE IS NEW?

I GUESS I CAN TRY AGAIN LATER. BUT I THINK I'D BETTER TAKE A BREAK, BEFORE I WRITE SOMETHING <u>REALLY</u> EMBARRASSING. LIKE HOW I'M PRETTY SURE I'M—

HA!

I'M RECKLESS, BUT I'M NOT <u>THAT</u> RECKLESS!

NOT THAT IT MATTERS. I'M GOING TO HIDE THIS NOTEBOOK SO WELL, I DOUBT <u>I</u>'LL EVEN BE ABLE TO FIND IT. AND I SHOULD PROBABLY DO THAT NOW BECAUSE MY RIDICULOUSLY ANNOYING BODYGUARD IS GETTING BORED. (YEAH, RO—I HEAR YOU LOUD-SIGHING OVER AND OVER. I'M PRETTY SURE EVERY PERSON ON THE PLANET CAN HEAR YOU!!) AND WHEN SHE GETS BORED, SHE GETS REALLY HUMILIATING IDEAS.

SO... HUNKYHAIR → OUT.

Novella

Hi again, everyone!

Yay—you're still here! I hope that means you enjoyed the first half of this book—though I have a feeling some of you have snuck back here before reading all of that other awesome stuff because you're dying to know what's going to happen next to Sophie and her friends. And that's fine. I won't judge.

BUT.

Like I said earlier, the novella you're about to read takes place right after the ending of *Legacy*, so I need to interrupt this letter for yet another gigantic *SPOILER ALERT*!

If you haven't read Legacy *yet—and don't want any of the twists and surprises spoiled—turn and flee immediately! Even the rest of this letter isn't safe!*

I'm going to pause one final time to make sure everyone has heeded my warning. . . .

. . .

Okay, back to what I was saying!

The novella you're about to read is what I'd originally planned as the beginning of Keeper #9—until I realized that I could tell this part of the story better if I broke the usual pattern for the series. The Keeper books are limited to Sophie's point of view, meaning the only scenes we see are scenes where Sophie is present, and the only thoughts we hear are Sophie's. And to show how Keefe discovers the ways he's been affected by what his mother put him through in the final scenes of *Legacy*, I needed to be able to include his thoughts and show certain moments that he would try to hide from the rest of his friends. So I decided to move this section of the story to here, where I can alternate between Sophie's and Keefe's POVs. Each chapter is labeled to let you know whose head we're in. And don't worry, this novella may be a little shorter than the Keeper books usually are, but it's packed with huge revelations! You also definitely need to read it before you read Book 9.

I hope you enjoy every single page. And I promise, I'm writing Keeper #9 as fast as I can!

Happy reading!

xo

Keefe

I CAN'T DO THIS."

The words felt desperate and terrifying—but Keefe could taste the truth behind them. So he didn't lie or take them back or try to twist them into a joke.

He wanted to.

He missed laughing and pulling pranks and messing around with his friends.

But he wasn't that guy anymore.

He didn't know *who* he was.

All he knew was that he'd changed.

And the powers he'd been given were *much* too dangerous.

He needed to accept that, and make everyone else accept it too.

They were too busy hoping and planning and pretending that everything was okay.

But it *wasn't* okay.

He couldn't control this—not unless he did something drastic.

Something he definitely didn't want to do.

But he would.

He *had* to.

He wasn't giving up.

He was fighting back his own way.

- ONE -
Sophie

SO . . . HOW DO WE ACCESS THE MEMORY?"
Sophie asked, pulling free from the deal-sealing hand-shake to uncover the clear, marble-size gadget that had been pressed between her palm and Councillor Oralie's.

The tiny blue jewel set into the center of the cache glinted in the afternoon sunlight seeping through the swaying Panakes branches.

Inside was a single Forgotten Secret.

Hopefully filled with the answers Sophie needed.

That was why she'd agreed to work with Oralie, despite barely being able to look at the pretty blond Councillor now that she knew the truth about her.

"Don't even *think* about telling me we have to wait," she warned when Oralie's delicate features pulled into a frown.

Sophie didn't have time to be patient anymore.

Or cautious.

Or afraid.

She needed to figure out how to help Keefe, then get back to the Healing Center.

"That's not what I was going to say," Oralie assured her.

But the crease between her perfectly arched eyebrows deepened, and she kept shifting the way she sat, streaking the skirt of her fluttery pink gown with mud and bits of grass.

"The cache is designed to erase itself if I perform the access sequence incorrectly," Oralie eventually admitted, "and I'm having a difficult time determining the proper order of the steps."

"Access sequence?" Sophie repeated. "I thought the memory just needed a password."

That was what Dex had told her when he was trying to access the secrets hidden in Fintan's cache—though he'd technically been trying to hack into a fake cache without realizing it at the time.

"The password's part of it," Oralie agreed. "But first I have to prove that I'm 'authorized.' And no, a Technopath won't be able to bypass any of the security, if that's what you're about to suggest. Even someone as talented as Dex."

Sophie groaned, wishing she could grab the cache and fling it off one of Havenfield's cliffs—or maybe at Oralie's head. But the memory inside had something to do with stellarlune—the term Keefe's mom had used for the creepy things she'd done to herself and her husband before she got pregnant.

An experiment of sorts.

Designed to make Keefe ready for whatever "legacy" his mom had been planning for him.

And there had turned out to be a second, horrifying step to the process.

Sophie tried everything to stop it, but in the end, all she could

do was watch as Lady Gisela forced Tam to use his ability as a Shade to dissolve the dwarven king's magsidian throne after Keefe had been bound to it—and then ordered a Flasher who called herself Glimmer to blast the ethertine crown that had been placed on Keefe's head. Exposing Keefe to massive amounts of shadowflux and quintessence to trigger . . .

Something.

Sophie had no idea what.

Lady Gisela had managed to escape—*again*—without giving any further insights into her son's condition. And Keefe had been unconscious ever since.

But Elwin could tell that Keefe's cells were going through some sort of *transformation*—which was the same horrible word that Lady Gisela kept using to describe what she hoped would happen to her son if he "embraced the change." And while Elwin seemed convinced that Keefe was simply manifesting a new special ability— that still sounded absolutely terrifying. Especially since Sophie had a feeling that would only be the beginning.

They wouldn't know for sure until Keefe woke up.

If he—

She managed to shut down that bleak thought before it could fully form. But she couldn't stop the bigger worries from screaming around her brain like a freaked-out banshee.

What if Keefe wasn't Keefe anymore?

What if he joined the Neverseen for real?

What if he turned into—

"No."

She said the word out loud to silence all the mental noise.

She'd stayed telepathically connected to Keefe the entire time the shadowflux and quintessence were tearing through his system, and he'd still been *him*.

He'd also been having some very Keefe-like dreams now that he was safely in the Healing Center.

Plus, Keefe was *much* too stubborn to ever let his mom win.

But Lady Gisela is just as stubborn, her brain had to remind her. *And she isn't done with Keefe yet.*

She'll never be done with him.

Not until she gets what she wants.

Or someone kills her . . .

"What are you doing?" Oralie asked as Sophie jumped to her feet, needing to move—pace—something.

"I don't understand why you didn't look up the sequence to open the cache before you came here," Sophie grumbled. "You knew we were going to need it."

Oralie's pink lips flickered with a hint of a smile. "It's not as if there's an instruction manual, Sophie. Quite the opposite, actually. The knowledge was divided into pieces and scattered throughout my consciousness—and sadly, using your telepathy won't help, since false instructions were buried with everything else, and you'd never be able to tell which are which."

"Okay," Sophie said, tugging out an eyelash as she walked a slow circle around the trunk of Calla's Panakes tree. "Then how do we figure it out?"

"*We* don't—though I appreciate your spirit of teamwork. And I understand your urgency. I feel it too. But I'm still going to need a minute to think."

Sophie gritted her teeth and went back to circling, tapping her fingers against the coarse, braided bark to distract herself.

But one minute turned into two.

Then three.

Four.

"You know, for years I've had to hear about how perfect and safe your world is supposed to be," Sophie muttered, kicking the grass. "And yet you guys sure did put a lot of obnoxiously complicated security measures into place."

"I think you mean *our* world," Oralie corrected.

Sophie shrugged.

The Lost Cities were her home now—and she wouldn't ever want to leave them.

But sometimes she felt . . . disconnected.

"You're not wrong about the contradiction," Oralie admitted, reaching for a fallen Panakes blossom. "We've been playing both sides for far too long. Convincing ourselves that we're above the problems plaguing the other intelligent species, all while still attempting to prepare for any worst-case scenarios—through rather convoluted methods, I'll even admit. We wanted to believe that we're superior. And we are, in certain ways. But . . . I can't help wondering if things would be different right now if we'd simply accepted from the beginning that the power we have is both our greatest asset and our largest vulnerability."

"Or maybe things would be different if you stopped trying to control everyone all the time," Sophie suggested.

That was what the whole mess boiled down to.

A ridiculous power struggle.

The Neverseen thought *they* should be in charge—and they'd convinced others to join their cause by pointing out the Council's mistakes.

Uncovering lies the Councillors had told.

Highlighting injustices they'd allowed.

And the scariest part was: The Neverseen weren't wrong.

They just had really cruel solutions to all of the problems—at least as far as Sophie could tell. She'd only uncovered tiny fragments of their plans, and she still had no idea how to fit the pieces together.

The Neverseen were too smart to give anything away until they were ready to put their schemes into action.

But Sophie *had* to get ahead of them this time—*had* to stop them from dragging Keefe in any deeper.

Unless she was already too late . . .

"Ruling this planet is no easy task," Oralie told her. "We do the best we can."

Maybe they did. But the Council's "best" didn't seem to be good enough anymore—assuming it ever had been. And Sophie was tempted to remind Oralie that no one had *asked* the elves to put themselves in charge.

But she needed to stay focused.

"What exactly do you remember from the instructions?" she asked, pointing to the cache.

Oralie stood, holding the tiny crystal up to eye level. "I know it needs my blood, sweat, and tears. I'm just not sure if that's the right order to give them in. It might be tears, sweat, then blood. Or sweat, tears, then blood. Or sweat, blood, and tears. Or blood, tears, then—"

"Is there someone you can ask?" Sophie cut in. "What about Bronte?"

"Councillor Bronte would not support my decision to come here. Nor would any of the other Councillors. They believe the Forgotten Secrets should remain forgotten."

"Then why bother storing the memories in the first place?" Sophie countered.

"Because it's important to have a record *somewhere*, in case of an extreme emergency."

"Well this—"

"*Isn't,*" Oralie finished for her. "At least not as far as the rest of the Council is concerned. In fact, several Councillors feel that the uncertainty behind Keefe's condition would best be managed medicinally—or by containing him."

Bile soured Sophie's tongue. "They wouldn't order Elwin to keep him sedated, would they? Or lock him away in Exile?"

Or both.

She couldn't bring herself to voice the last option, in case it gave the Council ideas.

Exile's somnatorium was *real.*

Sophie had walked through its disturbingly silent halls.

"I won't let that happen," Oralie promised. "But the more information we have about what the Neverseen are planning for him, the better. Why do you think I'm here? I told you, I'm done hiding from the darker truths in our world. I'm ready to face them—even if it means violating my oaths. I just can't count on any help from the rest of the Council. Particularly because I'm working with you."

Sophie frowned. "But, I'm a Regent now. And the leader of Team Valiant! If they don't trust me—"

"This isn't about trust. It's about *risk*. Like you said, you've become quite valuable to the Council. They've finally realized exactly how much they need you. So to put you in danger this way—"

"I'm always in danger!" Sophie pointed to where Sandor stood sentry by Verdi's pasture—then to where Flori watched them from the edge of the tree line.

She'd gotten so used to being shadowed by bodyguards that she could almost forget they were there—particularly since she was down to only two now that Nubiti was the new queen of the dwarves. Tarina was still ironing things out with her empress after the incident with the illegal troll hive, and Bo was protecting Tam and Linh.

"This is a different level of danger," Oralie insisted. "You've never dealt with a Forgotten Secret before."

"Uh, pretty sure I have," Sophie argued, loud enough to make sure Sandor heard the reminder. The last thing she needed was to have him think she was stepping into a new level of uncharted dangerous territory and shift into overprotective-goblin mode. "*Someone's* cache has to be filled with all of the things Vespera did to get herself locked up in Lumenaria's dungeon. But the Council didn't bother coming clean after she escaped, so I got to learn about her crimes the hard way."

The *very* hard way.

Like, having her human parents captured and tortured after Vespera went back to work on her evil experiments.

And Biana had scars all over her back, arms, and shoulders from when Vespera tried to kill her.

"I suppose you're right," Oralie murmured. "But that should

make you all the more cautious. Forgotten Secrets aren't erased simply to protect the sanity of the Councillors. They're often truths that could send our world spiraling into chaos."

"Yeah, well, what else is new?" Sophie's eyes locked with Sandor's, and thankfully he didn't argue.

But he did seem to be gripping the hilt of his giant black sword a whole lot tighter.

Oralie stepped closer. "I'm not telling you this because I'm going back on our deal—or because I'm trying to scare you. I just . . . need to make sure you're *truly* prepared for the turbulent waters ahead. I can't bear having any more regrets when it comes to you."

Sophie rolled her eyes.

The words were probably meant to be touching—but she knew all Oralie was *really* trying to do was allay her own guilt if something bad happened.

Oralie sighed. "I realize you're angry with me, Sophie. And I'm not trying to start another fight. But regardless of what you may think, I do . . . *care* about you. And someday I hope you'll understand the difficult position I—"

"I won't!"

"You *might*. Things feel so much bigger when you're young. So much more absolute. But . . . love isn't as black-and-white as you believe it to be. It comes in many colors, many forms—"

"Yeah, well, I'm pretty sure none of them involve lying to someone for years, or signing your daughter up to be part of a genetic experiment!"

"It can," Oralie whispered, wrapping her arms around her waist, "when that's the only way to *have* a daughter."

The last word sounded different than the others, and for a second, Sophie found herself meeting Oralie's stare and wishing the Black Swan had made her an Empath. Then she would've been able to tell if the sadness and longing she could see in Oralie's eyes were actually real.

But it didn't matter.

"It wasn't the *only* way," Sophie reminded her. "You just wanted to keep your precious position on the Council."

"I did," Oralie agreed, reaching up and tracing her fingers over the jewels in her circlet. "But that isn't just about me. It might've started out that way when I was first elected. But you have no idea what kind of chaos would ensue if I were to leave—especially for a scandal like this."

Sophie opened her mouth to argue, but . . .

She'd unfortunately already come to the same frustrating conclusion.

The Lost Cities were in turmoil, and losing another Councillor could give the Neverseen the opening they needed to finally take over.

That was why Sophie hadn't told anyone the truth about Oralie.

Not even Fitz.

Despite how much the secret had cost her.

Her heart turned sharp and heavy at the reminder, like a lump of shrapnel slowly shredding the inside of her chest.

She'd gotten used to their "breakup"—if that was even the right term for what had happened between her and Fitz. But that didn't mean she was over it. Or that part of her didn't still wish . . .

"I'm sorry," Oralie said, stepping closer. "I never meant to hurt you."

"Well, you have."

"I know. And . . . I have to live with that."

Oralie's voice cracked—and the sound made Sophie's resolve crack a little too.

But her shrapnel heart snapped her out of it.

Her hands curled into fists. "Yeah, well I get to live with being *unmatchable*. So I win."

Worst. Victory. Ever.

"I'm so sorry, Sophie. Truly."

Sophie jerked away when Oralie reached for her. "Just stop it, okay? You're wasting time."

"Actually . . . I'm not. We needed my tears, didn't we?" Oralie blinked, showing how glassy her eyes had gotten. "I knew the easiest way to trigger them was to remind myself of how much you hate me."

"Oh."

It was the only thing Sophie could think to say.

She was so tired of feeling sorry for people who didn't deserve her sympathy.

"How do you know that starting with tears is the right order for the cache?" she asked, getting back to a subject that actually mattered.

"Because my mind's been fixated on a phrase ever since I started trying to piece together the steps. *Truth starts below.*"

"Am I supposed to know what that means?"

"No, it's a clue I left for myself. And it's not about the words—though I'm sure I chose them because they sound mysterious enough to catch my attention. The secret's in their first letters. *T. S. B.* Tears, sweat, then blood."

"You're sure?" Sophie had to ask as Oralie reached up to wipe the corners of her eyes.

"Positive."

Her voice didn't waver—but Sophie noticed that Oralie held her breath as she smeared her damp fingertip across the curve of the cache.

"Should something be happening?" Sophie asked after several endless seconds.

"Not yet. I've only begun the sequence." Oralie swept the long tendrils of her hair over her left shoulder. "These ringlets are so heavy—they always make my neck glisten."

"Glisten?"

Oralie nodded, and Sophie begrudgingly had to admit that Oralie did look more shimmery than sweaty as she brushed her finger along her hairline and swiped it across the cache—which still didn't respond.

"Now for the part I've been dreading." Oralie bit her lip as she removed one of the golden pins securing her circlet. "The rational side of me knows I'll only feel a tiny prick, but . . . I think you must get your needle phobia from me."

"I'm pretty sure everyone hates needles," Sophie argued, refusing to feel even the tiniest connection to Oralie.

"I suppose." Oralie scowled at the sharp point for a beat before she lowered it toward her fingertip—and Sophie looked away until Oralie announced, "All done."

The cache was streaked with red when Sophie turned back—but nothing else had changed.

"There's one final step," Oralie explained. "*Now* it needs a password—and I actually have two, in case someone ever tried to force me to do this. One that opens the cache, and one that destroys it."

"And you're sure you know which is which?"

"Thankfully I made it easy for myself." She leaned closer, her breath clouding the crystal as she whispered, "Fathdon."

Sophie realized that was Councillor Kenric's last name the same moment the cache flashed glaringly bright and she found herself squinting right at him—or rather, squinting at a small projection of him that was hovering above the glowing orb like a tiny Kenric apparition. A projection of Oralie stood facing him, both of them silhouetted in moonlight, wearing long silver capes with hoods covering their circlets.

"I knew Kenric would be a part of this," the real Oralie murmured. "He always insisted on being involved in everything I did."

"But he doesn't look happy about it," Sophie noted.

The projections were slightly blurry, and some of the details were a little off with their features, since Oralie didn't have a photographic memory. But Sophie could still see the scowl on Kenric's usually smiling face.

"For once, would you please just trust that I know what's best?" he pleaded, knocking back his hood and tearing his hands through his vivid red hair.

"No! You don't get to drag me into this and then not tell me what's going on!" the projection of Oralie argued.

Kenric heaved a sigh. "It doesn't matter. Your memory is going to be erased anyway."

"Then that's all the more reason to keep me informed! The record in my cache should be a *complete* account of what we're up against, not whatever scattered pieces you feel like sharing. Otherwise, what use will it be if we need to reference it in the future?"

"Exactly!" Sophie said, hoping Kenric listened.

But his projection moved closer and reached for Oralie's hand. "Please, Ora. I need you to trust me on this. Can you feel how serious I am when I tell you that it's absolutely essential to keep everything about Elysian fragmented?"

The projection of Oralie frowned. "That's not the word you had me ask Fintan about."

"I know. And I can't tell you what it means, so don't ask. I shouldn't have mentioned it at all, but . . . I always say too much when I'm with you."

"And yet, here I stand, completely in the dark," the projection of Oralie noted.

"Good. You'll be safer that way."

"Elysian doesn't feel familiar," the real Oralie murmured as the projection of Kenric started to pace.

"Is it a place?" Sophie asked, remembering the myths she'd read back in her old school about the Elysian Fields.

Often there were glimmers of truth behind the stories humans told—remnants from the days when the elves and humans still had a treaty between their worlds. Or pieces of the elves' campaign of misinformation to make their existence sound too silly to be believed.

"I truly have no idea," Oralie admitted. "All of this feels strangely . . . detached. It's like I'm watching someone else's life instead of my own. I always thought accessing a Forgotten Secret would be like recovering any other memory, and after a few moments my brain would find enough cues to sync it back into my mental timeline. But this doesn't connect to anything."

"Not even to stellarlune?"

Past Oralie must've been thinking the same thing, because her projection asked Kenric, "Does this Elysian thing have something to do with whatever stellarlune is?"

Kenric sighed. "I can't tell you that, either."

"You can and you *will*." The tiny Oralie stalked forward, grabbing his wrist. "You don't get to show up at my door in the middle of the night, beg me to go with you to see a former Councillor—who seemed particularly unstable, by the way—ask him over and over about whatever stellarlune is, even after I told you he wasn't lying when he said he'd never heard of it, and then stand there, gray as a ghoul because you slipped and said something about this mysterious Elysian."

Kenric let out a soft chuckle. "*Gray as a ghoul*. You've always had a flair for the dramatic, Ora. It's one of my favorite things about you."

"Stop trying to distract me!"

"But I'm so good at it!" Kenric flashed a smug grin as he stepped closer—so close, the toes of their shoes touched. "I seem to remember you losing your train of thought twice the other day when I wore that gray jerkin with the emeralds on the collar. The one you've always said brings out the flecks of green in my eyes."

He batted his lashes and Sophie had to smile.

But the real Oralie looked ready to cry.

And her projection seemed eager to smack him.

"You're ridiculous," she whisper-hissed, reaching up to make sure her hood still covered her circlet before glancing over her shoulder. The memory was too shadowy for Sophie to tell where they were, but the silence in the background made it seem like they were alone. "Tell me about Elysian, Kenric! And stellarlune! And anything else you're investigating! You came to me for help, so let me help!"

"You already have, far more than you know," he assured her. "Fintan was calmer with you there, and that allowed me to finally slip past his guard."

"You breached his mind? Why?"

Kenric backed away, resuming his pacing. "The same reason I always breach someone's mind—but I didn't find the information I was looking for, in case you're wondering. That's probably good news, though. At least this mess is a little more contained than I'd feared. I just wish I could find the source of the leak."

"I'm getting tired of your vagueness and riddles," the projection of Oralie warned.

Sophie snorted. "Welcome to my world."

"The truly strange thing is," the real Oralie murmured, "I can't recall any part of the conversation I apparently had with Fintan. And if the Washers erased it, there should be a second jewel in my cache—or this memory should start much earlier. I suppose it's possible that Kenric washed it himself, but—"

"Kenric was a Washer?" Sophie interrupted.

"One of the best. It was often his job to wash the minds of the other Washers, to make sure they hadn't inadvertently learned anything from their assignments—but he was under oath to never wash the mind of anyone on the Council, even if they asked him to. And I can't see him breaking that vow—especially with me."

"I can, if he thought he was protecting you," Sophie argued.

"I suppose." Oralie studied the tiny versions of herself and Kenric, who seemed to have entered into some sort of epic staring contest. "Actually, now that I think about it, there was another time when my mind felt like it does right now. I woke up in my sitting room, and Kenric was there with . . . someone. I can't remember who—which is strange. I know we weren't alone, but . . ." She rubbed the center of her forehead, like she was trying to massage the detail loose. "I also have no memory of letting them in. But I remember Kenric teasing me about drinking too much fizzleberry wine. And I *had* indulged in a second glass that night with dinner, so that seemed like a logical enough explanation at the time. But . . . I do also remember thinking that something about his smile felt off. I was just too tired to ask him about it. My head was so . . . fuzzy." She frowned, rubbing her forehead harder. "I have that same fuzziness now. It's like . . . trying to feel my way through fog, except there's nothing on the other side, if that makes sense."

"Do you think that other memory has something to do with stellarlune?" Sophie asked. "Or Elysian?"

"It could. But let's not forget that it's equally possible that I truly did have too much wine."

Somehow Sophie doubted that. "And you have no idea what Elysian is—not even a guess?"

She wasn't surprised when Oralie shook her head—but that didn't make her any less ready to scream, *Just once, couldn't you guys call it something like "Our Massive Conspiracy to Control the World" and stop with all the fancy words that don't mean anything?*

"This is such a classic Kenric move!" Oralie huffed, glaring at his projection. "He always kept me out of anything he'd decided was 'too intense.' That's why there's only one Forgotten Secret in my cache."

"Um . . . it sounds like the real reason for that might be because Kenric stole some of your other memories," Sophie had to point out, which made her want to throw a full-fledged tantrum—complete with kicking and flailing.

Sometimes it felt like all she ever did was try to help fill in someone's mental gaps after someone else messed with their memories. It was enough to make her start hating Telepaths.

Oralie turned away, stretching out her hand to catch several of the pinkish, purplish, bluish petals raining around them. "I know what you're thinking, Sophie. But Kenric would never do anything malicious—especially to me. He and I . . ."

She didn't finish the sentence—but she didn't need to.

Kenric's feelings for Oralie had been incredibly obvious, and Sophie had long suspected that the feelings had been mutual.

But she still had to wonder if there'd been a lot more to Kenric than she'd originally realized.

She squinted at his face, wishing she knew more about him.

He'd always been her favorite Councillor—but that had mostly been because he tended to take her side. And that didn't necessarily mean she should've trusted him.

"Is that the end of the memory?" she asked.

"I can't tell," Oralie admitted.

The two projections were standing so still that the image almost looked frozen.

"Do you think—" Sophie started to ask, but Kenric's voice cut her off.

"I'm sorry for dragging you into this, Ora." He dropped his gaze toward the ground. "I tried to avoid it. But I didn't know who else to trust."

Oralie's projection reached for his hands. "If you *really* trust me, tell me what's going on."

For a second he looked tempted. But he shook his head. "I *can't*. And I swear, I'm doing you a favor by keeping you in the dark. I'm counting down the days until I can have the Washers clean this mess out of my brain."

"I can tell." Oralie closed her eyes in the memory. "I feel so much fear and frustration. And . . . is that disgust?"

Kenric pulled his hands away from her. "Let's just say that sometimes I'm not particularly proud to call myself a Councillor."

"It's that bad?" she whispered.

He looked pale when he nodded. "Some days I dream about walking away."

"You mean resigning?" Oralie clarified.

He hesitated before stepping closer. "I've done my share for my people, Ora. I'd have zero problem letting someone else take over. But . . . I won't go unless you resign with me."

Everyone sucked in a breath: Sophie, Oralie, Oralie's projection— even Kenric, as if he couldn't believe he'd just said that.

But he didn't take it back.

Instead, he reached for her face, gently cupping her cheek. "I may not be an Empath, but I know I'm not alone in this. Don't tell me you've never wished—"

"Please don't say it," Oralie begged—but there was no energy behind her plea.

She even leaned into his hand.

"Ora," Kenric breathed, sweeping back her hood, "you don't have to keep fighting this. We wouldn't be the first to walk away because of—"

Oralie shook her head. "Kenric, don't."

His jaw set and his eyes blazed with the same intensity as his voice when he told her, "Because of *love*, Ora. We both know that's what this is, no matter how hard we pretend otherwise."

The real Oralie covered her mouth, tears streaking down her face. Her projection just stood there shaking.

Kenric reached for her other cheek. "Think of how much simpler everything would be if we stopped trying to deny how we feel," he whispered. "How *happy* we could be. How *free*." His gaze shifted to her mouth. "We could have our own place. Our own lives. Maybe someday even our own family."

"Kenric . . ."

He leaned toward her, and her lips parted, like she might let him kiss her. But at the last second she turned her face away.

"I can't do this."

He turned her chin back toward him. "Can't? Or won't?"

"Both."

The word seemed to form a wall between them, growing thicker with every silent second that followed.

Kenric tilted his head. "There's something you're not telling me."

"No—"

"There is. I know you too well, Ora. In fact . . . I might even know what it is."

"There's nothing to know," Oralie swore.

Kenric laughed sadly, stepping back. "Empaths are terrible liars."

"Kenric—"

"That time when you were ill," he interrupted. "When you wouldn't let me take you to see any physicians. I stayed by your side the whole night, just to be safe. And there were a few moments when I couldn't tell if you were asleep or awake. You'd toss and turn and whisper something over and over. Something that sounded . . . a lot like *suldreen*."

Sophie felt her jaw fall open.

"*Suldreen*" was the proper term for a moonlark.

"That doesn't mean—" Oralie's projection tried, but Kenric cut her off.

"I saw how upset you were when Prentice was exiled. And I saw the look on your face when Alden brought us that strand of DNA. Everyone thought it was a hoax or a misunderstanding—but not you. Don't try to deny it, Ora. I saw you flinch when he used the phrase 'Project Moonlark.' And you've tried harder than anyone to stop Alden's search. You think I don't know that you're the one who convinced Bronte to place someone in Quinlin's office to keep an eye on things?"

"So he knew," Sophie said as both Oralies let out a strangled sob. "He knew you're my . . ."

"He must have," the real Oralie whispered. "But I had no idea. He never said . . ." She leaned closer to his projection, shouting, "*Why didn't you tell me when I'd remember it?*"

Kenric, of course, didn't answer.

And Sophie studied him, trying to decide if she wanted to laugh or cry or teleport somewhere far, far away.

Another person she'd trusted, who'd hidden things and lied to her every time she saw him.

That was the worst part of being the moonlark—aside from having enemies trying to kill her all the time.

No one was ever quite who they pretended to be.

"What did he mean about you being ill?" she asked, trying to piece together as much of the *real* story as she could.

Oralie pressed her hand against her stomach. "The process of giving the Black Swan what they needed for your genetics turned out to be more involved than I expected—physically *and* emotionally. And Kenric stopped by right after I returned home from the procedure. I tried to hide it from him, but I nearly fainted just answering the door. So he insisted on taking care of me. But . . . I woke up alone. He told me he went home after I finally fell asleep. Apparently not."

"And you're the reason Quinlin thought his receptionist was reporting on him to the Council?" Sophie verified, remembering the first time Alden brought her to Atlantis. "Not Bronte?"

"It wasn't like Bronte needed any convincing. All I did was suggest that Quinlin and Alden might be overstepping their authority—which they *were*. And then I made sure *I* received the reports on their activities so that I could monitor Alden's progress and also remove any notes about you from the record. I was trying to protect you!"

Sophie had no idea what to do with that information, except to shove it into another mental box of Things She'd Have to Deal with Later.

Her brain was getting pretty cluttered with those.

Someday she'd have to get brave and try to unpack them. But for now, she turned back to the memory, watching Kenric hold up a hand to silence Oralie.

"Don't bother with whatever lie you're about to give," he told her. "We both know I'm right. And . . . I understand. Or I'm trying to, anyway."

"Kenric—"

"And if that's why you have to stay, Ora, then I'm staying too." He tucked one of her ringlets gently behind her ear. "You're going to need all the allies you can get. Especially since someday the Black Swan is going to bring their moonlark into play. You know that, right?"

Oralie's mouth started to form one word. But at the last second she changed to a hushed "yes."

Kenric nodded gravely. "Do you know a lot of other things you aren't telling me?"

"No. I swear, Kenric. That was part of the deal." Her gaze shifted to her feet. "I'm completely separate."

"Good. It'll be easier to protect you that way."

"I don't need your protection!"

"Yes, you do. And you'll have it. I'll be right here by your side, even if I have to pretend that things between us are strictly professional. It's okay," he added, wiping away her fresh tears. "I knew this was how this conversation was going to go. Why do you think I've never said anything before? I just . . . had to say it—at least once. Just to see what would happen. And now seemed like a perfect time, since you won't remember it anyway."

Oralie closed her eyes, letting out a shaky breath. "You can't hide your feelings, Kenric. They're there—every time I'm around you."

His smile was heartbreaking. "I know. Empaths may be terrible liars—but they always find the deeper truth."

"We're not like Telepaths. We can't bury it—or wash it away," Oralie murmured.

"Very true." Kenric tucked another ringlet behind her ear before he pulled her hood back into place and pressed two fingers against her temple. "Still, it'll be hard for you to understand what you're feeling without the context, right? So how about I help you with that? I think it's time to put all of this behind us, don't you?"

"What are you doing? You're not supposed to—"

The projections blinked away, as if someone had flipped a switch. In a way, Kenric had.

"Well," Oralie said, curling her fingers around the cache and leaning against the trunk of the Panakes. "That . . . wasn't what I was expecting."

"Me neither," Sophie agreed, trying to figure out which emotion to go with.

The memory had been intense, and fascinating, and devastating—but also ridiculously disappointing, and maddening, and pointless.

That was all they had to help Keefe?

A new word that meant nothing, a vague mention of a conversation with Fintan about stellarlune—where he apparently didn't know anything—and Kenric and Oralie's star-crossed love story?

"It's okay," Oralie told her, slipping her cache into a pocket hidden in her gown. "This isn't the dead end you're thinking it is."

"Why? Did it finally trigger the other memories?"

"No. But I know where we can find them. Kenric's cache clearly has the information we need. That must be why he asked me to give it to you if something happened to him, and why he made sure I had a way to open it. It works differently than mine, since there are multiple memories inside, but the access sequence is actually a little easier." She held out her hand. "I'll show you."

Sophie's heart dropped into the sloshiest part of her stomach.

Oralie stepped closer, taking Sophie by her shoulders. "Please tell me the panic I'm feeling isn't because you lost Kenric's cache."

Oh, but it was so much worse than that.

Sophie stared at her boots, knowing she had no choice but to explain the whole miserable mess—from Keefe stealing the cache away from her and using it to bribe his way into the Neverseen, to him taking it back when he escaped and then finding out that he'd actually stolen a fake.

Oralie tightened her grip on Sophie's shoulders. "How could you not tell me about this sooner?"

"Uh, the Council hasn't exactly been super supportive and friendly, remember?" Sophie argued.

"*I* have. And I could've helped you get it back!"

"*How?*"

"I . . . don't know," Oralie admitted. "But that doesn't mean I wouldn't have found a way, or that you were right to keep this a secret!"

She had a point.

But Sophie wasn't in the mood to apologize.

Oralie dropped her hands and stepped back, letting out a long, heavy breath. "This has to stop, Sophie. We have to start working *together*. No more secrets. No more lies. You don't have to like me or forgive me—but you do have to trust me. And I'll do the same for you. There's too much at stake—and not just for Keefe. I don't know what Elysian is, or what it has to do with stellarlune, but the fear I can now remember feeling in Kenric was unlike anything I've ever experienced from him. He was always calm and collected, even under incredibly fraught circumstances. So for him to be *that* worried . . ." Her voice hitched and she turned away. "We have to find his cache—now."

"Okay, but *how?*" Sophie repeated.

Oralie stood taller, smoothing her gown. "I suppose we should start with you telling me everything you've already tried. Maybe that'll help us spot something you overlooked."

"We haven't really tried anything," Sophie reluctantly admitted. "There were too many other things going on. I did think about asking Fintan when I met with him, but our deal only allowed me to ask him one question, and there was something else I needed to know more. Plus, I'm sure the Neverseen moved the caches after he was captured, so anything he could've told me would be useless anyway. But . . . I guess we could try making another deal with him just in case—or wait. What about Glimmer? You guys have her in custody, right?"

"In a way, yes. We've placed her at Tiergan's house and made it clear that she's not allowed to leave—and Bo has been tasked with making sure she's constantly supervised. But . . . we've yet to schedule her Tribunal. She's being cooperative enough that we don't want to risk changing her attitude."

Sophie's jaw tightened. "Cooperative *enough* isn't the same as cooperative! Has she told you anything new about the Neverseen?

Like where any of their hideouts are, or any insights into their plans, or—"

"She's answered all of our questions honestly," Oralie assured her. "I've monitored her reactions closely during our conversations. But . . . so far, she hasn't shared anything particularly useful. Then again, neither has Tam. And neither did Keefe, after he escaped, as I'm sure you remember. The Neverseen are incredibly cautious with what they allow their members to know. And there's been no indication that Glimmer's holding anything back from us—at least not beyond her name and what she looks like."

"She still hasn't taken down her hood?"

"She says she doesn't feel safe—and yes, we *could* force her to," Oralie added before Sophie could make that exact suggestion. "But the Council feels she'll be more useful to us if we make her a *willing* ally—and I agree. So we're giving her a little space—a little time—to see if she'll choose to trust us before we try anything more drastic."

Sophie opened her mouth to argue—and realized she had no idea what she wanted to say.

She'd watched Glimmer *voluntarily* help Lady Gisela with her dangerous plans for Keefe—and heard Keefe's mom champion Glimmer's loyalty.

But.

Glimmer had also been the one to turn on Lady Gisela in Loamnore and set Tam free from the bonds that had been controlling him.

And yet . . .

Glimmer was the one who put those bonds on his wrists in the first place.

They also hadn't figured out how Lady Gisela had escaped.

Given her injuries, she would've needed *someone's* help—and while it was possible that a few dwarves remained loyal to her, it was also *just* as possible that Glimmer was trying to do exactly what Keefe had attempted when he ran off and joined the Neverseen, and was pretending to switch sides to try to take down her enemies from the inside out.

Tam seemed to trust her, though . . . and he barely trusted anybody.

So basically, Sophie had no idea what to believe.

"I want to meet with her," she decided, wishing she'd demanded it sooner.

She'd lost so many days sitting by Keefe's side in the Healing Center.

And yet, she needed to get back to him as soon as possible.

"I should be able to make that arrangement," Oralie agreed after a second. "But we need to keep pursuing other leads as well. There's a good chance that Glimmer knows nothing—or that what she knows is now outdated, just like Fintan."

"Okay, but *what* leads?" Sophie hated the whine in her voice, but she was done convincing herself they had something to go on when they didn't.

Oralie chewed her lip, pressing so hard that her teeth left tiny dents. "Well . . . do you think you can find Alvar again?"

The name hit like a thunderbolt, stirring up enough anger, sorrow, and regret to make Sophie dizzy.

"I don't even know if he's still alive," she mumbled.

The last time she'd seen Alvar, he'd looked . . . *grim*.

That'd been one of the reasons why she and Keefe were willing to let Alvar escape in exchange for a little information. The risk of him hurting someone before his time was up had seemed pretty small.

"Still, I think it's worth trying to track him down," Oralie told her. "Maybe Fitz or Biana would know some places he might go to die in peace."

"I suppose I can ask them," Sophie said, feeling ready to vomit just thinking about it.

Biana might not handle it *that* badly.

But Fitz?

Fitz had the *worst* temper.

Especially when it came to anything to do with his brother.

But . . . Alvar was a Vanisher. And he'd already admitted that he'd used his ability to sneak around the Neverseen's hideouts, trying to gain leverage in case he ever needed it. So he might know something about the caches.

Or maybe there was something he hadn't told them about stellarlune.

He might've even heard of Elysian.

"I'll talk to Fitz when I go back to the Healing Center," Sophie promised, reminding herself that they couldn't afford to waste any time.

And maybe because she was dreading that conversation so very much, it took her longer than it should have to realize that the crisp, accented voice shouting inside her head wasn't just a flashback from her memories.

SOPHIE!

SOPHIE!

SOPHIE!

FITZ? she transmitted back, stumbling over her feet when he responded with a brain-splittingly loud *FINALLY!*

WHAT'S WRONG? she asked. *IS KEEFE OKAY?*

If something happened . . .

HE'S FINE, Fitz assured her. *BETTER THAN FINE. THAT'S WHY I REACHED OUT. I FIGURED YOU'D WANT TO KNOW THE GOOD NEWS RIGHT AWAY.*

He paused long enough that she would've clobbered him if he'd been closer.

Then he told her, *KEEFE'S AWAKE.*

-TWO-
Keefe

OKAY, FOR THE TEN-ZILLIONTH TIME:
I'm *fine*," Keefe promised as Elwin snapped his
fingers and replaced the glowing blue orb around
Keefe's head with a neon yellow one. "You don't
have to keep testing me."

Especially with balls of superbright light, which were *not* helping
with all of the pounding going on in his brain.

The pounding didn't mean anything, by the way.

That's why he didn't bother mentioning it.

Of *course* he had a headache!

His mom had just tried to kill him—*again*!

Sure, she'd claimed it was simply the next part of her evil plan to
make him into her own personal super-elf—but that was basically
the same thing. And she could order Bangs Boy and the Flasher girl
with the weird nickname to blast him with as many freaky shadow-
bolts and light beams as she wanted.

It wasn't going to change anything.

He still hated his mom.

Still planned to destroy her creepy organization.

Still had notoriously awesome hair—even if he was probably rocking some major bed head at the moment.

So . . . he was good.

Everything was good.

Well. Maybe not *everything*.

He wasn't a fan of the way Elwin kept blocking him from getting up, because apparently he was supposed to "rest" for a couple of centuries. And he certainly wasn't enjoying the Headache of Doom. Or how twisty and churn-y his insides felt—but he didn't mention *that*, either, because he already knew why his spit tasted so sour.

His mom . . .

She must've gotten away again.

Otherwise he would've woken up to a whole lot of high-fiving and celebrating.

Instead, he'd found Fitz and Elwin staring at him with tired eyes and extra crinkly foreheads—and he didn't know why he was so surprised. Things hadn't exactly been going well before he blacked out, given that pretty much everyone on his side was unconscious and his mom had just gotten exactly what she wanted.

Honestly, he should've been relieved that he hadn't woken up trapped in a Neverseen hideout with Mommy Dearest standing outside of his cell.

But . . . some tiny part of him had still been hoping his friends would pull off a victory—probably because then whatever his mom had done to him wouldn't matter.

Now he was going to have to deal with it *and* deal with her at the same time. Which sounded . . . tiring.

He'd thought about asking Fitz what went wrong. But he wasn't in the mood to hear about all of the mistakes they'd made.

Okay, *fine*—he wasn't in the mood to hear about all of the mistakes *he'd caused everybody to make*, because his brilliant plan had turned out to be a little less-than-brilliant.

Apparently, he shared the Really-Bad-at-Scheming gene with his mom.

And yet somehow she always found a way to beat him.

He couldn't figure out how she kept pulling that off.

Was it ruthlessness, like Vespera had droned on and on about in one of her *Look—I'm-the-queen-of-all-things-evil!* speeches?

Or was it a deeper kind of desperation?

Or pure, random luck?

Or was it something more insidious than all of that?

Could his mom have built some sort of . . . *fundamental flaw* into him during her creepy experiments? A way to make sure that her little Legacy Boy would be just strong enough to do her bidding but not strong enough to take her down?

The possibility felt like an angry T. rex tearing through his already aching brain, and he had to press his arms against his sides to fight the urge to reach up and smack himself.

No way did his mom deserve that kind of credit.

She wasn't some gene-manipulating mastermind.

She was an evil, power-hungry, unstable murderer playing with things she didn't understand—and whatever she'd tried to do to him in Loamnore wasn't going to work.

It wasn't.

He'd make sure of that.

Plus, he had the moonlark on his side—and Foster was even more amazing than the Black Swan had designed her to be.

She was an overachiever like that.

In fact, he'd bet anything that Sophie was the one who'd gotten him safely away from the dwarven capital while he was unconscious.

Though . . . maybe if she hadn't had to do that, his mom wouldn't have escaped.

There was no way to know, so it was probably better not to wonder about it.

He just had to keep fighting and remember that the defeats they'd suffered were . . . mostly a timing issue. After all, his mom had been refining her plan for *years*, and he was stuck playing catch-up—*and* he had holes in his memory slowing him down.

But he was getting smarter every day.

And stronger.

And angrier.

So.

Much.

Angrier.

And all of that rage was going to keep fueling him while he finished this game once and for all.

Until then, he needed to focus on the smaller victories. Like the fact that this time all of his friends had made it through safely. That'd been the first thing he'd asked after he'd woken up—if waking up was the right way to describe the process. He hadn't necessarily been asleep. He'd been sort of . . . *drifting* through a strange mental space where past and present—dream and reality—all blurred together.

He probably should've clung to some of the images his mind had been replaying in case they turned out to be important. But hopefully they were tucked away in his photographic memory, because the only thing he could think about after his vision came into focus was "Where's Sophie? Is she okay?"

According to Elwin, she'd been sitting by his side in the Healing Center for days and had only gone home a few hours earlier because Fitz had convinced her to get a little sleep.

Keefe might've gotten choked up hearing that—but he'd pretended to cough to make sure no one noticed.

Then he'd gone through a list with Fitz name by name, checking that all the other people he cared about had made it out of Loamnore without any injuries. And Fitz had assured him that everyone was good. Even Shady McSilverbangs was back living at Tiergan's house again—not that Keefe necessarily counted Tam as a friend. But he was glad to hear that Tammy Boy hadn't officially turned into an *enemy*, either—mostly because the guy could do some seriously scary stuff when he put his mind to it.

Now if only Keefe could get Elwin to stop with All the Pointless Tests Ever.

It'd also be awesome if Fitz would quit staring at him like he was expecting him to sprout wings and a tail and morph into a gorgodon.

Keefe could practically feel the worry rippling off both of them in prickly little waves.

Actually . . .

Nope.

He had to be imagining that.

The only emotions he could feel automatically were Sophie's—well, and the alicorns'. And humans'. With everyone else, he had to *try* in order to take a reading. He also usually needed physical contact, unless Sophie was enhancing him. And most of the time he had to guess what people were feeling, since a lot of moods felt the same without context.

And thank goodness his empathy worked that way, because Foster's feelings were more than enough for him to handle—not that he didn't love catching glimpses of the *real* Miss F, instead of the brave face she tried to put on for everybody.

But being around Sophie could be *intense*. Particularly when she was worried about something.

It also wasn't a whole lot of fun when her heart got all pitter-pattery—though *that* might be changing.

Foster hadn't told him anything for certain, but he'd sure felt a whole lot of heartache when he'd asked what was going on between her and the Fitzster. She also hadn't corrected him when he'd said he was sorry—which he shouldn't be happy about.

He absolutely, one hundred percent, should *not* be glad that someone he cared about was experiencing any kind of emotional pain—two someones, actually.

But . . . if he was honest . . . he wasn't necessarily *sad*.

He glanced at his best friend, knowing it definitely *wasn't* the right time to grill him about troubles in Fitzphieland—and even if it was, that was the kind of conversation he should stay far, *far* away from for lots of practical, let's-not-turn-this-into-a-huge-mess-of-drama reasons.

But he couldn't seem to stop himself from blurting out, "I'm surprised Foster isn't here by now. I figured you'd do that

Team-Cognates-Forever! thing and telepathically tell her it's time to come yell at me for breaking my promises to stay away from Loamnore."

"Actually, I did," Fitz said, fidgeting with the end of his tunic. "I'm sure she'll be here any second."

And *WHAM!*

A giant gut-punch of feelings hit Keefe out of nowhere.

Sadness.

Nervousness.

Regret.

Loneliness.

Plus, a hefty dash of *anger.*

And as much as Keefe didn't want anything to be different after . . . *everything* . . . he had to admit that the emotions weren't *his.*

He could feel them zinging through the air.

Coming straight from Fitz.

"Sooooooo, how's the nausea?" Elwin asked, raising one of his eyebrows as he snapped his fingers and surrounded Keefe with a bubble of purple light. "Hmm, I guess I should also be asking how the headache's going—and think *very* carefully about how you answer. Remember: I can *see* your cells right now. So there's no use pretending that everything's normal. I know you want that to be true—and believe me, I wish it were. But what happened to you isn't something you can just pretend away. That's why I need you to be honest with me, so I can figure out the best means to help you. We're in this together, and I promise, I'm going to do everything in my power to get you through it. I just need you to cooperate."

He held Keefe's stare as something heavy crashed against Keefe's senses.

Concern.

Usually a tough emotion to recognize, because it felt like a bunch of different things. But Keefe didn't even have to *try* to translate the feeling—which made him want to curl into a little ball and pull the blankets over his head.

Instead, he leaned back against his pillow and propped up his feet.

If he was going to have to deal with . . . whatever *this* was, he wanted to figure it out on his own, without people fussing over him and asking all kinds of personal questions—or freaking out about what it all might mean.

So he twisted his lips into what he hoped was a convincing smirk and told Elwin, "I appreciate the pep talk, Dr. Worries-Too-Much. But really, *I'm fine.* I mean, yeah, I'm a little queasy, and I have a slight headache—but wouldn't you, if you hadn't eaten in two days? Or has it been three?"

Elwin sighed. "Actually, it's probably closer to four at this point."

"Okay, four," Keefe corrected, trying hard not to wince.

But almost *four days* unconscious in the Healing Center?

That was a Foster-Level of almost dying!

He'd have to make sure he returned the favor the next time he saw Mom of the Year.

Or finish her off entirely.

In the meantime, he needed to convince Elwin to let him go home, because he *really* wanted to talk to his dad—which kinda felt like proof that his mom actually *had* broken his brain.

But . . . his dad was an Empath. So maybe Lord Jerkface would know what was happening with Keefe's ability—especially since he'd also been a part of the creepy experiment in the beginning.

Keefe was trying not to think about that.

He was trying not to think about *lots* of things.

He just needed answers—even if he despised where they'd be coming from and dreaded the horrible bargains he'd have to make with Lord Jerkface to get them.

And the sooner he got those answers, the better. So he was careful to keep his voice perky as he told Elwin, "No wonder I have a headache! I mean seriously, what's a guy gotta do to get a meal around here? You'd think the near-death experience would count for at least a few snacks or something. Guess I'll just have to head home and see what weird food Daddy Dearest is making for dinner. He thinks he's some sort of culinary genius, but trust me, he's *not*."

Elwin crossed his arms. "Okay. If that's how you want to play this, I can have Fitz head to the Mentors' cafeteria and get you some butterblasts. I know how much you love those."

Keefe *did* love butterblasts.

But the thought of all that rich, sweet goo made his stomach turn a few backflips, and he had to lock his jaw to stop himself from hurling all over the blankets.

"That's what I thought," Elwin said, shaking his head. "You're not fooling anyone, Keefe. So how about we try this again? On a scale of one to ten, how bad are the nausea and the headache?"

"A two," Keefe tried—but even he didn't believe himself.

Time to switch to his ultimate defense mechanism.

"Okay, fine, maybe a four—but that's still not a big deal! And if you don't believe me, check out Bullhorn over there." He nudged his chin toward the purple-eyed banshee curled up in the corner. "He's *so* not interested in me right now. In fact, I swear, if he could talk, he'd be like"—he shifted his voice down a couple of octaves and added a hint of rasp as he said—*"yo, dudes, this guy is super boring—get him out of my Healing Center so I can get back to snoring!"*

"*That's* what you think a banshee would sound like?" Fitz asked, exactly the way Keefe hoped he would.

Humor made the perfect distraction.

"Hey, not everyone can have the fancy Vacker accent," Keefe said, switching to an impersonation of Fitz's crisp voice. "But you can't stop us from trying."

He nailed the intonations so perfectly that it almost felt . . .

Wrong.

He'd done hundreds of awesome impressions over the years. But this . . .

This was something else.

This felt like he'd channeled some sort of deeper instinct as he'd said the words.

Almost like—

NOPE!

He definitely wasn't going to let his mind go *there*—because there was no way *that* was possible.

None.

Less than none.

Negative infinity!

"Care to explain what just made you grind your teeth and turn so pale?" Elwin asked, snapping his fingers and switching to a bright orange light that felt like it was shredding Keefe's skull.

"If you must know," Keefe said, clearing his throat to make sure his voice sounded like *him* again, "I'm bummed that no one noticed the awesome rhyme I just pulled off. The Black Swan could learn a thing or two from me if they ever go back to the whole mysterious-notes strategy—anyone else miss those days? All the suspense! All the intrigue! All the—"

"Nice try," Elwin cut in, "but you're not going to distract me." He adjusted his glasses and narrowed his eyes as the light around Keefe flared brighter. "Based on what I'm seeing, your nausea has to be at least an eight. And I'd put the headache at a nine."

Keefe would've put them both at a ten.

Maybe an eleven.

But if he admitted that, he'd never get out of the Healing Center.

"Even if you're right," he argued, "and I'm not saying you are—you're missing my point, which was that Bullhorn's not even a tiny bit worried about me. And overreacting is pretty much what banshees live for. So whatever you think you're seeing is just . . . a misunderstanding."

That's all it was, he told himself.

It had to be.

But to be safe, he was never going to impersonate anyone ever again.

He also wished he could block the stinging waves of worry that were now slamming into him from *both* Elwin and Fitz.

And there was a new emotion scraping the edge of his senses, coming from someone who must've been somewhere behind him.

He realized it was impatience right as a much-too-familiar voice called out, "Our pretty little Blondie needs to get back here. She's the only one who can make Lord Funkyhair cooperate."

Keefe had been hoping to avoid that voice for at least a couple more hours.

Or days.

Maybe a year or two.

But sadly, he turned, and there was Ro, leaning against the doorway to the Healing Center.

She gave a mocking wave before reaching up to adjust one of her choppy pigtails, which she must've dyed again, because her hair was now the same vivid red that she'd painted her claws.

It looked like fresh-spilled blood. And her pointy-toothed smile promised *lots* of gleeful revenge. But Keefe could feel *all* of Ro's emotions whirling toward him like spinning daggers.

Anger.

Annoyance.

A tiny wisp of relief—which freaked him out more than the others.

Any goodwill Ro might be feeling toward him had to be buried *deep*.

"All right, you can drop the tough-guy act," Ro told him, stalking closer. "You're way too sweaty and shaky right now to pull it off. Plus, you've got this frantic look in your eyes, like a trapped baby bunny. So it's time to come clean to the nice elf-y doctor and let him give you a bunch of his weirdo medicines, okay? He's also more than welcome to subject you to any and all treatments that involve melting off your skin."

"Counteroffer," Keefe said, throwing back his covers. "I go home and—"

"Nope!" Ro shoved him back onto the cot and reached into her breastplate, pulling out a tiny glass vial that looked like it was filled with curdled snot. "If you insist on being difficult, we can try this another way: I was planning to use this for your first punishment—and you should note my use of the word 'first' there, Funkyhair, because believe me, I have *big* plans for you. But I'll happily change things up and force a few of these amoebas down your throat right now if—"

"No amoebas!" Elwin interrupted, snatching the vial out of Ro's hand with some fairly impressive reflexes.

"You're cute if you think I'm not going to steal that back in about three seconds," Ro warned. "And I'm sure I'll break a loooooooot of things in the process."

"And *you're* cute if you think I don't have an elixir that'll knock you out with a tiny whiff," Elwin countered, patting the satchel slung across his shoulder.

Ro cocked her head to study him. "Not sure I believe you."

"You should, since it'll also make you lose control of your bladder," he warned.

"Yeah, I'm going to need a vial of whatever that is," Keefe chimed in when Ro backed away from Elwin.

"Not going to happen." Elwin stuffed the vial he'd confiscated from Ro into his satchel and latched it closed. "I'll give this back to you later—well, depending on what it is. But in the meantime, I need you to promise me that you'll lay off the microbial punishments. I can't have you giving Keefe anything that could mess with my readings until he's back to normal."

Keefe knew that was his cue to insist that he already *was* back to normal. But . . .

A few weeks free from Ro's nasty microbes was kinda worth staying silent.

Ro heaved a giant sigh. "Fiiiiiiiiiiiiiiine. I suppose I can see the logic behind that. How about a good old-fashioned death threat, then?"

Elwin blocked her from unsheathing one of the knives strapped to her waist. "I'm sure that won't be necessary. Keefe's ready to start cooperating now, isn't he?"

Keefe tapped his chin. "That doesn't sound like me. . . ."

"It doesn't," Ro agreed, wrenching out of Elwin's grip—but Elwin caught her wrist and twisted her arm away from her weapons with a move that made Keefe wonder if Foxfire's physician had gotten some battle training.

"Sooner or later Keefe's going to realize that fighting my help only makes everything worse," Elwin assured Ro as he let her go, "including these symptoms he's trying to pretend aren't there." He turned to Keefe. "Your nausea and headache won't go away on their own, no matter how hard you try to ignore them. In fact, they're going to get progressively worse. So why don't you tell me what I need to know so I can get you some medicine before you pass out or throw up all over my nice, clean Healing Center?"

"See, but a vomit-fest sounds kind of awesome, doesn't it? Oooh! You guys could join in! Who's with me?" He held up his hand for a high five, but everyone left him hanging. "Boo, you're no fun. Seriously, *I'm fi*—"

"If you say 'fine' one more time," Ro interrupted, "I'll *grusom-daj* your scrawny butt into submission!"

Keefe smirked. "Bring it on, Princess. I'm—"

"Enough!" Elwin dragged his palms down his face. "Once again, Ro, I can't let you do anything that might affect Keefe's recovery—but don't look so smug there, Keefe. I have plenty of ways to make your life *very* unpleasant if you insist on being so stubborn."

Ro jumped up and down, clapping. "Please tell me they involve ooze!"

"Ooze sounds good to me," Keefe assured her. "But I'll take mine to go. That way I can ruin my dad's fancy rugs. Or maybe—"

"Ugh, just stop!" Fitz snapped, and Keefe assumed he was talking to Ro, since the ogre princess was blocking Keefe from getting up again. But apparently Fitz had zero BFF loyalty, because he turned to Elwin and said, "Keefe's freaking out right now because he can read all of our emotions without trying to—and without needing any kind of enhancing or contact. And I guess he's translating them way easier than he usually does too. He also ranked his headache and nausea at a ten or an eleven."

Keefe blinked. "You—"

"Yeah," Fitz cut him off. "I read your thoughts without your permission. I'm sorry. But we both know you were never going to tell us what's really going on—and Elwin *needs* to know, so . . ."

He shrugged like it wasn't *that* big of a deal—but Keefe could feel Fitz's sour guilt swirling through the air.

Good.

Fitz sighed. "Come on, don't look at me like that. You think I wanted to hear what you're thinking?"

"Are you still listening?" Keefe asked, trying not to wonder how long Fitz had been eavesdropping—or what *else* he might have heard—as he let his mind flood with an abundance of particularly creative insults.

Fitz tore a hand through his boringly perfect hair. "I get why you're mad. But I'm only trying to help. I know what you're going through—"

"Right—you totally know what it's like to have your mom do deadly experiments on you," Keefe muttered. "I must've forgotten that part of the Vacker history."

"Maybe not," Fitz conceded, "but I *do* know what it's like to have a traitor in the family. And I also remember how scary it is to wake up in one of these cots after being brutally attacked—just like I know how hard it is to talk about what's wrong, because it feels like you're admitting that the Neverseen beat you. But they only win if you keep pretending everything's normal, because you end up making the damage permanent."

"I'm not *damaged*—"

"You're right. That's the wrong word." Fitz blew out a breath. "Look, all I'm trying to say is that I wouldn't be walking right now if I hadn't let Elwin help me. I probably wouldn't even be alive. So I want to make sure you get the help you need—and you *do* need it, Keefe. No matter what you want to believe. But accepting help doesn't make you weak. It just means you're taking care of yourself."

Ro whistled. "What do you know? For a moment, I actually like Captain Perfectpants."

"Good, you can be *his* bodyguard," Keefe grumbled, well aware of how sulky he sounded.

But it was super annoying when people made valid points when he'd rather be mad at them.

Plus, he was now getting slammed with sour waves of his least favorite emotion.

"I *really* don't want your pity," he warned, squeezing his blankets so hard he could feel the fibers in the fabric stretching.

Elwin plopped down on the cot next to him. "Good. Because you're not going to get it."

Keefe snorted. "Uh, hate to break it to you, Dr. Pity-Party, but—like Fitz just told you—I *know* you're lying."

"You sure what you're picking up is pity?" Elwin countered as Keefe fanned the air. "Because from what I've heard, pity can feel a whole lot like empathy—and apparently empathy is an emotion a lot of Empaths struggle to distinguish. Don't ask me why—maybe the name throws you guys off? Either way, I can't speak for Fitz and Ro. But for me"—he held out his hand—"I think you should check your reading."

Keefe glared at Elwin's fingers, waiting for him to give up. But Elwin just sat there, raising one eyebrow until Keefe finally swiped his thumb across Elwin's pinky.

"*Focus,*" Elwin said when Keefe doubled over. "Take a deep breath if you need it."

Keefe closed his eyes and inhaled, struggling to sort through the emotions battering his senses.

He'd never felt a reading so strongly—not even while Sophie was enhancing him.

But as his breathing steadied and his mind sharpened, he realized Elwin was right.

There was no pity.

Only worry, and frustration, and concern, and sadness, and anger, and determination, and lots of other things that twisted together into something that felt . . . warm.

Elwin cared.

"I think you're starting to get it," Elwin said, waiting for Keefe to look at him before he added, "I understand why you're trying to push everyone away. You've had so many people let you down that it's hard for you to trust anybody. But I'm on your side, Keefe. No matter what happens. And I promise, I'll never give you any judgment or pity. I'm just here to help you through this, so will you please let me? We can even come up with one of those names you're always giving things. Team Sencen-Heslege?"

"Huh—I never knew your last name," Fitz mumbled.

"There's a *lot* you don't know about me," Elwin told him, before turning back to Keefe. "So, what do you say? Team Sencen-Heslege for the win? Or maybe Team Troublemaker and the Worrying Doctor?"

"Oh! Team Funkyhair and Funkyclothes!" Ro suggested, pointing to the krakens covering Elwin's sleeves.

"Hey, don't knock my special tunics!" Elwin told her. "I'm a trendsetter! In fact, I think Keefe and I should get matching outfits as our team uniform. Maybe gulons—or are you still trying to pretend you had nothing to do with that?" He frowned when Keefe didn't smile. "Come on, Keefe. Stop overthinking this. The more you sink into your head, the more you're going to keep missing important stuff. Like, oh . . . I don't know . . . how about the fact that what's going on with your empathy sure sounds a lot like what happens when everyone first manifests?"

Keefe sat up taller.

"Ha, didn't think about that, did you?" Elwin asked.

No.

He definitely hadn't.

And Elwin was right.

This was exactly how he'd felt when he'd manifested as an Empath.

Well, maybe not *exactly*—but it was close enough.

Special abilities were always disorienting in the beginning.

It was *normal* to be overwhelmed.

In fact, when his empathy first kicked in, he'd ended up laughing and crying at the same time—*and* he'd gotten majorly queasy that night. And sure, the nausea was partly because he suddenly had proof of how little his parents cared about him—but it was also because being an Empath is *rough* sometimes.

"You're feeling better now, aren't you?" Elwin asked.

He absolutely was.

He also wasn't sure if he wanted to kick himself for being so dense, or wrap Elwin up in a giant bear hug. But he settled for collapsing back onto his pillows, shaking with so much laughter that it was a little tough to breathe.

"Um . . . I think it might be time to give our boy a sedative," Ro noted.

"No, I'm fine," Keefe choked out—meaning it for the first time. "It's just . . . Don't you realize what this means? My mom almost killed me, *and* did painful experiments on herself and my dad, *and* took Bangs Boy prisoner, *and* made a really bad deal with King Enki—and who knows what other ridiculous stuff she did—all so she could *make me manifest as an Empath all over again*! It's like . . . the most epic fail of all epic fails!"

Another round of laughter took over, and he curled his knees into his chest as relieved tears streamed down his cheeks.

His mom hadn't changed him!

All he needed was a couple of days for his empathy to settle down and then he'd be back to his old self again!

Or that's what he'd started to believe—until Fitz had to go and prove that he was the worst best friend in the history of best friends by asking, "Okay, but . . . what about the mimicking?"

"Mimicking?" Elwin repeated as Keefe tried to calculate how many times he could smack the teal-eyed Wonderboy with his pillow before Elwin stopped him.

He should've just grabbed the pillow and started whomping, because then he could've stopped Fitz from adding, "That's why Keefe got so pale after he impersonated my voice. He thought it felt like he'd tapped into some sort of deeper instinct—which sounds like mimicking, doesn't it? And his mom *is* a Polyglot. And Polyglots usually have more than one ability, so . . ."

Keefe went back to strangling his blankets. "Might as well go ahead and say it, Fitzy, since you clearly already believe it."

Fitz kicked his toe into the side of his boot. "Even if I'm right, it's not like it's a bad thing. So you're a Polyglot *and* an Empath? That—"

"You are?" a new voice interrupted.

A beautiful voice.

Keefe's favorite voice—even when it was all squeaky with worry.

But he'd barely caught a glimpse of a pair of gold-flecked brown eyes before he called out, "'Bout time you got here, Foster!" before an emotional storm crashed against his senses.

Panic and *confusion* and *joy* and *fear* and *frustration*—plus a billion other things Keefe couldn't translate because it was way too much for his poor pounding brain.

"Uh, you should probably step back, Sophie," Fitz warned. "I think your emotions are too strong for him."

"No, they're not!" Keefe argued—and *wow*, did his voice sound strained. He cleared his throat and tried again. "Nothing's wrong. I swear, I'm fine."

"He keeps saying that," Fitz told her—because he was *begging* for a face-punch. And if the world hadn't gotten so spinny, Keefe might've given it to him when Fitz added, "But Keefe's been picking up all of our emotions without even trying. And he's always been able to do that with you, so I think you're overwhelming him right now."

"Okay, I'm done liking Captain Perfectpants," Ro announced.

Keefe was right there with her—which was probably why he blurted out, "Uh, for the record, most of the emotions are coming from you, Fitzy. You wouldn't happen to have some unresolved feelings for anyone in this room, would you?"

Agonizing silence followed—along with enough misery to make the room blurry. All Keefe could see were splotches of color, and he closed his eyes and reached up to rub his temples, trying to think of something to fix the mess he'd just made—but that only made the dizziness worse.

Elwin coughed. "Well. I think maybe visiting hours should—"

"No," Keefe interrupted, turning toward the blobby shape where

Elwin had been sitting a few seconds earlier. "It's okay. My senses just . . . need to adjust. Plus, I never took anything for the headache and nausea. I should have."

"Yes, you *should*," Elwin agreed, leaning in to whisper, "Guess Ro was right about what we needed to get you to cooperate—or *who* we needed."

Keefe felt his cheeks burn.

He wanted to snap back with some sort of clever denial, but witty banter was way too much for his spinning brain. So he settled for a shrug as Elwin's blurry shape moved toward the colorful shelves of elixirs, and the sound of glass vials plinking against each other echoed through the awkwardness.

If Fitz's grumpy resentment had been the only emotion churning around the room, Keefe would've let him stand there and stew in it—maybe even made another joke to amp it up. But Foster's feelings were such a brutal mix of hurt, heartache, and humiliation that he had to mumble, "Sorry. I didn't mean that the way it sounded. I just meant—"

"I think it's best if I don't let you finish that sentence," Ro jumped in. "The probability of you making things worse is muuuuuuuuuch too high. And since I'm being more helpful than you deserve, I'll also add that now might be a good time for you to tell us how you're feeling—and spoiler alert: 'Fine' is *not* the correct answer."

Keefe rolled his eyes. "Okay, how about this? My senses are a little overloaded—but it's definitely *not* anyone's fault."

"It got worse once I was here, though, right?" Sophie asked, sounding farther away.

Keefe followed her voice to a blurry blond shape lurking in the doorway, along with a gray blob that was probably Sandor. "It's *not* you, Foster. Trust me. The dizziness isn't getting any better with you standing way over there."

Which was true!

And supergood news—unless it meant she was still too close . . .

"I just need medicine," he insisted. "Elwin to the rescue!"

Too bad the first elixir Elwin gave him only succeeded in making him gag. And the sickeningly sweet one after that actually made his headache *worse*.

But then Elwin gave him a vial filled with something sour that felt strangely cold when it hit his tongue, and the brain-pounding faded to a soft pulse as the room sharpened into focus.

Elwin followed that with a bubbly elixir that helped Keefe's insides stop all the backflipping.

"Now we're getting somewhere," Elwin said, flashing lavender light around Keefe's head. "And you're probably right about needing to eat something. Think you can take down three squelchberries?"

He handed Keefe three purplish, reddish, fuzzy things that kind of looked like dead caterpillars, and Keefe's stomach tightened—but he shoved them into his mouth and . . .

"Guess I should've warned you not to do that," Elwin said as the evil fruits melted into an earthy-tasting slime that glued Keefe's jaw shut. "Sorry, I thought you were familiar with squelchberries. They have a whole meal's worth of nutrients in each bite—but they have to be eaten one at a time, otherwise there's too much juice."

"I wouldn't call this juice," Keefe said—or that's what he tried to say. With his teeth stuck together it sounded like "Hai-wunnit-hall-ish-oosh."

"Okay, I'm going to need about a thousand of those," Ro told Elwin.

"Me too!" Keefe added, but it came out like "Hee-oo!"

Elwin laughed. "I almost want to give you guys a bag and see what kind of chaos ensues. But I'm guessing I'd end up regretting that. And thankfully there's an easy fix. Tilt your head back, Keefe, and try to open your mouth as much you can."

Keefe did as he was told—though the Sticky Juice of Doom forced some strange combination of grinding teeth and fish lips. And when Elwin tried to pour in a little Youth, it mostly splattered Keefe's face.

"This may be the greatest thing I've ever seen," Ro informed everyone. "Can we try dunking his head next?"

"I'd be happy to help," Sandor volunteered in his strange, squeaky voice.

"I'm down," Fitz agreed.

"I'm just glad I'm not the only one who doesn't know everything about all the weird plants and foods here," Sophie added quietly—which was why she was Keefe's favorite.

"Hang in there, Keefe," Elwin said, drenching Keefe even worse than the first time. But a tiny bit seeped through the cracks in his teeth, making the gooey glue start to loosen. "A little more should do the trick."

He soaked Keefe again, and that time the cool water washed away enough goo to let Keefe wrench his jaw open.

"Wait!" Elwin warned when Keefe started to close his mouth.

"You have to rinse the rest of the juice down first, or you'll get stuck again."

It took *four* bottles of Youth before Elwin announced that the squelchberry slime was gone—and Keefe's stomach felt like he'd swallowed the entire ocean.

Ro let out a happy sigh. "Seriously—you *have* to give me some of those berries."

"Same!" Fitz flashed Keefe a wide smile, but Keefe could feel the tension lingering in the air between them.

He just didn't have the energy to deal with it right then.

Especially since the brain pain was back with a vengeance.

"How are you feeling?" Sophie asked, and Keefe's gaze shifted to where she stood in the doorway, looking wary and worried and . . .

Absolutely perfect.

Which was a dangerous thought to have around her telepathic, eavesdropping maybe-boyfriend, so he quickly added, *No sign of any injuries.*

"You don't have to stay back, Foster," he told her, scrubbing his fingers through his drenched hair, trying to bring a little life back to it. "Seriously. I'm much better now. Right, Elwin?"

Elwin snapped his fingers, wrapping orange light around Keefe's head. "I'd prefer you to take another dose of headache medicine first."

"Bring it on. Just no more squelchberries, okay? Let's save those to sneak into Ro's dinner, so we can all have a few hours of silence."

"Um, excuse me, Berry Boy—I think you're forgetting that I have *plenty* of ways to make your life miserable, even with the doc's restrictions." Ro shot a meaningful glance at Sophie that Keefe *really* hoped no one noticed.

Elwin saved him from having to reply by handing him another elixir, and Keefe sighed as the cold tingles made his skull-pounding fade.

"See, Foster?" he asked, offering what he hoped was a reassuring smile. "I'm all good. You don't have to keep hiding in the doorway."

He waved her over, and she chewed her lip for several seconds before taking the world's tiniest step closer—which would've been adorable if another worry storm hadn't slammed hard into Keefe's senses.

She scrambled back so fast that she crashed into Sandor. "It *is* my fault!"

"No, it's not what you think!" Keefe sucked in a shaky breath, trying to figure out how to explain it. "You got nervous about moving closer, right? *That's* what I felt. And it's not just you. I'm picking up *everyone's* mood swings right now, without trying—even Gigantor's, who, I gotta say, is a big old softie. Who knew our favorite goblin had so many fuzzy feelings?"

Sandor let out a squeaky growl.

But the joke mostly fell flat. And Sophie's worry surged even stronger.

"I'm seriously okay, Foster," Keefe promised. "It's always this way when Empaths first manifest—ask Elwin."

"Well, I'm not an Empath," Elwin corrected. "But . . . abilities do tend to be overwhelming in the beginning. And it seems like Keefe's empathy has been reset. I'm sure you understand better than any of us how intense that can be, right, Sophie?"

"Yeeesss," she agreed, dragging out the word as she tugged softly on her eyelashes.

She really was the cutest worrier ever.

"I'm *fine*, Foster," Keefe assured her, "and yes, Ro, I know I keep saying that. But I'm serious. In a couple of days, I'll be totally back to normal."

Sophie flicked an eyelash away. "But . . . Fitz said you're a Polyglot now. . . ."

Fitz at least had the decency to look uncomfortable as he mumbled, "Well . . . I don't know for sure if he is. But he mimicked—"

"No, I *thought* I mimicked," Keefe corrected. "That doesn't mean I was right."

"You realize there's a super-easy way to settle that, don't you?" Ro asked before Fitz could argue. "Do the pretty boy's snooty voice again!"

Keefe snorted. "Thanks, I'll pass."

As soon as the words left his mouth, the worry storm kicked up again, thrashing against his senses so hard, it felt like a hurricane.

"What's wrong?" he asked, struggling to focus on Sophie. "Why are you looking at me like that?"

She sacrificed another eyelash before she told him, "Because . . . you understood Ro. And you replied back in her same language."

Her same language?

He spun toward Ro. "You were speaking Ogreish?"

Ro nodded. "So were you. And your pronunciation was eerily perfect. Who knew you could growl like that?"

It was the perfect setup for a joke.

But Keefe couldn't find anything funny to say.

He couldn't find any words at all—except the ones he *really* didn't want to admit.

He made himself say them anyway.

"So . . . I guess I'm a Polyglot, then."

"Why is that bad?" Elwin asked as Keefe reached for his pillow and hugged it tight, wishing it was Mrs. Stinkbottom. "Your dad's an Empath. Your mom's a Polyglot. Now you have both of their abilities. That's honestly the way the matchmakers wish it would work all the time!"

Keefe squeezed his pillow tighter. "Awesome, because my goal in life has always been to make the matchmakers happy. Besides, we all know I wasn't a Polyglot yesterday—or the day before, or the day before that. And I wouldn't be one now if my mom hadn't attacked all of my friends, bound me to King Enki's throne, and . . ."

He shook his head, not wanting to relive the rest.

But his brain still gave him a full playback—and thanks to his photographic memory he got to witness the terror in Sophie's eyes as she watched the freaky shadows rush toward him, and the agony on Tam's face, and his mom's sickening smile.

He'd told himself not to look at her, but he'd stolen one quick glance, and . . .

She'd looked *triumphant*.

Like, *Yay, torturing my son is the greatest thing I've ever done!*

And now he was going to have to face her again someday and watch her celebrate how she'd gotten exactly what she wanted.

"Hey."

Sophie's voice sounded closer, and when Keefe followed the sound, she was standing only a few steps away.

His senses hadn't overloaded when she moved—which should've been good news.

But he was too busy freaking out to care.

"Hey," Sophie said again, closing the last of the space between them. "I know what you're thinking—and *not* because I read your mind. I just . . . I get it, okay? I've been experimented on too. I know what it's like to have *unnatural* abilities—how unsettling it is. And I've been lucky, since the Black Swan—"

"Aren't psychotic murderers?" Keefe interrupted, twisting his pillow into a stranglehold.

"Well . . . yeah," Sophie admitted. "That does make it a little easier. But I've also been lucky because they've been pretty good about reminding me of something I'm sure your mom is hoping you'll forget." She waited for him to look at her before she said, "You still have a choice, Keefe. Nothing your mom does will ever take that away. She can give you whatever abilities she wants, but she can't make you use them. You're not her puppet—you're Keefe Sencen: the most stubborn person I know."

Sandor snorted from the doorway. "Boy, is *that* the truth."

"Tell me about it," Ro agreed.

Keefe felt his lips twitch, like they *wanted* to smile.

"You should listen to your pretty little Blondie, Hunkyhair," Ro told him. "I honestly don't get what your mom is thinking. Like . . . she's met you. She has to know there's no way you're ever going to do what she wants you to. So why give you more elf-y powers to use against her?"

"And why a Polyglot?" Fitz added. "It's not exactly the most useful talent. Not that it's bad or anything," he added, glancing sheepishly at Sophie—which normally would've given Keefe an abundance of Fitzphie Fail jokes.

But he'd been wondering the same thing.

What did his mom think he was going to do for her now that he was a Polyglot?

Translate stuff?

Mimic voices?

She could already do all of that herself!

"Well . . . maybe this is proof that your mom's plan isn't very good," Sophie suggested.

"Yeah, most of the Neverseen's plans don't make a whole lot of sense," Fitz reminded him.

"And yet, they keep beating us," Keefe muttered, tossing his pillow aside, "usually because we can't figure out what they want until it's too late. Aaaaaaaaaaaaand here we are again."

"Wow, that's *quite* a pity party you're throwing for yourself," Ro told him.

"Uh, if anyone's heaping on any pity, it's you guys." Keefe fanned the air, which felt so thick and sour it made him want to vomit.

"I don't think your senses are as good as you think they are," Sophie said, offering him her hand, just like Elwin had earlier. "You're not getting any pity from me. Go ahead and check."

Keefe stared at her gloved fingers, very aware that holding her hand in front of the Fitzster was a terrible idea—even if it was just to take a reading.

But . . . he couldn't leave her hanging there, could he?

And he *was* curious about what she was feeling.

So he reached up and . . .

There were no words.

Keefe had never stood directly under a waterfall before, but he was pretty sure he knew what it felt like now as every possible emotion crashed against his senses with the force of a million stampeding mastodons.

He couldn't think.

Couldn't breathe.

Even after he yanked his hand back—assuming he actually did that.

He couldn't tell.

He couldn't feel his body anymore.

All he could feel was fear and fury and panic and pain and hate and horror and sadness and regret and things he didn't have words for—pounding and stretching and twisting and tearing and shredding.

His lungs screamed for air, and his brain screamed for help, and the rest of him just screamed the only word—the only thought—left in his exploding head.

The plea was fire and ice on his tongue, searing hot and cold as he ordered his senses to do the only thing that would save him.

"NUMB!"

And it worked.

The roaring faded.

The emotions vanished.

The nausea and headache eased.

And his starved lungs sucked in a trembling, grateful breath.

Then another.

And another.

His pulse followed the same steady rhythm, and his vision sharpened into focus, and he searched the room, realizing he was now surrounded by . . .

. . . blank stares.

Sophie.

Fitz.

Elwin.

Even Ro and Sandor.

They just stood there, slack-jawed and unblinking.

And he realized.

He wasn't numb.

Everybody else was.

- THREE -
Sophie

SOPHIE HAD BEEN DRUGGED BEFORE.

Lost days drifting in and out of a blurry haze.

But she'd never experienced anything like *this*.

There were no words to describe it.

No metaphors or comparisons.

Everything was just . . .

Blank.

She could hear her pulse pounding in her ears—see her chest rise and fall with each breath.

But she couldn't *feel* it.

Nor could she register any trace of the panic her brain kept telling her she should be experiencing.

She was empty.

She was nothing.

Life had become a memory.

All that remained was *existence*.

She realized her arms were moving and glanced down, watching a pair of hands jostle her wrists. The jarring motion should've startled her, but she couldn't feel that, either. She also couldn't tell when she lost her balance. The only clue was the ground rushing toward her—and some tiny part of her wanted to scream. But she didn't have the energy.

She couldn't even brace for the crash.

But the hands holding her wrists pulled her back up and steadied her as a familiar voice echoed in her ears.

"Sophie."

"Sophie!"

"SOPHIE!"

She didn't know how to answer.

Even when the calls turned to pleas.

Then commands.

"WAKE UP!"

"RELAX!"

"UNDO!"

Nothing made any difference.

"Please," the voice begged. "Please don't be numb anymore."

Still no change.

Time slowed to a crawl and Sophie tried to count her breaths. But she kept losing track after three or four.

She'd just started over again when the voice spoke, sounding sharper—*darker*—as it told her, *"FEEL!"*

Then it was like being dumped into a pool of hot *and* cold water.

Too many sensations.

Too many emotions.

All surging and swirling and churning—making her head spin and her heart race and her knees collapse again.

The hands holding on to her wrists came to her rescue once more as thumps and crashes thudded all around her. She tried to follow the sounds, but her brain and eyes weren't ready to focus.

She needed to start smaller.

She concentrated on that small point of contact—the gentle pressure of fingers against her skin, sharing their strength while her own failed her.

She knew those hands.

And she knew the voice they belonged to.

"Keefe?" she whispered as her vision slowly sharpened.

Her eyes traced the line of his arms up past his shoulders, to his pale, terrified face, and he nodded and burst into tears—and seeing his raw, unrestrained emotion unlocked something deep inside Sophie, flooding her with a softer, gentler rush that made her feel like *her* again.

A sob crawled up her throat, and she didn't try to swallow it down.

She'd never try to bury her emotions again.

They were *far* too precious.

"Keefe," she repeated, scrambling to grab his hand when he tried to back away. "What happened?"

He shook his head again, pulling free from her grasp.

"Whatever that was, it wasn't your fault," she promised as he sank onto his cot and dragged the covers up over his head.

"Yes, it was," a new voice declared—a voice Sophie didn't hear very often. And when she did, it usually meant problems.

She spun toward the sound and there was Councillor Alina, standing in the doorway wearing a ridiculously fancy purple gown, staring with narrowed eyes at the Keefe lump hiding under his blanket.

Sophie was more interested in the frilly pink figure beside her.

"You told the Council that Keefe was awake?" she asked Oralie, not bothering to hide her irritation.

She hadn't trusted Oralie *much*, but she'd thought after Oralie's *we have to start working together* speech, it was at least safe to explain why she had to rush back to the Healing Center.

Apparently not.

"Of course she told us," Alina said, adjusting her peridot circlet. "I realize this is a difficult concept for you to grasp, but we're your *leaders*. We expect to be apprised of *all* significant developments. And it's a good thing Oralie hailed me, because this is an even bigger disaster than I feared."

Oralie sighed. "There's no need to be so dramatic, Alina."

"Oh, really?" Alina pointed at something behind Sophie. "Then why do I see four unconscious bodies on the floor?"

"Bodies?" Sophie repeated, wheeling around and gasping. "Fitz!"

He was a tangle of arms and legs.

So was Elwin.

And Ro.

And Sandor—though he was flat on his stomach, as if he'd leaped to get to her and ended up face-planting instead.

"We're not unconscious," Elwin mumbled, his voice groggy and his glasses askew as he carefully sat up. "We're just moving a little slow, from . . . everything. Plus, this floor is definitely not as soft as I wanted it to be."

"No, it's not," Fitz agreed, wincing as he rose to his knees. He reached up to rub his left shoulder, but Sophie didn't see any other injuries.

Sandor seemed okay too, looking more dazed than hurt as he shakily rose to his feet.

Sophie wanted to kick herself for forgetting about them as she watched Elwin hand Fitz a vial of something that was probably a painkiller—and she felt even worse when she realized that Keefe had saved her from falling, but hadn't been able to help anyone else.

"Normally I'd give you some 'smooth points' for taking care of your pretty little Blondie and leaving Captain Perfectpants to fend for himself," Ro told Keefe as she stood and stretched. "But next time, how about a little help for the person who knows a hundred different ways to kill you?"

The Keefe lump under the blanket didn't respond.

"Shouldn't there be another bodyguard here?" Alina asked. "The female assigned to Fitz?"

"Grizel is doing a perimeter sweep," Sandor told her.

Sophie had bigger questions. "Does anyone know what happened?"

"No. But I'm guessing *this* is why Mommy Dearest gave her little Legacy Boy that weird ability that starts with a *P*," Ro muttered. "What's it again? A Polystar?"

"What I saw had nothing to do with being a *Polyglot*," Councillor Alina argued. "Polyglots simply have a capacity for language and intonation. They can't affect emotion."

"Does that mean Keefe's a Beguiler?" Fitz asked, and Sophie's mouth turned sour.

She didn't know much about the ability—only that Councillor Alina was one, and that Beguilers could use their voice to affect what people were feeling.

But the thought of Keefe being able to do something like that sounded . . . complicated.

Alina shook her head. "Beguiling is about suggestion—persuasion. Planting thoughts in someone's mind to guide them to a desired response, preferably without them even realizing what you're doing. That's not what happened here."

"How much did you see?" Elwin asked, straightening his glasses as he stood.

"Not much," Oralie told him.

"But *enough*," Alina insisted. "We arrived right before he gave the command that brought you all out of whatever strange trance he'd put you in."

"It wasn't a trance," Sophie argued. "I was conscious. I just couldn't . . ."

"*Feel*," Fitz finished for her, turning slightly pale.

Oralie shivered. "I've never experienced anything like that numbness."

"You could sense it?" Elwin asked.

Oralie nodded. "There was a strange emptiness in the air. And when he snapped you out of it, the deluge of emotion felt like it was drowning me."

"I had to steady her," Alina added, the silky fabric of her gown swishing as she stalked closer to Keefe's cot. "Care to shed any further insights on the situation, Mr. Sencen?"

Keefe's only response was to pull the blanket even tighter around his head.

"He's scared to talk," Fitz explained, "in case something goes wrong again."

Alina frowned. "I'm assuming you know this from communicating with him telepathically?"

"Well, he's mostly ignoring me," Fitz admitted. "But that's what he was worrying about when I checked his thoughts—and now he's grumbling about eavesdropping Telepaths."

Sophie couldn't necessarily blame Keefe for that—even if part of her also wished she'd thought to reach out to him that way.

Her brain felt like it was five steps behind everybody.

"It just . . . doesn't make sense," she said quietly. "Keefe said all kinds of other stuff that didn't have any effect on us. He was talking like normal until . . ." She stared at her hands.

"Did you enhance him?" Fitz asked, voicing the same question she'd been about to ask herself.

She replayed her memories. "I don't think so. I feel like I'd know if I had. And I can control the ability now—*and* I'm wearing gloves as backup. Plus, Keefe was holding my wrists—not my hands—when he snapped us all out of it, so there's no way I could've enhanced him for that."

"Yeah, I guess." Fitz dragged a hand through his hair. "Seems like you must've done *something*, though, since he was fine until . . ."

He didn't finish the sentence. But he didn't need to.

"Until I showed up," Sophie mumbled miserably.

Her emotions had overwhelmed Keefe the moment she'd walked into the Healing Center. So . . . maybe the physical contact had pushed him over the edge.

"Okay, I'm definitely not an expert on your freaky elf-y abilities," Ro jumped in, "but I don't think it's anything you did, Blondie."

"Of *course* you don't," Fitz grumbled.

"Uh, because I know how to use my brain," Ro snapped back. "I've watched her and Hunkyhair together more than anyone, and they always have a calming influence on each other."

"Maybe," Fitz conceded. "But that was before . . ."

Once again, he didn't finish the sentence. And once again, he didn't need to.

Before Keefe's mom changed him.

It was time to start acknowledging that, wasn't it?

He was a Polyglot now.

And he could do . . . whatever it was that had made them all go numb.

"I think part of the problem," Elwin said, yanking back the blanket covering Keefe's head, "is that we don't know what Keefe actually did, so we're just speculating and making assumptions."

He snapped his fingers, flashing an opalescent orb around Keefe's entire body as Keefe rolled to his side, keeping his back to everyone.

"It was his tone," a hushed voice said from the doorway, and Sophie turned to find a third Councillor watching them.

It took her brain a second to recognize him as Councillor Noland—one of the Councillors she rarely interacted with. His dark hair had been slicked back into a very tight ponytail, and he had the most sculpted eyebrows she'd ever seen.

His eyebrows scrunched together as he repeated, "It was his tone. Keefe's inflection shifted when he gave the command that brought back your emotions. So it's safe to assume he did the same when he numbed you."

"You're sure?" Alina asked.

Noland nodded. "I know voices."

He did.

He was a Vociferator—another talent Sophie didn't fully understand. All she knew was that Noland could make some painfully loud sounds when he wanted to. Which might explain why he was speaking so softly.

"So . . . you're saying Keefe's a Vociferator?" Fitz asked.

"No, I'm saying he can give his words power—which also means he can take that power away and let his words simply be words. It all depends on his tone." He made his way to Keefe's cot. "I understand how it feels to fear your own voice," he whispered when Keefe didn't turn to face him. "But hiding behind silence is not the answer. You must learn control. Restraint. Master *when* and *how* to use this ability."

"Are you volunteering to train him?" Alina asked.

Noland shook his head. "I doubt I will be of much use. As I said, he's not a Vociferator."

"Okay, so . . . what *is* he?" Sophie asked.

Everyone waited for Noland's answer—even Keefe peeked over his shoulder.

So the room filled with a collective groan when Noland told them, "Honestly, I have no idea. This is something new to me."

"A *new* ability?" Alina clarified.

"Why do you say that like it's a bad thing?" Noland wondered. "Every ability begins somewhere."

"Yes, but most begin *naturally*," Alina argued. "And there was nothing natural about this."

"There wasn't," Noland agreed, shifting his gaze to Sophie. His eyes had a slight purplish tint, like the tanzanites in his circlet, and they seemed to twinkle as he added, "But I'm staring at someone else with *unnatural* abilities. And she's proven to be quite a valuable asset. Hopefully this boy will be the same."

He placed his hand on Keefe's wrist, and the warm, burnished tone of Noland's skin made Keefe look extra pale.

"Look at me, Keefe," he ordered, and after several long breaths Keefe slowly rolled toward him. "It's time to stop fearing this change. You need to speak again. Trust me—*this* we have in common. You need to prove to yourself that you can do it—still be normal. Still be *you.*"

He's right, Sophie transmitted when Keefe pressed his lips together. *Nothing bad is going to happen.*

Keefe's eyes met hers, and she took that as permission to open her mind to his thoughts.

Nothing bad is going to happen, she promised again.

You don't know that, he argued.

Yes, I do. What happened was a fluke. Just . . . don't say "numb," and you'll be good. And maybe don't hold my hand.

She flashed a smile he didn't return. But that might've been because hers was a little forced.

It wasn't your fault, he told her.

She wanted that to be true.

Otherwise . . . what? She'd never be able to touch his hand again without triggering some horrible reaction?

But this wasn't about *her.*

It wasn't your fault either, Keefe, she transmitted. *It was just . . . an accident.*

Maybe, he reluctantly agreed. *But that doesn't mean it won't happen again. Or something even worse.*

It won't be as bad as you're thinking.

She was doing her best to ignore the images screaming around Keefe's head, but it was hard to skip past the flashbacks of her blank, dazed face—or the images of things he was afraid would happen. Visions of everyone screaming and thrashing from some imagined terror he'd forced upon them. Or inconsolably sobbing.

Emotions are powerful, Keefe told her.

I know. But . . . even if something like that DID happen, it would only be temporary—just like the numbness was. You'd figure out how to undo it. And it's not like you're the only person to struggle after manifesting. Marella set fire to her bedroom. Linh flooded everything. Jensi said his brother got stuck half-phased in the floor. I thought I'd gone insane because of the voices in my head—and I inflicted on Sandor. Sometimes it takes time and practice to get the ability under control.

But what if I never get control?

You WILL. Everyone does.

Okay, but what if—

"Ugh, are you guys done with your mental conversation yet?" Fitz interrupted.

Ro snorted. "Boy, is *that* an ironic question coming from Captain Cognate. And I'm surprised you weren't eavesdropping."

Sophie was too.

Unless he *had* been and just didn't want to admit it . . .

Not that it mattered.

She turned back to Keefe and switched to talking, so Keefe would have to use his voice too. "Just try one word. Something random, like . . . aardvark. Or mallowmelt. Or boobrie. How could anything bad happen from saying 'boobrie'?"

Ro sighed when Keefe shook his head. "Looks like we need to try a different kind of motivation. So here's the deal. I'm going to give you to the count of five to say something—and if you don't, *I'll* start talking. And I think we both know which of your secrets I'm going to share first."

Keefe's eyes narrowed.

"Is that glare supposed to scare me?" Ro asked him, followed by a big, fake yawn.

"It might be unwise to antagonize him," Oralie warned.

"Nah, Hunkyhair's harmless. That's what he's forgetting. Nothing's going to change the fact that he's a great big softie. Meanwhile, *I* am not. So when I make a threat, I mean it." She flashed a pointy-toothed smile at Keefe. "One . . ."

Come on, Keefe, Sophie transmitted when Ro got to "three." *Say "alicorn." Or "gulon." Or better yet—tell me what the Great Gulon Incident was!*

"Four," Ro warned.

Keefe bit his lip so hard it looked ready to draw blood. But before Ro got to five, he whispered, "Mrs. Stinkbottom."

Sophie had to laugh at his word choice.

But the best part was: *Nothing happened.*

"See?" Noland told Keefe. "It's that easy. Now say something else—a little louder this time. Your power doesn't come from volume. It comes from tone."

Keefe shook his head.

Ro groaned. "Come on, Hunkyhair. I *know* you have about fifty different jokes you're *dying* to make. Especially with Captain Cognate over there. Give us your best one!"

Keefe shook his head again, and Sophie tried to imagine what it would be like if he stayed quiet like this all the time.

He wouldn't be Keefe anymore.

You're really going to let your mom win like this? she asked. *Give her this kind of control?*

No. I'm just trying to be responsible—for once. If I'd tried that a few days ago, I would've listened to Tammy Boy—and you—and stayed out of Loamnore. But I did what I always do, ignored everyone, and look how awesome that worked out for me.

Except you're still ignoring everyone, Sophie argued. *Do you really think Noland would tell you to try this if he was worried it would put him—and two other Councillors—in danger?*

Probably not, Keefe conceded. *Unless he's looking for an excuse to send me to Exile.*

A cold shiver rippled down Sophie's spine, and she turned to study the Councillors, wondering if they would sink that low.

They definitely would.

But . . . that wasn't what this was.

They already have a reason to exile you, she reminded him, fighting another shiver. *They know you numbed five people. That's more than enough to lock you up.*

I guess. He blew out a breath. *But . . . maybe I should be. I know what happened, okay? The emotions got overwhelming, and I needed them to stop—so I MADE them stop. And with my empathy so sensitive right now, we both know that could happen again. Especially when I'm with . . .*

The thought trailed off, but Sophie knew exactly what he'd stopped himself from saying.

"His mood is sinking," Oralie announced before Sophie could figure out what to say. "So perhaps we should hold off on any more practice for now? I suspect his emotional state is directly tied to this new ability."

"You can feel his emotions?" Alina asked. "Without any contact?"

Oralie nodded. "And in case you're wondering, that's definitely a new development."

"Have there been any *other* developments?" Alina asked Elwin. "Aside from Keefe's stronger emotions, becoming a Polyglot, and whatever this new ability is?"

Elwin snapped his fingers, flashing orange light around Keefe. "Well, he's been battling a headache and nausea since he woke up. Guessing that's from stress, though—and from being unconscious for three and a half days, and almost dying."

Alina's jaw tightened. "You know that's not what I meant."

She tapped her shoe against the floor—*tap tap tap tap tap*—until Fitz told her, "Keefe's empathy is stronger too."

"Thank you, Mr. Vacker," Alina told him. "I appreciate *someone* cooperating—even if it *should* have been our Regent."

"I'm *cooperating*," Sophie argued. "I'm just not sure if Keefe's empathy *is* stronger, or if it's just extra sensitive right now because the ability reset."

"Well, how about you try giving me *all* of the information and let me decide what I do and don't need to know?" Alina countered.

Sophie crossed her arms. "Fine. Want me to describe how he

accidentally glued his jaw shut with squelchberries, too?"

"I love when our sweet little Blondie shows her claws," Ro said—which earned a soft snort of laughter from Keefe and an epic eye roll from Councillor Alina.

A staring contest followed—until Oralie murmured, "I wonder if this new ability isn't an ability at all."

"What do you mean?" Noland asked her.

Oralie's cheeks flushed. "I'm not certain. It just seems significant that Keefe is now a Polyglot and an Empath, and used his *voice* to control *emotion.* That almost sounds like the two abilities *merged* somehow—or synchronized. Which would make sense, given that Keefe was exposed to shadowflux and quintessence. Elements trigger *change.* They rarely create something entirely new. But I'd need to do more research to know for sure."

"We all need more research," Noland said, smoothing the sides of his ponytail. "Particularly when it comes to the larger question. New ability—merged abilities—whatever *this* is, what we need to be focusing on is the *why.* Why would Lady Gisela go to so much trouble to give her son these powers?"

"Technically, we don't know that she did," Sophie reminded him. "Just because this is what happened, doesn't mean it's what she wanted. There are a bunch of things about me that the Black Swan never planned."

"I suppose," Noland said slowly. "But I think it's safe to assume that the majority of these changes *are* a part of her scheme—just as the majority of your genetics *are* in line with Project Moonlark's goals, which are still unclear, by the way. But *that* is a conversation for another time. For now, I think it's best if we treat each of these developments as though they're clues to what the Neverseen is planning, and see how much we can learn."

"Who wants to bet we'll learn a whole lot of nothing?" Ro asked, raising her hand.

The question was probably meant to be rhetorical. But Sophie raised her hand too.

So did Keefe.

And Sandor.

And Fitz.

Alina clicked her tongue. "So little faith in your powers of deduction."

"More like we've played Guess Their Evil Plan enough times to know it doesn't work," Ro snapped back. "And I don't know about you guys, but I'm done caring what they want. I say we focus on what *we* want and figure out how to use our Legacy Boy's new elf-y powers to take Mommy Dearest and her band of black-cloaked losers down!"

"She has a point," Oralie admitted. "But with either approach, the first step remains the same. We need to learn as much about Keefe's new abilities and sensitivities as we can."

"And he needs to be trained," Noland added. "To gain proper control."

"He also needs to be moved," Alina said, turning to check her reflection in one of the shinier bottles of medicine. "We're about to reopen Foxfire and—"

"You are?" Fitz interrupted.

Alina nodded. "It hasn't been announced yet—but it will be soon. Normalcy needs to return to the Lost Cities, and our children

588   UNLOCKED

need to focus on their education. And we cannot have prodigies returning to a place where someone with an unknown, uncontrolled new ability—or merged abilities, whatever you want to call it—triggered by two of the most unstable elements is hiding in the Healing Center."

"But he still needs more treatment," Elwin argued, flashing a blue orb around Keefe's head.

"He's well enough to light leap, isn't he?" Alina demanded.

Elwin squinted through his glasses. "Yeah, I guess."

Alina smiled triumphantly. "Good. Then there's no reason he can't be relocated. You can continue any additional medical care at the new location."

"Which is where?" Elwin asked, and Sophie shifted her weight to the balls of her feet.

If anyone said "Exile," she would grab Keefe and run so fast, her newly improved teleporting would get them *far* away from there.

"We haven't worked out the details," Alina said, glancing at the other Councillors. "We needed to assess the specifics of Mr. Sencen's condition before we instructed the gnomes what to build."

"Build," Sophie repeated. "You mean like the prisons you created for Fintan and Alvar?"

Alina smoothed her gown. "No need to be so dramatic, Miss Foster. It wouldn't be a prison. It would be a *facility*."

"And I maintain that it's unnecessary," Oralie informed everyone. "Keefe's father's home is sufficiently isolated. And Lord Cassius is an Empath, so he can help with his training. And—"

"Uh, much as I'm *not* on board with the whole Special

Sparkletown Facility idea, since I'll be stuck there too," Ro interrupted, "I gotta say, I'm pretty sure if you put our boy in a house with Lord Bossypants right now and make them train in emotional stuff, it's *not* going to go well."

"I have to agree," Elwin said, shifting the light around Keefe to green. "Keefe needs to be somewhere calming—and that's *not* anywhere near his dad, or any isolated, confining place you guys build for him."

"So what would you suggest?" Noland asked.

Elwin scratched his chin. "Well . . . what if I take Keefe home with me? My house is about as isolated as it gets. And I'll be able to monitor his recovery there, nice and easy. *And* I have lots of different elixirs I can give him if he starts to lose control."

"Oh! Oh! I vote for that!" Ro said. "Bonus points if there aren't any sparkles!"

"Sadly for you, I'm a sparkle fan. But you'll get used to it." Elwin turned to Keefe. "What do you think of that plan?"

Keefe shrugged—but it didn't quite hide his relief.

Sophie felt the same way.

"Fine," Alina huffed, glancing at the other Councillors for confirmation. "We can *try* that for now. And reassess if needed."

Noland cleared his throat. "So now we just need to figure out who should mentor the boy. I would offer, but I fear my training won't be much help, since nothing I do affects emotion."

"I could—" Oralie started to offer, but Alina cut her off.

"He needs more than just an Empath."

Oralie rolled her eyes. "Yes, I'm aware. Which is why I was going to say that I could talk to Lady Cadence—or Councillor Clarette—and see if either of them would mentor Keefe with me, so he'd have a Polyglot *and* an Empath."

Alina tilted her chin up. "I suppose that's not a *terrible* idea. But I think he should receive some lessons from me, as well. My ability has some overlaps that should be considered."

Ro snickered. "Yeah, you two training together sounds like the perfect way to keep Hunkyhair calm."

Alina smiled, and her voice took on a soft, sugary tone when she told Ro, "Oh, I can be very soothing when I want to be."

Ro blinked. "Whoa. That's freaky."

"No," Alina corrected, checking her reflection again, "that's how *true* power works. It's not weapons or muscles or unhinged brutality. It's natural talent."

"And yet *I'm* in charge of keeping Hunkyhair safe," Ro reminded her. "If you guys are so powerful, how come you hide behind your bodyguards?"

"Everything's settled, right?" Elwin jumped in before Alina could respond.

Oralie and Noland said "yes" at the same time Alina and Sophie said "no."

"What's your problem with this arrangement?" Noland asked Sophie.

"It's not the arrangement," Sophie explained. "It's the fact that no one made sure Keefe's okay with it. He should get a choice in his training." Tiergan had given her one before he became her telepathy Mentor. So she asked Keefe, "Are you okay training with Alina and Oralie and whoever else?"

Keefe considered that for a second before he nodded.

Noland clapped his hands. "Good, then we're settled. I'll inform the rest of the Council and—"

"We're not settled," Alina interrupted. "I still have one final requirement." She pointed to Sophie. "It's already been proven that you're capable of triggering a disturbing aspect of Keefe's ability. And I'm not convinced you can fully control your enhancing, either. So until we understand more about what we're dealing with—and Keefe gains some level of control—you need to stay away. No visits. No hailing each other or sneaking off or whatever else you two do."

Noland tugged at the collar of his jerkin. "I suppose that *is* a valid precaution. Don't you agree, Oralie?"

A beat of silence followed, and Sophie stared at her feet, already knowing Oralie's answer.

But when Oralie spoke, she told Noland, "I think this should be up to Keefe. He knows his limits better than any of us—and he's shown his desire for caution by refusing to talk, despite all of our urging. So what do you say, Keefe? Do you want Sophie to stay away from Splendor Plains for now?"

"Splendor Plains?" Fitz asked.

"That's the name of my estate," Elwin explained.

He said something else, too. But Sophie wasn't listening. She was too busy studying Keefe's face.

He was the most stubborn, rebellious person she'd ever met.

But there was no fight left in his eyes.

He looked only tired and shattered as he turned toward Oralie and nodded that yes, he wanted Sophie to stay away.

- FOUR -
Keefe

"WELCOME TO SPLENDOR PLAINS!"
Elwin said as the scenery glittered into
focus and Keefe turned to study the sprawling mansion in front of them, which
somehow managed to be both super colorful and really, really boring.

The walls were floor-to-ceiling windows, and each pane was a
different shade of glass, arranged in vibrant, alternating patterns of
the light spectrum.

But the architecture itself was pretty basic.

Flat roof.

Square rooms stacked on top of each other.

Lots of sharp angles.

Even the wide, straight flight of stairs that Elwin led them up
was made of dull, square stones. And the door was a simple sliding
sheet of glass.

Inside, the huge main room was almost entirely empty. The only
furniture was a swiveling white armchair and a small, round table,
both arranged precisely in the center.

"I'm guessing this isn't what you were expecting," Elwin told Keefe, setting Bullhorn down so that the slinky banshee could duck down some tiny gap in the glass floor and scurry away under their feet.

It was and it wasn't.

Honestly, Keefe had never really given a whole lot of thought to where Elwin went when he wasn't at Foxfire.

He knew Elwin had to live *somewhere*.

He'd just never had a reason to imagine it.

And now . . . he lived here too—at least temporarily.

Life just kept getting weirder and weirder.

But it was *way* better than going back to the Shores of Solace and Daddy Dearest, with his constant demands and criticism— especially since his dad would *love* that Keefe couldn't snap back with any jokes or insults.

And it was *definitely* better than letting the Council build him a "facility."

Plus, Elwin had a steady supply of sedatives, and Keefe did *not* share Foster's aversion to drug-induced sleep. He'd actually been planning to beg Elwin to knock him out for a few more days— or weeks, whatever it took—hoping he'd wake up and his senses would be back to normal.

But as soon as the Councillors left, Elwin started scrambling to pack up and get them out of there, so that sleep-away-the-troubles plan would have to wait.

Elwin claimed he was worried that the rest of the Council would try to change the plan once they knew what was happening, so he wanted to get Keefe settled in so they could see how well things were going. But Keefe was pretty sure Elwin was mostly just trying to find some way to fill the excruciating silence that followed Foster's sudden departure.

She'd raised her home crystal to the light and disappeared as soon as Keefe had agreed to Alina's condition—without even saying goodbye.

Keefe couldn't blame her.

He closed his eyes, forcing himself to remember the look on her face—the hurt and betrayal and sadness and anger.

Even if he wasn't an Empath, he would've felt each emotional blow.

And he deserved to, because he knew she was already blaming herself for what happened, and he'd basically told her that he blamed her too.

It *wasn't* her fault.

It was *his* fault—and his mom's fault.

He'd only told Sophie to stay away because . . . he was scared.

And embarrassed.

And what if he discovered more horrible changes?

He needed some time and space to figure out how to hide everything that had happened—and he wasn't going to be able to do that with Miss Worries-Too-Much watching him with a crinkly-forehead stare.

So . . . he'd told her to go away—and then he'd been too big of a jerk to even tell Fitz he should go after her.

He'd thought about it, so maybe Fitz had been eavesdropping again, and that's where he went when he left a few minutes later.

But Keefe doubted it.

Fitz could be pretty dense when it came to things like that.

And some tiny, selfish part of Keefe secretly hoped he was right. Because if Fitz couldn't figure that out on his own, he didn't deserve Foster.

Then again, neither did he.

Ro heaved a sigh. "I hope you have some cures for 'mopey boy' in that little satchel of yours, Doc. Otherwise it's going to be one big sulkfest around here. And I never thought I'd say this, but it's even worse without Hunkyhair talking."

"Sadly, there's no cure for teenage angst," Elwin told her, motioning for them to follow him to a glass staircase tucked into the far corner. "Though baked goods can help—and I always have some fresh ripplefluffs in my pantry. Today's are chocolate peanut butter."

Keefe shook his head as hard as he could.

His stomach was still recovering from the squelchberries.

"Aaaaaaaand *there's* the sparkle-overload," Ro said when they reached the top of the stairs and found themselves in a hall where the windows were draped with crystal-beaded curtains and the doors were each positioned near fancy chandeliers.

"Told you I was a fan. The bottom level is my *quiet space*, so I kept things simpler. But up here is where I *live*." Elwin pushed open the first door, revealing a room packed with so many stuffed animals, Keefe almost wanted to swan-dive into them and drown in fuzzy snuggles. "This is my Emotional Support Stuffed Animal collection. Mrs. Stinkbottom used to be right there." He pointed to a small gap near a stuffed griffin and a stuffed ghoul. "But I thought she'd be happier with you. I'll make sure your dad sends her over here tomorrow, along with some clothes and anything else you want. But if you need a snuggle buddy stand-in for tonight, might I suggest Boo Boo the boobrie?"

He pointed to a black-and-yellow stuffed bird with a mohawk and long, curled eyelashes.

"See, and I think Hunkyhair might prefer cuddling with that," Ro said, pointing to a shimmering silver moonlark.

Keefe rolled his eyes as Elwin coughed to cover his laugh.

"Come on, seriously! An eye roll is all I get for that?" Ro tapped the top of Keefe's head. "I know you have about a billion snarky comebacks dancing around this brain. Bet you're composing another verse of *The Ballad of Bo and Ro*, too. What do you think is going to happen if you say it? I'm going to fall madly in love with him? Actually, you know what? Let's not test that, just to be safe. But come on, Hunkyhair, hit me with something. I deserve it for that moonlark comment!"

Keefe turned away.

Somehow the longer he stayed quiet, the scarier it felt to speak. Like his words might be storing up power.

"I'm not going to let anything happen, Keefe," Elwin assured him, grabbing Boo Boo the boobrie and leading them down the hall to the far door. "But if you need a little time to process all of this, I'm not going to fight you. Right now, I want you to settle in and get some rest."

He pulled open the door and Ro groaned. "Okay, now you're just messing with me."

"Kind of," Elwin agreed. "But not completely. I call this my 'prism room.' Everything is designed to catch the light differently."

"Yeah, and it's sparkle overload," Ro grumbled, shielding her eyes.

She wasn't wrong.

The walls were covered in tiny crystal beads that refracted so many glints of light, the floor and ceiling looked like a hologram. And the bed was piled with dozens of jewel-encrusted pillows.

"If it's too much, we can move you to another room tomorrow," Elwin told him, "but for tonight, I thought it might be good to have you sleep in here. Because the best part about the prism is . . ."

He snapped his fingers, turning off the chandeliers and transforming the room into a tiny universe. Each fleck of light was now a star, twinkling steadily though the inky darkness.

"Ohhhhh," Ro breathed. "Now *these* are my kind of sparkles." She ran a hand gently down the wall, watching the stars shimmer on her skin. "This reminds me of my father's palace. Some of the microbes he cultivates there look just like this."

Keefe might've imagined it, but Ro sounded a little choked up. And normally he would've teased her about it. So he was actually kind of glad he had a reason to stay quiet.

He never really thought about what it must be like for Ro, living somewhere so different and far away from her own world— particularly because it was also somewhere people sometimes judged her or mistreated her or tried to kill her.

"Okay, this is officially freaking me out!" Ro said, grabbing Keefe's wrists and shaking his arms. "Stop looking at me all sappy like that! And stop with the thoughtful silence! It's time to be *you* again. Bring on the insults! Bring on the rhymes. Bring on the bets!"

"He'll get there," Elwin said when Keefe pressed his lips tighter together. "He just needs some time to process. And sleep will help too. I'm guessing you don't want any dinner?"

Keefe shook his head so hard, it hurt his neck a little.

"Then I'll leave you to settle in. But I want you to take these before you go to bed." He dug through his satchel, pulled out five vials in various shades of blue, and set them on the round table beside the bed. Then added a deep purple one. "That last one's a sedative, since I have a feeling you're going to want one—but I'll leave that up to you. The others aren't optional, but that one is. And if you need anything else . . . well, I was about to say 'holler,' but I think we both know that's not going to happen. So just come find me. I'll be in my lab for the next few hours, which is the third door on the other side of the hall."

"You gonna make something to fix our boy?" Ro asked.

"It's not about *fixing*." His eyes shifted to Keefe. "You're not broken, Keefe. I know it feels like it. But right now, you're just . . . adjusting. And I have a few ideas for some elixirs that might help smooth out the process. *That's* what I'll be working on—though I might need to wait until I speak to Kesler Dizznee tomorrow morning. I don't usually work with amarallitine, and it can be a little volatile. Plus, I need to go to Slurps and Burps to get some supplies. Anyway, none of that really matters to you. Sorry, I think out loud a lot when I'm home, so it's a little strange having someone around here who can hear me. Try to get some rest. And if you want to dim the lights more, just keep snapping. I figured you might not enjoy darkness right now, so I have it on the brightest setting. But if you can't sleep with all that light, there are ten other levels, including absolute pitch black. I wouldn't recommend that one unless you take the sedative—and then it won't really matter since you'll be knocked out cold anyway. Aaaaaaaand I'm rambling again. Sorry. Gonna take some getting used to, having company."

He gave some sort of awkward wave as he turned to leave.

"Wait."

It took Keefe's brain a second to process that the whispered voice had come from him, and he squeezed his eyes shut for a beat, hoping hoping hoping he wouldn't find Elwin frozen in place when he opened them again.

"Everything okay?" Elwin asked when Keefe dared a peek.

Keefe released the breath he'd been holding and nodded.

But he needed to use his voice again to say two things.

First, "Thank you."

He wanted to add more, since Elwin deserved a lot more gratitude than that for taking him in and saving him from ending up in one of the Council's facilities.

But each word was a risk, and he'd thought of something much more important to communicate—something that might be another way to help him take control of his new abilities.

He cleared his throat, telling himself to keep his tone neutral as he whispered, "Tell Dex."

Elwin frowned. "Tell Dex what?"

Ro knew what he meant. "Actually, that's a good idea. Your techy friend made something to help Blondie with some of her abilities, didn't he?"

Keefe nodded.

Technically, some of the gadgets had been made by Tinker—the Black Swan's Technopath—but Dex had designed some bracelets that would've helped Sophie with her enhancing if he hadn't used crush cuffs and made it awkward.

Dex had even invented an ability restrictor—which . . . had seemed like a really horrible idea. Particularly after the Council forced Foster to wear it.

But it might be good to have Dex build a backup, just in case, and key it to his DNA so there was no way the gadget could be used on anyone else.

"Tell Dex," Keefe repeated, and that time Elwin got it.

"I will," he promised. "Now take your medicine and go to bed."

FIVE

Sophie

I BROUGHT YOU SOME BREAKFAST," EDALINE said as she made her way over to Sophie's enormous canopied bed—even though the tray she was carrying of sliced purple fruit and sugar-sprinkled pastries pretty much spoke for itself.

And what the tray said was: *I know I'm a Conjurer and could've snapped my fingers and made this appear in your room, but I'm using breakfast as an excuse to check on you.*

Which was sweet.

Sophie knew that.

She also knew how lucky she was to have such caring, supportive adoptive parents.

But . . . she *really* wasn't in the mood to talk.

"I know," Edaline told her, proving that mom-intuition could sometimes be just as powerful as telepathy. "And I'll leave you alone if you want me to. But . . . Elwin hailed me last night and told me what happened, so I have to at least make sure you're okay."

Sophie buried her face between Ella's floppy blue elephant ears. "I'm fine. It wasn't a big deal."

That's what she'd been telling herself ever since she'd fled the Healing Center.

Keefe was just trying to be extra careful until he figured out how to control his new ability—she should be grateful for that!

He was being cautious instead of reckless.

And it wasn't like he'd told her to stay away *forever*.

But . . . her mind kept replaying that nod he gave Oralie. The set of his jaw and the determination in his eyes almost felt like . . .

Like he wasn't even going to miss her.

Like he didn't care at all.

Which was a really weird—really pointless—thing to be thinking about when she should be trying to figure out what Lady Gisela was planning, and what Elysian was, and how to find Kenric's cache.

And yet, there she sat, strangle-hugging her stuffed elephant instead of getting up and getting dressed and doing something productive.

She'd also barely slept, despite the soothing images of meadows and mountains and endless starry skies that Silveny kept flooding her mind with—and she'd thought about camping out under the Panakes with Wynn and Luna, but . . . she didn't feel like snuggling. Even with adorable baby alicorns.

She just wanted to be alone.

Okay, fine, maybe she wanted to sit there feeling sorry for herself for a few more hours—but in her defense, it had been a rough couple of weeks.

She'd sorta broken up with Fitz. Found out Councillor Oralie was her genetic mother. Watched helplessly as Keefe nearly died from his mom's horrible experiments. Spent days sitting by his side in the Healing Center, worrying he'd never wake up. And now that he had, he'd basically told her to go away.

"Must've been pretty scary," Edaline said as she set the tray on the bed next to Sophie and carefully sat down beside her. "Feeling numb like that."

Sophie shrugged. "The thing about being numb is, you can't feel *anything*."

"I guess that's true. But it sounded like what happened afterward was . . . intense." She stopped there, as if she were hoping Sophie would fill in the rest of the details. But Sophie was sure that Elwin had already told her more than enough.

Edaline sighed. "Fine, I won't force you to talk about it. But you do need to eat something. You went to bed without dinner." She nudged the tray closer. "At least try one of the sugarknots—I guarantee they'll be one of your new favorites. And Flori brought the fruit from her personal garden. I don't actually know what it is, but she *insisted* you try it."

Sophie stared at the neatly arranged slices, which were such a dark purple, they looked like they would stain her teeth. "Maybe later."

Edaline blocked her from pushing the tray away. "Flori also wanted me to tell you that the fruit came from a very special tree—a tree she grew using seeds that Calla sent her right before she chose to sacrifice herself. And the seeds came with a note that said, 'Grow these for my moonlark.'"

Sophie sat up straighter, setting Ella aside. "Really?"

Edaline smiled and held up the plate.

Sophie reached for a slice, and maybe she was imagining it, but she could've sworn she heard one of Calla's soft songs as she lifted the fruit to her lips—a gentle melody about how shedding leaves helps a tree survive the harsh winter.

She closed her eyes, savoring that tiny connection to her lost friend before she took a taste and . . .

It was like eating sunshine.

Warm and sweet and a tiny bit tingly on her tongue.

She tried to savor each bite, but all too soon the fruit was gone. So she moved on to the sugarknots, which turned out to be flaky—like croissants—and were filled with some sort of rich brown-sugar custard.

"Thank you," she told Edaline, dusting the extra sugar off her hands. "And thank Flori, too."

"You're welcome!" Flori called from the hallway. "I was so excited when that tree finally started to produce! I decided to name the fruits dawnlings, since they have to be harvested at sunrise. And I have a good crop growing now, so I can bring you some whenever you need another boost."

"I'm sure that'll be soon," Sophie called back, feeling her mood already sinking.

Edaline snapped her fingers, making the empty tray disappear so she could scoot close enough to wrap her arm around Sophie's shoulders. "I'm guessing you still don't want to talk about it."

"Not really." Sophie tilted her head forward, hiding behind her hair before she added, "It's just been . . . a lot."

"I know." Edaline tucked Sophie's hair behind her ear. "*That's* why I'm here. I wish you'd let me help. I doubt I can do anything for Keefe. But I might be useful for whatever you and Oralie are working on—and don't even think about telling me you guys aren't up to something. She was here for way too long yesterday. She also came alone, so I'm guessing this project is a bit less official than your Team Valiant assignments."

"It is," Sophie admitted, trying to figure out how much to say. "But I'm not working on it with Oralie anymore."

Not since Oralie had proven that anything Sophie shared with her would go straight to the Council.

Plus, it wasn't like they'd had much of a plan to find Kenric's cache, anyway. All she was supposed to do was talk to Fitz about Alvar—and she'd left the Healing Center in such a rush that she'd forgotten to do that.

She could hail Fitz now, of course, but . . . if he knew anything, he would've already tracked down his brother, wouldn't he?

She also wasn't in the mood to get yelled at again.

Really, she'd be way better off looking for Alvar by herself. She just . . . didn't know where to start.

"You can trust me, Sophie," Edaline pressed. "I'm not going to freak out—and I know how to keep a secret. You can tell me *anything*."

Sophie really wished that was true.

But there were lots of things she could never tell Edaline.

Being the moonlark meant being lied to *and* lying to everybody.

"I'm also not going to stop you from taking risks," Edaline promised, reaching for Sophie's hand. "I just want to know what's going on, in case I can help. It's nice to have a partner."

"It is," Sophie agreed, glancing at the Cognate ring on her thumb.

She wasn't sure if she and Fitz could actually *be* Cognates anymore, with all the awkwardness between them. Which made her shrapnel heart shred even deeper.

"You shouldn't do this alone," Edaline said gently. "Even if you can't tell me the specifics, I still might be able to help you come up with a strategy. I do that with Grady sometimes, when he's stumped by a classified assignment. He gives me a vague explanation of the problem, and we put our heads together and brainstorm solutions. Can you at least let me try?"

Several long seconds passed before Sophie told her, "Well . . . I need to find someone. And I don't know where to start."

Edaline tightened her grip. "If you're thinking of going after Keefe's mom—"

"I'm not," Sophie interrupted. "Really, I'm *not*."

Edaline relaxed her hold. "Okay, good. I can deal with you taking risks, but they have to be *smart* risks. Tracking down *anyone* in the Neverseen needs to be a team effort—and by 'team,' I mean bodyguards and adults and Councillors and—"

"I know," Sophie cut in, resisting the urge to point out that they'd tried that in Loamnore and still ended up trapped and helpless while Lady Gisela got exactly what she wanted. "I'm not trying to find anyone in the Neverseen. I mean . . . they used to be—but they're not anymore."

Edaline's eyes narrowed, and Sophie had a feeling that meant she'd guessed who Sophie was talking about. But all Edaline said was, "And you can't use your telepathy to help track them down?"

"I wish. I can't track thoughts without having some idea of where I'm searching. And transmitting won't work either, because the person would have to choose to respond to me."

Which seemed like poor planning on the Black Swan's part, if she was being honest.

Sometimes it felt like they just . . . hadn't made her strong enough.

They'd genetically engineered everything about her—why not go *big*?

Though . . . if they *had* done that—assuming it was actually possible—her life would've been even more complicated and weird. So she should probably be grateful the Black Swan let her have a tiny bit of normal.

She doubted Keefe's mom had done the same for him.

And Keefe seemed to know it.

That's why he'd hidden under his blankets.

Refused to talk.

Sent her away . . .

What if—

"Do you know the last place this person was seen?" Edaline asked, reminding her to focus.

Sophie nodded. "But I saw them leave, and I can't imagine they'd go back."

"Okay, but have you searched the place since then? They might've left something behind that could help you figure out where they went."

"I suppose it's possible."

It seemed like a long shot, but . . .

Candleshade was pretty enormous.

And Alvar had been hiding there for a while—and he left in a hurry.

Maybe it was worth checking.

Definitely sounded better than hailing Fitz and getting shouted at for things she couldn't change.

"Thank you," she told Edaline, throwing back her covers. "I guess I'll give it a try."

Edaline smiled. "Good. And don't worry, I won't ask where you're going, or try to convince you to let me go with you—but I *am* going to insist that you take *both* of your bodyguards."

Sophie knew better than to argue. Plus, having Flori there might be a good idea. Gnomes had different senses than goblins. They could even see Vanishers after they'd disappeared.

"I also want you to take this." Edaline snapped her fingers, making a silver melder appear in her palm. "And have Sandor give you some throwing stars just in case."

Sophie nodded.

A few years ago, she might've cringed at the idea of carrying weapons.

But she wasn't that girl anymore.

"I'll be careful," she promised, taking the melder and heading for her closet to change into one of her special tunics with lots of pockets.

"I know," Edaline told her. "But I'm still going to worry. So I think I deserve *all* the mom points for letting you do this."

"You do," Sophie agreed.

It hit her then. The contrast between her different mothers.

Her human mom never quite knew what to do with her.

Oralie had abandoned her and betrayed her.

But Edaline *truly* trusted her—even when she knew Sophie was hiding stuff.

Which made Sophie wish she could sit back down and unload *everything*—and made Sophie resent Oralie even more. Especially since it was only a matter of time before she'd have to lie to Edaline to protect Oralie's secrets.

"What's this for?" Edaline asked when Sophie turned back and threw her arms around her.

"Because I know it's not easy being my mom—"

"Wrong," Edaline interrupted, leaning back to meet Sophie's eyes. "I'll admit, the abundance of near-death experiences can be a *bit* stressful—but being your mom is *easy*."

"Really?" Sophie whispered, blinking back tears.

She didn't like to think about how it felt growing up hearing her human parents' thoughts all the time, knowing how much they struggled to understand her. And it was even worse realizing how easily Oralie had cast her aside, as if having a daughter were just some item she'd checked off her to-do list.

"Really," Edaline promised, kissing Sophie's cheek. "You're the single greatest gift I've ever been given, Sophie. And I'm so incredibly grateful that you trust me enough to be my daughter. I love you so much—and I always will. No matter what."

"I love you too." Sophie buried her face in Edaline's hair and wished she could stay like that and never let go.

But she had work to do, so she forced herself to drop her arms and stand, promising one more time, "I'll be careful, Mom."

She didn't use that title for Edaline very often—but she should.

"I know you will," Edaline assured her. "I'll be here when you get back."

Sophie changed quickly, pulling her hair into a simple ponytail and stuffing her pockets with weapons before making her way to the stairs.

"You're not going to use the Leapmaster?" Edaline asked when Sophie started going down instead of up. "I thought you might be heading somewhere we have a crystal for."

"I am," Sophie agreed, deciding to give her mom that tiny clue. "But I need to practice my teleporting."

Sandor groaned as he followed. "You're really going to make us jump off a cliff when we could light leap?"

Sophie shook her head. "Not this time. All you'll have to do is run beside me."

Or she hoped that was how it would work.

She wasn't 100 percent certain, since the times she'd teleported the other way, she'd either been alone or carrying somebody.

But they were about to find out.

She pulled open the front door and studied Havenfield's pastures. Most of the longer paths went uphill, but the one that led to the cliffs stayed mostly flat, which would hopefully make it easier to build up momentum—and if it didn't work, they could always change plans and jump off the edge.

"Okay," she said, reaching for Sandor with one hand and Flori with the other. She closed her eyes, taking a deep breath to rally her concentration. "Here goes nothing."

"For the record," Sandor grumbled as they struggled to stop their sprint, "that was worse than jumping off a cliff."

Sophie disagreed—though she also wasn't sure if she knew exactly what had happened.

One second she'd been running—channeling energy to her legs to go faster, faster, faster. Then Sandor and Flori had started to lag behind, so she'd tightened her grip and pushed herself even harder. Next thing she knew, her feet were barely touching the ground, and Sandor and Flori were half floating, half flailing as she dragged them into the void.

Then she pictured Candleshade, and they were there, stumbling along the overgrown path that led to the main entrance.

"I thought it was exhilarating," Flori breathed. "Such a special glimpse of the moonlark's strength and power."

"I don't know about that," Sophie mumbled, bending to lower her head between her knees.

Now that she'd stopped running, everything was spinning and her lungs felt like they were going to explode.

"I do," Flori insisted. "You carried both of us as though we were dandelion seeds caught on a breeze. And while *I* may be small, Sandor definitely isn't."

Sandor straightened to his full height, and Sophie had to admit that it *was* kind of amazing that she'd been able to drag him along so easily. Her arms didn't even feel sore—though that might change once the adrenaline wore off.

"Impressive or not," Sandor said, arching his back into a stretch, "I prefer free-falling. Particularly since it encourages you to limit the ability to absolute necessity."

"What he means," Flori told Sophie, "is he doesn't like that you can now go anywhere, anytime, without needing one of your crystals, or a cliff, or me to sing to the roots to carry you. All you need is a bit of speed. And I'm happy for you to have that freedom—and proud to watch the moonlark find her wings. I just hope you'll continue carrying me with you."

"I don't *hope*, I *insist*," Sandor corrected, gripping the hilt of his sword. "I go where you go."

Sophie wanted to roll her eyes. But her lips curled into a small smile instead. "Believe me, I know. I didn't argue about bringing you with me today, did I? And all I'm doing is searching an empty house!"

She straightened up, needing a few more breaths for her vision to clear enough to focus on the enormous, multi-spired crystal tower in front of them, which was probably designed to be equally impressive and intimidating. But all Sophie felt was sadness.

So many horrible, traumatic things had happened to Keefe inside those shimmering walls, and she found herself wishing she could tear them down, block by block.

Maybe someday she would.

For now, she was about to waste an afternoon searching through dusty, abandoned rooms and finding nothing useful—which was a terrible attitude, she knew. But she'd done these kinds of searches too many times to have any real hope.

Still, she made her way to the front door, which looked disproportionately small compared to the two-hundred-story structure.

"Do you think we should knock?" she wondered.

Sandor sniffed the air. "Yes. Because we're not the only ones here."

Sophie reached for her melder. "Who—"

Before she could finish the question, the door opened, and there was Lord Cassius, looking as arrogant and pristine as ever.

But the real surprise was the boy standing beside him, staring guiltily at his feet as she whispered, "Fitz?"

SIX

KEEFE

"WOW, YOU'RE REALLY NOT GOING to talk?" Dex asked, resting his hands on his hips as he turned a slow circle to study Keefe's extra sparkly new bedroom. "I figured Elwin was either exaggerating that part, or you were messing with him."

Keefe pressed his lips tighter and shook his head.

His throat felt thick and scratchy from the lack of use. But he wasn't going to risk it, because even with the sedative, he'd spent most of the night dreaming about Sophie's eerie blank stare.

Was *that* what his mom wanted?

Was *he* her way of neutralizing the Black Swan's moonlark?

Or was that only the beginning?

His mom craved power and control—and now she'd given him an ability that let him turn everyone around him into useless, mindless shells.

People with no feelings.

No fear.

No guilt.

And if they were given the right commands?

Boom—instant ruthless army!

Ro sighed and turned to Dex. "In case you were wondering, he's overthinking everything right now. I don't know what he's imagining, but he keeps getting all shuddery, so I'm guessing it's something super melodramatic, like him single-handedly destroying the world with the sound of his voice. Who knew our Hunkyhair was an even bigger worrier than Blondie?"

Dex grinned. But his dimples faded when his gaze shifted back to Keefe. "Elwin said you needed my help?"

Keefe nodded—then swallowed back a belch, which tasted like the awful, gurgley elixir Elwin had given him that morning.

His new superstrong empathy had faded after the numbing disaster, but the little sleep he'd gotten had apparently brought it back with a vengeance. And Elwin had made the elixir specifically to try to dull his senses—but the mix of curiosity and confusion drifting from Dex's general direction made it pretty clear that the medicine had been a fail.

Hopefully Keefe would have better luck with Dex's help.

He pointed to his throat, and then his forehead, trying to show Dex what he needed.

"Some Nogginease?" Dex guessed.

Keefe shook his head and tried pulling on the choker-style band of his registry pendant.

"Um . . . you want to hack into the registry again?" Dex tried.

Ro snorted. "Wow, you guys are *super* bad at this. How about I save us all some time and speak for my boy? Okay, so Councillor Sparkle-Eyebrows—"

"Who?" Dex interrupted.

Ro shrugged. "No idea. Can't remember his name. You guys have way too many leaders to keep them all straight. All I know is the dude had these huge hairy things above his eyes and a jewel from his crown rested right between them, so I'm calling him Councillor Sparkle-Eyebrows. Anyway, he said my boy's new elf-y ability is linked to the tone of his voice, and he seemed pretty sure about it. So, assuming he's right, we need you to use your techy skills to build a gadget that'll give Hunkyhair better control over that, kinda like you did for Blondie to help with her power-boost-touch thing. And *personally*, I vote for something that makes his voice extra high-pitched and squeaky—although it could also be fun to make him sound super creepy. Ooo, is there a way to have it switch back and forth?"

She smirked at Keefe, daring him to contradict her. But he honestly wouldn't care if Dex made him sound like a screeching siren, if it made talking safe again.

"Welllll," Dex said, dragging out the word. "I bet I can figure out how to make something like that. But . . . would it really help? There's a difference between *voice* and *tone*, you know? Look at Sandor. He sounds all cute and cuddly—until he gives an order. Then he's terrifying. But his voice doesn't change. Just his tone."

"Okay, first: I'm *so* telling Gigantor you called him cuddly," Ro told him. "Second: If you think *he's* terrifying, you should hear my dad command his Mercadirs. And third: I . . . guess that's a fair point. So, fine, make something that tweaks Hunkyhair's tone."

Dex reached up, mussing his strawberry-blond hair. "I mean . . . I can definitely try. But tone is way more complicated, since it's connected to emotion."

"It is?" Keefe asked—then clapped his hands over his mouth.

Ro pumped her fist. "He speaks! And look—the world didn't end! No one got all dazed or numb or anything! Try it again! Try it again!"

Keefe pressed his hands tighter against his lips and glanced at Dex, hoping the look in his eyes said *Please ignore my annoying bodyguard and answer the question I accidentally asked, because emotion might be a clue to what's happening with this ability.*

"Think about it," Dex told him. "When you feel sad or angry, your tone changes, right?"

Keefe nodded slowly.

He hadn't really considered what *he'd* been feeling when he'd numbed everybody. He'd been more focused on how Sophie's emotions had overloaded his brain.

But . . . when he'd touched Sophie's hand and everything turned overwhelming, some part of him had been terrified that he'd never be able to get close to her again. And *that* made him desperate to do anything to stop the chaos.

He'd also been just as scared and desperate when he was trying to figure out how to snap everyone out of it.

Though . . . the first few words he'd tried hadn't worked, and he'd been just as emotional when he said those. So there had to be some other variable—some other connection—between the two effective commands.

His mind drifted back to the moment right before he'd finally found the word that brought everyone out of the daze.

What had he done differently for that command?

He'd made himself stop, take a deep breath, and *think*. And then . . .

He seriously had no idea.

Somehow he just *knew* the word he needed to say—*knew* it would work even before he said it.

Was that . . . *confidence*?

Maybe—but that couldn't be the connection either, since he definitely hadn't been feeling confident when he numbed everyone.

There had to be something else.

And then he realized . . .

It was all about *him*.

His *wants*—or maybe it made more sense to call it his *needs*. Either way, it was that craving—that desire—that took over and made him do whatever it took to get his way.

Which was actually super terrifying, since his mom could *easily* use that to manipulate him.

She knew his hopes and fears and dreams.

And she knew exactly how to stack them against him.

He sank onto the edge of his bed, burying his head in his hands and closing his eyes.

"Oh goody, looks like we're back to the overthinking," Ro announced, and a burst of her annoyance hit Keefe like a gutpunch.

It took all of his willpower not to shout back, *Of course I'm overthinking—I could turn everyone into mindless murderers for my mommy if I don't figure out how to stop this!*

"Hey," Dex said—and when Keefe didn't respond, the bed shifted, like Dex had sat down beside him. "I'll see what I can come up with, okay? And if I can't figure it out, I'll check with Tinker. Or I can always have Sophie enhance me. Sometimes that helps me find the right answer."

The promise should've made Keefe feel better—especially since he wasn't picking up any pity in the air.

But his brain was too stuck on the word "enhance."

What would happen if Sophie enhanced *his* ability?

He did *not* want to find out.

And there were only two ways to make sure that never happened.

He could stay away from Sophie from now on, or . . .

He cleared his throat and raised his head, trying to focus on calm, steady breaths.

"Wait—I think he's going to speak again!" Ro called out.

He *was*, because this request was too important to risk any misunderstanding.

In fact, it required a whole sentence.

He cleared his throat again, lowering his voice to something barely more than a whisper as he said, "I need you to make me an ability restrictor."

And *whoa*, did he get hit with worry, anger, and panic.

His ears rang and his vision dimmed and he sucked in a long, deep breath as Dex jumped to his feet and told him, "I'm *never* making one of those again!"

Keefe wasn't surprised.

The other ability restrictor that Dex had made was an epic disaster and had left Sophie powerless and in a whole lot of pain. Their entire group also had to flee the Lost Cities after Dex defied the Council and destroyed the gadget.

But this was different.

This new ability *needed* to be restricted.

And it was only a matter of time before the Council realized that and locked Keefe away somewhere.

"*Please,*" he whispered, keeping the word barely audible. "You can find a way to key it to my DNA, so it'll only work on me."

Dex shook his head so hard it made his ears jiggle. "Then the Council could have one of their Technopaths figure out a way around that. Or copy my design and build a bunch more—why do you think I threw the other one into the fire?"

His resolve felt like a wall between them.

"*Please,*" Keefe begged again, trying to wear Dex down with as few words as possible.

But Dex's determination strengthened, and Keefe could tell that nothing he could say would get through.

Unless . . .

His heart started racing and his palms started sweating and he felt a thought start itching in the back of his brain.

No—not a thought.

A *word.*

A word that Keefe refused to acknowledge because he knew it was his need taking over again, and if he said the word, it would smash through Dex's doubts and *make* him cooperate.

But he couldn't shove the word out of his mind either, because the need kept reminding him that if Dex wouldn't make him an ability restrictor, he could never see Sophie again.

He'd probably never be able to see anyone.

Those were his only options.

He had to make Dex understand.

Had to. Had to. Had to.

The command burned on his tongue, but he swallowed it back, hacking and coughing as the unspoken word caught in his throat.

His instincts were screaming at him to stop resisting, but he slammed his fist into his chest, and the pain distracted him enough to make the word fade.

"Whoa, easy, boy," Ro said, grabbing Keefe's arm to stop him from hitting himself again. "It's okay. You're okay."

Keefe shook his head, feeling tears pour down his cheeks as the rest of him collapsed into Ro, clinging to her as hard as he could.

"Uh, I'm not much of a hugger," Ro warned.

But she also twisted Keefe's head so it rested on her shoulder, away from the spikes on her armor. And mixed with her surprise and awkwardness was a tangle of anger and concern so tightly woven together that they felt almost solid.

Protective.

Which was good, because Keefe couldn't let go.

Couldn't move.

Could barely open his eyes—but he made himself focus on Dex, pouring the full force of his plea into his stare.

Ro whistled. "Wow, now *that's* what desperation looks like."

"It is," Dex agreed, dragging his hands down his face so hard, his fingers left little red lines. "But you don't understand what you're asking for, Keefe. You weren't there in Magnate Leto's office when the Council made me put the ability restrictor back on Sophie. Even with the adjustments I made, I could tell it was super painful—and I don't think I can fix that. I also can't control which abilities it blocks. I'd have to restrict *all* your abilities."

"I don't think my boy cares," Ro said quietly. "But you know what, Hunkyhair?" She grabbed Keefe's shoulders and leaned him back, so he'd have to look at her. "I think you *should* care. I mean, don't get me wrong—I'll always think you elves put way too much emphasis on your little ability things. But I've also been here long enough to see how much drama it causes if you don't have them—and you have enough drama in your life already. Plus . . . you *do* have abilities. They're part of you. It never goes well trying to fight who you are—trust me on that."

Keefe jerked away and sank onto his bed, curling into a ball and wishing he could shout, THIS ISN'T WHO I AM—MY MOM CHANGED ME.

But . . . did she?

Or had she just activated something that had always been there?

Some awful, creepy thing she'd planned from the beginning?

And did it matter?

This was his life now.

He had to deal with it.

Dex sank onto the bed next to him again. "Wow. You're *really* scared. I'm not even an Empath, and I can feel it."

"So can I," Ro mumbled, and the protective energy in the air ramped up a bit.

Which made Keefe want to deny it—want to smirk and crack a joke like he always did.

But those things felt like they belonged to a different life.

Seconds ticked by.

Finally Dex said, "Okay. I get it. Elwin described what happened yesterday, and . . . yeah, it's pretty terrifying. But . . . you just manifested *yesterday*, you know? You haven't given the ability any time to settle. You don't even know exactly what the ability *is*, or have a name for it yet! And you haven't tried whatever concoctions Elwin and my dad are making right now. You also haven't let me see if I can come up with some gadgets to help—or some elixirs. I make a lot of those, too—and I'm pretty good at it. *And* you haven't tried training. So . . . can't we start with all of that? Before we try anything more drastic?"

"Come on, Hunkyhair," Ro said, shaking his shoulder. "Your techy friend is right. You're giving up *way* too easily. Where's the stubborn guy who set the record for detentions at your fancy elf-y academy? The guy who's spent years finding creative ways to annoy his jerk of a dad instead of giving in and cooperating?"

"The guy who spent weeks setting up for the Great Gulon Incident," Dex added, nudging Keefe with his elbow. "I know I wasn't there for that, but I've heard *lots* of stories. And I know you planned it so perfectly that Dame Alina never found enough proof to nail you for it."

Ro laughed. "Sounds like someone needs to give me the details on this gulon thing I keep hearing about someday. But right now"—she dragged Keefe up to a sitting position—"you need to get your fight back. I didn't leave my home and suffer all these months in Sparkle Town so I could protect some boy who gives up the second things get tough. I came here to protect the scrawny elf who beat *my dad* in a sparring match, because I figured that guy might be someone worth keeping around. And I'll deny saying this later, but . . . you *are* worth keeping around."

Keefe looked away, not sure if the tears burning his eyes were from Ro's pep talk—or the fact that he couldn't quite believe it.

Ro shook him until he turned back to face her. "I know you think your mom won, but trust me, this *isn't* over. You have an infinite number of ways to keep resisting her. Don't give up. And don't hide from the power she gave you. Learn how to use it against her."

"Exactly," Dex agreed, placing a hand on Keefe's shoulder. "And remember, you're not in this alone."

Keefe had never felt more alone in his entire life.

But . . . when he read Dex's emotions, all he felt was determination and confidence and hints of the same warmth he'd felt from Elwin.

Dex was on his side.

So was Ro, strangely enough.

Her protective vibes were stronger than anything he'd ever experienced before.

He didn't want to let them down.

And he *definitely* didn't want to let his mom win.

So maybe if he was careful, and stayed hidden, and didn't talk, and worked super hard—maybe he could get a handle on this new power in a more manageable way.

He'd already resisted using a command on Dex.

That had to be a good sign.

So he sat up taller and nodded—but he also grabbed Dex's wrist when Dex started to pull away, took a steadying breath, and risked nine more whispered words.

"If it doesn't work, you have to help me."

He didn't specify *how*—too afraid it would turn into a command. But Dex seemed to know he meant the ability restrictor.

Dex sighed. "I'll think about it. That's all I'll agree to."

Keefe tightened his grip as the itch surged back in his brain—the word so loud this time that he could almost hear it, almost *know* what to say.

But he closed his eyes and breathed until he'd buried it again.

That was twice now.

Twice he'd kept control.

So maybe there *was* hope.

If not, he'd make Dex take the ability away.

By any means necessary.

SEVEN

Sophie

"WHAT ARE YOU DOING HERE?" Fitz asked as Lord Cassius flashed an oily smile and said, "To what do I owe my sudden popularity?"

Sophie ignored both questions.

"What are *you* doing here?" she asked Fitz.

"Providing me with an update on my son," Lord Cassius told her, "since no one else seems to have considered that to be a priority—unless that's why you're here." He fanned the air. "No, it feels like you were very much hoping I wouldn't be home."

"I'm always hoping you won't be anywhere I'm going," Sophie snapped back, deciding she was done trying to be polite to Keefe's father. She should've used every word—every conversation—to shame him for the countless ways he'd hurt his son. "If you wanted updates on Keefe, you could've shown up at the Healing Center. He was there for three days. So was I. Where were you?"

Lord Cassius narrowed his eyes. "I don't need to explain myself to anyone—least of all to a teenager with an inflated sense of self-importance. *But,* since you seem to think you have everything all figured out, it might interest you to know that I've been working on an assignment from the Black Swan."

He paused to let that sink in—let her wonder what the Black Swan might be hiding from her.

Sophie refused to ask any questions.

"Your stubbornness has gotten much stronger since you first arrived in our world," Lord Cassius noted. "Perhaps this new separation from my son will help you learn better deference and respect."

"You told him about that?" she asked Fitz—then realized she probably should've transmitted the question.

Lord Cassius looked much too pleased with her response.

She couldn't take the words back, though, so she decided to remind Fitz, "He went along *willingly* with Lady Gisela's plans for Keefe's legacy. So he's just as much to blame for what's happening to Keefe as she is."

"The only thing I'm to *blame* for," Lord Cassius argued, "is wanting the best for my son."

Sophie rolled her eyes. "No, you wanted the best for *yourself.* You wanted to be the father of someone powerful and important and special, so that maybe people would think *you* were powerful and important and special too—but all they're going to think is that you're a creepy jerk who let his wife experiment on his family. And the really sad thing is, Keefe would've been all of those things without you messing with his abilities. So you put him through this nightmare for no reason."

Lord Cassius's glare felt colder than staring down a Froster. But when he spoke, all he said was "Interesting."

"What is?" Fitz demanded when Sophie stayed silent.

Lord Cassius kept his focus on Sophie. "Should I tell him what you're feeling right now?"

"Don't bother." She turned to Fitz. "I'm trying to decide if I'd rather inflict on him or zap him a few times with this melder."

She patted the pocket hiding her weapon.

"Interesting," Lord Cassius repeated, his lips twitching with something between a smile and a scowl. "Seems you've also picked up my son's habit of using jokes to deflect attention. But they never fully mask what you're hiding, do they?" He waved his hands through the air again before shaking his head and dropping his arms to his sides. "Actually, it seems like you're even hiding these feelings from yourself—and I have neither the patience nor the desire to deal with adolescent drama. So I'm just going to say this: Hate me all you want—blame me all you want. It won't change anything. And it won't make you feel any better."

"Probably not. That's why I'm leaning toward using the melder." Sophie patted her pocket again. "It's so much less exhausting than inflicting, but equally painful."

"Okay, it's official," Grizel said, applauding as she stepped out of the shadows near Candleshade's vortinator. "I'm a *big* fan of this new Sophie. Don't get me wrong—you've always been a fierce little force of nature," she added when Sophie frowned. "But this is a whole other level of confidence—and I'm *here* for it!"

"So am I," Flori agreed.

"Me too."

Fitz's voice was quiet enough that Sophie almost wondered if she'd imagined it. But she dared a quick look at his face and found him focused right on her.

And when their eyes met?

Man, she'd missed having him smile at her.

His smile was more tentative than it used to be—and her heart was too shrapnel-filled to react.

But it was still a nice change.

A tiny shift that helped her believe they could save their friendship.

"*Anyway*," Lord Cassius said, reaching up to smooth his hair, "you still haven't explained why you're here—with *two* bodyguards, no less. Clearly it wasn't to see me, even though this is my home."

"Before we get to that," Grizel cut in, "how about we finish the conversation *we* were having, before we were interrupted?" She side-eyed Sandor with the last word.

"If you'd told me that you were coming here, I could've coordinated our arrival," Sandor reminded her.

"That argument applies just as easily to you, Captain Cuddles," Grizel countered, bopping his flat nose with her finger.

"Captain Cuddles?" Flori asked, giggling as Sandor's gray skin took on a pinkish hue. "Can we all use that title?"

"*No*," Sandor told her, at the same time Grizel said, "Absolutely!"

Sandor let out a squeaky growl. "Can we focus?"

"I suppose we can try." Grizel turned back to Lord Cassius. "In case you've forgotten, you were about to tell us about your wife's abilities."

"No, I was about to reiterate that—as far as I know—she only has *one*. And yes, I'm sure it *is* possible that she's been hiding a second ability, since, as you know, Gisela has no problem erasing memories—or lying. *But*, I do remember asking her once if she was bothered by the fact that most Polyglots have an additional talent, and the disappointment and frustration I felt from her would be hard to fake."

"Unless she was disappointed and frustrated that she couldn't tell you about her other ability," Fitz suggested.

"I suppose that's possible," Lord Cassius admitted. "But the *real* question is: Why does it matter? I assure you, if my wife could've affected people with her voice the way you say my son now can, there's no way she would've been able to resist using the ability for all this time."

He had a point.

And Sophie tried to find that comforting, since Lady Gisela would be almost unstoppable if she could do what Keefe did.

But it also meant that Lady Gisela must have an elaborate plan for how to make Keefe use his new ability the way she wanted.

And her plans usually succeeded.

"It matters," Fitz told Lord Cassius, "because Councillor Oralie thinks the numbing command that Keefe used might not be a sign of a new ability. She thought it sounded more like the elements made his empathy merge with his new Polyglot senses, and that's why he's able to affect emotions with his voice. So I figured it'd be smart to make sure there aren't any other abilities that Keefe might've inherited."

"*Merged* abilities," Lord Cassius said quietly.

"Did that word trigger any memories?" Sophie asked when he turned to pace the foyer.

"I wish." He reached up to rub his temples, crossing the length of the room twice more before he added, "But it does feel . . ."

"Feel?" Fitz prompted.

When Lord Cassius stayed silent, he added, "Would it help if we did another probe? Or I could try to do it myself, if . . ."

His eyes darted to Sophie, like he wasn't sure if he should suggest working together.

But Sophie was more interested in the way Lord Cassius had frozen midstep—foot dangling in the air—the second Fitz had mentioned searching his mind.

"Is there a problem?" she asked him.

"Of course not." But his voice was as tense as his features. "I just . . . need time to process."

"You realize how suspicious you sound, right?" Grizel asked as Lord Cassius reached under his cape, fumbling with his sleeve. "Especially with how pale you've gotten?"

"Suspect whatever you want. I'm sure you're all very used to being wrong about me." He pulled out a pathfinder and spun the crystal back and forth. "And I need to go."

"Go where?" Sophie asked.

"It doesn't concern you."

"We'll decide that," Sandor told him.

But Lord Cassius locked the crystal into place and leaped away without another word.

Fitz glanced at Sophie. "So . . . that was super weird, right?"

Sophie nodded, wishing she'd thought to shove her way into Lord Cassius's mind before he'd left. They deserved answers *way* more than he deserved privacy.

"You don't think he'd try to protect Lady Gisela, do you?" Fitz asked.

"I was just wondering the same thing," she admitted. "But . . . I feel like the only person he cares about is himself."

"True. Though, what if protecting her also protects some embarrassing secret he doesn't want anyone to know?" Fitz suggested—which definitely sounded like something Lord Cassius would do.

Sophie sighed. "We need to figure out where he went. I don't suppose you saw which facet he used on his pathfinder?"

"You can't really tell by looking at them. It's about counting the turns of the crystal and feeling the cuts and angles." Fitz dragged a hand through his hair. "I guess Grizel and I can go wait at the Shores of Solace and confront him as soon as he gets back."

"That's assuming he actually goes home. He might not." She tugged her eyelashes a little harder than she needed to. "Ugh, why does *everything* have to be so hard? Like . . . is it really asking so much for people to be honest about what they're doing? Even if they're doing something wrong, at least own it, you know?"

"That would definitely make life easier." Fitz kicked the side of his boot a few times. "Though . . . that sounds a little funny coming from *you*, since . . . you know . . . you still haven't said why you're here right now."

He had a point.

And Sophie was absolutely not in the mood to get into another huge fight—especially since it had felt like some of the awkwardness between them was *finally* fading.

But . . .

Lying did make everything way more complicated.

Plus . . . how could they ever be friends again if she kept hiding things from him?

"Okay," she said, taking a deep breath. "If you really want to know . . . Oralie and I unlocked the Forgotten Secret in her cache—and we didn't really learn much from the memory. But it seemed like the information we need is actually in Kenric's cache. So I'm trying to get that back."

"And you think it's here in Candleshade?" Fitz asked.

"No, I wish." She fought the urge to tug out another itchy eyelash before she added, "We don't know where to look. So we thought it might be good to see if any members of the Neverseen have any information that they'd be willing to share."

She stopped there, clinging to the *tiny* hope that Fitz might not be able to guess the rest of her plan.

But of course he immediately said, "So . . . you came here looking for Alvar."

Sophie forced herself to nod. "Well . . . mostly I'm looking for anything he might've left behind that could tell me where he's hiding."

She focused on her feet, bracing for a whole lot of shouting.

But when Fitz finally spoke, his voice was calm and steady— maybe even a little sad as he said, "And you didn't ask me for help."

"I—"

"It's okay," he interrupted. "I'm not mad. I just . . . wish I knew why." He blew out a breath before he added, "Was it because of all the awful stuff I said when you told me you let Alvar go? Or was it because of . . . the other thing?"

Grizel coughed. "You know, I think it's high time we do another grounds patrol, don't you?"

"I do," Flori agreed.

"I'll keep watch here," Sandor told them—then let out a squeaky yelp. "Or . . . I'll be right outside the main door."

Fitz cleared his throat when they were alone. "Goblins aren't great at being subtle, are they?"

"Definitely not," Sophie agreed, wondering if her cheeks were as red as the sash on her tunic. "Though . . . they're better than ogres."

"Very true. Ro's the worst."

"She can be," Sophie admitted. "But in her own way, she can be kind of sweet."

"I guess." Several painful seconds passed before Fitz added, "You didn't answer my question."

Sophie cringed. "Caught that, huh?"

"It's pretty hard to miss. Just like all of this awkwardness."

Sophie dared a quick peek at his face and was stunned that he didn't look angry.

He looked . . . sad.

Also ridiculously handsome—but that wasn't something she needed to be thinking about.

That would only bring up the *almost*s and the *what-if*s, and make her start wishing for things that wouldn't be a good idea.

Fitz took a small step closer. "I really miss you, Sophie. Not just as . . . whatever. I hate how it feels like we're not even friends anymore."

"I know," she whispered, trying not to wonder if any of that meant he still . . .

Because it didn't matter.

She'd been the one to end things.

It had all gotten so complicated—and things were *still* complicated.

None of that had changed.

But she did need him to know, "I miss you, too."

That earned her his glorious, movie-worthy smile.

He took another step closer, running a hand that looked a little shaky through his hair before he said, "Do you think we can maybe just . . . start over? Forget everything else and just try working together again?"

Sophie's brain was screaming, *YES!*

But when she actually used her voice, she found herself asking, "Are you going to get mad at me about Alvar again?"

His smile faded, and he turned away, curling and uncurling his hands for several deep breaths.

"Anything with my brother is always going to be hard for me," he eventually admitted. "But . . . I'm going to try to keep my anger directed at him, and no one else."

It wasn't the *most* reassuring answer.

But it did feel *real*—and wasn't that what they'd been striving for during all of their Cognate training?

Truth.

Trust.

Open communication.

"Okay," she whispered. "Let's try it."

He turned back, flashing another beautiful smile—though it was back to being a bit more reserved.

But that felt real, too.

So did the fact that neither of them reached for the other's hand.

They still had a long way to go—a lot of healing and figuring things out.

But it felt like a good beginning.

"So . . . how do you want to do this?" Sophie asked, trying to get back to the more urgent problems they were facing. "We'd cover more ground if we split up and searched by ourselves, but—"

"Okay, don't get mad at me for saying this," Fitz interrupted. "But . . . I think this is a waste of time."

"I know," Sophie admitted. "I'm sure it's going to be too. But . . . it's still better than doing nothing, right?"

"See, but I think we have another option." He stepped closer, lowering his voice to a whisper. "You want to talk to someone from the Neverseen, right? What about Glimmer? I'm sure she'd know *way* more than my brother."

"I actually suggested that," Sophie told him. "But Oralie seemed pretty convinced that Glimmer doesn't know anything—just like Keefe didn't know anything when he left the Neverseen. And neither did Tam."

"Yeah, but Keefe and Tam weren't *trusted* members of the order," Fitz reminded her. "The Neverseen knew Keefe was trying to play them, just like they knew Tam was basically a prisoner. But Lady Gisela thought Glimmer was super loyal, didn't she? Do you really think she didn't tell Glimmer *anything*? And isn't talking to her better than spending hours searching this depressing, dusty house for something we both know we're not going to find?"

Sophie sighed. "Yeah, I guess. Do you think we should go now?

I don't have a crystal to go to Tiergan's house—and I've never been there, so I can't picture it well enough to teleport."

"Candleshade has a Leapmaster we could use. But honestly? I think we should wait until tomorrow. Don't take this the wrong way, but you look super exhausted. Did you sleep at all last night?"

"Not really."

"That's what I figured. So why don't you go home, get some sleep, and we'll go to Tiergan's house in the morning? Actually, it'd probably also be good to let Tam know we're coming, since I hear he's been a little . . . protective."

"But—"

"It's not wasting time," Fitz interrupted. "I know it feels like it is, but seriously, Sophie. You've barely slept at all in days. And I know you're probably thinking that you're just going to toss and turn or have nightmares, but that doesn't mean you don't need to try to rest. Plus . . ."

"What?" Sophie asked when he didn't continue.

He dragged a hand through his hair. "Well . . . I think I know something that might help you sleep—and no, I don't mean taking a sedative. I mean . . . Keefe."

Sophie straightened up, crossing her arms. "What about him?"

"Come on, Sophie. I saw the look on your face when he agreed to Councillor Alina's demand, and then you leaped out of the Healing Center as fast as you could. And I get it—it was pretty harsh of him to do that. Especially after you spent all that time sitting by his side in the Healing Center, waiting for him to wake up." He cleared his throat. "But . . . that's why I think you might feel better if you guys talked it out."

"Yeah . . . well . . . he doesn't want to talk to me."

"Not with his voice," Fitz agreed. "But you could use your telepathy."

Sophie crossed her arms tighter, basically hugging herself.

She'd actually thought about doing that the night before. But she wasn't sure if Keefe would respond. And the thought of him ignoring her . . .

"He told me to stay away," she mumbled, focusing on her feet.

Fitz sighed. "I know. But he was afraid he might lose control of his new ability. It'll be way different if you use your telepathy. Trust me—I'm his best friend. I know these things. Plus, I saw the look on his face after you left, so I'm sure he'd feel better if you talked everything through. He's probably been waiting for you to reach out, since you guys talk that way a lot."

"No we don't," Sophie argued, not sure why her voice had gotten so high-pitched. "Seriously, we don't."

"Well, even if that's true, you guys are . . . close."

"We're friends," Sophie clarified, cringing when her voice turned squeaky again.

The conversation was just so . . . awkward.

"I know you are," Fitz told her. "That's not what I'm saying. I just . . . I know you're super worried about him. And I know you're probably thinking he's mad at you or something. And the only way your brain is going to quiet down enough to let you sleep is if you talk to Keefe. So just . . . try it, okay? You're going to need the rest. I have a feeling meeting with Glimmer tomorrow is going to be pretty intense."

He was right, of course.

Sophie knew that.

But that didn't make the idea any less . . . scary.

"It'll be okay," Fitz promised. "Trust me."

She met his eyes, remembering all the times she'd done exactly that. Fitz had been her first friend—her first guide—in this scary, shimmering new world she'd had to figure out how to belong to. The person she'd called for help after her kidnapping, who'd shown up just in time to save her. Someone she'd survived fires and battles and banishment with, and who'd faced down cold, cruel monsters with her over and over and over.

"Okay," she whispered. "But we meet up *early* tomorrow."

"Deal," Fitz agreed. "I'll head to Havenfield as soon as you're awake."

Sophie stalled a little longer before she leaped back to Havenfield—then stalled a whole lot more once she got there, not sure she was ready to find out if Keefe would ignore her.

But outside, under Calla's Panakes, with Wynn and Luna snuggled against her, she finally found the courage to stretch out her mind.

Keefe?

She was only going to try three times—that was the deal she'd made with herself. Three times, and if he didn't answer, then . . . that was that.

KEEFE?

She pushed the call as far as it could go, holding her breath.

Still no answer.

One more time, she told herself. *One more time, then count to five.*

She rallied her mental strength. *KEEFE!*

One second passed.

Two.

Three.

And before she got to four, a familiar voice flooded her mind.

Has anyone told you you're starting to sound like Silveny?

Sophie let out a breath. *Hey, Keefe.*

- EIGHT -
Keefe

SOOOOOOOOOOOO, KEEFE THOUGHT, mentally dragging out the word, *I guess this means you're still talking to me.*

Funny, Sophie transmitted, *I was about to say the same thing to you.*

Keefe winced.

"What's wrong?" Ro asked. "Need me to get Elwin?"

He shook his head.

Ro leaned closer. "Then why do you look all sweaty and nervous?"

Keefe shrugged.

Ro gritted her teeth. "If you don't start talking soon, I'm going to tie you up in your blankets and use you for tackling practice."

He shrugged again, earning a growl that rattled the walls.

Are you still there? Sophie transmitted in a soft, worried tone that made Keefe imagine her tugging on her eyelashes.

Yeah, sorry. Ro was distracting me.

He smirked at his bodyguard as he sat up and tried to fix his hair—then wanted to smack himself since it wasn't like Sophie could see him. And it was a good thing she couldn't, because *wow*—he didn't realize his hair could bend that many different directions at the same time.

He was also pretty sure the tingling in his cheek was from big, red pillow creases.

He'd tunneled under his blankets after Dex left, and he'd been there ever since, tossing and turning and flailing and thrashing and generally feeling sorry for himself.

Elwin had brought him dinner at some point—something he called Cosmic Explosion, with all kinds of weird, colorful fruits cut into stars and moons and planets and suns. It even had sparkly silver dust sprinkled on top. And it tasted as amazing as it looked, but Keefe had only been able to choke down a few bites before his insides knotted up.

So . . . how are you doing? Sophie asked.

Oh . . . you know.

He wanted to tell her he was great—convince her that things were already going back to normal.

But then she might want to visit.

I've been better, he said, flopping back onto his pillow. He pulled his blankets over his head before he added the words he didn't even like admitting to himself. *I think this ability is getting stronger. I almost used a command on Dex today. Twice.*

Several seconds crawled by before Sophie asked, *But you didn't, right?*

Yeah, I fought it off. But it was a STRUGGLE.

What was the command?

I'm not sure. I couldn't let myself acknowledge the word, because I knew if I did, I'd HAVE to say it.

More painful silence. Then Sophie told him, *Well . . . that sounds like good news.*

Keefe snorted a laugh. *You're cute when you try to be optimistic, Foster. But we both know if I were there, I'd be seeing that little crinkle you get between your eyebrows when you're worried. You're reaching up to smooth it right now, aren't you?*

Actually, I'm rolling my eyes. You don't have to get rid of the power, Keefe—you just have to learn how to control it. And that's what you did today, right?

Keefe couldn't bring himself to agree.

He wasn't ready to feel optimistic—not when his throat hurt from the words he'd choked back, and his stomach hurt from all the failed medicines, and his head hurt from the constant emotional overload, and his heart hurt worse than anything.

At least he could do something about the last one.

I haven't said I'm sorry yet, have I? he asked quietly.

No, Sophie admitted. *But you don't—*

Yes, I do. He pulled his blankets tighter around himself, into a Cocoon of Shame. *I'm really sorry, Sophie. I didn't mean to make it seem like I don't want to be around you, or like I think any of this is your fault. I definitely don't.*

Endless silence followed.

When Sophie finally responded, the thought was barely a whisper. *It kinda seems like you do. I mean . . . you hung out with Dex—*

I wouldn't call it "hanging out," he corrected. *It was more like he lectured me and I fought the urge to use some creepy command on him. And he was only here because I'm hoping he might be able to make me a gadget like those fingernail things Tinker made for you—but, you know, for my voice.*

Ohhhhh, that's an awesome idea! She sounded so sweetly hopeful when she added, *Does Dex think he can make something?*

He wasn't sure. But he's going to try. And I guess Elwin and Kesler are working on some elixirs that might help too.

He decided not to mention the whole ability restrictor option, since he had a feeling Sophie would hate that idea even more than Dex did—and he wouldn't blame her.

Plus, he was trying to apologize.

So . . . are we okay? he asked carefully. *Or do I need to do some begging? I will. I'll even write an apology poem if I have to. I just need to figure out what rhymes with "total jerkface."*

Her mental voice somehow carried her laughter. *I think I'm good.*

Hmm, that wasn't very convincing. Apology poem it is! Imagine me clearing my throat now for dramatic effect, and . . . "Forgive me, Lady Foster. I never meant to make you mad—"

I wasn't mad, Sophie interrupted.

Fine, we'll switch it to "sad." Is that better?

Sort of. It was more like . . . I don't know. It just felt like you didn't want to be my friend anymore.

Keefe sank deeper into his Cocoon of Shame. *I know. I felt that when you left. And it totally killed me. I just . . . I didn't know what else to do. I need a little more time to get control of whatever this ability is—then I promise I'll be around so much, you'll be trying to find ways to get rid of me. And I'll be like, "NO WAY—TEAM FOSTER-KEEFE IS FOREVER."*

He could tell she was smiling when she said, *I hope so.*

So did he.

But they didn't need to have his doubts in the mix.

So he told her, *No need to hope, Foster. That will definitely be happening. I may even get us tunics that say "Foster-Keefe is back—and better than ever!" And*—

Ro yanked back the blanket over Keefe's head. "You're doing that elf-y mind trick thing to talk to your pretty little Blondie, aren't you? I knew it! It's like I can feel the angst cloud lifting! So, I'm guessing you groveled enough to get her to forgive you?"

Keefe reluctantly nodded.

"THANK ALL THE SPARKLES FOR THAT! Now you just need to tell her you're helplessly in love with her so she can be like"— Ro shifted her voice up an octave and clasped her hands against her heart—"'Oh, Hunkyhair, I never realized you felt that way, even though it was ridiculously obvious to everyone else. And I've been in love with you forever—I just didn't know it because I'm super oblivious. I'm sorry I wasted so much time crushing on Captain Perfect—come here, let's do all the smooching ever!'"

She followed that with kissing sounds, and Keefe opened his mouth to tell Ro exactly where she could go.

But he caught himself at the last second.

"Gah, I almost had you!" She slumped into a dramatic sigh. "Fine. Get back to your little Blondie before she starts worrying that you're ignoring her."

Sorry, Keefe told Sophie. *Ro distracted me again.*

I figured. Everything okay?

Oh yeah. I'm just going to need to find some prank elixirs to punish her. I'm sure Elwin must have a stash somewhere.

I'd be stunned if he didn't. What's his house like?

Super Elwin-y in some ways. Mellower than I expected in others.

He almost added, *You'll have to see it sometime*, but that would probably bring back the awkwardness.

So he went with a safer *Definitely way better than being stuck with Daddy Dearest.*

Yeah, I bet. And that reminds me . . . I don't suppose you have any idea why your dad would get all weird about the term "merged abilities," do you?

Nope. But what do you mean by "weird"?

It's probably easier if I show you.

Her memories crashed into his mind in loud, vivid detail, and he found himself grinning at her snarky comebacks even as his stomach turned extra churn-y at the sight of his dad.

Keefe had always disliked his father—but that dislike was slowly morphing into fist-clenching hate. And he couldn't decide if he wanted to grab his dad and shake him as hard as he could or punch him dead in the face.

"Everything okay, Hunkyhair?" Ro asked. "You're getting a little twitchy. You haven't wrecked things with Blondie, have you?"

Keefe shook his head.

To Sophie he added, *Yeah, I have no clue what that was all about. But you can bet Daddio and I will be talking about it as soon as it's safe for me to do that.*

Or maybe before.

He definitely wouldn't feel guilty about numbing his father—though his father was such a cold, emotionless shell, it probably wouldn't make any difference.

You'll let me know if you find out more? he asked.

Of course. Though . . . we're not really focusing on him right now.

He tried not to let that "we" sting, but of course his brain had to remind him that she was talking about Fitzphie time.

But that was good. Fitz had botched things majorly, but he definitely still cared. So hopefully he'd get his act together and figure out how to be the kind of boyfriend that Foster deserved.

He had a way better chance of pulling that off than Keefe ever would.

You okay? Sophie asked, and Keefe tried to shove those thoughts away, hoping he hadn't accidentally let her hear any of them.

Yep. All good. So, what are you and the Fitzster working on?

He wished he hadn't asked when she told him, *Well . . . we really need to find Kenric's cache.*

It was the mistake that kept on giving.

The betrayal Keefe never seemed to be able to fix.

Got any good leads? he asked, pretty sure he already knew the answer.

Not really. But . . . we're going to try talking to Glimmer tomorrow. Maybe she'll know something.

She didn't sound convinced.

Keefe couldn't blame her for that. But . . . who knew? Maybe Glimmer would surprise them.

He wasn't sure he believed that Glimmer had truly turned against his mom, but his mom was also pretty creepy and evil, so maybe she finally scared Glimmer off.

Will you let me know what she says? he asked.

Of course. Anything you want me to ask—or tell her?

Oh, he had quite a list—most involving words that would make Foster's innocent little ears burn.

Nah, I'm sure you and Fitzy have it covered. Just . . . keep me in the loop.

Will do.

They fell back into slightly painful silence before she added, *What are you going to do tomorrow? Draw more memories?*

He probably should.

He needed to sketch what happened in Loamnore, see if it helped him figure out what was happening to him right now.

But he wasn't in the mood to relive it all yet.

You know what might help? Sophie asked. *Maybe you should try writing about the memories after you draw them. I remember learning that words and images are processed by different parts of the brain, so using both might help you discover new things.*

She went on for a few more sentences about the power of words, but Keefe spent most of the speech imagining how she looked as she was saying it. She was so adorable when she was trying to get him excited about something.

I guess I can give it a try, he agreed when she finally finished.

You should. And you should also get some rest. You sound . . . tired.

So do you, he noted. And that was probably his fault. *I think you need a Wynn-and-Luna snugglefest tonight.*

I'm actually with them right now.

UM, EXCUSE ME—YOU'VE BEEN CUDDLING WITH BABY ALICORNS THIS WHOLE TIME AND YOU DIDN'T TELL ME? I NEED A MENTAL PICTURE OF THIS IMMEDIATELY.

Okay, hang on.

His mind filled with what might've been the cutest thing he'd ever seen—Foster leaning against the Panakes's trunk with Wynn's head resting in her lap and Luna lying on her back beside her, getting a major belly rub. Flowers drifted all around them, and the sky was that perfect dusky purple, with tiny stars just starting to break through.

Wish I was there, he told her, hoping it wasn't too sappy of a thing to admit.

Sophie's reply was a soft, sweet whisper. *Me too.*

For a second, Keefe could imagine himself right there beside her, with her head resting gently on his shoulder—but he shoved that thought away as fast as he could, hoping she didn't notice.

Get some rest, Foster.

I will if you will.

Keefe smiled. *Deal.*

He wasn't sure how long their minds stayed connected after that, but at some point he drifted off to sleep—and he didn't have a single nightmare.

"He looks so peaceful—I feel bad waking him," someone said—a voice that sounded familiar, but Keefe's snoozing brain couldn't recognize it.

"Well then, I guess it's a good thing *I* don't have any problem with it," someone else added, followed by a bone-shaking shout of "WAKE UP, HUNKYHAIR!"

Keefe bolted upright, struggling to catch his breath as his heart slammed against his ribs and the room sharpened into focus.

Ro grinned. "Looks like I need to start calling you Droolyhair."

Keefe gave her an *I-will-make-you-suffer-later* glare as he reached up to wipe his chin.

"Oh . . . hey," he mumbled when he noticed Dex hiding in the doorway—then sucked in a sharp breath and clamped his hand over his mouth.

"HE SPEAKS!" Ro shouted. "And once again, the world did NOT end! MORE! MORE! MORE!"

Keefe gave her a less-than-friendly gesture instead.

Dex laughed. "Sorry. Elwin sent me up here to wake you. My dad and I stopped by with a few things we wanted to test to see if they help."

Keefe was on his feet immediately, wobbling as his body adjusted to being vertical.

"Hang on," Ro said, putting out her arms to block him. "Shirt first. And maybe do something about that morning breath?"

Keefe glared at her.

But she had a point, so he grabbed the nearest tunic and pulled it on before chugging some Youth to rinse his mouth.

Dex snorted. "Nice pajamas."

Keefe hadn't even noticed what he was wearing, but it must've been something Elwin had given him. The bright blue fabric was covered in colorful murcats, which had all been dusted with glitter.

He shrugged, dragging a hand through his wild hair as he followed Dex into the hall.

"Uh, just so you know, it's about to get really loud," Dex warned. "My dad thought it would be a good idea to bring the triplets for this, so . . ."

He didn't need to finish the sentence.

Keefe could already hear the screaming.

"DAD—LEX KEEPS LOOKING OUT MY WINDOW!"

"IT'S NOT *YOUR* WINDOW!"

"YES, IT IS—I'M STANDING IN FRONT OF IT!"

"SO AM I!"

"NOW YOU'RE NOT!"

"DAD—REX SHOVED ME INTO BEX. AND SHE SMELLS LIKE ROTTING FLOWERS!"

"YEAH, WELL, YOU SMELL LIKE YOU'VE BEEN ROLLING IN POOP!"

"HE WAS!"

"NO, I WASN'T!"

"OW, DON'T POKE ME!"

Dex rubbed his temples as they headed downstairs. "My mom keeps promising they'll calm down when they get older, but they're twelve now, so I don't think it's going to happen. And I'm pretty sure they're going to beat your detention record this year."

"Not if I can help it," Ro jumped in. "Hunkyhair and I still have plenty of chaos to cause, don't we?"

She held out her hand for a high five, but Keefe kept right on walking.

He couldn't imagine life ever being that normal again.

"Over here!" Elwin called, gesturing for them to join him in the center of the giant main room, where he stood with Kesler in front of the swiveling armchair.

The triplets were way on the other side of the room, making different shadow animals in the multicolored light filtering in through the windows—which was good, since Keefe could already feel crackly waves of their enthusiasm slamming against his senses.

He was going to have *quite* the headache when they got closer.

"Sorry we woke you," Kesler told Keefe. "I was hoping you'd already be up."

Keefe shrugged, trying to tell Kesler it wasn't a big deal.

"Okay, take a seat." Kesler patted the armchair. "I'll try to make this quick. It's hard to know if I'm on the right track with something until I see how the elixir actually works—and these formulas are so specific to what you're dealing with that I have to test them on you."

"I thought it'd be smart to test my prototype, too," Dex added, pulling something small and silver out of his pocket, which kind of looked like a tiny metal egg. "I'm sure it still needs some tweaks, but I'm hoping I'm close."

He tapped the top of the egg, and the gadget split open, revealing all kinds of cogs and circuitry neatly arranged inside.

Ro whistled. "You made that in one night?"

Dex shrugged. "It's not as complicated as it looks."

Keefe doubted that. And when he studied Dex closer, he could see dark shadows under his eyes.

Dex must've stayed up all night working.

And Kesler and Elwin looked just as exhausted.

"You okay there, Hunkyhair?" Ro asked.

Keefe nodded, but his eyes felt a little watery.

He wasn't used to people making those kinds of sacrifices for him—and he could feel their concern drifting through the air, with no trace of any pity.

"I should probably explain how this is going to work," Kesler said, pointing to three vials on the small table next to the armchair—one green, one purple, and one orange. "The plan is—"

"GIVE IT BACK!" one of the triplets shouted, followed by a whole lot of squealing.

"DAAAAAAAAAAAD!"

"STOP CRYING TO DAD ALL THE TIME!"

"I'M NOT CRYING—YOU'RE CRYING!"

"I'LL MAKE YOU BOTH CRY!"

"AHHHHHH!"

Kesler sighed as Rex, Bex, and Lex charged past them like a strawberry-blond stampede. "Sorry. I know the triplets can make things a little chaotic—"

"A *little*?" Dex cut in.

Kesler rumpled Dex's hair, making the resemblance between the two of them even more noticeable. "Okay, fine—a *lot* more chaotic. But that's why they're here." His periwinkle eyes focused on Keefe as he said, "I need you to get overwhelmed. I won't know if anything's working until you start to lose control—and for the record, I won't mind at all if you end up numbing my kids. I might even have you leave them that way. I could use a little quiet."

"Relax," Elwin said, blocking Keefe from getting up. "If all goes well, no one will end up numbed—and if they do, it's totally painless, and you already know how to fix it."

"Rex, Bex, and Lex also know what might happen," Kesler added, "and they're good with it."

"YEAH—DO YOUR WORST!" one of them shouted. "YOU'LL NEVER BE ABLE TO NUMB ME!"

"OR ME!"

"OR ME!"

Keefe shook his head, even though he could definitely feel their conviction.

"I know there's a chance you might end up giving a different command," Elwin told him, before Keefe could figure out how to convey that exact argument. "That's why I'll be wearing earplugs, so I can step in if needed."

"So will I," Kesler promised.

"Me too," Dex agreed.

"Me three!" Ro winked when she added, "And I'll happily smack you around to snap you out of it."

"And yes, we realize there's still a small risk," Kesler admitted, "but . . . that's pretty normal for us."

"Yeah, my dad's always making us test his Slurps and Burps elixirs," Dex explained. "One time he made all my hair fall out and gave the triplets explosive farts. And my mom got stuck with bloodred teeth for a week."

"Ohhh, I might have to try that bloody teeth one!" Ro cut in, puckering her red lips.

"And let's not forget that Dex has almost electrocuted me *several* times," Kesler noted, "not to mention that hole in the roof."

Dex shrugged. "It happens."

"So see? Nothing out of the ordinary around here," Kesler added. "No need to look so worried."

Keefe shook his head again.

He could definitely tell from everyone's emotions that none of them were the least bit concerned by this plan they'd come up with. But that didn't mean it wasn't a super-bad idea.

"LOOK HOW SCARED HE IS!" one of the triplets shouted as the stampede charged closer.

"YEAH, WHO KNEW THE GREAT KEEFE SENCEN WAS SO BORING!"

"HE'S NOT BORING! HE'S CUTE!"

"EWWWW, BEX LIKES KEEFE!"

"SO WHAT IF I DO?"

Keefe had never been so relieved to not have to come up with a reply.

Especially when Rex and Lex started making a bunch of really loud kissy noises and chanting, "BEX WANTS TO SMOOCH HIM!"

Dex snort-laughed. "Welcome to my life. Try not to be envious."

Keefe grinned at the joke. But honestly?

When he looked at the crinkly smile on Kesler's face and the way he rested his hand on Dex's shoulder, Keefe *was* envious.

He would've fit in so much better with a loud, chaotic family. Instead, he'd been stuck with—

His thoughts were cut off when the triplets sprinted over, hitting him with such a strong blast of excitement, smugness, and pure *energy* that Keefe felt his eyes start to glaze.

"Okay, let's get this going," Kesler told everyone. "Earplugs in!"

"Remember, this is the best way to find something to help you deal with this. It'll be okay," Elwin promised before popping two glittery blobs into his ears.

Dex and Kesler did the same.

Ro sighed and crammed hers in too. "Even your *earplugs* are sparkly. You elves have serious issues."

Kesler clapped his hands. "All right. We'll start with the green and go from there. You guys remember what to do, right?" he asked the triplets.

"YEP!" they all said in unison, and the three of them lunged for Keefe with flailing arms, like some sort of mutated kraken.

Keefe jolted as Bex grabbed his hand and the two boys each grabbed his shoulders—but it wasn't just from the emotional bombardment.

One of the boy's hands felt like ice searing his skin. Bex's grip felt weirdly squishy. And the third boy's touch was . . . Keefe didn't even know how to describe it.

There was something hollow about it.

Or maybe "empty" was a better word.

All Keefe knew was, he didn't like it.

He tried to twist away, but the triplets clung tighter than a jaculus feasting on a T. rex. And the more he struggled, the more they squealed and slammed him with more emotions and tightened their unsettling grips.

He wanted it to stop.

Needed it to stop.

And the moment he had that thought, a word started burning in his throat.

"Drink this!" someone ordered, and Keefe felt a vial press against his lips.

He choked down the bitter liquid, coughing and hacking.

"Is that any better?" the voice asked.

Keefe shook his head.

If anything, the unspoken command seemed to burn even hotter.

He locked his jaw and pressed his lips tighter, sucking air in through his nose.

"Okay, how about this one?"

Keefe cracked his mouth open enough to gulp down something sludgy and sweet, which made his head feel like he was being stepped on by a mastodon.

The command turned to fire in his throat, getting hotter and hotter and hotter.

It had to stop.

Someone, please make it stop.

He gritted his teeth, biting back the plea.

But his brain kept rattling with the word.

Stop, stop, stop, stop, stop.

"I don't think that one helped either," the voice said. "But I feel like the last one will do the trick."

Keefe gagged as the cloying sweetness hit his taste buds.

Somehow he managed to choke the medicine down, and as it streamed across his throat, it did ease some of the burning.

But it also made his heart race and his head spin.

And the command was still there.

It was just . . . shifting into something else.

He didn't need it to stop this time.

He needed it to . . .

No.

He couldn't let himself think the word.

He was too tired to choke it back.

No. No. No. No. No.

"All right, let's try it my way," a new voice said, and Keefe felt something brush against his neck. "I just clamped my gadget around your registry pendant, and it should obscure your tone if you try to give a command right now."

"It's okay," someone added as Keefe shook his head. "Remember, this is a test. Use your voice."

Keefe shook his head harder.

Which made everyone start chanting, "USE YOUR VOICE! USE YOUR VOICE! USE YOUR VOICE!"

The triplets tightened their grips and rocked his shoulders—thrashed his arms—as their emotions brewed into a frenzy.

Keefe couldn't breathe.

Couldn't think.

Couldn't fight anymore as the command shifted back to the most basic need.

"STOP!" he screamed, then slumped with sweet relief when the room fell blissfully silent.

He took a slow, deep breath, reveling in the quiet, before he forced his eyes open to see what he'd done.

And there they were.

All three of the triplets, looking sort of . . . stuck.

Their eyes were wide, mouths open, limbs stiff—as if they'd been frozen somehow.

"Well," Dex said through the fog of panic slowly filling the air, "looks like we'll all have to go back to the drawing board."

- NINE -
Sophie

I THINK I'M STARTING TO UNDERSTAND WHY the Council let Glimmer stay here," Sophie grumbled as she bent to catch her breath. "I swear this place is harder to get to than Exile. At least *those* stairs go down."

It also didn't help that she couldn't see their destination.

Somewhere up ahead—much farther than Sophie wanted to think about—the stone staircase they were climbing disappeared into the misty clouds.

Tiergan's house hopefully wasn't too far beyond that.

Fitz arched his back in a stretch. "I still think we should try levitating."

"Not in these winds," Biana told him. "We'd be swept so far out to sea, we'd never get back."

"Yeah, I guess." He lunged to stretch his quads, rubbing his left knee when he straightened.

"Is your leg hurting?" Sophie asked, realizing that was the same leg that Umber injured when she attacked Fitz with shadowflux.

"It's fine," Fitz promised.

"You're *sure*?" Biana pressed. "I saw you limping a little while ago."

"I wasn't *limping*. I was just . . . taking slower steps." He glanced at Sophie, who must've looked as unconvinced as Biana, because he raked his fingers through his hair. "I'm out of shape, okay? Thanks for making me feel bad!"

Sophie let him off the hook. "Clearly we're *all* out of shape."

"Hey—speak for yourself!" Biana sprinted up the next few steps, blinking in and out of sight with each movement. "I run laps around Everglen every morning—and I'm always faster than Woltzer!"

"It's my *job* to stay behind you," Woltzer muttered from a few steps back. "I can't protect you if I race ahead."

"Then how come Sandor and Grizel are ahead of us right now?" Biana countered.

"Because they know I'm covering the rear!" Woltzer shouted. "Don't you know *anything* about battle strategy?"

"Of course I do." Biana flashed her loveliest grin. "It's just so much fun to mess with you."

Fitz snorted. "It's *amazing* your bodyguard hasn't strangled you."

"Nah, Woltzer loves me!" She blew him a kiss over her shoulder.

Honestly, Woltzer should've won the prize for Most Patient Bodyguard.

"So, are you losers rested enough to keep going?" Biana asked, tossing her dark, wavy hair. "Or do you need to waste more valuable time?"

Fitz sighed. "Who invited her?"

"That would be *you*," Biana informed him. "You thought having a Vanisher would come in handy."

"No, I just knew you'd sneak along anyway, since you're nosy like that—and dying to see Tam." He stage-whispered to Sophie, "My sister's a fan of silver bangs."

Sophie raised her eyebrows, glancing at Biana.

Biana's cheeks flushed—but Sophie couldn't tell if that was confirmation or irritation.

Or both.

"Really, Fitz?" Biana snapped. "*You* want to talk about crushes? Because you . . ."

Her voice trailed off, and she turned even redder when she glanced back at Sophie.

They hadn't really talked about the breakup—mostly because Sophie hadn't talked much about the whole dating thing with Biana in the first place.

Yet another reason having a crush on her friend's brother made things *super* awkward.

Fitz cleared his throat but didn't seem to know how to break the silence.

Neither did Sophie.

But she forced her tired legs to start trudging up the stairs again—and the momentum helped her find a change of subject. "I think we should run through our plan."

"There's a plan?" Fitz asked. "I thought we were just going to ask Glimmer what she knows about the caches."

"Right, but we're going to need to make her trust us before she'll tell us anything," Sophie reminded him.

"See, and I think Glimmer should be making *us* trust *her*," Biana argued. "She's the one hiding behind a cloak, probably hoping we won't ask how many times she helped plan the Neverseen's attacks."

She traced her fingers over one of the deeper scars running down her arm and shoulder.

"I know," Sophie told her, cringing over her next words even before she said them. "But I think Councillor Oralie was right about something she told me. *Willing* allies are way more useful than forced ones. If we make Glimmer trust us, she'll tell us stuff she'd hold back otherwise."

"*Or* we poke around her head and find out everything we need to know in one easy probe," Fitz countered.

Sophie sighed. "Yeah, but you and I both know probes are never that easy—especially with the Neverseen. I'm sure Gethen's trained her to block Telepaths, and she probably has all kinds of false information in her head."

"Yeah, I guess." They climbed in silence for several steps before Fitz mumbled, "You know, I thought being Cognates would make us way more powerful than we are."

"So did I," Sophie admitted, trying not to wonder if he was blaming her for that.

Her struggles with the whole total-trust-and-honesty thing always got in the way of their training.

"Hey," Biana said quietly, "you guys are being too hard on yourselves. You've done some *amazing* things. The problem's just bigger than that."

"What do you mean?" Fitz asked.

Biana traced more scars on her shoulder. "Well . . . we've kind of been set up to fail, you know? *Nothing* we've learned prepared us for what we're dealing with—not our Foxfire lessons, or our ability training, or even the stories we were told about what it would be like when we grew up. We're not supposed to have enemies trying to kill us, or massive, evil conspiracies destroying everything we know. Our world was supposed to be safe and happy and perfect, like it was for our parents. But it's not—and it turns out it wasn't like that for them, either. They just didn't let themselves see the problems. So now we're stuck figuring out how to fix this giant mess—while fighting against people who've been planning this stuff for longer than we've been alive. So of *course* they keep beating us. Of *course* we don't feel powerful enough. We aren't!"

"Are you saying it's hopeless?" Sophie had to ask.

"Are you kidding? I *know* we're going to win this." There wasn't a hint of doubt in Biana's voice. "I think we just need to remember that we're doing something no one has ever had to do before—and all the advice we've been given isn't necessarily *good*. So yeah, we don't always do everything perfectly, and it can feel like we're not strong enough. But that doesn't mean we aren't powerful and awesome and amazing. We're doing our best. We just need to keep fighting. And we should probably stop listening to what everyone's telling us and try finding our own way."

She was right, of course.

But when she put it like that, it sounded even more exhausting than all the stairs they were currently climbing.

"Sorry," Biana mumbled. "Didn't mean to derail the conversation."

"No, you're right," Fitz told her, rushing up the next few stairs and turning to face them. "Okay, I want to preface this by saying I'm *not* a fan of it, but . . . maybe we need to come at this totally differently than we normally would. So instead of focusing on getting her to cooperate with *us*, we act like we're *willing allies* with her."

"What does that mean?" Sophie asked. "We act like we want to join the Neverseen?"

Fitz shook his head. "Nope. It means acting like we can't wait to work with her—showing her why she should've been on our side this whole time. I know it'll be tough. But maybe if we act like she's already a part of our team, she'll cooperate."

"Okaaaaaaaay," Biana said slowly. "You really think we can pretend to be her friend, though? She's going to be sitting there in one of those creepy black cloaks, probably giving us lots of attitude."

"Well . . . we don't have to be *friends*," Sophie realized. "I doubt she'd believe that. But we could treat her like an *equal*. She kind of is. She could've just as easily been working with the Black Swan if we'd reached out to her before the Neverseen recruited her."

"You really think that's true?" Biana asked.

"I don't know," Sophie admitted. "But it's at least possible. Both groups exist because of a lot of the same problems. They just have very different solutions."

"Like murdering," Biana mumbled.

"I know," Fitz told her. "That's why I hate this plan. But . . . it's definitely a different approach than we normally use. And I'm pretty sure Glimmer will be expecting us to march in there and treat her like the enemy, so it might throw off her guard if we don't."

Biana sighed. "Ugh, I guess I can't be mad, since I'm the one who started us down this path. Fine . . . Let's go be besties with Little Miss Neverseen!"

"Not besties," Sophie corrected. "Equals."

Not that she really wanted to be *equals* with someone who'd put bonds on Tam's wrists and blasted Keefe with light to trigger the changes he was now struggling with.

But Sophie kept those thoughts to herself.

Her feet were ready to scream at her for the abuse they'd endured when Tiergan's house finally came into view—sturdy stone towers peeking over fortresslike walls.

Sandor and Grizel were waiting outside the only entrance—a wide, rectangular door carved with elaborate filigree woven around the word "Solreef."

"I want to make one thing clear before we continue," Sandor said, holding out his arms as a barricade. "No matter what this Glimmer person tells you, you are taking that information and going home. I mean it!" he added when Sophie opened her mouth to respond. "She could tell you that every member of the Neverseen was drugged, tied up, and ready for capture as long as someone heads there in the next five minutes, and you will say, 'Good to know, but we're going to listen to my bodyguard because he will lock me in my room for the rest of eternity.' Are we clear?"

"I already promised that," Sophie reminded him. She'd been through the endless *Is-it-safe-to-meet-with-Glimmer?* conversation that morning. "We won't do anything without discussing it with you."

"Not discussing," Sandor corrected. "*Agreeing.* We all need to *agree* on the next move."

"Fine. Can we go in now?" She reached around him to pull the rope for the chimes, and a tinkling melody filled the air.

Sophie was stunned to realize she recognized it.

"Was that . . . the Beatles?" she asked when Tiergan pulled open the door.

His lips curled into a smile as he stepped aside to let them in. "No one's ever recognized it before. But I suppose I should've known you would. Ready for your meeting? Your guest is waiting."

He led them down a brightly lit hallway, past rooms that looked surprisingly warm and cozy. All the couches and chairs were covered in soft, squishy pillows, and the tables and shelves were filled with worn books and framed photos and carefully selected knickknacks.

Sophie wondered how Tiergan felt about having a former member of the Neverseen staying in a place he'd worked so hard to make feel like a *home*—especially since they had no idea if Glimmer was involved with the Neverseen's abduction of Wylie. But it wasn't the right time to be thinking about things like that.

They stopped at a carved wooden door, and Tiergan knocked in six very specific places before the door swung open, revealing Bo with his sword drawn like he'd expected some sort of trickery.

He had no smile for his former charge, but Sophie wasn't expecting one.

Bo wasn't a fan of making friends.

"The space is small, so it's best if you wait out here," he told Sandor, Grizel, and Woltzer. "Don't worry, if she makes any threats, I will end her."

"There won't be any threats," Tam grumbled from somewhere behind Bo.

He was still rolling his silver-blue eyes when Sophie made her way into the narrow sitting room.

His smile also looked guarded—but this was the first time Sophie had seen him since Loamnore.

It probably felt even weirder for him than it did for her.

"Where's Linh?" she asked, trying to ease some of the tension—but Tam's shoulders went rigid again.

"She's still at Choralmere," he mumbled. "She thought it was too crowded around here."

"No, she just doesn't like me," a new voice said—one that was both familiar and not familiar enough.

It came from the corner of the room that Sophie had been trying her best to ignore—trying to prepare herself for the sight of a black cloak and the Neverseen's creepy eye symbol. But she couldn't avoid it anymore.

Glimmer rested on a chaise near the window, her face completely obscured by her hood, and her head was turned as if she was staring outside and not paying them the slightest bit of attention.

"To save us all time," she said without turning toward them, "I don't know where Gisela is—or anyone else, for that matter. I also don't know what they're planning. Or what's happening to your friend."

"Good," Sophie said, turning back to Tam. It made it easier to sound cheerful when she added, "That's not what we're here to talk about."

"Yeah, well, I'm not telling you who I am either," Glimmer informed her.

"Also not why we're here," Sophie promised.

"We *are* curious about why you joined the Neverseen, though," Biana jumped in—which seemed to catch Glimmer's attention.

"Why?" she demanded, turning toward Biana. "So you can tell me how misguided I am?"

Tam sighed. "Glimmer—"

"It's fine," Fitz assured him. "We're not here to judge you, Glimmer. We're here to see if we can work together."

Glimmer snorted and turned back to the window. "No, you're here because you want something."

"You're right," Sophie agreed, taking a breath to steady her temper.

Her brain kept replaying the moment when Glimmer unleashed that light beam toward Keefe's head—but she couldn't let herself fixate on that.

"We need help," she said quietly. "Lots of it. And since we probably wouldn't have gotten out of Loamnore without you, we thought you might be willing to work with us."

"I won't be working with you, though, will I?" Glimmer snapped. "I'll still be stuck right here, waiting for the next group of people to show up to ask me a bunch of endless questions even though I don't know anything!"

"Somehow I doubt that," Biana told her—but her tone was friendly. Teasing, even. "I mean, I get it. I'm always grumbling about how the Black Swan never tells us anything. But if I really think about it, there *is* stuff I know. Things I've seen. Comments I've overheard. All kinds of tiny little pieces that add up, you know?"

Sophie could practically hear the eye roll in Glimmer's voice when she said, "Yeah, well, the Neverseen are too smart for that."

"Then why did you leave them?" Fitz wondered. "You joined for a reason, right? And you had to know that leaving would mean you'd end up in a room like this—which, by the way, doesn't have to stay that way. We want you on our side, Glimmer. You just have to trust us."

"Oh good, we're finally to the part where you tell me I can prove myself by sharing this wealth of information you all seem to think I'm hiding—except I'm not. And no one believes me, and instead everyone acts like I'm just being uncooperative. So here I sit, locked in a room with an ogre who keeps reminding me that he can end me anytime."

"I can," Bo agreed unhelpfully.

Sophie sighed and glanced at Tam, whose shrug seemed to say, *She's not wrong.*

"Fine, you know what?" Sophie said. "There *is* one piece of information we're hoping you might have—but if not, it won't change us wanting to work together. So let's just put it out there so we can move on, okay?"

She paused for Glimmer to agree but was met with only silence.

"Okay, I'll take that as a yes," Sophie pressed on. "We need to find Councillor Kenric's cache. Keefe stole it from me to prove his loyalty when he joined the Neverseen, and he thought he stole it back when he left, but it turns out that was a fake. So now we need to track down the real one—and we have no idea where to look, so if you have *any* information that might steer us in the right direction, that'd be awesome."

"Doesn't have to be anything huge," Biana added. "We realize it's probably asking too much for there to be some sort of secret Neverseen storehouse where they hide all their important things."

Biana was probably trying to lighten the mood with a joke.

But Glimmer flinched.

Even Tam noticed.

"What?" he asked her. "And don't say 'nothing.'"

The silence stretched and stretched and stretched.

Tam moved to sit beside her. "These are my friends, Glimmer. You really can trust them. And if you know something that might help, it'll be better for everyone."

"No, it'll be better for *you*," Glimmer argued. "All it'll do for me is prove that I need to stay in this room and have more people annoy me with questions. Maybe they'll even order a memory break—"

"They won't," Sophie assured her. "And even if they did, they'd order me or Fitz to do it, and we won't." She took a cautious step closer, like she would if she were approaching a frightened animal. "We're not lying about wanting to work with you. We need your help."

A whole lot more silence followed.

"Come on, Glimmer," Tam pleaded. "If you don't trust them— trust *me*."

Glimmer sighed. "I . . . heard Gisela mention something to Vespera about a storehouse one time. She didn't say much else. But it sounded like it was part of the Lodestar network."

Sophie closed her eyes, wishing she hadn't let herself get her hopes up.

It felt like a total gut-punch having to admit, "All the Lodestar hideouts were destroyed."

"Were they?" Glimmer asked. "Or is that what the Neverseen wanted you to believe? I mean, do you *really* think they'd destroy everything they'd built just because you guys cracked their little symbol? Especially when they're so good at hiding things with illusions?"

A sharp intake of breath echoed around the room as the gravity of that revelation settled in.

"You know this for sure?" Tam clarified.

"No," Glimmer admitted. "But . . . it makes sense, right?"

It definitely did.

"I mean . . . I know they *did* destroy some stuff," Glimmer hedged. "There was this whole annoying power struggle going on, and Fintan was changing up some of the plans and decided to get rid of the stuff he was abandoning. But some of it was left. And it sounded like the storehouse was part of that."

A tiny spark of hope flared inside Sophie as she whispered, "Where do we find it?"

Glimmer turned to her, and Sophie could hear her sharp smile when she said, "You're the one who said you wanted to work together. So here's your chance. I'll tell you which hideout to go to—but only if you take me with you."

- TEN -
KEEFE

OKAY, LET'S TRY THIS AGAIN!" KESLER said, clapping his hands to get everyone's attention. "And I gotta say, I have a good feeling this time. I think we're finally onto something! But we'll know soon enough. Everybody—earplugs in!"

Keefe cringed as Kesler, Elwin, Ro, and Dex shoved the glittering blobs into their ears.

He couldn't believe he'd let them talk him into sitting through more tests after what happened that morning.

It had taken *several* panic-filled minutes for him to find the right command to snap the triplets out of whatever weird trance he'd put them in—and even though they'd laughed about how cool it was to watch everyone freaking out while they were stuck like statues, Keefe was pretty sure he was going to have nightmares about frozen Dizznees for the next few centuries.

Especially since it seemed like whatever he'd done to the triplets had been different from when he'd numbed everyone—more like he'd ripped their emotions away, instead of dulling them. Which made sense, since he'd given a different command. But he didn't like having *multiple* ways to turn people into empty shells.

And he *definitely* didn't want to discover any other methods.

That was why he'd crawled into bed the second the Dizznees left, hoping they'd give up on the whole project.

But hours later they were back—and Keefe had felt so much hope and conviction in the air that he didn't have the heart to tell them to go away.

Plus . . . he wasn't quite ready to give up on the chance of finding some kind of solution.

So he'd climbed onto Elwin's armchair, seriously questioning his life choices—particularly after he saw that Kesler had brought *five* new elixirs to test.

Dex also had *two* new gadgets.

And the triplets must've eaten a *lot* of sugar.

So basically, there was no way this was going to end well.

"Ready, kids?" Kesler asked, and when the triplets responded with an ear-rattling "YES!" he told them, "Okay—go ahead and grab on!"

"Gah! Why are your hands always so freezing?" Keefe asked as Lex grabbed his left wrist—or he thought it was Lex. It was *really* hard to tell the triplets apart.

"ARE THEY?" Lex grabbed his brother's hand.

"NAH, HE'S JUST WHINING 'CAUSE HE'S SCARED!" Rex pulled his hand free and grabbed Keefe's elbow, flooding Keefe with that strange empty feeling again.

And Bex's hand still seemed weirdly squishy.

But Keefe didn't mention any of that, since it was probably

another way this new ability was getting stronger and he wasn't in the mood to think about what that meant.

He wasn't in the mood to think at all, now that he was getting hit with lightning bolts of the triplets' exuberance, mixed with tingly giddiness and rippling confidence and a heated sort of curiosity. It all kept building and building and building, like water rising up around him, drowning out all the air.

"It seemed like the orange elixir helped a *little* last time," Kesler shouted over the roaring in Keefe's ears, "so these first three are all variations of that same formula. The other two go in a totally different direction, in case we're still on the wrong path—but I don't think we are."

Spoiler alert—they *definitely* were.

The first elixir made everything spin and spin and spin so fast that Keefe might've vomited if the command he was choking back hadn't closed off his throat.

The second made his head pound so hard, he was ready to beg for relief—but he bit his tongue instead, letting the iron taste of blood distract him from the word crackling inside his brain.

The third made him itchy.

So so so so so so itchy that Elwin had to pin his arms to stop him from scratching off his skin.

Keefe's eyes watered and his legs thrashed and he knew there was only one way to end the agony—but he refused to say it.

Refused to even let himself think it.

"It's all right," Kesler told him, placing a hand on Keefe's shoulder. "You're doing great. We're going to get you through this."

But that wasn't true.

It couldn't be.

Not with Kesler's hand triggering that same hollow, empty feeling as Rex's grip.

Keefe knew what that was now.

It had to be his body's way of telling him to give up.

Stop fighting.

Surrender to his new horrible reality.

"Hey—don't you give up," Kesler told him, like he knew what Keefe was thinking. He pressed a cool vial against Keefe's lips. "We still have two more tries."

Keefe shook his head so hard, he spilled at least half of the medicine.

"Come on, Keefe," Elwin told him. "I know this is hard, but we're learning a lot."

A laugh slipped through Keefe's lips, and it felt as bitter as the elixir he swallowed, which burned like magma, making his eyes water as it seared his throat.

But all that boiling pain at least scorched the word that had been forming, making it crumble to ash and dust.

"Well . . . that's something," Kesler said as Keefe slumped against his chair. "Though it might not be an ideal solution. Last one—for now. And this one should be gentler."

Keefe didn't deserve *gentle*.

But he definitely craved it.

So he drank every drop, sighing as his body turned very, very heavy.

His eyelids drooped, his limbs hung limp, and his breathing slowed and slowed and slowed some more.

It felt like falling—and the darkness raced up to catch him.

A soothing pool of black that swallowed him whole, until there was nothing left.

Now he was safe.

Everyone was safe.

And the world was blissfully quiet.

So was his tired brain, which slowly shut down.

The darkness turned thicker and thicker while Keefe sank as far as he could go.

Hoping he'd never find a way back.

"HE'S FINALLY AWAKE!" someone shouted, making Keefe groan as the much-too-loud voice sliced through his brain.

He cracked his eyes open, sucking air through his teeth when the brightness blasted out everything.

It took several painful blinks before the world faded into focus again, and Keefe realized he was back in his room—and if the crick in his neck was any indication, he'd been there for a while.

"You've been out for about five hours," Elwin said, and Keefe's eyes darted toward the doorway to find the physician standing with a plate of food and a bottle of Youth. "Figured it'd be good to get some nutrients in your system before I give you any medicine for the headache and nausea."

Keefe groaned. "No more medicine."

"Hey, he speaks!" Ro said.

She didn't sound nearly as enthusiastic as she had been.

"Yeah, I know," Elwin told Keefe. "We've done a number on your system. But I'm only using normal remedies now. They'll help, I promise."

Keefe was too tired to argue.

The food and Youth and elixirs actually did make him feel more normal. He even managed to sit up and comb his fingers through his sweaty hair.

"In case you're wondering," Elwin said as he gathered the empty plates and vials, "Kesler and I have decided to take a break from trying to treat your ability medicinally. I suppose we should've known better. Abilities are a part of who we are. They don't get affected by elixirs. We just thought yours might be different, since it's so . . . unique."

The better word would've been "unnatural."

But it wasn't safe for Keefe to say that.

It was *never* going to be safe for him to speak.

Or to be around people.

Or to have any sort of physical contact.

Or a life.

"Hey," Elwin said, plopping down onto the bed. "That doesn't mean we're giving up. In fact, Dex left something he wants you to test."

Keefe shook his head harder, but Elwin grabbed his hand, pressing something flat and cool and square into his palm. "Relax—it's not one of his inventions. Dex wanted to make more tweaks to those before we try them. But he also had a theory that sounded pretty valid."

Elwin pulled back his arm, and Keefe stared at the small silver Imparter.

"Dex thinks your commands will only work on people in the same room with you, since tone comes from emotion," Elwin explained. "He said you're probably transmitting some sort of emotional energy when you say the word, and that's what causes the reaction—or helps, at least. And that's something that can't happen in an Imparter conversation."

"He also said he knows you're going to shake your head when we tell you to test it, because you're scared and tired and convinced nothing is ever going to help," Ro added. "So he said to tell you to *trust the Technopath* and hail him once you wake up so he can say, 'I told you so.' And I gotta say, I'm liking techy boy more and more. I think you should listen to him."

"So do I," Elwin agreed. "If you do end up commanding him, I'll be right here with earplugs in to help you figure out a counter command—but I don't think you're going to need me. Every time you've used your ability, I've felt a strange ripple pass through the room. So I think Dex is onto something with this theory. You also won't be able to feel what Dex is feeling—which is what seems to overwhelm you. But . . . there's only one way to know for sure."

Keefe tightened his grip on the Imparter, knowing the smarter, safer move would be to toss it against the wall as hard as he could, let it shatter into so many pieces, he'd never be able to use it.

But a tiny spark of hope had been kindled again.

"Go on, Hunkyhair," Ro told him. "I have a good feeling about this."

Keefe definitely didn't.

But he still took a slow, calming breath, promising himself that if this failed, it would be his *last* test.

He was giving one final try—one final push against what his mom had done to him.

If it didn't work . . . it was ability restrictor time.

He closed his eyes, trying to keep himself as relaxed as possible before he held the Imparter up to his lips. His mouth was parched and his voice sounded raw and crackly as he whispered, "Show me Dex."

NOPE—WE'RE *NOT* HAVING THIS argument again!" Sophie said, waiting for the room to quiet down before she added, "You guys *have* to stop freaking out any time something sounds a tiny bit dangerous—"

"This is more than a 'tiny bit dangerous,'" Grady interrupted, pacing to the wall of windows and staring out at Havenfield's pastures.

Sophie had kept her promise to Sandor and went straight home after Glimmer made her offer.

But that didn't mean she was planning on staying there for very long.

"You're talking about going to a Neverseen hideout *with* a member of the Neverseen," Edaline gently reminded her.

"No, Glimmer's a *former* member of the Neverseen," Sophie corrected.

"So she *claims*," Sandor snorted. "This whole thing could be a trap."

"Glimmer wouldn't do that!" Tam argued.

"Sadly, I don't think that you—or anyone else here—can truly speak for what Glimmer would or wouldn't do," Tiergan said quietly.

Tam and Tiergan had insisted on being part of the conversation—as had Fitz and Biana. And Sophie was sure it was only a matter of time before Mr. Forkle showed up.

And the rest of the Black Swan.

And more of her friends.

And Sophie was done wasting that kind of time.

Especially since none of their planning and arguing and worrying and explaining ever seemed to save them from almost dying. That's why she'd had the we-need-to-stop-overthinking-things fight with them before.

And still, here she stood, staring down a bunch of stubborn, worried faces.

She knew they were only trying to keep her safe—but she was really getting sick of having everyone question her and doubt her all the time and try to hold her back.

She was the moonlark.

This was what she was supposedly *made* for.

Wasn't it time for people to start trusting her?

And didn't the fact that she *wasn't* dead—despite how many times the Neverseen had tried to kill her—prove that she was strong enough and smart enough and capable enough to know when a risk was worth taking and roll with whatever happened next?

Or . . . was she just getting more desperate and reckless?

"Look," Sophie said, climbing up a few of the stairs on the curved central staircase to make it easier for everyone to see her. "We *finally* have an actual lead—and it's for something we totally overlooked, so we're lucky we're getting a second chance. Whatever's in that storehouse has been hidden right under our noses this entire time—probably while the Neverseen laughed at us for falling for their trick."

"That's no reason to go rushing over with only five minutes of planning," Grady argued.

"Actually, it is. The Neverseen know we have Glimmer. So I'm sure they're scrambling to protect anything she might know. They're probably moving stuff and hiding stuff right now—as we speak. And we have this *tiny* window of a chance left—assuming we're not already too late. So we need to move quickly. And stealth needs to be our priority. The bigger our group is, the harder it's going to be to sneak around. So I'm fine bringing Sandor and Flori—and Bo can come too, since he's in charge of Glimmer. But other than that, it should just be me, Tam, and Glimmer."

Biana sighed. "You're seriously going to make me remind you that I'm a Vanisher?"

"That doesn't mean you can't set off their sensors," Sophie countered. "We're going to a Lodestar hideout—those had lots of security."

"Yeah—didn't you need to have some sort of little black disk etched with the right piece of the Lodestar symbol on it to not set off all their sensors?" Fitz asked. "And now that I think about it, how are you going to get there? I doubt Glimmer's going to know exactly which piece of the symbol matches the storehouse she mentioned—and even if she did, you'd need one of those gadgets that project the symbol, like we found in the Silver Tower."

Those were unfortunately very valid questions.

Sophie didn't have a good answer, except to say, "I guess if that's all true, then we won't be going to the Neverseen's storehouse today. But I doubt Glimmer would've made the offer if she didn't know how to get there."

"She wouldn't," Tam agreed. "She's way too smart for that."

"I don't know," Biana muttered. "She did support the Neverseen for a pretty long time, so she's not necessarily the shiniest jewel in the tiara, if you know what I mean. She may not even realize how complicated it is to reach any of the Lodestar hideouts. It didn't sound like she'd actually been to one."

"And if that's true," Sophie jumped in, "then that'll mean we don't end up going anywhere with Glimmer."

They'd just go to each Lodestar hideout one by one instead—which they'd need to do eventually anyway, since it sounded like there were others that weren't destroyed.

Though . . .

The Neverseen would probably figure out what they were doing pretty quickly and destroy the rest of the hideouts—or set up an ambush.

So they'd be *way* better off if Glimmer was able to make good on her promise.

"The truth is," Sophie said, standing taller and squaring her shoulders, "this is our best option right now. If it works, it works. If it doesn't, it doesn't. But I'm ready to stop talking about it and go find out."

"You still won't have the little black disks you need," Fitz reminded her—though he looked like he felt a little bad about it. "So the Neverseen are going to know there are intruders."

"That's why we'll have bodyguards," Sophie argued. "And weapons. Plus, Tam can hide us with shadows, like he did when we snuck into Ravagog. And if it gets too intense, I can teleport us to safety."

"You say all of that like it counts as an actual plan," Grady told her. "It doesn't."

"Maybe. But we'll figure out the rest as we go along. Trust our brains and our powers—and our bodyguards—and . . . hope for the best."

She wished she could've come up with a stronger way to wrap up her response, but . . . hope was really all they ever had. And Sophie refused to treat it like it wasn't enough.

If she let her mind go down that path, she'd want to give up.

She *had* to hope that they'd track down Kenric's cache, and figure out what stellarlune and Elysian were, and find a way to help Keefe, and finally stop the Neverseen.

And all of that was only going to happen if she kept taking risks.

"We're going now," Sophie said, making her way over to Tam.

She was done asking permission.

"Hang on there," Grady told her. "Relax, I'm not going to stop you. But I *am* going with you to Solreef, and you're going to tell me exactly where Glimmer's taking you before you guys leave. Then you'll have fifteen minutes to look for the cache and get back—and if you're gone a second longer, I'm coming after you."

"Me too," Fitz added.

"And me!" Biana agreed.

"Fifteen minutes isn't much time," Tam argued.

"Then I suggest you work fast," Tiergan told him, "because at fifteen minutes and one second, I'm going after you too."

Sophie and Tam exchanged a look, neither needing to check the other's thoughts to know it was the best offer they were going to get.

"Deal," Sophie said, glancing at Sandor, who was obviously *not* thrilled with the arrangement, even though he was invited to go. "Just let me run upstairs and change. I'm going to need a tunic with more pockets."

If things went well, she'd be filling one of them with Kenric's cache.

And if things went badly, hopefully they could deal with it.

Assuming Glimmer even knew how to get them there . . .

The doubt whispered around Sophie's head as she dressed for the mission and grabbed as many weapons as she could carry—and it was still in the back of her mind when their group made it back to Solreef.

Tam must've been just as concerned, because the first thing he said after Bo let them in to see Glimmer was "Don't make a promise you can't keep."

Glimmer sat up taller. "Does that mean you're taking me up on my bargain?"

"Only if you actually know what you're talking about," Sophie told her. "We know what the Lodestar security is like—the question is, do you?"

"Ugh, I almost want to take my hood down so you can see me roll my eyes." Instead she stood and bent over, grabbing the bottom corner of her cloak. "I never planned to leave the order. But I knew if I did, I'd have to abandon everything, and that they'd likely move my belongings to their storehouse. So I made sure I had one of these."

She ripped open the seam at her hem, and Sophie expected her to hold up one of those black disks Fitz had been talking about.

Instead she held up a small, silver hairpin.

And set among the metal filigree at the end was a smooth starstone.

TWELVE

KEEFE

S O . . . THE POINT OF THIS IS FOR YOU TO talk, remember?" Dex said, glancing over his shoulder before he turned back to Keefe. "Hey, don't look at me like that! *You* hailed *me*! I could be doing lots of other things right now instead of sitting here, watching you pout. Rex has been doing enough of that!"

"He's not pouting—he's brooding," Ro corrected. "*Pouting* would have his shoulders hunched and his lip jutting out more. And *sulking* would have his eyes all downcast. *Wow.* I kind of hate myself for knowing that. Clearly I've been spending too much time with a silent, moody boy."

Dex cracked up.

But his smile faded when Keefe pressed his lips tighter.

"You need to say something," he told Keefe. "That's the only way we're going to know if this works. And it *will*. Trust me."

Elwin nudged Keefe with his elbow. "Remember, I can't hear a thing with these earplugs in. So I can help if it starts to get funky."

Keefe snorted.

"Funky" made this ability sound like it was just a silly little quirk he was learning to live with.

"I know you're scared," Dex told him. "And I know our other tests haven't gone very well. But I swear, this one will be different."

Keefe sighed.

It better be different.

Otherwise hard changes were coming—he had to hold himself to that.

"Maybe you need some topic ideas!" Ro suggested. "Let's see. I mean, you're both elves, so you could probably talk about sparkles for days—but who wants to listen to that? Oh, you're both pretty good at pranking! Not as good as *me*, of course. But who is? Ooo! Ooo! We could plan something for when school starts—make that Great Gulon thing seem like child's play! Who's game?"

Keefe shook his head.

Dex glanced over his shoulder again, looking distracted.

"Okay, fine, you're clearly intimidated by my pranking genius. Can't blame you for that. Let's see . . . what else is there?" Ro tapped her chin with one of her red claws. "It needs to be something that'll get Hunkyhair fired up, so he'll be able to see if using this gadget thing is safe. Which means our best bet is probably Blondie."

"You mean Sophie?" Dex asked, whipping back around to face them.

"Yep! I'm sure you both have *lots* to say about her."

Dex cleared his throat. "Not really. I mean . . . she's my best friend, but—"

"Aw, come on, Dexy," Ro interrupted. "You're among friends.

And Hunkyhair told me about your smoochfest with the Mysterious Miss F! High five, by the way!"

Dex turned so red, it looked like flames were about to curl out of his ears.

"Wait, was that a secret?" Ro asked. "I figured you must've been shouting that from the rooftops! Especially since Captain Perfectpants hasn't gotten any lip action—and he probably won't, now that Fitzphie's unraveling."

"It is?" Dex asked.

Ro's eyebrows shot up. "You haven't noticed? Wow. Obliviousness is rampant here in Sparkle Town!"

"I'm not *oblivious*," Dex argued. "It's just . . . none of my business."

"Really? Huh. I thought she was your best friend. Ohhh, does the smooching thing make it awkward for you guys?"

Dex sank lower in his chair. "Why are we talking about this?"

"Because I'm trying to get a rise out of my boy." Ro put a hand on Keefe's shoulder, jostling him. "*Nothing* you want to say, Hunkyhair? I bet Dexy could relate, if you wanted to unload on him. In fact, you guys should *totally* do one of those dude-commiseration convos. I bet it would help with all the angst."

Keefe tried to decide if he wanted to shove his Imparter down her throat or slither under his bed and never come back out.

Slithering seemed like the best option when Dex asked, "What angst?"

But he thankfully got distracted by whatever seemed to be going on behind him.

"Is this a bad time?" Keefe asked.

Dex whipped back around. "Hey—you talked! And see? Nothing happened!"

"Not *yet*," Keefe mumbled.

Ro poked him in the side with her claw. "You need to speak up. Enunciate, like you do when you're getting all command-y. I'm also happy to help overwhelm you so we can see if that changes anything."

She poked his side again.

And again.

And again.

"Okay, I think I see a flaw in this plan," Elwin cut in as a word started to bubble up Keefe's throat. "The test is supposed to see if *Keefe* is affected by *Dex*—or if *Dex* is affected by *him*. So they should probably be talking alone."

"Aw, but that sounds like way less fun!" Ro whined.

Elwin dragged her toward the door. "We'll be right out here in the hall," he told Keefe. "Just remember—I can't hear you, so if something happens, you'll need to come get me."

"Or me!" Ro added. "But I'll totally be eavesdropping because I'm not scared of your elf-y abilities!"

Dex cleared his throat when the door slammed shut. "Your bodyguard is . . . interesting."

"That's one way of putting it," Keefe muttered—then froze.

"I'm fine," Dex told him. "Seriously, talk as much as you want. It's not going to affect me."

Keefe swallowed, trying to get some moisture back into his mouth again. But his voice still crackled when he said, "I swear, I'm starting to forget how to do this."

"I bet." Dex reached into his pocket, pulling out some piece of circuitry to fidget with. "You've had a rough few days. Well . . . I guess it's been a rough few *years*, huh?"

"Pretty much my entire life," Keefe corrected. He hated how whiny that sounded, so he added, "But . . . it is what it is."

"You don't have to do that," Dex told him. "It's okay to talk about it. I'm happy to—"

He whipped his head around again.

"Looks like there's something else you should be dealing with right now," Keefe noted.

"Nah, I'm enjoying a break from the madness. You can't hear all the squealing and crashes because I added noise canceling to my Imparter. But it's full-fledged mayhem downstairs. Bex and Lex manifested a couple of hours ago."

"Wow, both of them at the same time?"

"Yep. It was super unexpected—and awesome, of course. Especially since so many people . . ."

He didn't finish the sentence. But Keefe was well aware of how judgy everyone was about the Dizznee triplets, since their parents were a bad match.

"Rex didn't manifest?" he asked.

"Not yet—which is normal," Dex added quickly. Maybe even a little defensively. "Just because they're triplets doesn't mean they do everything the same, you know? Bex started walking days before the others. And Rex is still the only one who can do cartwheels."

"Makes sense," Keefe agreed.

"But . . . that's why Rex has been pouting," Dex admitted. "And

I can't really blame him. Especially since Lex keeps pelting him with snowballs."

"So Lex is a Froster?" Keefe asked.

"Yep. Just like my mom. The whole downstairs looks like a blizzard tore through the house. He's actually showing pretty solid control—which may not be a good thing, since I'm pretty sure it means I'm going to wake up trapped in a giant ice cube."

Keefe laughed. "Sounds about right."

Dex sighed. "Yep. My life is about to get even more chaotic. I don't even want to *think* about the pranks Bex is going to pull once she figures out how to walk through walls without getting stuck."

"She's a Phaser?"

"Yeah, and she's definitely still getting the hang of it. My dad's down there trying to help her pull her feet out of the floor. So weird, right?"

It was.

But Keefe didn't understand why he felt so twitchy all of a sudden.

If felt like . . .

Like he was missing something.

He sat up straighter. "Wait—*that's* why their hands felt so weird!"

"What do you mean?"

"Remember how I said Lex's hand felt freezing? Bex's hand also felt sorta squishy. I didn't mention it because there was so much else going on. But they must've already been manifesting."

Dex frowned.

"What?" Keefe asked, lowering his voice. "Have I been talking too much?"

He'd gotten so distracted that he'd forgotten to watch his tone.

"No . . . it's fine. I told you—using the Imparter protects me. I just . . . I was always taught that manifesting was like flipping a switch. One second you don't have any power. And the next second—boom."

"Well, but it might be different for some people," Keefe reminded him.

"Truuuuuuuue." Dex fidgeted with the piece of circuitry, twisting one of the wires so tight it looked ready to snap. "But . . . I held their hands when we leaped home, and I didn't notice anything squishy or freezing about them. And Rex didn't think Lex felt cold either, remember?"

It was Keefe's turn to frown. "What are you saying?"

"I don't know." Dex leaned closer and lowered his voice before he added, "It just . . . It kinda sounds like you *sensed* that they were going to manifest. And you even knew their exact abilities."

Keefe sucked in a breath. "But that's not a thing. No one can do that—not even the ability detecting Mentors!"

"Right—but new powers happen sometimes," Dex reminded him. "Maybe all the changes to your empathy allow for it or something. I don't know—it definitely sounds weird, but so is what happened to you, you know? And it sorta makes sense, doesn't it?"

No.

Nothing about this made sense.

"You don't think *I* triggered their abilities, do you?" Keefe asked quietly.

"I was just wondering that—but I don't think so, because Rex still hasn't manifested, remember? Did you feel anything when you held his hand?"

Keefe closed his eyes and replayed the memory—then replayed it again.

He wanted to be absolutely certain before he answered.

"Well . . . I actually did feel something," he admitted. "But I don't really know how to describe it. It was kinda hollow, somehow. A little . . . empty."

"Empty," Dex repeated. "I'm trying to think of what that could be. A Shade, maybe? Or a Vanisher? Have you been around Tam or Biana to compare?"

"No. But I don't know that it matters. I didn't feel anything with you or Elwin or Fitz—or even Sophie. Only the triplets. Well, and . . ."

"What?" Dex asked.

Keefe shook his head, desperately searching all of his recent memories, hoping to find some other sensation he'd missed.

"*What?*" Dex repeated. "Come on, Keefe—you have to tell me."

Technically, Keefe didn't *have* to do anything.

He could lie.

Switch off his Imparter.

Flee the Lost Cities forever.

All of that sounded way better than answering. Because if he was right, then this was so much huger than sensing someone manifesting.

It was even bigger than numbing people with his commands.

But maybe he was wrong. . . .

So he told Dex, "I felt the same emptiness when your dad put his hand on my shoulder . . . and I think that means I can only feel something when it's someone who *hasn't* manifested."

"Okay," Dex said, dragging out the word. "But . . . my dad's Talentless."

Keefe nodded.

Dex swallowed hard and nodded too.

He opened his mouth, and Keefe wanted to beg him not to say whatever he was thinking, because once he said it, it'd be this real thing they'd have to deal with.

But Dex still mumbled, "So . . . you're saying Rex is going to be Talentless?"

WHERE DID YOU GET THAT?"
Sophie asked, shaking with something
that was part shiver, part shudder as
she squinted at the familiar blue-white
aura around Glimmer's starstone.

Tam asked the smarter question: "How do you know where
it goes?"

Glimmer sighed. "You guys love to act like everything's so complicated. It was Gisela's—where else would I get it? And I know
where it goes because I watched her use it to retrieve something
from the storehouse. After she got back, I used a light trick to
make her think something had damaged the starstone, so she
threw it away. Then I went back later, dug it out of the trash, and
hid it in the hem of my cloak."

"That sounds like a lot of work for someone who claims she wasn't
planning on leaving the Neverseen," Sophie felt the need to point out.

"No, it was a lot of work for someone who likes to be *prepared for
anything*," Glimmer corrected.

Which made Sophie wonder what Glimmer had done to prepare for where she was about to take them.

Not that it mattered.

Whatever happened, Sophie would deal with it.

She *had* to.

"Time to go," she said, holding out her hand for the hairpin.

"Hang on," Grady called from the doorway. "You'll need to leave that with me, since it's the only way to get there. And remember: You get fifteen minutes—not a second longer."

Glimmer dropped the starstone into Sophie's palm. "What happens after fifteen minutes?"

"We come get you," Grady told her as Sophie brought the starstone over to him.

Glimmer snorted. "*That's* your plan?"

"Yep!" Sophie was already getting sick of Glimmer's attitude.

Grady squinted at the gem, watching the blue glow flare brighter. "You ready for this, kiddo?"

"Almost." She moved to Tam's side and whispered. "Are *you* ready?"

He hadn't had to face any of the Neverseen since he'd escaped— and hopefully that wouldn't change. But she wanted to make sure he was mentally prepared.

Tam tugged on his bangs, pulling the silver tips over his eyes. "Yeah, I'm good. Let's do this."

Sophie reached for his hand and laced their fingers together.

Tam offered Glimmer his other hand, and she took it, mumbling, "I hope you guys know what you're doing."

"We do," Sandor assured her, grabbing Sophie's arm.

Flori and Bo completed their circle.

"You'll need this, too," Tiergan said, clasping a silver chain around Sophie's neck. "The pendant will leap you back here, where we'll be waiting—unless we need to come after you."

"You won't," Sophie assured him.

"And even if you do, you won't be able to find us," Glimmer warned.

Tiergan smiled. "You'd be surprised at what we can do."

"I hope so," Glimmer told him. "Because so far, I'm not impressed."

And on *that* encouraging note, Sophie tightened her grip and told Grady, "Okay, we're ready."

Grady looked *far* from pleased—but he obediently held the starstone up to the light, creating a milky-blue path.

"Be careful," he ordered. "Your fifteen minutes start *now*."

"Where's the storehouse?" Sophie shouted, not sure if anyone could hear her above the roar of the waterfall that cascaded over the edge of a nearby cliff and crashed into a raging river *far* below.

The ground trembled beneath their feet, and mist hung thick in the air, turning everything cold and dreary and making it hard to see more than a few feet ahead—which was probably better. The ledge they'd reappeared on seemed like it was both narrow and *very* steep, since it was near the top of the falls.

"See the rainbow?" Glimmer called back, pointing to the colorful arch refracting across the mist. *"That's our path!"*

"How can a rainbow be a path?" Sophie had to ask.

"Like this!" Glimmer stepped off the ledge.

Everyone screamed—even Glimmer. But instead of plummeting into the torrents, she hovered like an eerie black-cloaked ghost. The wet fabric clung to her frame, making her look smaller than Sophie had been imagining—maybe even a little frail. But Glimmer's voice boomed with strength and authority when she told them, *"Trust the colors, not your eyes!"*

"I'll go first!" Flori offered. And Sophie tried to feel reassured by how easily the tiny gnome followed Glimmer's steps. But she had a horrible feeling that whatever path they were taking would be very slippery.

She let Bo go next.

Then Tam.

"I'll follow you!" Sandor told her when she gestured for him to go ahead. *"And don't worry, if you start to fall, I'll catch you!"*

Sophie doubted he'd be able to do anything except watch her drown—but she appreciated the sentiment as she focused on the rainbow, imagining it was a wide, sturdy bridge and *not* a simple illusion that happened when light shone through water droplets.

"I'm trusting the colors," she told herself, thinking about all of the other impossible things she'd been able to do since arriving in the Lost Cities. Then she took a small step and . . .

. . . found solid footing.

Or *sorta* solid.

The ground was squishy and uneven, and her legs shook from the effort of keeping her balance. But somehow she caught up to everyone without tripping.

"That must be why the Black Swan believed the hideout was destroyed!" Tam shouted, pointing at something far below.

Sophie decided to take his word for it.

Looking down seemed like a *very* bad idea.

"Now what?" she asked.

Glimmer had stopped a few steps away from where the rainbow was swallowed by the falls—and Sophie had a horrible feeling she knew what that meant.

Sure enough, Glimmer told her, *"Now we cross through!"*

"At least we don't have to jump off the edge!" Flori reminded everyone.

Which was a good point.

But it didn't make Sophie any more excited when Glimmer told them, *"Hold your breath, keep your arms up, and stay as close to me as you can!"*

"How do you know all of this?" Tam asked.

"I told you—I like to be prepared!" She fanned out her fingers—as if they could somehow shield her from the thunderous wall of water. And Sophie could hear Glimmer's squeal as she was swallowed by the surging white streams.

Flori held her arms up and followed, twirling as she passed through.

Bo used his sword to cover his head.

Tam glanced at Sophie. *"I really wish we'd brought Linh!"* he shouted before charging after the others.

Sophie definitely agreed—which made her realize that the reason Linh wasn't there was because she didn't trust Glimmer.

That *could* mean that Linh was much smarter than they were.

"You're next!" Sandor shouted, placing his hand on her shoulder. *"Don't worry—I have your back!"*

He always did.

And Sophie hoped he knew how grateful she was for that.

She also hoped it would be enough if they were racing into a trap.

"Here goes!" she said, raising her arms and trying to prepare herself for the overwhelming rush of the waterfall. But when she shoved herself into the stream, it was more like . . .

. . . stepping into the shower.

Her hair became plastered to her face, and her clothes suctioned onto her skin, and the water felt tepid and frothy—but *way* gentler than she'd been expecting.

Then it was gone—and so was most of the noise and all of the mist. The ground actually felt dry and crackly, as if she'd slipped through some sort of force field and entered a space completely shielded from the falls.

She rubbed the water out of her eyes as Glimmer told her, "Welcome to the Neverseen's storehouse. It's . . . not as big as I'd imagined."

It also wasn't fancy, like Sophie had been picturing. It was just a dim, dusty cave lined with shelves.

There wasn't even a door!

Just two small balefire sconces framing the archway they'd passed through when they'd entered—which seemed like a shocking oversight in the Neverseen's security.

But then Sophie remembered the black disks they were supposed to be carrying and couldn't help wondering if an alert had already gone out.

Were the Neverseen on their way?

"Okay, let's get started," Tam said as if he'd been worrying about the same thing. "How do you want to do this?"

The flickering blue flames cast just enough light to show that the shelves were crammed with trunks and scrolls and books and boxes, and there didn't seem to be any rhyme or reason to anything.

"I guess we should fan out," Sophie decided. "The cache is a round, clear crystal about this big"—she looped her fingers to demonstrate the size of a marble—"and there might be two of them together, since Fintan's cache should be here too. Grab both if you find them—and try not to touch much else. We don't know if any of this stuff is booby-trapped."

"The Neverseen wouldn't do that," Glimmer argued.

"How do you know?" Sophie countered.

Glimmer shrugged. "They'd rather capture you themselves. Or kill you."

Bo cleared his throat. "I'll guard the entrance—and I'll be watching both directions, in case anyone is thinking of escaping."

"Oh please," Glimmer told him. "Where would I go?"

"I guess we'll never know." Sandor drew his sword. "I'm doing a perimeter check. Everyone, stay where I can see you."

He disappeared into the darkest corner of the cave.

Sophie shared a look with Tam before they headed for the shelves. Flori and Glimmer followed, each of them choosing different places to search.

Sophie's section seemed to be filled with bin after bin of tiny glass vials, each a different color. None of them were labeled to tell her what they were—but that didn't matter. She wasn't there to find out what elixirs the Neverseen were making.

"Hey, do you think this is that soporidine stuff?" Tam called out.

Sophie spun to where he was pointing and noticed a stack of barrels lined up on their sides, tucked into the shadows. A quick count told her there were twenty, which matched how many dusty circles they'd seen on the floor of the first Nightfall facility.

"Probably," she realized—which made her wonder if any of the vials she was searching were filled with the antidote.

She shoved a few in her pockets just in case.

"You need to hurry!" Sandor warned—as if they didn't already know—and Sophie forced herself to skip past the next section, which was crammed with scrolls.

Part of her was dying to unroll them and see what she could learn about the Neverseen's plans. But she was there for one thing and one thing only.

"You're looking for Kenric's cache," she mumbled as she tore through a pile of fabric on the next shelf. It seemed like a bunch of scraps, until she noticed the white eye symbol and realized it was more of the Neverseen's cloaks.

Dozens of them.

Maybe hundreds.

Goose bumps prickled her skin as she imagined facing *that* many enemies.

They'd barely survived battling a few of the Neverseen at once.

How were they supposed to—

"Is that what you're looking for?" Glimmer asked, tossing something tiny and black at Sophie's head, which turned out to be a velvet satchel.

The size was right—and Sophie could feel two small items inside—but her fingers were shaking so badly, she couldn't unknot the strings.

"Here," Flori said, using her green teeth to rip the fabric before pouring two clear orbs into Sophie's palm.

"YES! THIS HAS TO BE THEM!"

Sophie honestly couldn't believe it.

Things never went this smoothly—which made her glance over her shoulder, waiting for cloaked figures to leap out at her.

But the cave stayed silent, except for the muffled rumble of the waterfall—and the pounding of her heart as she tucked the caches safely into her pocket.

"Okay, time to go," she said, taking one last longing look around the cave as she pulled out the crystal Tiergan had given her.

"That's it?" Glimmer asked, and Sophie noticed that she was holding a small blue bundle.

"What's that?" she demanded.

"My *stuff*. You know, the reason I made this deal in the first place? Don't look at me all suspicious like that! I told you this was why I went to so much trouble to be able to find this place! Plus, we all know your little bodyguards are going to search it as soon as we're out of here. But we're *seriously* leaving? Already?"

"Our time is almost up," Sophie reminded her.

Glimmer shook her head. "Wooooooooooooow. That's . . . I don't even know what to say to that. This whole time I've been thinking there had to be more to the plan than what you were telling me. But you're seriously ready to grab the caches and go? You realize you're standing in the Neverseen's *storehouse* right now, don't you? You think you're going to get another chance like this? The Neverseen are going to have guards crawling all over this place anytime now."

"Yeah, and *that's* why we need to leave," Sophie argued.

"No, that's why you should be grabbing everything while you can—though, honestly, what you *should've* done is come here with your own little army and seized this place. Showed the Neverseen it was *your* storehouse now, and let them cry while you go through all their stuff. But you didn't even *think* of that, did you?"

"No," Sophie admitted, feeling her stomach knot up.

The knots twisted tighter when Glimmer told her, "And *that's* why you guys always lose."

"Glimmer," Tam warned.

"No—I mean it," Glimmer told him. "You keep telling me I should join your side because you guys are right about everything and fair and keep your word and blah blah blah. And maybe you do—but you also *lose*. *Every* time. And now I know why! Do you think the Neverseen would leave a single thing behind if they found *your* storehouse? They'd grab it all—and keep some dwarves here to ambush whoever finally showed up to find out what was going on. *That's* why they win."

"That's also why they're creepy," Sophie muttered.

"Maybe," Glimmer agreed. "But what's the point of being 'better' if you keep getting beaten? You want to do some actual good in this world? You need to take them *down*. And sorry, but from what I've seen, you guys just don't have it in you."

Sophie opened her mouth, dying to tell Glimmer she was wrong.

But . . . Glimmer had a point.

"Fine," she said, racing back to the shelves. "Everyone, grab as much as you can."

She wished she'd brought a Conjurer who could snap their fingers and send everything into the void. But she hadn't thought of that, either.

The best she could do was stuff her pockets with all the vials she could carry, then load up her arms with scrolls.

Tam had a similar haul.

So did Glimmer.

But Sandor and Bo informed her that they needed their hands free to be able to draw their weapons.

And Flori was struggling to carry a thick black book—though Sophie's pulse raced when she recognized it.

"That's Lady Gisela's Archetype!" she shouted. "Be super careful with that!"

She couldn't believe they'd almost left that behind.

"And we should be good now—let's go," she said, holding Tiergan's crystal up to the light. "We need to get out of here."

Glimmer clicked her tongue. "You're really going to leave the rest of this behind?"

"We don't have a choice! We can't carry any more, and we're running out of time, and—"

"If I learned one thing from Gisela," Glimmer interrupted, "it's that there's *always* a choice. And you're about to make the wrong one—*again*. You already made a bunch of bad choices when you planned this mission, but it's not too late to fix that."

"How?" Sophie demanded.

"You tell me," Glimmer argued. "You're the moonlark, aren't you? The one who's supposed to lead everyone to victory. So *lead!*"

"*How?*" Sophie repeated. *"What do you want from me?"*

"I want you to prove that you guys have *any* chance of winning this thing! And I think you know what you need to do—you just don't want to do it. And that's fine. I don't even blame you for that. I probably wouldn't want to either. But don't ask me to sign up for your little cause, because I'm done losing. I've lost more than enough already!"

Sophie stared into the cowl of Glimmer's cloak, wishing she could see the girl behind it. It might've made it easier to know if Glimmer was *right* or just egging her on.

But did she really need to see Glimmer's face to know that everything she'd just said was true?

Hadn't she already felt just as lost—just as hopeless—just as convinced that they were losing this fight?

And didn't some tiny, angry part of her already have an idea for what she needed to do?

Her eyes drifted to the balefire sconces, watching the blue flames flicker.

They were designed to be contained.

To burn forever, without needing any fuel.

But she wondered what would happen if someone set them free.

Would they fizzle out?

Or grow much, *much* stronger?

"What is my moonlark thinking?" Flori wondered as Sophie set down her scrolls and reached for the Archetype, tracing her fingers over the metal lock.

They'd already found the key. So if she brought this home, she could study it—memorize everything Gisela had been planning and come up with a strategy to fight back.

Or . . .

"I'm thinking like the Neverseen," Sophie told her, glancing at Glimmer as she added, "and changing the game."

This is for Kenric! she thought as she swung the Archetype at one of the balefire sconces.

And Mr. Forkle!

And Keefe!

And all of the scars and tears and nightmares and threats and fear and pain!

She'd been fighting the Neverseen's fires since the moment she'd arrived in the Lost Cities.

Now it was time for *them* to burn.

She smashed the other sconce and held the pages of the Archetype in the shower of blue sparks until they caught fire—then flung the burning book into the pile of black cloaks.

"Whoa," Glimmer breathed as the fabric erupted with blue flames. "I did *not* see that coming. But *that's* what I'm talking about."

"Time to go," Tam said as Sophie grabbed the scrolls she'd dropped.

And he was right.

The smoke was already burning her throat and eyes.

But she had to take one last look at the burning storehouse, wondering if she was going to regret losing all of that intel and evidence.

Let it burn, she told herself. *Let the Neverseen see how it feels to scramble.*

All their plans.

All their soporidine.

She was destroying everything.

And it felt *good.*

"Seriously, come on," Sandor said, coughing as he dragged Sophie away from the fire. "We have to go—now!"

Sophie nodded, holding Tiergan's crystal up to the light—but before she stepped into the path, she scratched a few lines in the dirt with her heel.

It wasn't a perfect symbol, but it kinda looked like a moonlark with spread wings.

She hoped the mark survived the inferno.

She wanted the Neverseen to know *she* did this.

She wasn't scared.

She was strong.

And she was ready to start winning.

- FOURTEEN -
Keefe

YOU CAN'T TELL REX!" DEX SNAPPED— then disappeared from his Imparter's screen, making Keefe wonder if that meant that he was too upset to talk.

Keefe wouldn't blame him.

But Dex reappeared a few seconds later, mumbling, "Sorry—had to lock my door. Didn't want to risk that anyone might hear us."

"Probably a good call," Keefe told him, cringing a little.

Just when he'd finally found a way to talk, he'd managed to ruin it—though that was a ridiculous, selfish thought to be having after the bomb he'd just dropped on poor Dex.

Dex's skin looked pale and sweaty, like he might hurl any second.

"There has to be a mistake," Keefe mumbled. "Rex can't be . . ."

He didn't even want to repeat the word.

"You're *sure* you felt the same thing from my dad?" Dex asked. "Like . . . it couldn't have been . . . I don't know, that one of the elixirs got on my dad's skin, and maybe it had some numbing ingredients in it—and that felt *similar* to holding Rex's hand, but wasn't *exact*?"

Keefe sighed. "I guess it's possible."

He closed his eyes and covered his ears, not letting anything distract him as he replayed both memories—focusing on each moment separately and trying to pick the sensations apart down to the tiniest detail.

But . . . as much as he was dying to tell Dex, *You're right! There actually were a bunch of differences!*

He just . . . couldn't.

The more he thought about it, the more convinced he became that both touches had been *exactly* the same. He'd never felt anything like that strange emptiness before—and he hoped he'd never feel it ever again.

You will, though, his brain reminded him. *Every time you're around someone who—*

He shook his head, refusing to finish the thought.

But that didn't make it any less real.

Any less horrible.

And when he opened his eyes, Dex looked absolutely *wrecked*.

His whole body trembled, and he wrapped his arms around himself and whispered, "We seriously can't tell Rex."

Keefe nodded. "I know. We won't."

"It's going to be so hard lying to him," Dex mumbled. "He's going to talk about manifesting all the time—especially as he gets older and starts to worry about it. But I can't tell him! I *can't*."

"You can't," Keefe agreed.

Dex hugged himself tighter. "He was crying earlier—did I tell you that? Bex and Lex had been teasing him like they always do—and he usually doesn't care. But this was bigger, and he got all upset and ran upstairs and slammed the door to his room. My mom was busy trying to stop Lex from burying everything we own in snow, and my dad was trying to help Bex free her feet from the floor, so I went to check on him, and I found him curled up on his bed, sobbing about how unfair it was. And I told him . . ." Dex swallowed hard. "I told him that it would be his turn soon enough. And . . . he didn't believe me. He looked right at me and whispered, 'What if I never manifest?'"

Keefe turned away.

Dex choked a little as he added, "I told him he was being ridiculous. I said he was only twelve, and he still had *tons* of time left—and that just because Bex and Lex got their abilities early didn't mean he wouldn't get one too. And then I said his ability would probably be way cooler than theirs and that's why it was taking a little longer—and he sat up and asked, 'Like a Technopath?' And I remember thinking how weird that was, since I was actually bummed about my ability at first. But he told me, 'Think of all the cool stuff we could build together!'"

His voice broke with a sob, and Keefe had to scrub away a few tears of his own.

He tried to think of something to say—something to fix this.

The best he could come up with was "We could still be wrong. Just because the two feelings were the same doesn't mean . . ."

"Yeah, I know," Dex said quietly. "*That's* why we can't tell him. Maybe once you get a little more used to the ability, you'll realize it was just . . . a misunderstanding."

"Exactly," Keefe agreed.

But neither of them sounded convinced.

Dex sniffled. "The thing is, though . . . even if we knew for *sure* . . . we'd still have to hide it for as long as we could. I mean . . . think about what it would do to him—to his *life?* He'd probably get expelled from Foxfire. And *everyone* would start treating him even worse than they already do. Gossiping about how there's another *Talentless* Dizznee—they've all been waiting for that since the triplets were born. So once they have their confirmation, they're going to focus all their judgment on Rex and make him feel defective and worthless and inferior—like he shouldn't exist, and—"

"And they're *wrong*," Keefe interrupted. "You and I both know that. So will everyone who matters."

Dex sniffled again. "Yeah, but we also know that doesn't make it any easier to deal with."

Keefe sighed. "Very true."

Several agonizing seconds passed before Dex murmured, "And I do realize that if you're right and Rex is . . . you know . . . then all of that is going to happen eventually, anyway. I can't change that. But . . . if we don't tell him, at least he'll get a few more good years before he has to deal with it, right? It's not like I'm keeping the secret for *me*—it's actually going to be *brutal* hiding it. I honestly don't know how I'm going to pretend to be excited when he talks about the abilities he wants—or how I'm not going to strangle Lex and Bex when they tease him about not manifesting yet. And if he ever finds out that I hid this . . . I don't know. I can't decide if I'd be grateful or furious if someone kept something like this from me. Probably a little of both. But I'd also feel super betrayed and foolish, like . . . *You listened to me cry about how bad ability detecting was going, and you never said anything!* He may even hate me for it. But . . . I *can't* tell him. I can't do that to him—not yet."

Keefe stared at his hands, wishing he had something to squeeze or throw or punch. "I'm sorry I dumped this on you," he whispered, wondering if he should smack himself. "I shouldn't have said anything."

He'd kept his mouth shut for *days*, trying to make sure he didn't say anything to hurt someone.

And the first time he lets himself talk, what does he do?

Dex would never look at his brother the same now.

There'd always be a little bit of weirdness between them.

All because he had to tell Dex—

"It's not your fault," Dex said, like he knew what Keefe was thinking. "*You* didn't do this to him. It's just . . . genetics."

"I still didn't have to tell you about it," Keefe argued.

"Well . . . I asked," Dex reminded him.

And it looked like he wished he hadn't.

Which made Keefe wonder what he was supposed to do the next time this happened—the next time he felt that strange emptiness and knew exactly what it meant.

Should he tell the person?

Hide it?

Would he even be able to pull that off?

Or would they know right away that something was wrong?

Wrong with HIM—not THEM, he clarified.

He shouldn't be able to know these things. And if people found out, it would turn into a serious nightmare.

Every kid who hadn't manifested would swarm him, wanting to find out what they were going to be.

The parents would be even pushier.

And what if it turned out that he actually could trigger their abilities?

He hadn't ruled out that possibility yet.

In fact, it seemed pretty likely.

Was *that* what his mom wanted?

But . . . *why*?

Why give him that ability? Since there was no way it manifested by accident.

She definitely planned this.

So . . . what was in it for her?

Power, he realized.

That's always what it went back to with his mom.

And in a world where abilities were the single most defining thing in someone's life, having any kind of knowledge about what was going to happen to them—or *making* it happen for them—was the ultimate advantage.

She could demand anything she wanted for a meeting with her talented little son, and people would pay it—swear it. And she'd get to pick and choose who got the chance.

Or . . .

Was it bigger than that?

He hadn't forgotten what his mom called her plan.

The Archetype.

An original model, that all other things were copied from or compared against.

He'd thought that was just her obnoxious way of saying, *I'm smarter than everyone else, and this is why they all need to listen to me!*

But what if the title was about *him*?

What if *he* was her Archetype—and she was going to use him to measure everybody?

Judge them.

Sort them.

Gather up the best of the best.

Form her own superior elite class and use them to dominate everyone else.

Was *that* his legacy?

But if it was . . . wasn't his power limited?

It wasn't like he could *stop* people from manifesting.

Or . . . could he?

Was there some word—some command—he could give that would strip someone's ability away?

He didn't know—and he didn't *want* to know.

Keefe pulled himself into a tight little ball and buried his head.

"I can't do this," he whispered.

"Do what?" Dex asked.

"All these freaky, unnatural things my mom did to me. I can't control these abilities—"

"Yes, you can," Dex argued. "I've seen you do it. I mean, sure, you're still getting the hang of it, but I've watched you choke back commands. And this is the first time you've let yourself talk in days—and only because you know it's safe."

"Yeah, but what happens when my mom shows up again? She knows everyone I care about, and how to use them to manipulate me and—"

"And you're stronger than her," Dex assured him. "Trust me, I know you—you'll never give in. She could have ogres pry your jaw open, and you still wouldn't give a command."

Well, *there* was a lovely mommy-son image.

But Keefe wouldn't put it past her.

And Dex was right—he'd fight that for sure.

But what if she did that to one of his friends?

Or to Sophie?

And . . . did it even matter?

This new ability wouldn't need anything drastic like that.

All his mom would have to do is strap him to a chair and keep a Telepath around while people touched his hands. Then she'd know everything Keefe felt and what it meant—even trigger their abilities or maybe take them away—and there was nothing he'd be able to do to stop that.

Even wearing an ability restrictor wouldn't be enough, because his mom would just have her Technopath remove it—and probably put it on Sophie instead.

"I can't do this," Keefe repeated, glancing around his room like he was hoping some magic solution would appear in the glittering walls.

Or maybe a hole to disappear into.

"You can," Dex promised. "Because you won't have to do it alone."

Keefe shook his head, hating that he was making this all about him after what he'd just put Dex through.

But he had to be *very* clear. "You can't tell anyone about this, Dex. No one. Not Elwin. Not the Black Swan. Not even Sophie! Especially not her."

"Okay," Dex told him. "I wasn't planning on it."

"I need you to *promise*," Keefe pressed.

Dex held his stare. "I *promise*, I won't tell anyone about this new ability."

"About *any* of my new abilities," Keefe clarified. "I know a few people already know a little bit—and I can't change that. But just . . . downplay that part as much as you can—and don't tell them *anything* else."

"I won't. I promise." He must've known that Keefe was still worried because he added, "It's better for my brother that way."

"It's better for everyone," Keefe told him.

Every. Single. Person would be happier and safer if no one ever found out what he could do.

"Where are you going?" Dex asked as Keefe reached to click off the Imparter.

"I don't know. I just . . . need to think. This is so huge, you know? I need some time to process it all."

Dex nodded slowly. "But . . . you're okay?"

"No," Keefe admitted. "Are you?"

Dex sighed. "No, not really."

And it was those three words that sealed it.

Dex wasn't okay.

And it was his fault.

He had to make sure he never did that to anyone else.

No matter what that meant.

"Okay," Keefe said, dragging a hand down his face. "I have to go, but . . . thanks. For all the help with this voice thing. And . . . for everything else."

"Sure." Dex frowned and tilted his head. "You know we're not done, right? We can figure all of this out—I'm not giving up."

"Neither am I," Keefe said, his eyes burning as he turned away.

He *wasn't* giving up.

But he couldn't keep pretending everything would be okay, either.

"Thanks again," he told Dex. "And . . . I'm sorry."

"Don't be. I'll talk to you soon."

Keefe bit his lip to stop himself from agreeing. "Bye, Dex."

He clicked the Imparter off before he could say anything else, staring at the silent silver screen.

He knew what he needed to do.

He just needed to make himself do it.

Someone cleared their throat behind him, and he whipped around, cringing when he found Ro standing there studying him.

"I feel like this is a good time to remind you that I didn't put any earplugs in like Elwin did," she told him. "So yeah, I heard that whole conversation. Elwin didn't, in case you're worrying. I even talked him into going downstairs because I know you well enough to know you're probably planning something super melodramatic and reckless right now. So make sure you're keeping in mind that I go where you go."

Keefe shook his head.

She sighed. "Riiiiiight, we're back to the whole 'not talking' thing now that your little gadget is switched off. Fine—I'll do the talking for both of us. I know what you're thinking right now. You want to stop your creepy mom—make sure she doesn't use you to make a giant mess out of Elf-y Land so it all comes crumbling down and she can swoop in, take over, and rebuild it the way she wants. And I gotta admit, I'm not happy about that plan either. So I repeat—*I go where you go*. It's my job to keep you alive and out of trouble, but if you want to hunt down Mommy Dearest together, I'm game. It's not *ideal*—and your pretty little Blondie is going to be *so mad* at us. But if you want to try to end this now, we can."

Keefe shook his head again, and Ro blocked him when he stood.

"I don't think you're hearing what I'm saying, Hunkyhair. So let's try this again. You're not going anywhere without me. *Seriously*," she said when he tried to shove past her. "Fight me all you want. I'm stronger than you and smarter than you. And you *need* me. You're not a killer. *I* am."

She let the words hang there for a beat, probably waiting to see if he'd flinch.

He didn't.

"Interesting," she said. "I think you're finally ready. But you're still getting my help—whether you want it or not. I'm in control here."

She usually was.

Usually, he needed tricks or schemes to get the upper hand with Ro.

But there was nothing *usual* about him anymore.

So he closed his eyes and let the fear and worry and desperation build and build, until a command burned his tongue—and he didn't try to hold it back.

"*Sleep.*"

Instantly, Ro collapsed in a heap of tangled limbs.

Keefe watched her snore for a second, taking in the full gravity of his power—reminding himself that this is why he had no other choice.

Then he tore the sheets and blankets off his bed and used them to restrain her before he gathered up his meager possessions.

His dad hadn't sent much—just some clothes and notebooks and Mrs. Stinkbottom.

But that was all he needed.

Probably more than he deserved.

Still, he slung the bag over his shoulder and checked Ro's bed-sheet bonds one more time.

They wouldn't hold her for long.

But he only needed a few seconds.

Just enough time to step into the light.

He took one last look around the room, wondering if he should leave Elwin a note to thank him for trying so hard. But he didn't have time.

Plus, his brain was too busy composing the harder letter he needed to write.

"Sorry, Elwin," he whispered, focusing on Ro as he breathed another "sorry."

Then he closed his eyes and gathered the energy to tell her, *"Wake."*

She tried to jolt upright, but the bonds held her in place—and in the split second it took Keefe to raise his crystal, he watched her realize what was happening.

"You're going to regret this," she warned.

He nodded.

He had zero doubt about that.

But he still stepped into the path, letting the warmth carry him away.

WHY DO YOU SMELL LIKE SMOKE?"
Grady demanded when Sophie's group
reappeared at Solreef—thankfully at the
top of the stairs, instead of the bottom.
"What happened?"

Sophie knew she should be the one to answer.

But her brain got a little stuck on the fact that Grady was still
there.

So was Tiergan.

And Fitz.

And Biana.

And Grizel and Woltzer.

No one had gone after them yet—which should've been obvious,
since no one had shown up at the storehouse.

But Sophie hadn't really thought about what that meant.

They . . . hadn't even been gone the full fifteen minutes.

She'd destroyed the Neverseen's storehouse—and hopefully most
of their plans—in less than a quarter of an hour.

If only she could wipe out the rest of their organization as quickly.

Grady took her by the shoulders, turning her to face him. "Are you okay? Were you attacked?"

"No," she told him—then realized how that sounded. "I mean, *yes*, I'm okay—*no*, we weren't attacked. But before we left, I . . . It's hard to explain."

It was probably going to take her longer to tell him what she'd done than it had for her to decide to do it.

She wasn't sure how to feel about that.

"You should go inside for this conversation," Sandor told her before turning to the other bodyguards and adding, "Grizel? I need you and Flori to do a security sweep with me. And Woltzer? I need you to cover the interior. Be extra vigilant."

"Sounds like the mission was *eventful*," Tiergan noted, gesturing to the scrolls cradled in Sophie's and Tam's arms.

"Discuss it *inside*!" Sandor ordered, practically shoving them through the front door.

The look he gave Sophie before he drew his sword and marched away was completely unreadable.

Furious?

Scared?

Proud?

All of the above?

Bo took Glimmer's wrist. "I'll make sure your *guest* is secured— and I suggest keeping any items away from her until they've been thoroughly inspected."

"Hey!" Glimmer protested as Bo yanked her blue bundle out of her hands, along with everything else she'd collected. "I don't care if you search my stuff—but you don't have to be such a jerk about it!"

"I'll take that," Tam offered, adjusting the scrolls he was carrying to make room.

"I think it might be best if we move everything to my office," Tiergan told him, taking Glimmer's things from Bo and motioning for everyone to follow him down a different hallway.

"If you break my cat statue, I'm going to be super mad!" Glimmer shouted after them.

No one said anything else as they made their way up a spiral staircase to an enormous oval room, which looked like the kind of office that Sophie kept imagining someone in the Black Swan would have—complete with a giant fireplace, shelves full of strange, whirling gadgets, and an imposing desk covered in meticulously arranged stacks of paperwork. But the twisted tree sprouting from the center of the floor with flowering branches stretching toward the arched skylight was a bit of a surprise.

"Everything you took will be safe in here," Tiergan assured them, setting Glimmer's things in a neat pile on the floor behind his desk and gesturing for them to copy him. "I'll make sure it's properly examined and cataloged before it's relocated to somewhere more permanent."

"Like a storehouse?" Tam asked. "'Cause, uh, that may not be the smartest strategy."

"Why not?" Grady, Tiergan, Fitz, and Biana all asked in unison.

Sophie had a different question. "Are you going to give it back to us—and tell us *everything* you learn?"

"Of course, Sophie. Just like you're going to tell us *everything* that happened today, aren't you?" Tiergan countered. He smiled when she nodded. "Good, I'm looking forward to it. But first"—he pointed again to the spot behind his desk—"please trust me. You don't need the burden of having to protect these things."

She didn't.

And what was she going to do?

Hide the stuff under her bed?

Still, the second she set the scrolls and vials down, she wanted to grab them all back.

Instead she shoved her hand in her pocket and tightened her grip on the caches.

Tam added the scrolls and gadgets he'd taken, and everyone stared at the final pile.

"Quite a haul," Tiergan told them. "Particularly since you went there for a single cache—which I'm assuming you recovered."

Sophie nodded.

She was surprised by how impressed Tiergan sounded—and how excited Fitz and Biana were.

All she could think when she studied the pile was how insignificant it looked—and how useless it would all probably turn out to be.

And how glad she was that she'd sparked that fire.

Glimmer was right—they'd planned that mission completely wrong from the beginning.

How many other times had they made that mistake—thought too small and set themselves up to fail?

Tiergan cleared his throat. "So . . . I believe you have a story to share with us?"

He motioned for everyone to take a seat on the colorful ottomans arranged around the tree.

Sophie stayed standing, needing to move as she explained what happened.

The smoke scent clinging to her clothes seemed to get stronger as she talked, and by the end her throat had turned thick and her eyes were burning—though maybe that also had something to do with the way everyone's smiles had faded into the same unreadable expression she'd seen on Sandor. Even Tam—who'd been there with her.

He'd heard what Glimmer had said.

And he trusted Glimmer.

"It was the right move," she told him before shifting her focus to everyone and adding, "This is how we're going to have to fight if we want to win."

Tiergan cleared his throat again, drawing out the sound. "Well . . . that explains Sandor's emphasis on security."

"You think the Neverseen will come *here*?" Tam asked.

"It's possible. My estate's hardly a secret. Neither is the fact that Glimmer's being kept here. And surely the Neverseen will assume she's the one who led us to their storehouse. So they may decide she poses too great of a threat and try to retrieve her—or end her."

Grady stood. "Or they'll go to Havenfield. I should warn the rest of the goblin patrols—and Edaline."

"I guess I should warn my parents too," Fitz said quietly. "The Neverseen will probably assume Biana and I were a part of it."

"We'll need to warn *everyone*," Biana corrected. "Keefe, Dex, Linh, Wylie, Marella, Maruca, Stina."

"Also the Council," Tiergan added. "And the Collective. And—"

"Okay, whoa!" Sophie interrupted, holding out her hands like stop signs as everyone reached for their home crystals or path-finders. "You guys didn't act like this after we went to Nightfall or Loamnore—or after the newborn troll fight at Everglen. Or after any of the Neverseen's other attacks."

"Yes, but those were *their* attacks," Tiergan reminded her. "This was *ours*. Well . . . *yours*. And it was unprovoked."

"*Unprovoked?*" Sophie repeated. "You're kidding, right?"

"No, Sophie—none of us think this is a joke," Grady said quietly. "And I'm really hoping you don't either. Because you just turned this into a war."

Sophie blinked. "*I* did? *Me?*"

She glanced at her friends, expecting them to look just as affronted.

But they mostly looked nervous and fidgety.

"This was already a war," she said, turning back to Grady. "It has been since the moment I was kidnapped. Actually, no, it started much earlier. Lady Gisela was already working on her stellarlune thing before Keefe was born. And they killed Jolie way before that."

Grady flinched.

"Sorry," Sophie mumbled, realizing how harsh that sounded. "Just . . . look at how much they've hurt us. How many scars we all have—how many times we've almost died! Tam was their *prisoner*! Keefe's afraid to talk because he has all these scary new abilities. Kenric is *dead*—and so is Mr. Forkle. And you're accusing *me* of escalating this?"

"Yes," Tiergan said simply. "Though 'accusing' is the wrong word. 'Informing' is better. Making sure you understand that you haven't just changed the game for the Neverseen—you've changed it for *everyone*. Up until now, we haven't *attacked*. We've defended ourselves. But raiding their hideout—and then destroying it—is an *attack*, Sophie. And that means we're now officially at war."

The word echoed around the room.

War. War. War.

And for some reason, Sophie found herself staring at the tree, wishing she could hear its song whisper through its leaves.

Maybe it would tell her what to think or feel or say or do.

But the tree stayed silent.

So did her friends.

"If I'd stuck to our plan," Sophie said quietly, "the Neverseen would've just moved all their stuff to a new storehouse and carried on like nothing happened. Now they have to change their strategy. Now *they're* the ones scrambling. So, even if I did start . . . whatever . . . I also brought us a victory. A *real* one—not just a Yay-we-didn't-die! kind of thing."

She didn't understand why they couldn't see that.

It made her wish Keefe were there—he would've backed her up.

In fact, he probably would've helped her spark the flames at the storehouse.

"No one's denying any of that," Tiergan told her gently. "But . . . you should be careful of that word."

"Victory?" Sophie asked.

Tiergan shook his head. *"I."*

Sophie stood up taller. "You think I did this for *me?*"

"No. I think you acted alone. And I realize you're going to argue that there wasn't time for a big debate or discussion—and I'm certain there wasn't. But that doesn't change the fact that you made an enormous decision that will affect everyone entirely on your own."

"You even made sure the Neverseen knew it was you," Sandor said from the doorway. "I saw the mark you left before we leaped away."

"What mark?" Grady asked.

Sandor held Sophie's stare when he answered. "It looked like a flying moonlark."

"Oh wow," Biana whispered.

Grady sighed.

"Hey—the Black Swan puts the sign of the swan on everything!" Sophie argued.

"But we are a *group*," Tiergan countered.

"And I'm a part of that group," Sophie reminded him.

"But that wasn't the symbol you used," he reminded her. "You made your own, positioning yourself as the threat and the victor. Not the Black Swan. Not your friends. *You.*"

Sophie backed up several steps, needing air—space. "You seriously think I did this for attention?"

"Whether that was your goal is irrelevant," Tiergan told her. "My point is that you've now made yourself a true target. So you need to be prepared for the Neverseen to come after you."

"They're always *after me!*"

"Not like this," Sandor warned. "The most dangerous time in any movement is when a new leader first takes their place. They're still fledgling and weak and full of mistakes. Not ready for the onslaught they'll be facing."

Sophie's mouth went dry, and it took her several seconds to find enough voice to tell him, "I'm not trying to be anyone's leader."

"And yet, it's what you were made for," a new voice said.

A voice that always managed to fill Sophie with hope *and* dread—and now there was also a healthy amount of wariness as Sandor stepped aside to let Mr. Forkle shuffle into the office.

He looked less swollen and wrinkled than usual—like he'd rushed there after finishing some other assignment. And his piercing blue eyes seemed tired when he focused on Sophie and said, "If all of you wouldn't mind, I think it's time for Miss Foster and I to have a talk."

Sophie's stomach turned sloshy somersaults as everyone stood.

Fitz's and Biana's expressions were still unreadable, and Tam's half smile mostly seemed to say, *Glad I'm not you.* And as they all glittered away, Sophie couldn't shake the feeling that something fundamental had changed for all of them.

"I'll see you at home, kiddo," Grady told her, pulling her in for a hug and whispering, "We'll get through this. Just be careful. And know that I love you *so* much."

"I love you too," she whispered back, then remembered to add, "Dad."

He kissed her forehead, begging her to be careful one more time before he disappeared in a shower of sparkle.

Tiergan and Mr. Forkle exchanged a look—probably communicating telepathically—before Tiergan left with Sandor and Flori, telling them he'd like to discuss Solreef's security.

Mr. Forkle closed the door behind them, and Sophie sank onto one of the ottomans, trying not to feel like a scared kid in the principal's office.

"I don't want to be the leader," she said, deciding to go preemptive-strike on him. "That wasn't what I was trying to do today."

"I know." He huffed out a heavy breath as he lowered himself to the ottoman across from her. "And I realize how overwhelming this all must be, and how hard you're trying to do the right thing. That's why I want to make sure you're truly ready for what lies ahead."

"I don't want to be the leader," Sophie insisted. "I *don't*."

"I *know*," he agreed. "And yet . . . it's rather interesting, isn't it?"

He stopped there, waiting for her to ask what he meant—and she *really* didn't feel like playing along.

But she finally rolled her eyes and said, "What's interesting?"

His smile brightened. "You kids can be so stubborn. But I suppose that's also what makes you so strong. And what's *interesting* is that you chose to leave your own symbol—which sounds like quite a powerful image, I might add—when no one has ever asked you or advised you to do that."

Sophie slumped a little. Shrinking in on herself. "I didn't do it because I want to send some sort of message that I'm in charge or anything. I just . . . wanted the Neverseen to know it was me—that *I* dealt that blow to them—after everything they've done to me. That's it, that's all it was. And maybe it was a bad idea. I don't know. I didn't put much thought into it."

"And *that's* what I want to talk to you about," he told her, shifting his weight to lean closer. "Whether or not you *want* to be a leader, Miss Foster, you *are* one—and I'm not saying that because I designed you to be that way. The leadership simply comes from who you are. You're a powerful, brilliant, determined, inspiring young lady. People naturally look to you. And they're going to do that more and more, the stronger you become. Today was a huge part of that. I'm proud of the stand you took. And for the record, I think you made the right call."

"You do?" Sophie whispered.

"Absolutely. You saw the mistake we'd all made, and a path to correct it, and you did what needed to be done. *But*," he had to add, right when she was starting to feel a little better, "you also made some fairly significant mistakes."

She slumped lower. "Like what?"

"Well . . . for starters, did you warn the others about what you were doing, and make them all step back before you sparked the fire?"

"No," Sophie admitted. "But they were already far enough away."

"Yes, but people do *move*, you know. It's always best to communicate. And what about the larger danger? Did you take any measures to ensure that the fire wouldn't spread anywhere else beyond the Neverseen's hideout?"

"No," Sophie had to admit again. "But I didn't need to—the storehouse was behind a giant waterfall!"

"Did you actually consider that, though?" he pressed. "And what I mean is, did you have a conscious thought about there being an abundant water supply nearby that would safely extinguish the blaze before it could spread? Because if you didn't, you don't get to take credit for the waterfall's safety. That's what we call random luck."

Sophie reached for her eyelashes, giving them a soft tug. "It wasn't like I had a lot of time to think—"

"There's never enough time to think in war," he interrupted. "That doesn't mean you don't need to do it. Believe me, Miss Foster, I understand the complexity of the situation you faced today better than anybody. But since it's only the first of *many* complex situations you're going to find yourself in, I need to make sure you're truly prepared for the responsibility you're going to face. Because if it weren't for the random luck of being near a water-fall today, you could've set off an enormous firestorm and caused untold collateral damage."

Sophie shuddered and closed her eyes, trying to fight back the painful flashbacks.

But she could still hear the screams.

Still see the neon yellow flames.

Still remember the last time she saw Kenric's face.

"You're right," she admitted. "I'm sorry."

"Don't be sorry. Be *better*. And remember that mistakes don't have to be mistakes if you correct them quickly. You could've alerted someone about the fire the second you arrived at Solreef—had them go back to the hideout to monitor the blaze and contain it if necessary. But you didn't do that, either."

She wanted to point out that Tam and Flori and Sandor and Bo and Glimmer could've done that too, and hadn't. But . . .

They weren't the ones who smashed those sconces.

"None of this is easy," he told her. "And sadly, it's going to get harder. But you must never let yourself forget that winning won't matter if you sink fully to the Neverseen's level."

"Glimmer thinks that's the only way we're going to win," Sophie mumbled.

"Yes, well, Glimmer has much to learn as well. There's a way to be bold and brave and stand up to your enemies without forgetting that actions have consequences."

Sophie nodded, twisting a loose string on the edge of her sleeve as she worked up the courage to ask, "What consequences are going to come from what I did today?"

Mr. Forkle blew out a breath. "I wish I knew. But that's how it always goes with hard decisions. I had no idea what would happen when I helped create a powerful young girl—a fearless moonlark. I just knew she was going to change the game. And now . . . she has. *You* have. And I'm proud of you. I believe in you. And I'm here to help you and guide you as much as I can."

Sophie couldn't think of what to say to that.

Was she supposed to say "thanks"?

Be grateful he'd dumped this impossible responsibility on her shoulders?

Maybe.

And maybe someday she'd even feel that way.

Someday when this was all over and life was normal again, maybe she'd look back and be glad she got to play a part.

Assuming that day ever happened.

But for now, she let her silence speak for itself—let it hold all her fear and uncertainty.

"I believe in you," he repeated. "I believe in my moonlark. In fact, I'd love to see the symbol you created. Will you show it to me?"

Sophie stood, making her way to Tiergan's desk and grabbing a pen and paper. She wasn't an awesome artist like Keefe, but she sketched the simple lines she'd carved into the ground, adding a few extra curves and flourishes before she handed the page to Mr. Forkle.

His lips curled with another smile. "Now, *that's* a symbol. You should start using this."

"For what?" Sophie asked.

"You'll know when the time comes," he told her, which was such a cheating way to answer.

He laughed when she scowled.

"Just let it bring fear *and* hope to people, Miss Foster. And let it remind you to be strong *and* smart. Use it to change the game—but make sure you win the *right* way. And never forget that moonlarks can't do everything on their own. Not even you."

Sophie nodded.

"Good." He stuffed the paper into one of the pockets in his cape. "I'm keeping this. And I'm going to let you keep those caches—but don't think we're not going to talk about your plans for those very soon."

"I don't actually have any plans," Sophie told him.

Which was true, since she really didn't want to have to go back to working with Oralie.

But she would probably have to.

"I know you don't," he told her. "But you will. You'll figure it all out in time. That's what leaders do. For now, how about you sit back down and tell me more about destroying this storehouse?"

"Why?" Sophie asked—but she still returned to one of the ottomans.

He smiled his widest smile yet. "Because we need to celebrate the victories."

- SIXTEEN -
KEEFE

I HAVE NO IDEA WHAT I'M DOING," KEEFE whispered, "but it's going to be okay."

He'd said those words to himself several dozen times since he'd fled Elwin's house. And now he was saying them again to a tiny, caged imp—who narrowed his watery green eyes, looking about as dubious as Keefe felt.

"Trust me, this will be your best look yet—you'll see," he promised, keeping his voice extra soft in case his new ability worked on furry creatures. Plus, it'd be super bad if he got caught sneaking into Foster's room and messing with her pet. "Just give this a little drinky-drink for me, and let the awesomeness happen."

He pressed a vial against Iggy's lips, and the feisty imp unleashed a cage-rattling fart to punish him. But he also slurped down the thick syrup—a mix of five different elixirs, which Keefe had concocted from one of his prank stashes during the quick stop he'd made at the Shores of Solace.

Thankfully, Daddy Dearest hadn't been home, so he'd been able to grab the final thing he needed and get away without any drama.

"Ooo, it's working—what did I tell you?" Keefe scratched Iggy's fuzzy cheeks, filling the room with the sound of squeaky purring as Iggy's fluffy fur slowly changed colors—green in some patches. Blue and purple in others.

Some spots even merged into a soft teal tone, which made Keefe want to roll his eyes and grumble about Fitzphie.

But Foster would love it.

And honestly, he hoped Fitz would step up and become whoever and whatever she needed him to be.

She deserved that.

She deserved to be happy.

"Huh, that's unexpected," he said as tiny black tiger stripes streaked across Iggy's body. Keefe wasn't sure which of the elixirs had caused something like that. He'd just thrown his favorites together, trying to create something memorable.

At least he'd gotten *that* right.

"You look fabulous," he assured Iggy. "I'm definitely going to win the prize for Best Imp Stylist."

Not that he'd be around to claim his victory.

Or to see Foster's reaction.

But that was probably better, since a colorful, stripy imp wasn't the only surprise he was leaving for her.

He pulled the letter he'd written from his pocket and carried Iggy's cage over to the giant canopied bed, setting both on the pillow so there was no way anyone would miss them.

His brain kept screaming at him to tear the letter up and rewrite it. But there was no time for that.

Plus . . . it was better to be honest, wasn't it?

"If you chew this," he warned, showing Iggy the crinkled envelope, "I will shave you bald—you hear me?"

Iggy burped in his face.

"I'll take that as a yes." But just to be extra safe, he slid the cage on top of the letter to weigh it down.

And . . . that was it.

There was nothing left for him to do.

Except leave.

"Bite anyone who tries to hurt her, okay?" he told Iggy. "Or better yet, just fart in their face."

Iggy burped again, making the room smell like rotting umber leaves.

Keefe gagged. "Burping works too. Just . . . take care of her."

He might've been imagining it, but he could've sworn the tiny imp nodded.

"Thanks," he whispered.

And now he was definitely stalling, so it was time to go.

But . . . his legs wouldn't cooperate.

Or they wouldn't until a familiar voice behind him said, "Keefe?"

Then Keefe was ready to smash a Keefe-shaped hole through the wall.

Instead, he squared his shoulders and forced himself to turn and face Sophie's adoptive father—who looked . . .

Extra murder-y.

"What are you doing in my house—in my daughter's room—without permission?" Grady demanded, which made it pretty clear the conversation was *not* going to go well.

Keefe couldn't risk using his voice, so he shrugged and pointed at Iggy's cage, wiggling his hands like, *Ta-da—fancy new imp colors!*

"That's right—I heard you aren't talking now." Grady's eyes focused on the sealed envelope with Sophie's name written across it. "Is that what the letter's for? Trying to keep in touch?"

Nodding would've been easier.

Grady probably would've dropped the subject.

But for some reason, Keefe shook his head.

Grady sighed. "Yeah. I was afraid of that. And I'm guessing I don't want to know what you wrote in there."

That time Keefe definitely nodded.

Grady's jaw tightened—and his teeth made a painful grinding sound when he took a longer look at Keefe, focusing on Keefe's backpack. "Going somewhere?"

Keefe nodded again.

"For how long?"

Keefe shrugged.

However long it took for all of this to be over.

That time Grady's sigh sounded more like a growl. "You tried this already, remember? And it was a total disaster! So why don't you do everyone a favor and tear that letter up, go home, and *not* do whatever you're planning? We'll say you came here to change Iggy's color and that's it. Deal?"

He held out his hand for Keefe to shake, and Keefe *really* wished he could take it.

But he backed a step away, trying to think of some combination of gestures that would explain why this plan was way different from the last one.

"Look," Grady told him, stalking closer and grabbing Keefe's shoulders. "I'm sure you think you're doing the right thing—but you're not. This is *not* the time to run off and do something reckless."

"I know," Keefe whispered, deciding to risk using the two tiny words.

He wanted to say so much more, but he could feel Grady's emotions swirling—a whole lot of stinging anger and bitter frustration—and didn't trust his voice to stay even.

Grady shook his head and dropped his hands. "You don't understand, Keefe. Everything's about to get *really* messy. Sophie burned down the Neverseen's storehouse today."

Keefe's eyebrows shot up so high, they felt like they were stretching his face.

"Yeah," Grady said quietly. "Apparently she gets in even more trouble without you there. Who knew?"

Keefe's lips pulled into a smile, even though it really wasn't funny.

He closed his eyes, taking several calming breaths before chancing one quick question. "Is she okay?"

"For now." Grady made his way over to the bed and sank down on the edge, looking more exhausted than Keefe had ever seen him when he added, "I'm sure it won't be long before the Neverseen retaliate. And I have a horrible feeling it'll be their cruelest attack yet. Sandor's working on new security strategies, but you and I both know how stubborn Sophie can be about that kind of thing. And . . . honestly . . . as much as I don't understand your friendship . . . she does listen to you sometimes. And rely on you. And . . . I think she's going to need you for this next part."

Keefe wasn't sure that was true.

But Grady had to be pretty desperate to tell him that.

In fact, he could feel Grady's worry hanging over them like heavy storm clouds.

It made him want to shred that letter and run back to Elwin's and tell Ro, *JUST KIDDING—DON'T BE MAD.*

But he was right this time.

He could *feel* it.

"I really have to go," he whispered.

Grady closed his eyes.

"I'm not going to pretend like I know what you're going through," he told Keefe. "But . . . I do know what it's like to have a daunting power. And I respect how hard you're fighting to get control. You just need to believe in yourself. You *will* figure this out, with time and training and practice and—"

Keefe grabbed Grady's arm, waiting for him to look at him before he shook his head.

"I *have* to go," he said, risking that tiny bit of emphasis. "I'm sorry. I wish . . ."

There were so many ways he wanted to finish that sentence—so many hopes and dreams and fears and frustrations.

But he kept them all to himself.

None of them were options anymore.

He had one choice left.

And he *had* to make it.

No matter what it cost him.

Grady tilted his head to study him, like he was trying to solve a riddle.

He must've found some sort of answer because he stood and

said, "Okay. If that's what you need to do, I'm not going to stop you."

Keefe nodded, feeling his chest tighten and his eyes burn as reached into his pocket for his pathfinder.

He had to get out of there before he broke down crying.

But Grady put a hand on his shoulder. "Wait, I need you to take this with you." He reached into his pocket and pulled out his Imparter. "I promise, I'll only use it for an emergency. I just . . . I have a feeling Sophie's going to need you before this is all over. So please, keep it in your pocket—and swear to me that you'll answer if I hail you."

Keefe swallowed hard, clearing his throat several times to make sure the words were a request, not a command, before he said, "You can't tell Foster you have a way to reach me."

"I won't tell anyone," Grady promised.

Keefe nodded, grabbing the Imparter and shoving it into his pocket as Grady's words replayed in his head.

Sophie's going to need you.

He didn't think she would.

He knew she would keep right on being her brave, powerful, awesome self and show his mom why the moonlark would always be better and smarter and stronger than anyone else.

"Thank you," Grady said, giving Keefe's arm a gentle squeeze before letting him go.

Keefe took one last look around the room, and when he got to Iggy's cage—and the letter underneath—he realized he'd reached another point of no return.

He'd had a lot of those in his life.

But this was a big one.

And the *right* one.

He just had to be brave.

"Take care of yourself," Grady told him as Keefe pulled out the pathfinder he'd stolen from his dad. And it was obvious that Grady noticed that the crystal was cobalt blue.

"I'll try," Keefe promised.

It was the best he could do.

Then he stepped into the path and let the blue light carry him far away.

To the Mysterious Miss F!

Ugh—I'm already regretting starting this letter that way. But I don't have any extra paper, and crossing it out would look worse, so . . . I guess we'll just have to add it to my list of mistakes.

And I know you're going to think that everything I'm about to say should also be on that long list of Keefe Fails. But I swear—that's NOT what this is. I'm not trying to fix everything or save everyone this time. I'm just trying to make sure I don't hurt anyone.

I can't tell you more than that without putting you in danger, so just . . . trust me when I say that the powers my mom gave me are super bad. There seriously aren't strong enough words to explain how horrible they are. And I CAN'T control them—just like I can't stop my mom from forcing me to use them.

So . . . this is the only way. I don't want to do it. But I have to.

And I'm not going to ask you not to hate me. In fact, it might be better if you do, because I need you to PROMISE that you won't try to find me. My mom will be waiting for you to track me down—and since I know how stubborn you are, I want to make sure you understand who you'd be putting in danger.

I'm going to be hiding the same way the Black Swan hid you.

That's why you have to stay away. Well, there are lots of reasons. So again, please, just . . . trust me, okay?

And since this is the last time I'll ever talk to you, I just . . . I want to say that I'm really going to miss you. You mean a lot to me, Foster. More than you'll ever know.

Please be careful. Please be happy. And PLEASE forget all about me.

It'll be better for everyone that way. You'll see.

Love,
Keefe

ACKNOWLEDGMENTS

I'm sure you guys all turned the page thinking, *There's absolutely no way Shannon Messenger would end this book without showing us Sophie's reaction to Keefe's letter! Even with all her evil cliff-hangers, she would never do THAT!*

And yet . . . ☺

Don't worry, we'll pick up Sophie's story in Book 9—which I'm writing as fast as I can.

AND I REALLY DO LOVE YOU GUYS. I SWEAR!!! YOU'RE ALL AMAZING AND AWESOME AND FABULOUS AND BRILLIANT—AND HAVE I MENTIONED YOU'RE ALSO PATIENT AND FORGIVING???

considers going into hiding

Torturous endings aside, I hope you guys loved this book as much as I do. I've never written a project like this, and it was such an amazing experience working with a truly incredible team. So many brilliant people shared their time and talent to make *Unlocked Book 8.5* come together, I don't even know where to begin! But I guess I'll start with the phenomenal illustrators who contributed their stunning art to this book.

To Francesca Baerald: Thank you for taking that horrible sketch I sent you and creating the most gorgeous map I've ever seen. You truly are a genius for figuring out how to organize everything.

To Jason Chan: Thank you, thank you, *thank you* for another perfect cover. Not gonna lie, I got a little teary seeing my brave girl flying all by herself on her alicorn.

To Felia Hanakata: Thank you for taking on the daunting task of trying to make drawings of plants and clothes and foods seem exciting—and then knocking it out of the park on every illustration. (Also: Those stuffed animal drawings have made my *life*.)

To Laura Hollingsworth: You seriously outdo yourself with every piece and have managed to capture my characters so perfectly that sometimes I wonder if you peeked inside my brain. (You're not a Telepath, are you???)

Of course I also have to thank the myriad of people at Simon & Schuster who managed to make such a complicated project happen—and during such an especially complicated year, no less—including Liesa Abrams Mignogna and Jessica Smith (who truly were the wonder editing team!), Rebecca Vitkus and Elizabeth Mims (my copyediting and fact-checking geniuses, who—it should be noted—also helped compile everything I'd need to write the guide section, which was a Herculean task!), Karin Paprocki and Mike Rosamilia (who are the reason this book looks so beautiful), Jon Anderson, Valerie Garfield, Chelsea Morgan, Sara Berko, Adam Smith, Stacey Sakal, Lauren Hoffman, Caitlin Sweeny, Alissa Nigro, Anna Jarzab, Nicole Russo, Cassie Malmo, Michelle Leo, Mara Anastas, Chriscynethia Floyd, Jenn Rothkin, Ian Reilly, Christina Pecorale, Victor Iannone, and the entire sales team.

I also couldn't do this job without the invaluable guidance from my agent, Laura Rennert (as well as everyone else at Andrea Brown Literary and Taryn Fagerness Agency).

And while all of my foreign publishers are seriously *The Best*, I have to give special thanks to Cécile Pournin and Mathilde Tamae-Bouhon—and everyone else at Lumen éditions—for taking such good care of me when I've visited you in France (and for always doing such fantastic work on my books).

I'll never be able to properly thank all the booksellers, teachers, librarians, bloggers, and #bookstagrammers who spread the love for this series—but that doesn't mean I won't keep trying! You truly are the best people ever!

And I have to thank Katie Laird, my assistant extraordinaire, for being my second brain and helping me finally get organized and caught up.

Of course I also have to thank the friends who've been there for all of my brainstorming, commiserating, venting, panicking, and procrastinating needs, including Roshani Chokshi, Debra Driza, Faith Hochhalter, Jenn Johansson, Amie Kaufman, Kelly Ramirez, C. J. Redwine, Brandi Stewart, Amy Tintera, Kasie West, and Sarah Wylie.

I also owe a special shout-out to Alexander Morelli—even though he technically already got one in the dedication—because this book wouldn't be what it is without him. So thank you, Alex, for all your patience and plotting and planning and pep talks. (I could say more, but I think I'll stop with that awesome alliteration. ☺)

And last but *never* least, I have to thank my family—Allison, Jeff, Nadia, and Roland, who manage to make me feel cool *and* tease me so unfailingly that it keeps me humble. And Mom and Dad: I absolutely could not do this super-tricky, exhausting, wonderful, complicated job without you! I promise, I really will *try* to sleep more next year!